THE LESSON OF THE MASTER

was born in New York, April 15th, 1843.
He lived most of his life in England, and
was eventually naturalised in 1915. He
died in Chelsea on February 28th, 1916.

THE LESSON
OF THE
MASTER

AND OTHER STORIES BY

HENRY JAMES

JOHN LEHMANN

MCMXLVIII

THIS EDITION FIRST PUBLISHED IN 1948 BY
JOHN LEHMANN LTD
MADE AND PRINTED IN GREAT BRITAIN BY
PURNELL AND SONS LTD
PAULTON (SOMERSET) AND LONDON

NOTE TO THE PRESENT EDITION

WITH THE exception of *The Lesson of the Master* and *The Figure in the Carpet* the stories in this collection were written for *The Yellow Book*, *The Death of the Lion* appearing in the April, 1894 number, *The Coxon Fund* in July of the same year and *The Next Time* in the July of the following year. Henry James himself was a little troubled by his appearance in the organ of the Aesthetic Movement, a movement with which he had so much and so little in common, and which had till then shown little interest in his work, except for *Daisy Miller*. In a letter to his brother William he excuses himself for not sending a copy of *The Yellow Book* containing *The Death of the Lion* because, "although my little tale . . . appears to have had, for a thing of mine, an unnatural success, I hate the horrid aspect and company of the whole publication." But his objection seems to have relaxed enough by the following July for him to allow *The Coxon Fund* to appear in the same company. It is interesting to note in passing that James said in a letter that this story was to be "an Impression—as one of Sargent's pictures is an impression."

The Lesson of the Master was the first to be written of the stories reprinted here. It appeared in *The Universal Review* during July and August, 1888. Lady Jersey, on reading it, suspected that the "Summer-soft" of the tale was intended to be her own Osterley, and wrote to James for confirmation. He answered, with that kind of baroque humour which he reserved for his women correspondents, that the resemblance "was only a matter of the dear old cubic sofa-cushions and objects of the same delightful order, and not of the human furniture of the house."

The Lesson of the Master was collected in *The Lesson of the Master and other Tales* in 1892, *The Death of the Lion* and *The Coxon Fund* in *Terminations*, 1895, and *The Next Time* and *The Figure in the Carpet* (which had originally appeared in *Cosmopolis* for January-February, 1896) in *Embarrassments*, 1896.

All the stories printed in this edition comprise Vol. XV of the New York Edition of 1909.

MICHAEL SWAN

MICHAEL SWAN

PREFACE

PREFACE

MY CLEAREST remembrance of any provoking cause connected with the matter of the present volume applies, not to the composition at the head of my list—which owes that precedence to its greatest length and earliest date—but to the next in order, an effort embalmed, to fond memory, in a delightful association. I make the most of this passage of literary history—I like so, as I find, to recall it. It lives there for me in old Kensington days; which, though I look back at them over no such great gulf of years—"The Death of the Lion" first appeared but in 1894—have already faded for me to the complexion of ever so long ago. It was of a Sunday afternoon early in the spring of that year: a young friend, a Kensington neighbour and an ardent man of letters, called on me to introduce a young friend of his own and to bespeak my interest for a periodical about to take birth, in his hands, on the most original "lines" and with the happiest omens. What omen could be happier, for instance, than that this infant *recueil*, joyously christened even before reaching the cradle, should take the name of *The Yellow Book*?—which so certainly would command for it the liveliest attention. What, further, should one rejoice more to hear than that this venture was, for all its constitutional gaiety, to brave the quarterly form, a thing hitherto of austere, of awful tradition, and was indeed in still other ways to sound the note of bright young defiance? The project, modestly and a little vaguely but all communicatively set forth, amused me, charmed me, on the spot—or at least the touchingly convinced and inflamed projector did. It was the happy fortune of the late Henry Harland to charge everything he touched, whether in life or in literature, with that influence—an effect by which he was always himself the first to profit. If he came to me, about *The Yellow Book*, amused, he pursued the enterprise under the same hilarious star; its difficulties no less than its felicities excited, in the event, his mirth; and he was never more amused (nor, I may certainly add, more amusing) than when, after no very prolonged career, it encountered suddenly and all distressfully its term. The thing had then been to him, for the few years, a humorous uneasy care, a business attended both with other troubles and other pleasures; yet when, before the too prompt harshness of his final frustration, I reflect that he had adventurously lived, wrought and enjoyed, the small square

7

lemon-coloured quarterly, "failure" and all, figures to me perhaps his most beguiling dream and most rewarding hours.

The bravest of the portents that Sunday afternoon—the intrinsic, of course I mean; the only ones to-day worth speaking of—I have yet to mention; for I recall my rather embarrassed inability to measure as yet the contributory value of Mr. Aubrey Beardsley, by whom my friend was accompanied and who, as his prime illustrator, his perhaps even quite independent picture-maker, was to be in charge of the "art department." This young man, slender, pale, delicate, unmistakably intelligent, somehow invested the whole proposition with a detached, a slightly ironic and melancholy grace. I had met him before, on a single occasion, and had seen an example or two of his so curious and so disconcerting talent—my appreciation of which seems to me, however, as I look back, to have stopped quite short. The young *recueil* was to have pictures, yes, and they were to be as often as possible from Beardsley's hand; but they were to wear this unprecedented distinction, and were to scatter it all about them, that they should have nothing to do with the text—which put the whole matter on an ideal basis. To those who remember the short string of numbers of *The Yellow Book* the spasmodic independence of these contributions will still be present. They were, as illustrations, related surely to nothing else in the same pages—save once or twice, as I imperfectly recall, to some literary effort of Beardsley's own that matched them in perversity; and I might well be at peace as to any disposition on the part of the strange young artist ever to emulate *my* comparatively so incurious text. There would be more to say about him, but he must not draw me off from a greater relevance—my point being simply that he had associated himself with Harland that brave day to dangle before me the sweetest aid to inspiration ever snatched by a poor scribbler from editorial lips. I should sooner have come to this turn of the affair, which at once bathed the whole prospect in the rosiest glow.

I was invited, and all urgently, to contribute to the first number, and was regaled with the golden truth that my composition might absolutely assume, might shamelessly parade in, its own organic form. It was disclosed to me, wonderfully, that—so golden the air pervading the enterprise—any projected contribution might conform, not only unchallenged but by this Circumstance itself the more esteemed, to its true intelligible nature. For any idea I might wish to express I might have space, in other words, elegantly to express it—an offered licence that, on the spot, opened up the millennium to the "short story." One had so often known this product to struggle, in one's hands, under the rude prescription of brevity at any cost, with the opposition so offered to its really becoming a story, that my friend's emphasised indifference to the arbitrary limit of length struck me, I remember, as the fruit of the finest artistic intelligence. We had been at one—that we already knew—on the truth that the forms of wrought things, in this order, *were*, all exquisitely and effectively, the things; so that, for the delight of mankind, form might compete with form and might correspond to fitness; might, that is, in the given case, have an inevitability, a marked felicity. Among forms, moreover, we had had, on the dimensional ground—for length and breadth—our ideal, the beautiful and blest *nouvelle*; the generous, the enlightened hour for which appeared thus at last to shine. It was under the star of the *nouvelle* that, in other languages, a hundred interesting and charming results, such studies on the minor scale as the best of Turgenieff's, of Balzac's, of Maupassant's, of Bourget's, and just lately, in our own tongue, of Kipling's, had been, all economically, arrived at—thanks to their authors, as "contributors," having been able to count, right and left, on a wise and liberal support. It had taken the blank misery of our Anglo-Saxon sense of such matters to organise, as might be said, the general indifference to this fine type of composition. In that dull view a "short story" was a "short story," and that was the end of it. Shades and differences, varieties and styles, the value above all of the idea happily *developed*, languished, to extinction, under the hard-and-fast rule of the "from six to eight thousand words"—when, for one's benefit, the rigour was a little relaxed. For myself, I delighted in the shapely *nouvelle*—as, for that matter, I had from time to time and here and there been almost encouraged to show.

However, these are facts quite of the smaller significance and at which I glance only because I seem still to recognise in those of my three bantlings held by Harland at the baptismal font—"The Death of the Lion" (1894), "The Coxon Fund" (1894), "The Next Time" (1895), *plus* a paper not here to be reproduced—something of the less troubled confidence with which they entered on their first state of being. These pieces have this in common that they deal all with the literary life, gathering their motive, in each case, from some noted adventure, some felt embarrassment, some extreme predicament, of the artist enamoured by perfection, ridden by his idea or paying for his sincerity. They testify indeed, as they thus stand together, to no

9

general intention—they minister only, I think, to an emphasised effect. The particular case, in respect to each situation depicted, appealed to me but on its merits; though I was to note with interest, as my sense more and more opened itself, that situations of the order I speak of might again and again be conceived. They rose before me, in fine, as numerous, and thus, here, even with everything not included, they have added themselves up. I must further mention that if they enjoy in common their reference to the troubled artistic consciousness, they make together, by the same stroke, this other rather blank profession, that few of them recall to me, however dimly, any scant pre-natal phase.

In putting them sundry such critical questions so much after the fact I find it interesting to make out—critically interesting of course, which is all our interest here pretends to be—that whereas any anecdote about life pure and simple, as it were, proceeds almost as a matter of course from some good jog of fond fancy's elbow, some pencilled note on somebody else's case, so the material for any picture of personal states so specifically complicated as those of my hapless friends in the present volume will have been drawn preponderantly from the depths of the designer's own mind. This, amusingly enough, is what, on the evidence before us, I seem critically, as I say, to gather—that the states represented, the embarrassments and predicaments studied, the tragedies and comedies recorded, can be intelligibly fathered but on his own intimate experience. I have already mentioned the particular rebuke once addressed me on all this ground, the question of where on earth, where round about us at this hour, I had "found" my Neil Paradays, my Ralph Limberts, my Hugh Verekers and other such supersubtle fry. I was reminded then, as I have said, that these represented eminent cases fell to the ground, as by their foolish weight, unless I could give chapter and verse for the eminence. I was reduced to confessing I couldn't, and yet must repeat again here how little I was so abashed. On going over these things I see, to our critical edification, exactly why—which was because I was able to plead that my postulates, my animating presences, were all, to their great enrichment, their intensification of value, ironic; the strength of applied irony being surely in the sincerities, the lucidities, the utilities that stand behind it. When it's not a campaign, of a sort, on behalf of the something better (better than the obnoxious, the provoking object) that blessedly, as is assumed, *might* be, it's not worth speaking of. But this is exactly what we mean by operative irony. It implies and projects the possible other case, the case rich and edifying where the actuality is pretentious and vain. So it plays its lamp; so, essentially, it carries that smokeless flame, which makes clear, with all the rest, the good cause that guides it. My application of which remarks is that the studies here collected have their justification in the ironic spirit, the spirit expressed by my being able to reply promptly enough to my friend: "If the life about us for the last thirty years refuses warrant for these examples, then so much the worse for that life. The *constatation* would be so deplorable that instead of making it we must dodge it: there are decencies that in the name of the general self-respect we must take for granted, there's a kind of rudimentary intellectual honour to which we must, in the interest of civilisation, at least pretend." But I must really reproduce the whole passion of my retort.

"What does your contention of non-existent conscious *exposures*, in the midst of all the stupidity and vulgarity and hypocrisy, imply but that we have been, nationally, so to speak, graced with no instance of recorded sensibility fine enough to react against these things?—an admission too distressing. What one would accordingly fain do is to baffle any such calamity, to *create* the record, in default of any other enjoyment of it; to imagine, in a word, the honourable, the producible case. What better example than this of the high and helpful public and, as it were, civic use of the imagination?—a faculty for the possible fine employments of which in the interest of morality my esteem grows every hour I live. How can one consent to make a picture of the preponderant futilities and vulgarities and miseries of life without the impulse to exhibit as well from time to time, in its place, some fine example of the reaction, the opposition, or the escape? One does, thank heaven, encounter here and there symptoms of immunity from the general infection; one recognises with rapture, on occasion, signs of a protest against the rule of the cheap and easy; and one sees thus that the tradition of a high aesthetic temper needn't, after all, helplessly and ignobly perish. These reassurances are one's warrant, accordingly, for so many recognitions of the apparent doom and the exasperated temper—whether with the spirit and the career fatally bruised and finally broken in the fray, or privileged but to gain from it a finer and more militant edge. I have had, I admit, to project *signal* specimens —have had, naturally, to make and to keep my cases interesting; the only way to achieve which was to suppose and represent them eminent. In other words, I was inevitably committed, always, to the superior case; so that if this is what you reprehensively mean, that I have been thus beguiled into citing celebrities without analogues and painting portraits without models, I plead guilty to the critical charge. Only what I myself mean is that I carry my guilt lightly and have really in face of each perpetrated licence scarce patience to defend myself." So I made my point and so I continued.

"I can't tell you, no, who it is I 'aimed at' in the story of Henry St. George; and it wouldn't indeed do for me to name his exemplar publicly even were I able. But I none the less maintain his situation to have been in *essence* an observed reality—though I should be utterly ashamed, I equally declare, if I hadn't done quite my best for it. It was the fault of this notable truth, and not my own, that it too obscurely lurked—dim and disengaged; but where is the work of the intelligent painter of life if not precisely in some such aid given to true meanings to be born ? He must bear up as he can if it be in consequence laid to him that the flat grows salient and the tangled clear, the common —worst of all !—even amusingly rare, by passing through his hands. Just so when you ask who in the world I had in mind for a victim, and what in the world for a treasure, so sacrificed to the advertisement not even of their own merits but of all sorts of independent, of really indifferent, exhibitory egotism, as the practically harried and hunted Neil Paraday and his borrowed, brandished and then fatally mislaid manuscript, I'm equally confident of having again and again closely noted in the social air all the elements of such a drama. I've put these elements together—that was my business, and in doing this wished of course to give them their maximum sense, which depended, for irony, for comedy, for tragedy, in other words for beauty, on the 'importance' of the poor foredoomed monarch of the jungle. And then, I'm not ashamed to allow, it was *amusing* to make these people 'great,' so far as one could do so without making them intrinsically false. (Yes—for the mere accidental and relative falsity I don't care.) It was amusing because it was more difficult—from the moment, of course I mean, that one worked out at all their greatness; from the moment one didn't simply give it to be taken on trust. Working out economically almost anything is the very life of the art of representation; just as the request to take on trust, tinged with the least extravagance, is the very death of the same. (There may be such a state of mind brought about on the reader's part, I think, as a positive desire to take on trust; but that is only the final fruit of insidious proceedings, operative to a sublime end, on the author's side; and is at any rate a different matter.) As for the all-ingenious 'Figure in the Carpet,'

12

let me perhaps a little pusillanimously conclude, nothing would induce me to come into close quarters with you on the correspondences of this anecdote. Here exactly is a good example for you of the virtue of your taking on trust—when I have artfully begotten in you a disposition. All I can at this point say is that if ever I was aware of ground and matter for a significant fable, I was aware of them in that connexion."

My plea for "correspondences" will perhaps, however, after all, but bring my reader back to my having, at the outset of these remarks, owned to full unconsciousness of seed dropped here by that quick hand of occasion that had elsewhere generally operated; which comes to saying, no doubt, that in the world of letters things don't at this time of day very strikingly happen. Suggestive and illuminating incident is indeed scarce frequent enough to be referred to as administering the shake that starts up afresh the stopped watch of attention. I shouldn't therefore probably have accumulated these illustrations without the sense of something interchangeable, or perhaps even almost indistinguishable, between my own general adventure and the more or less lively illustration into which I was to find this experiment so repeatedly flower. Let it pass that if I am so oddly unable to say here, at any point, "what gave me my idea," I must just a trifle freely have helped myself to it from hidden stores. But, burdened thus with the imputation of that irregularity, I shall give a poor account of my homogeneous group without the charity of a glance, however brief, at its successive components. However I might have been introduced in fact to Henry St. George, of "The Lesson of the Master," or however I might have been deprived of him, my complete possession of him, my active sympathy with him as a known and understood and admired and pitied, in fine as a fully measured, quantity, hangs about the pages still as a vague scent hangs about thick orchard trees. The great sign of a grasped warrant—for identification, arrest or whatever —is, after all, in the confidence that dissipates vagueness; and the logic of such developed situations as those of the pair commemorated at the head of my list imposed itself all triumphantly. Hadn't one again and again caught "society" in the very fact of not caring in the least what might become of the subject, however essentially fine and fragile, of a patronage reflecting such credit on all concerned, so long as the social game might be played a little more intensely, and if possible more irrelevantly, by this unfortunate's aid? Given the Lion, his "death" was but too conceivably the issue of the cruel exposure thus involved for him; and if it be claimed by what I can but feel rather a pedantic view that so precious an animal exactly *couldn't*, in our conditions, have been "given," I must reply that I yet had met him—though in a preserve not perhaps known in all its extent to geographers.

Of such a fantasy as "The Next Time" the principle would surely soon turn up among the consulted notes of any sincere man of letters —taking literature, that is, on the side of the money to be earned by it. There are beautiful talents the exercise of which yet isn't lucrative, and there are pressing needs the satisfaction of which may well appear difficult under stress of that failure of felicity. Just so there are other talents that leave any fine appreciation mystified and gaping, and the active play of which may yet be observed to become on occasion a source of vast pecuniary profit. Nothing then is at moments more attaching, in the light of "comparative" science, than the study of just where and when, just how and why recognition denies itself to the appeal at all artfully, and responds largely to the appeal coarsely enough, commingled. The critical spirit—with leisure indeed to spare —may well, in its restlessness, seek to fix a bit exactly the point at which a beautiful talent, as I have called it, ceases, when imperilled by an empty pocket, to be a "worldly" advantage. The case in which impunity, for the *malheureux* ridden by that questionable boon, insists on breaking down would seem thus to become susceptible of much fine measurement. I don't know, I confess, that it provably is; but the critical spirit at all afraid of so slight a misadventure as a waste of curiosity is of course deplorably false to its nature. The difficulty here, in truth, is that, from the moment a straight dependence on the broad-backed public is a part of the issue, the explicative quantity to be sought is precisely the mood of that monster—which, consistently and consummately unable to give the smallest account of itself, naturally renders no grain of help to inquiry. Such a study as that of Ray Limbert's so prolonged, so intensified, but so vain continuance in hope (hope of successfully growing in his temperate garden some specimen of the rank exotic whose leaves are rustling cheques) is in essence a "story about the public," only wearing a little the reduced face by reason of the too huge scale, for direct portrayal, of the monstrous countenance itself. Herein resides, as I have hinted, the anxious and easy interest of almost any sincere man of letters in the mere vicinage, even if that be all, of such strained situations as Ray Limbert's. They speak of the public, such situations, to whoever it may concern. They at all events had from far back insidiously beset

14

the imagination of the author of "The Next Time," who can scarce remember the day when he wasn't all sympathetically, all tenderly occupied with some presumed literary watcher—and quite of a sublime constitution—for that postponed redress. Therefore in however developed a state the image in question was at last to hover before him, some form of it had at least never been far to seek.

I to *this* extent recover the acute impression that may have given birth to "The Figure in the Carpet," that no truce, in English-speaking air, had ever seemed to me really struck, or even approximately strikable, with our so marked collective mistrust of anything like close or analytic appreciation—appreciation, to *be* appreciation, implying of course some such rudimentary zeal; and this though that fine process be the Beautiful Gate itself of enjoyment. To have become consistently aware of this odd numbness of the general sensibility, which seemed ever to condemn it, in presence of a work of art, to a view scarce of half the intentions embodied, and moreover, but to the scantest measure of these, was to have been directed from an early day to some of the possible implications of the matter, and so to have been led on by seductive steps, albeit perhaps by devious ways to such a congruous and, as I would fain call it, fascinating case as that of Hugh Vereker and his undiscovered, not to say undiscoverable, secret. That strikes me, when all is said, as an ample indication of the starting-point of this particular portrayal. There may be links missing between the chronic consciousness I have glanced at—that of Hugh Vereker's own analytic projector, speaking through the mouth of the anonymous scribe—and the poor man's attributive dependence, for the sense of being understood and enjoyed, on some responsive reach of critical perception that he is destined never to waylay with success; but even so they scarce signify, and I may not here attempt to catch them. This too in spite of the amusement almost always yielded by such recoveries and reminiscences, or to be gathered from the manipulation of any string of evolutionary pearls. What I most remember of my proper process is the lively impulse, at the root of it, to reinstate analytic appreciation, by some ironic or fantastic stroke, so far as possible, in its virtually forfeited rights and dignities. Importunate to this end had I long found the charming idea of some artist whose most characteristic intention, or cluster of intentions, should have taken all vainly for granted the public, or at the worst the not unthinkable private, exercise of penetration. I couldn't, I confess, be indifferent to those rare and beautiful, or at all events odd and attaching, elements

15

that might be imagined to grow in the shade of so much spent intensity and so much baffled calculation. The mere quality and play of an ironic consciousness in the designer left wholly alone, amid a chattering unperceiving world, with the thing he has most wanted to do, with the design more or less realised—some effectual glimpse of that might by itself, for instance, reward one's experiment. I came to Hugh Vereker, in fine, by this travelled road of a generalisation; the habit of having noted for many years how strangely and helplessly, among us all, what we call criticism—its curiosity never emerging from the limp state—is apt to stand off from the intended sense of things, from such finely-attested matters, on the artist's part, as a spirit and a form, a bias and a logic, of his own. From my definite preliminary it was no far cry to the conception of an intent worker who should find himself to the very end in presence but of the limp curiosity. Vereker's drama indeed —or I should perhaps rather say that of the aspiring young analyst whose report we read and to whom, I ruefully grant, I have ventured to impute a developed wit—is that at a given moment the limpness begins vaguely to throb and heave, to become conscious of a comparative tension. As an effect of this mild convulsion acuteness, at several points, struggles to enter the field, and the question that accordingly comes up, the issue of the affair, can be but whether the very secret of perception hasn't been lost. That is the situation, and "The Figure in the Carpet" exhibits a small group of well-meaning persons, engaged in a test. The reader is, on the evidence, left to conclude.

The subject of "The Coxon Fund," published in *The Yellow Book* in 1894, had long been with me, but was, beyond doubt, to have found its interest clinched by my persual, shortly before the above date, of Mr. J. Dyke Campbell's admirable monograph on S. T. Coleridge. The wondrous figure of that genius had long haunted me, and circumstances into which I needn't here enter had within a few years contributed much to making it vivid. Yet it's none the less true that the Frank Saltram of "The Coxon Fund" pretends to be of his great suggester no more than a dim reflexion and above all a free rearrangement. More interesting still than the man—for the dramatist at any rate—is the S. T. Coleridge *type*; so what I was to do was merely to recognise the type, to borrow it, to re-embody and freshly place it; an ideal under the law of which I could but cultivate a free hand. I proceeded to do so; I reconstructed the scene and the figures —I had my own idea, which required, to express itself, a new set of relations—though, when all this is said, it had assuredly taken the recorded, transmitted person, the image embalmed in literary history, to fertilise my fancy. What I should, for that matter, like most to go into here, space serving, is the so interesting question—for the most part, it strikes me, too confusedly treated—of the story-teller's "real person" or actual contemporary transplanted and exhibited. But this pursuit would take us far, such radical revision do the common laxities of the case, as generally handled, seem to call for. No such process is *effectively* possible, we must hold, as the imputed act of transplanting; an act essentially not mechanical, but thinkable rather—so far as thinkable at all—in chemical, almost in mystical terms. We can surely account for nothing in the novelist's work that hasn't passed through the crucible of his imagination, hasn't, in that perpetually simmering cauldron his intellectual *pot-au-feu*, been reduced to savoury fusion. We here figure the morsel, of course, not as boiled to nothing, but as exposed, in return for the taste it gives out, to a new and richer saturation. In this state it is in due course picked out and served, and a meagre esteem will await, a poor importance attend it, if it doesn't speak most of its late genial medium, the good, the wonderful company it has, as I hint, aesthetically kept. It has entered, in fine, into new relations, it emerges for new ones. Its final savour has been constituted, but its prime identity destroyed—which is what was to be demonstrated. Thus it has become a different and, thanks to a rare alchemy, a better thing. Therefore let us have here as little as possible about its "being" Mr. This or Mrs. That. If it adjusts itself with the least truth to its new life it can't possibly be either. If it gracelessly refers itself to either, if it persists as the impression not artistically dealt with, it shames the honour offered it and can only be spoken of as having ceased to be a thing of fact and yet not become a thing of truth. I am tempted to add that this recommemorative strain might easily woo me to another light step or two round about "The Coxon Fund." For I find myself look at it most interestedly to-day, after all, in the light of a significance quite other than that just noted. A marked example of the possible scope, at once, and the possible neatness of the *nouvelle*, it takes its place for me in a series of which the main merit and sign is the effort to do the complicated thing with a strong brevity and lucidity—to arrive, on behalf of the multiplicity, at a certain science of control. Infinitely attractive—though I risk here again doubtless an effect of reiteration—the question of how to exert this control in accepted conditions and how yet to sacrifice no real value; problem ever dearest to any economic soul desirous to keep renewing, and with a frugal splendour, its ideal of economy. Sacred altogether to memory, in short, such labours and such lights. Thus "The Coxon Fund" is such a complicated thing that if it still seems to carry itself—by which I mean if its clearness still rules here, or still serves—some pursued question of how the trick was played would probably not be thankless.

HENRY JAMES

CONTENTS

	PAGE
THE LESSON OF THE MASTER	21
THE DEATH OF THE LION	79
THE NEXT TIME	113
THE FIGURE IN THE CARPET	149
THE COXON FUND	185

THE LESSON OF THE MASTER

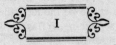

I

HE HAD been told the ladies were at church, but this was corrected by what he saw from the top of the steps—they descended from a great height in two arms, with a circular sweep of the most charming effect —at the threshold of the door which, from the long bright gallery, overlooked the immense lawn. Three gentlemen, on the grass, at a distance, sat under the great trees, while the fourth figure showed a crimson dress that told as a "bit of colour" amid the fresh rich green. The servant had so far accompanied Paul Overt as to introduce him to this view, after asking him if he wished first to go to his room. The young man declined that privilege, conscious of no disrepair from so short and easy a journey and always liking to take at once a general perceptive possession of a new scene. He stood there a little with his eyes on the group and on the admirable picture, the wide grounds of an old country-house near London—that only made it better—on a splendid Sunday in June. "But the lady, who's *she*?" he said to the servant before the man left him.

"I think she's Mrs. St. George, sir."

"Mrs. St. George the wife of the distinguished——" Then Paul Overt checked himself, doubting if a footman would know.

"Yes, sir—probably, sir," said his guide, who appeared to wish to intimate that a person staying at Summersoft would naturally be, if only by alliance, distinguished. His tone, however, made poor Overt himself feel for the moment scantly so.

"And the gentlemen?" Overt went on.

"Well, sir, one of them's General Fancourt."

"Ah yes, I know; thank you." General Fancourt was distinguished, there was no doubt of that, for something he had done, or perhaps even hadn't done—the young man couldn't remember which—some years before in India. The servant went away, leaving the glass doors open into the gallery, and Paul Overt remained at the head of the wide double staircase, saying to himself that the place was sweet and

21

promised a pleasant visit, while he leaned on the balustrade of fine old ironwork which, like all the other details, was of the same period as the house. It all went together and spoke in one voice—a rich English voice of the early part of the eighteenth century. It might have been church-time on a summer's day in the reign of Queen Anne: the stillness was too perfect to be modern, the nearness counted so as distance, and there was something so fresh and sound in the originality of the large smooth house, the expanse of beautiful brickwork that showed for pink rather than red and that had been kept clear of messy creepers by the law under which a woman with a rare complexion disdains a veil. When Paul Overt became aware that the people under the trees had noticed him he turned back through the open doors into the great gallery which was the pride of the place. It marched across from end to end and seemed—with its bright colours, its high panelled windows, its faded flowered chintzes, its quickly-recognised portraits and pictures, the blue-and-white china of its cabinets and the attenuated festoons and rosettes of its ceiling—a cheerful upholstered avenue into the other century.

Our friend was slightly nervous; that went with his character as a student of fine prose, went with the artist's general disposition to vibrate; and there was a particular thrill in the idea that Henry St. George might be a member of the party. For the young aspirant he had remained a high literary figure, in spite of the lower range of production to which he had fallen after his three first great successes, the comparative absence of quality in his later work. There had been moments when Paul Overt almost shed tears for this; but now that he was near him—he had never met him—he was conscious only of the fine original source and of his own immense debt. After he had taken a turn or two up and down the gallery he came out again and descended the steps. He was but slenderly supplied with a certain social boldness—it was really a weakness in him—so that, conscious of a want of acquaintance with the four persons in the distance, he gave way to motions recommended by their not committing him to a positive approach. There was a fine English awkwardness in this—he felt that too as he sauntered vaguely and obliquely across the lawn, taking an independent line. Fortunately there was an equally fine English directness in the way one of the gentlemen presently rose and made as if to "stalk" him, though with an air of conciliation and reassurance. To this demonstration Paul Overt instantly responded, even if the gentleman were not his host. He was tall, straight and elderly and had, like the great house itself, a pink smiling face, and into the bargain a white moustache. Our young man met him halfway while he laughed and said: "Er—Lady Watermouth told us you were coming; she asked me just to look after you." Paul Overt thanked him, liking him on the spot, and turned round with him to walk towards the others. "They've all gone to church—all except us," the stranger continued as they went; "we're just sitting here—it's so jolly." Overt pronounced it jolly indeed: it was such a lovely place. He mentioned that he was having the charming impression for the first time.

"Ah, you've not been here before?" said his companion. "It's a nice little place—not much to *do*, you know." Overt wondered what he wanted to "do"—he felt that he himself was doing so much. By the time they came to where the others sat he had recognised his initiator for a military man—such was the turn of Overt's imagination —had found him thus still more sympathetic. He would naturally have a need for action, for deeds at variance with the pacific pastoral scene. He was evidently so good-natured, however, that he accepted the inglorious hour for what it was worth. Paul Overt shared it with him and his companions for the next twenty minutes; the latter looked at him and he looked at them without knowing much who they were, while the talk went on without much telling him even what it meant. It seemed indeed to mean nothing in particular; it wandered, with casual pointless pauses and short terrestrial flights, amid names of persons and places—names which, for our friend, had no great power of evocation. It was all sociable and slow, as was right and natural of a warm Sunday morning.

His first attention was given to the question, privately considered, of whether one of the two younger men would be Henry St. George. He knew many of his distinguished contemporaries by their photographs, but had never, as happened, seen a portrait of the great misguided novelist. One of the gentlemen was unimaginable—he was too young; and the other scarcely looked clever enough, with such mild undiscriminating eyes. If those eyes were St. George's the problem presented by the ill-matched parts of his genius would be still more difficult of solution. Besides, the deportment of their proprietor was not, as regards the lady in the red dress, such as could be natural, toward the wife of his bosom, even to a writer accused by several critics of sacrificing too much to manner. Lastly, Paul Overt had a vague sense that if the gentleman with the expressionless eyes bore the name that had set his heart beating faster (he also had contradictory conventional whiskers—the young admirer of the celebrity had never in a mental vision seen *his* face in so vulgar a frame) he would have given him a sign of recognition or of friendliness, would have heard of him a little, would know something about "Ginistrella," would have an impression of how that fresh fiction had caught the eye of real criticism. Paul Overt had a dread of being grossly proud, but even morbid modesty might view the authorship of "Ginistrella" as constituting a degree of identity. His soldierly friend became clear enough: · he was "Fancourt," but was also "the General"; and he mentioned to the new visitor in the course of a few moments that he had but lately returned from twenty years' service abroad.

"And now you remain in England?" the young man asked.

"Oh yes; I've bought a small house in London."

"And I hope you like it," said Overt, looking at Mrs. St. George.

"Well, a little house in Manchester Square—there's a limit to the enthusiasm *that* inspires."

"Oh I meant being at home again—being back in Piccadilly."

"My daughter likes Piccadilly—that's the main thing. She's very fond of art and music and literature and all that kind of thing. She missed it in India and she finds it in London, or she hopes she'll find it. Mr. St. George has promised to help her—he has been awfully kind to her. She has gone to church—she's fond of that too—but they'll all be back in a quarter of an hour. You must let me introduce you to her—she'll be so glad to know you. I daresay she has read every blest word you've written."

"I shall be delighted—I haven't written so very many," Overt pleaded, feeling, and without resentment, that the General at least was vagueness itself about that. But he wondered a little why, expressing this friendly disposition, it didn't occur to the doubtless eminent soldier to pronounce the word that would put him in relation with Mrs. St. George. If it was a question of introductions Miss Fancourt—apparently as yet unmarried—was far away, while the wife of his illustrious confrère was almost between them. This lady struck Paul Overt as altogether pretty, with a surprising juvenility and a high smartness of aspect, something that—he could scarcely have said why—served for mystification. St. George certainly had every right to a charming wife, but he himself would never have imagined the important little woman in the aggressively Parisian dress the partner for life, the *alter ego*, of a man of letters. That partner in general, he knew, that second self, was far from presenting herself in a single type:

observation had taught him that she was not inveterately, not necessarily plain. But he had never before seen her look so much as if her prosperity had deeper foundations than an ink-spotted study-table littered with proof-sheets. Mrs. St. George might have been the wife of a gentleman who "kept" books rather than wrote them, who carried on great affairs in the City and made better bargains than those that poets mostly make with publishers. With this she hinted at a success more personal—a success peculiarly stamping the age in which society, the world of conversation, is a great drawing-room with the City for its ante-chamber. Overt numbered her years at first as some thirty, and then ended by believing that she might approach her fiftieth. But she somehow in this case juggled away the excess and the difference—you only saw them in a rare glimpse, like the rabbit in the conjuror's sleeve. She was extraordinarily white, and her every element and item was pretty; her eyes, her ears, her hair, her voice, her hands, her feet—to which her relaxed attitude in her wicker chair gave a great publicity—and the numerous ribbons and trinkets with which she was bedecked. She looked as if she had put on her best clothes to go to church and then had decided they were too good for that and had stayed at home. She told a story of some length about the shabby way Lady Jane had treated the Duchess, as well as an anecdote in relation to a purchase she had made in Paris—on her way back from Cannes; made for Lady Egbert, who had never refunded the money. Paul Overt suspected her of a tendency to figure great people as larger than life, until he noticed the manner in which she handled Lady Egbert, which was so sharply mutinous that it reassured him. He felt he should have understood her better if he might have met her eye; but she scarcely so much as glanced at him. "Ah here they come—all the good ones!" she said at last; and Paul Overt admired at his distance the return of the churchgoers—several persons, in couples and threes, advancing in a flicker of sun and shade at the end of a large green vista formed by the level grass and the overarching boughs.

"If you mean to imply that *we're* bad, I protest," said one of the gentlemen—"after making one's self agreeable all the morning!"

"Ah if they've found you agreeable——!" Mrs. St. George gaily cried. "But if we're good the others are better."

"They must be angels then," said the amused General.

"Your husband was an angel, the way he went off at your bidding," the gentleman who had first spoken declared to Mrs. St. George.

"At my bidding?"

"Didn't you make him go to church?"

"I never made him do anything in my life but once—when I made him burn up a bad book. That's all!" At her "That's all!" our young friend broke into an irrepressible laugh; it lasted only a second, but it drew her eyes to him. His own met them, though not long enough to help him to understand her; unless it were a step towards this that he saw on the instant how the burnt book—the way she alluded to it!—would have been one of her husband's finest things.

"A bad book?" her interlocutor repeated.

"I didn't like it. He went to church because your daughter went," she continued to General Fancourt. "I think it my duty to call your attention to his extraordinary demonstrations to your daughter."

"Well, if you don't mind them I don't!" the General laughed.

"*Il s'attache à ses pas.* But I don't wonder—she's so charming."

"I hope she won't make him burn any books!" Paul Overt ventured to exclaim.

"If she'd make him write a few it would be more to the purpose," said Mrs. St. George. "He has been of a laziness of late—— !"

Our young man stared—he was so struck with the lady's phraseology. Her "Write a few" seemed to him almost as good as her "That's all." Didn't she, as the wife of a rare artist, know what it was to produce *one* perfect work of art? How in the world did she think they were turned off? His private conviction was that, admirably as Henry St. George wrote, he had written for the last ten years, and especially for the last five, only too much, and there was an instant during which he felt inwardly solicited to make this public. But before he had spoken a diversion was effected by the return of the absentees. They strolled up dispersedly—there were eight or ten of them—and the circle under the trees rearranged itself as they took their place in it. They made it much larger, so that Paul Overt could feel—he was always feeling that sort of thing, as he said to himself—that if the company had already been interesting to watch the interest would now become intense. He shook hands with his hostess, who welcomed him without many words, in the manner of a woman able to trust him to understand and conscious that so pleasant an occasion would in every way speak for itself. She offered him no particular facility for sitting by her, and when they had all subsided again he found himself still next General Fancourt, with an unknown lady on his other flank.

"That's my daughter—that one opposite," the General said to him without loss of time. Overt saw a tall girl, with magnificent red hair, in a dress of a pretty grey-green tint and of a limp silken texture, a garment that clearly shirked every modern effect. It had therefore somehow the stamp of the latest thing, so that our beholder quickly took her for nothing if not contemporaneous.

"She's very handsome—very handsome," he repeated while he considered her. There was something noble in her head, and she appeared fresh and strong.

Her good father surveyed her with complacency, remarking soon: "She looks too hot—that's her walk. But she'll be all right presently. Then I'll make her come over and speak to you."

"I should be sorry to give you that trouble. If you were to take me over *there*——!" the young man murmured.

"My dear sir, do you suppose I put myself out that way? I don't mean for you, but for Marian," the General added.

"*I* would put myself out for her soon enough," Overt replied; after which he went on: "Will you be so good as to tell me which of those gentlemen is Henry St. George?"

"The fellow talking to my girl. By Jove, he *is* making up to her—they're going off for another walk."

"Ah is that he—really?" Our friend felt a certain surprise, for the personage before him seemed to trouble a vision which had been vague only while not confronted with the reality. As soon as the reality dawned the mental image, retiring with a sigh, became substantial enough to suffer a slight wrong. Overt, who had spent a considerable part of his short life in foreign lands, made now, but not for the first time, the reflexion that whereas in those countries he had almost always recognised the artist and the man of letters by his personal "type," the mould of his face, the character of his head, the expression of his figure, and even the indications of his dress, so in England this identification was as little as possible a matter of course, thanks to the greater conformity, the habit of sinking the profession instead of advertising it, the general diffusion of the air of the gentleman—the gentleman committed to no particular set of ideas. More than once, on returning to his own country, he had said to himself about people met in society: "One sees them in this place and that, and one even talks with them; but to find out what they *do* one would really have to be a detective." In respect to several individuals whose work he was the opposite of "drawn to"—perhaps he was wrong—he found himself adding, "No wonder they conceal it—when it's so bad!" He noted that oftener than in France and in Germany his artist looked like a gentleman—that is, like an English one—while, certainly outside a few exceptions, his gentleman didn't look like an artist. St. George was not one of the exceptions; that circumstance he definitely apprehended before the great man had turned his back to walk off with Miss Fancourt. He certainly looked better behind than any foreign man of letters—showed for beautifully correct in his tall black hat and his superior frock coat. Somehow, all the same, these very garments—he wouldn't have minded them so much on a week-day—were disconcerting to Paul Overt, who forgot for the moment that the head of the profession was not a bit better dressed than himself. He had caught a glimpse of a regular face, a fresh colour, a brown moustache and a pair of eyes surely never visited by a fine frenzy, and he promised himself to study these denotements on the first occasion. His superficial sense was that their owner might have passed for a lucky stockbroker—a gentleman driving eastward every morning from a sanitary suburb in a smart dog-cart. That carried out the impression already derived from his wife. Paul's glance, after a moment, travelled back to this lady, and he saw how her own had followed her husband as he moved off with Miss Fancourt. Overt permitted himself to wonder a little if she were jealous when another woman took him away. Then he made out that Mrs. St. George wasn't glaring at the indifferent maiden. Her eyes rested but on her husband, and with unmistakable serenity. That was the way she wanted him to be—she liked his conventional uniform. Overt longed to hear more about the book she had induced him to destroy.

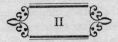

II

As THEY all came out from luncheon General Fancourt took hold of him with an "I say, I want you to know my girl!" as if the idea had just occurred to him and he hadn't spoken of it before. With the other hand he possessed himself all paternally of the young lady. "You know all about him. I've seen you with his books. She reads everything—everything!" he went on to Paul. The girl smiled at him and then laughed at her father. The General turned away and his daughter spoke—"Isn't papa delightful?"

"He is indeed, Miss Fancourt."

"As if I read you because I read 'everything'!"

"Oh I don't mean for saying that," said Paul Overt. "I liked him from the moment he began to be kind to me. Then he promised me this privilege."

"It isn't for you he means it—it's for me. If you flatter yourself that he thinks of anything in life but me you'll find you're mistaken. He introduces every one. He thinks me insatiable."

"You speak just like him," laughed our youth.

"Ah but sometimes I want to"—and the girl coloured. "I don't read everything—I read very little. But I *have* read you."

"Suppose we go into the gallery," said Paul Overt. She pleased him greatly, not so much because of this last remark—though that of course was not too disconcerting—as because, seated opposite to him at luncheon, she had given him for half an hour the impression of her beautiful face. Something else had come with it—a sense of generosity, of an enthusiasm which, unlike many enthusiasms, was not all manner. That was not spoiled for him by his seeing that the repast had placed her again in familiar contact with Henry St. George. Sitting next her this celebrity was also opposite our young man, who had been able to note that he multiplied the attentions lately brought by his wife to the General's notice. Paul Overt had gathered as well that this lady was not in the least discomposed by these fond excesses and that she gave every sign of an unclouded spirit. She had Lord Masham on one side of her and on the other the accomplished Mr. Mulliner, editor of the new high-class lively evening paper which was expected to meet a want felt in circles increasingly conscious that Conservatism must be made amusing, and unconvinced when assured by those of another political colour that it was already amusing enough. At the end of an hour spent in her company Paul Overt thought her still prettier than at the first radiation, and if her profane allusions to her husband's work had not still rung in his ears he should have liked her—so far as it could be a question of that in connexion with a woman to whom he had not yet spoken and to whom probably he should never speak if it were left to her. Pretty women were a clear need to this genius, and for the hour it was Miss Fancourt who supplied the want. If Overt had promised himself a closer view the occasion was now of the best, and it brought consequences felt by the young man as important. He saw more in St. George's face, which he liked the better for its not having told its whole story in the first three minutes. That story came out as one read, in short instalments—it was excusable that one's analogies should be somewhat professional—and the text was a style considerably involved, a language not easy to translate at sight. There were shades of meaning in it and a vague perspective of history which receded as you advanced. Two facts Paul had particularly heeded. The first of these was that he liked the measured mask much better at inscrutable rest than in social agitation; its almost convulsive smile above all displeased him (as much as any impression from that source could), whereas the quiet face had a charm that grew in proportion as stillness settled again. The change to the expression of gaiety excited, he made out, very much the private protest of a person sitting gratefully in the twilight when the lamp is brought in too soon. His second reflexion was that, though generally averse to the flagrant use of ingratiating arts by a man of age "making up" to a pretty girl, he was not in this case too painfully affected: which seemed to prove either that St. George had a light hand or the air of being younger than he was, or else that Miss Fancourt's own manner somehow made everything right.

Overt walked with her into the gallery, and they strolled to the end of it, looking at the pictures, the cabinets, the charming vista, which harmonised with the prospect of the summer afternoon, resembling it by a long brightness, with great divans and old chairs that figured hours of rest. Such a place as that had the added merit of giving those who came into it plenty to talk about. Miss Fancourt sat down with her new acquaintance on a flowered sofa, the cushions of which, very numerous, were tight ancient cubes of many sizes, and presently said: "I'm so glad to have a chance to thank you."

"To thank me——?" He had to wonder.

"I liked your book so much. I think it splendid."

She sat there smiling at him, and he never asked himself which book she meant; for after all he had written three or four. That seemed a vulgar detail, and he wasn't even gratified by the idea of the pleasure she told him—her handsome bright face told him—he had given her. The feeling she appealed to, or at any rate the feeling she excited, was something larger, something that had little to do with any quickened pulsation of his own vanity. It was responsive admiration of the life she embodied, the young purity and richness of which appeared to imply that real success was to resemble *that*, to live, to bloom, to present the perfection of a fine type, not to have hammered out headachy fancies with a bent back at an ink-stained table. While her grey eyes rested on him—there was a widish space between these, and the division of her rich-coloured hair, so thick that it ventured to be smooth, made a free arch above them—he was almost ashamed of that exercise of the pen which it was her present inclination to commend. He was conscious he should have liked better to please her in some other way. The lines of her face were those of a woman grown, but the child lingered on in her complexion and in the sweetness of her mouth. Above all she was natural—that was indubitable now; more natural than he had supposed at first, perhaps on account of her æsthetic toggery, which was conventionally unconventional, suggesting what he might have called a tortuous spontaneity. He had feared that sort of thing in other cases, and his fears had been justified; for, though he was an artist to the essence, the modern reactionary nymph, with the brambles of the woodland caught in her folds and a look as if the satyrs had toyed with her hair, made him shrink, not as a man of starch and patent leather, but as a man potentially himself a poet or even a faun. The girl was really more candid than her costume, and the best proof of it was her supposing her liberal character suited by any uniform. This was a fallacy, since if she was draped as a pessimist he was sure she liked the taste of life. He thanked her for her appreciation—aware at the same time that he didn't appear to thank her enough and that she might think him ungracious. He was afraid she would ask him to explain something he had written, and he always winced at that—perhaps too timidly—for to his own ear the explanation of a work of art sounded fatuous. But he liked her so much as to feel a confidence that in the long run he should be able to show her he wasn't rudely evasive. Moreover, she surely wasn't quick to take offence, wasn't irritable; she could be trusted to wait. So when he said to her, "Ah don't talk of anything I've done, don't talk of it *here*; there's another man in the house who's the actuality!" —when he uttered this short sincere protest it was with the sense that she would see in the words neither mock humility nor the impatience of a successful man bored with praise.

"You mean Mr. St. George—isn't he delightful?"

Paul Overt met her eyes, which had a cool morning-light that would have half-broken his heart if he hadn't been so young. "Alas I don't know him. I only admire him at a distance."

"Oh you *must* know him—he wants so to talk to you," returned Miss Fancourt, who evidently had the habit of saying the things that, by her quick calculation, would give people pleasure. Paul saw how she would always calculate on everything's being simple between others.

"I shouldn't have supposed he knew anything about me," he professed.

"He does then—everything. And if he didn't I should be able to tell him."

"To tell him everything?" our friend smiled.

"You talk just like the people in your book," she answered.

"Then they must all talk alike."

She thought a moment, not a bit disconcerted. "Well, it must be so difficult. Mr. St. George tells me it *is*—terribly. I've tried too— and I find it so. I've tried to write a novel."

"Mr. St. George oughtn't to discourage you," Paul went so far as to say.

"You do much more—when you wear that expression."

"Well, after all, why try to be an artist?" the young man pursued. "It's so poor—so poor!"

"I don't know what you mean," said Miss Fancourt, who looked grave.

"I mean as compared with being a person of action—as living your works."

"But what's art but an intense life—if it be real?" she asked. "I think it's the only one—everything else is so clumsy!" Her companion laughed, and she brought out with her charming serenity what next struck her. "It's so interesting to meet so many celebrated people."

"So I should think—but surely it isn't new to you."

"Why, I've never seen any one—any one: living always in Asia."

The way she talked of Asia somehow enchanted him. "But doesn't that continent swarm with great figures? Haven't you administered provinces in India and had captive rajahs and tributary princes chained to your car?"

It was as if she didn't care even *should* he amuse himself at her cost. "I was with my father, after I left school to go out there. It was delightful being with him—we're alone together in the world, he and I—but there was none of the society I like best. One never heard of a picture—never of a book, except bad ones."

"Never of a picture? Why, wasn't all life a picture?"

She looked over the delightful place where they sat. "Nothing to compare to this. I adore England!" she cried.

It fairly stirred in him the sacred chord. "Ah of course I don't deny that we must do something with her, poor old dear, yet!"

"She hasn't been touched, really," said the girl.

"Did Mr. St. George say that?"

There was a small and, as he felt, harmless spark of irony in his question; which, however, she answered very simply, not noticing the insinuation. "Yes, he says England hasn't been touched—not considering all there is," she went on eagerly. "He's so interesting about our country. To listen to him makes one want to do something."

"It would make *me* want to," said Paul Overt, feeling strongly, on the instant, the suggestion of what she said and that of the emotion with which she said it, and well aware of what an incentive, on St. George's lips, such a speech might be.

"Oh you—as if you hadn't! I should like so to hear you talk together," she added ardently.

"That's very genial of you; but he'd have it all his own way. I'm prostrate before him."

She had an air of earnestness. "Do you think, then, he's so perfect?"

"Far from it. Some of his later books seem to me of a queerness —— !"

"Yes, yes—he knows that."

Paul Overt stared. "That they seem to me of a queerness——?"

"Well yes, or at any rate that they're not what they should be. He told me he didn't esteem them. He has told me such wonderful things —he's so interesting."

There was a certain shock for Paul Overt in the knowledge that the fine genius they were talking of had been reduced to so explicit a confession and had made it, in his misery, to the first comer; for though Miss Fancourt was charming what was she after all but an immature girl encountered at a country-house? Yet precisely this was part of the sentiment he himself had just expressed: he would make way completely for the poor peccable great man, not because he didn't read him clear, but altogether because he did. His consideration was half composed of tenderness for superficialities which he was sure their perpetrator judged privately, judged more ferociously than any one, and which represented some tragic intellectual secret. He would have his reasons for his psychology *à fleur de peau*, and these reasons could only be cruel ones, such as would make him dearer to those who already were fond of him. "You excite my envy. I have my reserves, I discriminate —but I love him," Paul said in a moment. "And seeing him for the first time this way is a great event for me."

"How momentous—how magnificent!" cried the girl. "How delicious to bring you together!"

"*Your* doing it—that makes it perfect," our friend returned.

"He's as eager as you," she went on. "But it's so odd you shouldn't have met."

"It's not really so odd as it strikes you. I've been out of England so much—made repeated absences all these last years."

She took this in with interest. "And yet you write of it as well as if you were always here."

"It's just the being away perhaps. At any rate the best bits, I suspect, are those that were done in dreary places abroad."

"And why were they dreary?"

"Because they were health-resorts—where my poor mother was dying."

"Your poor mother?"—she was all sweet wonder.

"We went from place to place to help her to get better. But she never did. To the deadly Riviera (I hate it!), to the high Alps, to Algiers, and far away—a hideous journey—to Colorado."

"And she isn't better?" Miss Fancourt went on.

"She died a year ago."

"Really?—like mine! Only that's years since. Some day you must tell me about your mother," she added.

He could at first, on this, only gaze at her. "What right things you say! If you say them to St. George I don't wonder he's in bondage."

It pulled her up for a moment. "I don't know what you mean. He doesn't make speeches and professions at all—he isn't ridiculous."

"I'm afraid you consider, then, that I am."

"No, I don't"—she spoke it rather shortly. And then she added: "He understands—understands everything."

The young man was on the point of saying jocosely: "And I don't—is that it?" But these words, in time, changed themselves to others slightly less trivial. "Do you suppose he understands his wife?"

Miss Fancourt made no direct answer, but after a moment's hesitation put it: "Isn't she charming?"

"Not in the least!"

"Here he comes. Now you must know him," she went on. A small group of visitors had gathered at the other end of the gallery and had been there overtaken by Henry St. George, who strolled in from a neighbouring room. He stood near them a moment, not falling into the talk but taking up an old miniature from a table and vaguely regarding it. At the end of a minute he became aware of Miss Fancourt and her companion in the distance; whereupon, laying down his miniature, he approached them with the same procrastinating air, his hands in his pockets and his eyes turned, right and left, to the pictures. The gallery was so long that this transit took some little time, especially as there was a moment when he stopped to admire the fine Gainsborough. "He says Mrs. St. George has been the making of him," the girl continued in a voice slightly lowered.

"Ah he's often obscure!" Paul laughed.

"Obscure?" she repeated as if she heard it for the first time. Her eyes rested on her other friend, and it wasn't lost upon Paul that they appeared to send out great shafts of softness. "He's going to speak to us!" she fondly breathed. There was a sort of rapture in her voice, and our friend was startled. "Bless my soul, does she care for him like *that*?—is she in love with him?" he mentally inquired. "Didn't I tell you he was eager?" she had meanwhile asked of him.

"It's eagerness dissimulated," the young man returned as the subject of their observation lingered before his Gainsborough. "He edges toward us shyly. Does he mean that she saved him by burning that book?"

"That book? what book did she burn?" The girl quickly turned her face to him.

"Hasn't he told you, then?"

35

"Not a word."

"Then he doesn't tell you everything!" Paul had guessed that she pretty much supposed he did. The great man had now resumed his course and come nearer; in spite of which his more qualified admirer risked a profane observation. "St. George and the Dragon is what the anecdote suggests!"

His companion, however, didn't hear it; she smiled at the dragon's adversary. "He *is* eager—he is!" she insisted.

"Eager for you—yes."

But meanwhile she had called out: "I'm sure you want to know Mr. Overt. You'll be great friends, and it will always be delightful to me to remember I was here when you first met and that I had something to do with it."

There was a freshness of intention in the words that carried them off; nevertheless our young man was sorry for Henry St. George, as he was sorry at any time for any person publicly invited to be responsive and delightful. He would have been so touched to believe that a man he deeply admired should care a straw for him that he wouldn't play with such a presumption if it were possibly vain. In a single glance of the eye of the pardonable master he read—having the sort of divination that belonged to his talent—that his personage had ever a store of friendly patience, which was part of his rich outfit, but was versed in no printed page of a rising scribbler. There was even a relief, a simplification, in that: liking him so much already for what he had done, how could one have liked him any more for a perception which must at the best have been vague? Paul Overt got up, trying to show his compassion, but at the same instant he found himself encompassed by St. George's happy personal art—a manner of which it was the essence to conjure away false positions. It all took place in a moment. Paul was conscious that he knew him now, conscious of his handshake and of the very quality of his hand; of his face, seen nearer and consequently seen better, of a general fraternising assurance, and in particular of the circumstance that St. George didn't dislike him (as yet at least) for being imposed by a charming but too gushing girl, attractive enough without such danglers. No irritation at any rate was reflected in the voice with which he questioned Miss Fancourt as to some project of a walk—a general walk of the company round the park. He had soon said something to Paul about a talk—"We must have a tremendous lot of talk; there are so many things, aren't there?"—but our friend could see this idea wouldn't in the present case take very immediate effect. All the same he was extremely happy, even after the matter of the walk had been settled—the three presently passed back to the other part of the gallery, where it was discussed with several members of the party; even when, after they had all gone out together, he found himself for half an hour conjoined with Mrs. St. George. Her husband had taken the advance with Miss Fancourt, and this pair were quite out of sight. It was the prettiest of rambles for a summer afternoon—a grassy circuit, of immense extent, skirting the limit of the park within. The park was completely surrounded by its old mottled but perfect red wall, which, all the way on their left, constituted in itself an object of interest. Mrs. St. George mentioned to him the surprising number of acres thus enclosed, together with numerous other facts relating to the property and the family, and the family's other properties: she couldn't too strongly urge on him the importance of seeing their other houses. She ran over the names of these and rang the changes on them with the facility of practice, making them appear an almost endless list. She had received Paul Overt very amiably on his breaking ground with her by the mention of his joy in having just made her husband's acquaintance, and struck him as so alert and so accommodating a little woman that he was rather ashamed of his *mot* about her to Miss Fancourt; though he reflected that a hundred other people, on a hundred occasions, would have been sure to make it. He got on with Mrs. St. George, in short, better than he expected; but this didn't prevent her suddenly becoming aware that she was faint with fatigue and must take her way back to the house by the shortest cut. She professed that she hadn't the strength of a kitten and was a miserable wreck; a character he had been too preoccupied to discern in her while he wondered in what sense she could be held to have been the making of her husband. He had arrived at a glimmering of the answer when she announced that she must leave him, though this perception was of course provisional. While he was in the very act of placing himself at her disposal for the return the situation underwent a change; Lord Masham had suddenly turned up, coming back to them, overtaking them, emerging from the shrubbery —Overt could scarcely have said how he appeared—and Mrs. St. George had protested that she wanted to be left alone and not to break up the party. A moment later she was walking off with Lord Masham. Our friend fell back and joined Lady Watermouth, to whom he presently mentioned that Mrs. St. George had been obliged to renounce the attempt to go further.

"She oughtn't to have come out at all," her ladyship rather grumpily remarked.

"Is she so very much of an invalid?"

"Very bad indeed." And his hostess added with still greater austerity: "She oughtn't really to come to one!" He wondered what was implied by this, and presently gathered that it was not a reflexion on the lady's conduct or her moral nature: it only represented that her strength was not equal to her aspirations.

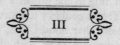

III

THE SMOKING-ROOM at Summersoft was on the scale of the rest of the place—high, light, commodious and decorated with such refined old carvings and mouldings that it seemed rather a bower for ladies who should sit at work at fading crewels than a parliament of gentlemen smoking strong cigars. The gentlemen mustered there in considerable force on the Sunday evening, collecting mainly at one end, in front of one of the cool fair fireplaces of white marble, the entablature of which was adorned with a delicate little Italian "subject." There was another in the wall that faced it, and, thanks to the mild summer night, a fire in neither; but a nucleus for aggregation was furnished on one side by a table in the chimney-corner laden with bottles, decanters and tall tumblers. Paul Overt was a faithless smoker; he would puff a cigarette for reasons with which tobacco had nothing to do. This was particularly the case on the occasion of which I speak; his motive was the vision of a little direct talk with Henry St. George. The "tremendous" communion of which the great man had held out hopes to him earlier in the day had not yet come off, and this saddened him considerably, for the party was to go its several ways immediately after breakfast on the morrow. He had, however, the disappointment of finding that apparently the author of "Shadowmere" was not disposed to prolong his vigil. He wasn't among the gentlemen assembled when Paul entered, nor was he one of those who turned up, in bright habiliments, during the next ten minutes. The young man waited a little, wondering if he had only gone to put on something extraordinary; this would account for his delay as well as contribute further to Overt's impression of his tendency to do the approved superficial thing. But he didn't arrive—he must have been putting on something more extraordinary than was probable. Our hero gave him up, feeling a little injured, a little wounded, at this loss of twenty coveted words. He wasn't angry, but he puffed his cigarette sighingly, with the sense of something rare possibly missed. He wandered away with his regret and moved slowly round the room, looking at the old prints on the walls. In this attitude he presently felt a hand on his shoulder and a friendly voice in his ear: "This is good. I hoped I should find you. I came down on purpose." St. George was there without a change of dress and with a fine face—his graver one—to which our young man all in a flutter responded. He explained that it was only for the Master —the idea of a little talk—that he had sat up, and that, not finding him, he had been on the point of going to bed.

"Well, you know, I don't smoke—my wife doesn't let me," said St. George, looking for a place to sit down. "It's very good for me— very good for me. Let us take that sofa."

"Do you mean smoking's good for you?"

"No, no—her not letting me. It's a great thing to have a wife who's so sure of all the things one can do without. One might never find them out one's self. She doesn't allow me to touch a cigarette." They took possession of a sofa at a distance from the group of smokers, and St. George went on: "Have you got one yourself?"

"Do you mean a cigarette?"

"Dear no—a wife!"

"No; and yet I'd give up my cigarette for one."

"You'd give up a good deal more than that," St. George returned. "However, you'd get a great deal in return. There's a something to be said for wives," he added, folding his arms and crossing his outstretched legs. He declined tobacco altogether and sat there without returning fire. His companion stopped smoking, touched by his courtesy; and after all they were out of the fumes, their sofa was in a faraway corner. It would have been a mistake, St. George went on, a great mistake for them to have separated without a little chat; "for I know all about you," he said. "I know you're very remarkable. You've written a very distinguished book."

"And how do you know it?" Paul asked.

"Why, my dear fellow, it's in the air, it's in the papers, it's everywhere." St. George spoke with the immediate familiarity of a confrère—a tone that seemed to his neighbour the very rustle of the laurel. "You're on all men's lips and, what's better, on all women's. And I've just been reading your book."

"Just? You hadn't read it this afternoon," said Overt.

"How do you know that?"

"I think you should know how I know it," the young man laughed.

"I suppose Miss Fancourt told you."

"No indeed—she led me rather to suppose you had."

"Yes—that's much more what she'd do. Doesn't she shed a rosy glow over life? But you didn't believe her?" asked St. George.

"No, not when you came to us there."

"Did I pretend? did I pretend badly?" But without waiting for an answer to this St. George went on: "You ought always to believe such a girl as that—always, always. Some women are meant to be taken with allowances and reserves; but you must take *her* just as she is."

"I like her very much," said Paul Overt.

Something in his tone appeared to excite on his companion's part a momentary sense of the absurd; perhaps it was the air of deliberation attending this judgement. St. George broke into a laugh to reply. "It's the best thing you can do with her. She's a rare young lady! In point of fact, however, I confess I hadn't read you this afternoon."

"Then you see how right I was in this particular case not to believe Miss Fancourt."

"How right? how can I agree to that when I lost credit by it?"

"Do you wish to pass exactly for what she represents you? Certainly you needn't be afraid," Paul said.

"Ah, my dear young man, don't talk about passing—for the likes of me! I'm passing away—nothing else than that. She has a better use for her young imagination (isn't it fine?) than in 'representing' in any way such a weary wasted used-up animal!" The Master spoke with a sudden sadness that produced a protest on Paul's part; but before the protest could be uttered he went on, reverting to the latter's striking novel: "I had no idea you were so good—one hears of so many things. But you're surprisingly good."

"I'm going to be surprisingly better," Overt made bold to reply.

"I see that, and it's what fetches me. I don't see so much else—as one looks about—that's going to be surprisingly better. They're going to be consistently worse—most of the things. It's so much easier to be worse—heaven knows I've found it so. I'm not in a great glow, you know, about what's breaking out all over the place. But you *must* be better, you really must keep it up. I haven't of course. It's very difficult—that's the devil of the whole thing, keeping it up. But I see you'll be able to. It will be a great disgrace if you don't."

"It's very interesting to hear you speak of yourself; but I don't know what you mean by your allusions to your having fallen off," Paul Overt observed with pardonable hypocrisy. He liked his companion so much now that the fact of any decline of talent or of care had ceased for the moment to be vivid to him.

"Don't say that—don't say that," St. George returned gravely, his head resting on the top of the sofa-back and his eyes on the ceiling. "You know perfectly what I mean. I haven't read twenty pages of your book without seeing that you can't help it."

"You make me very miserable," Paul ecstatically breathed.

"I'm glad of that, for it may serve as a kind of warning. Shocking enough it must be, especially to a young fresh mind, full of faith—the spectacle of a man meant for better things sunk at my age in such dishonour." St. George, in the same contemplative attitude, spoke softly but deliberately, and without perceptible emotion. His tone indeed suggested an impersonal lucidity that was practically cruel—cruel to himself—and made his young friend lay an argumentative hand on his arm. But he went on while his eyes seemed to follow the graces of the eighteenth-century ceiling: "Look at me well, take my lesson to heart—for it *is* a lesson. Let that good come of it at least that you shudder with your pitiful impression, and that this may help to keep you straight in the future. Don't become in your old age what I have in mine—the depressing, the deplorable illustration of the worship of false gods!"

"What do you mean by your old age?" the young man asked.

"It has made me old. But I like your youth."

Paul answered nothing—they sat for a minute in silence. They heard the others going on about the governmental majority. Then "What do you mean by false gods?" he inquired.

His companion had no difficulty whatever in saying, "The idols of the market; money and luxury and 'the world'; placing one's children and dressing one's wife; everything that drives one to the short and easy way. Ah the vile things they make one do!"

"But surely one's right to want to place one's children."

41

"One has no business to have any children," St. George placidly declared. "I mean of course if one wants to do anything good."

"But aren't they an inspiration—an incentive?"

"An incentive to damnation, artistically speaking."

"You touch on very deep things—things I should like to discuss with you," Paul said. "I should like you to tell me volumes about yourself. This is a great feast for *me*!"

"Of course it is, cruel youth. But to show you I'm still not incapable, degraded as I am, of an act of faith, I'll tie my vanity to the stake for you and burn it to ashes. You must come and see me—you must come and see us," the Master quickly substituted. "Mrs. St. George is charming; I don't know whether you've had any opportunity to talk with her. She'll be delighted to see you; she likes great celebrities, whether incipient or predominant. You must come and dine—my wife will write to you. Where are you to be found?"

"This is my little address"—and Overt drew out his pocket-book and extracted a visiting-card. On second thoughts, however, he kept it back, remarking that he wouldn't trouble his friend to take charge of it but would come and see him straightway in London and leave it at his door if he should fail to obtain entrance.

"Ah you'll probably fail; my wife's always out—or when she isn't out is knocked up from having *been* out. You must come and dine—though that won't do much good either, for my wife insists on big dinners." St. George turned it over further, but then went on: "You must come down and see us in the country, that's the best way; we've plenty of room and it isn't bad."

"You've a house in the country?" Paul asked enviously.

"Ah not like this! But we have a sort of place we go to—an hour from Euston. That's one of the reasons."

"One of the reasons?"

"Why my books are so bad."

"You must tell me all the others!" Paul longingly laughed.

His friend made no direct rejoinder to this, but spoke again abruptly. "Why have I never seen you before?"

The tone of the question was singularly flattering to our hero, who felt it to imply the great man's now perceiving he had for years missed something. "Partly, I suppose, because there has been no particular reason why you should see me. I haven't lived in the world—in your world. I've spent many years out of England, in different places abroad."

42

"Well, please don't do it any more. You must do England—there's such a lot of it."

"Do you mean I must write about it?"—and Paul struck the note of the listening candour of a child.

"Of course you must. And tremendously well, do you mind? That takes off a little of my esteem for this thing of yours—that it goes on abroad. Hang 'abroad'! Stay at home and do things here— do subjects we can measure."

"I'll do whatever you tell me," Overt said, deeply attentive. "But pardon me if I say I don't understand how you've been reading my book," he added. "I've had you before me all the afternoon, first in that long walk, then at tea on the lawn, till we went to dress for dinner, and all the evening at dinner and in this place."

St. George turned his face about with a smile. "I gave it but a quarter of an hour."

"A quarter of an hour's immense, but I don't understand where you put it in. In the drawing-room after dinner you weren't reading— you were talking to Miss Fancourt."

"It comes to the same thing, because we talked about 'Ginistrella.' She described it to me—she lent me her copy."

"Lent it to you?"

"She travels with it."

"It's incredible," Paul blushed.

"It's glorious for you, but it also turned out very well for me. When the ladies went off to bed she kindly offered to send the book down to me. Her maid brought it to me in the hall, and I went to my room with it. I hadn't thought of coming here, I do that so little. But I don't sleep early, I always have to read an hour or two. I sat down to your novel on the spot, without undressing, without taking off anything but my coat. I think that's a sign my curiosity had been strongly roused about it. I read a quarter of an hour, as I tell you, and even in a quarter of an hour I was greatly struck."

"Ah the beginning isn't very good—it's the whole thing!" said Overt, who had listened to this recital with extreme interest. "And you laid down the book and came after me?" he asked.

"That's the way it moved me. I said to myself, 'I see it's off his own bat, and he's there, by the way, and the day's over, and I haven't said twenty words to him.' It occurred to me that you'd probably be in the smoking-room and that it wouldn't be too late to repair my omission. I wanted to do something civil to you, so I put on my coat and came down. I shall read your book again when I go up."

Our friend faced round in his place—he was touched as he had scarce ever been by the picture of such a demonstration in his favour. "You're really the kindest of men. *Cela s'est passé comme ça?*—and I've been sitting here with you all this time and never apprehended it and never thanked you !"

"Thank Miss Fancourt—it was she who wound me up. She has made me feel as if I had read your novel."

"She's an angel from heaven !" Paul declared.

"She is indeed. I've never seen any one like her. Her interest in literature's touching—something quite peculiar to herself; she takes it all so seriously. She feels the arts and she wants to feel them more. To those who practise them it's almost humiliating—her curiosity, her sympathy, her good faith. How can anything be as fine as she supposes it ?"

"She's a rare organisation," the younger man sighed.

"The richest I've ever seen—an artistic intelligence really of the first order. And lodged in such a form !" St. George exclaimed.

"One would like to represent such a girl as that," Paul continued.

"Ah there it is—there's nothing like life !" said his companion. "When you're finished, squeezed dry and used up and you think the sack's empty, you're still appealed to, you still get touches and thrills, the idea springs up—out of the leap of the actual—and shows you there's always something to be done. But I shan't do it—she's not for me !"

"How do you mean, not for you ?"

"Oh, it's all over—she's for you, if you like."

"Ah much less !" said Paul. "She's not for a dingy little man of letters; she's for the world, the bright rich world of bribes and rewards. And the world will take hold of her—it will carry her away."

"It will try—but it's just a case in which there may be a fight. It would be worth fighting, for a man who had it in him, with youth and talent on his side."

These words rang not a little in Paul Overt's consciousness—they held him briefly silent. "It's a wonder she has remained as she is; giving herself away so—with so much to give away."

"Remaining, you mean, so ingenuous—so natural ? Oh she doesn't care a straw—she gives away because she overflows. She has her own feelings, her own standards; she doesn't keep remembering that she

44

must be proud. And then she hasn't been here long enough to be spoiled; she has picked up a fashion or two, but only the amusing ones. She's a provincial—a provincial of genius," St. George went on; "her very blunders are charming, her mistakes are interesting. She has come back from Asia with all sorts of excited curiosities and unappeased appetites. She's first-rate herself and she expends herself on the second-rate. She's life herself and she takes a rare interest in imitations. She mixes all things up, but there are none in regard to which she hasn't perceptions. She sees things in a perspective—as if from the top of the Himalayas—and she enlarges everything she touches. Above all she exaggerates—to herself, I mean. She exaggerates you and me !"

There was nothing in that description to allay the agitation caused in our younger friend by such a sketch of a fine subject. It seemed to him to show the art of St. George's admired hand, and he lost himself in gazing at the vision—this hovered there before him—of a woman's figure which should be part of the glory of a novel. But at the end of a moment the thing had turned into smoke and out of the smoke—the last puff of a big cigar—proceeded the voice of General Fancourt, who had left the others and come and planted himself before the gentlemen on the sofa. "I suppose that when you fellows get talking you sit up half the night."

"Half the night ?—*jamais de la vie !* I follow a hygiene"—and St. George rose to his feet.

"I see—you're hothouse plants," laughed the General. "That's the way you produce your flowers."

"I produce mine between ten and one every morning—I bloom with a regularity !" St. George went on.

"And with a splendour !" added the polite General, while Paul noted how little the author of "Shadowmere" minded, as he phrased it to himself, when addressed as a celebrated story-teller. The young man had an idea *he* should never get used to that; it would always make him uncomfortable—from the suspicion that people would think they had to—and he would want to prevent it. Evidently his great colleague had toughened and hardened—had made himself a surface. The group of men had finished their cigars and taken up their bedroom candlesticks; but before they all passed out Lord Watermouth invited the pair of guests who had been so absorbed together to "have" something. It happened that they both declined; upon which General Fancourt said: "Is that the hygiene ? You don't water the flowers ?"

"Oh I should drown them !" St. George replied; but, leaving the room still at his young friend's side, he added whimsically, for the latter's benefit, in a lower tone: "My wife doesn't let me."

"Well I'm glad I'm not one of you fellows !" the General richly concluded.

The nearness of Summersoft to London had this consequence, chilling to a person who had had a vision of sociability in a railway-carriage, that most of the company, after breakfast, drove back to town, entering their own vehicles, which had come out to fetch them, while their servants returned by train with their luggage. Three or four young men, among whom was Paul Overt, also availed themselves of the common convenience; but they stood in the portico of the house and saw the others roll away. Miss Fancourt got into a victoria with her father after she had shaken hands with our hero and said, smiling in the frankest way in the world, "I *must* see you more. Mrs. St. George is so nice; she has promised to ask us both to dinner together." This lady and her husband took their places in a perfectly-appointed brougham—she required a closed carriage—and as our young man waved his hat to them in response to their nods and flourishes he reflected that, taken together, they were an honourable image of success of the material rewards and the social credit of literature. Such things were not the full measure, but he nevertheless felt a little proud for literature.

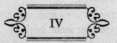

IV

BEFORE A week had elapsed he met Miss Fancourt in Bond Street, at a private view of the works of a young artist in "black-and-white" who had been so good as to invite him to the stuffy scene. The drawings were admirable, but the crowd in the one little room was so dense that he felt himself up to his neck in a sack of wool. A fringe of people at the outer edge endeavoured by curving forward their backs and presenting, below them, a still more convex surface of resistance to the pressure of the mass, to preserve an interval between their noses and the glazed mounts of the pictures ; while the central body, in the comparative gloom projected by a wide horizontal screen hung under the skylight and allowing only a margin for the day, remained upright dense and vague, lost in the contemplation of its own ingredients. This contemplation sat especially in the sad eyes of certain female heads, surmounted with hats of strange convolution and plumage, which rose on long necks above the others. One of the heads, Paul perceived, was much the most beautiful of the collection, and his next discovery was that it belonged to Miss Fancourt. Its beauty was enhanced by the glad smile she sent him across surrounding obstructions, a smile that drew him to her as fast as he could make his way. He had seen for himself at Summersoft that the last thing her nature contained was an affectation of indifference; yet even with this circumspection he took a fresh satisfaction in her not having pretended to wait his arrival with composure. She smiled as radiantly as if she wished to make him hurry, and as soon as he came within earshot she broke out in her voice of joy : "He's here—he's here ; he's coming back in a moment ! "

"Ah your father?" Paul returned as she offered him her hand.

"Oh dear no, this isn't in my poor father's line. I mean Mr. St. George. He has just left me to speak to some one—he's coming back. It's he who brought me—wasn't it charming ? "

" Ah that gives him a pull over me—I couldn't have ' brought ' you, could I ? "

" If you had been so kind as to propose it—why not you as well as he ? " the girl returned with a face that, expressing no cheap coquetry, simply affirmed a happy fact.

" Why he's a *père de famille*. They've privileges," Paul explained. And then quickly : " Will you go to see places with *me* ? " he asked.

" Anything you like," she smiled. " I know what you mean, that girls have to have a lot of people——!" Then she broke off : " I don't know; I'm free. I've always been like that—I can go about with any one. I'm so glad to meet you," she added with a sweet distinctness that made those near her turn round.

"Let me at least repay that speech by taking you out of this squash," her friend said. "Surely people aren't happy here !"

"No, they're awfully *mornes*, aren't they ? But I'm very happy indeed and I promised Mr. St. George to remain on this spot till he comes back. He's going to take me away. They send him invitations for things of this sort—more than he wants. It was so kind of him to think of me."

"They also send me invitations of this kind—more than *I* want. And if thinking of *you* will do it——!" Paul went on.

"Oh, I delight in them—everything that's life, everything that's London!"

"They don't have private views in Asia, I suppose," he laughed. "But what a pity that for this year, even in this gorged city, they're pretty well over."

"Well, next year will do, for I hope you believe we're going to be friends always. Here he comes!" Miss Fancourt continued before Paul had time to respond.

He made out St. George in the gaps in the crowd, and this perhaps led to his hurrying a little to say: "I hope that doesn't mean I'm to wait till next year to see you."

"No, no—aren't we to meet at dinner on the twenty-fifth?" she panted with an eagerness as happy as his own.

"That's almost next year. Is there no means of seeing you before?" She stared with all her brightness. "Do you mean you'd *come?*"

"Like a shot, if you'll be so good as to ask me!"

"On Sunday then—this next Sunday?"

"What have I done that you should doubt it?" the young man asked with delight.

Miss Fancourt turned instantly to St. George, who had now joined them, and announced triumphantly

"He's coming on Sunday—this next Sunday!"

"Ah my day—my day too!" said the famous novelist, laughing, to their companion.

"Yes, but not yours only. You shall meet in Manchester Square; you shall talk—you shall be wonderful!"

"We don't meet often enough," St. George allowed, shaking hands with his disciple. "Too many things—ah too many things! But we must make it up in the country in September. You won't forget you've promised me that?"

"Why, he's coming on the twenty-fifth—you'll see him then," said the girl.

"On the twenty-fifth?" St. George asked vaguely.

"We dine with you; I hope you haven't forgotten. He's dining out that day," she added gaily to Paul.

"Oh bless me, yes—that's charming! And you're coming? My wife didn't tell me," St. George said to him. "Too many things— too many things!" he repeated.

"Too many people—too many people!" Paul exclaimed, giving ground before the penetration of an elbow.

"You oughtn't to say that. They all read you."

"Me? I should like to see them! Only two or three at most," the young man returned.

"Did you ever hear anything like that? He knows, haughtily, how good he is!" St. George declared, laughing, to Miss Fancourt. "They read *me*, but that doesn't make me like them any better. Come away from them, come away!" And he led the way out of the exhibition.

"He's going to take me to the Park," Miss Fancourt observed to Overt with elation as they passed along the corridor that led to the street.

"Ah does he go there?" Paul asked, taking the fact for a somewhat unexpected illustration of St. George's *mœurs*.

"It's a beautiful day—there'll be a great crowd. We're going to look at the people, to look at types," the girl went on. "We shall sit under the trees; we shall walk by the Row."

"I go once a year—on business," said St. George, who had overheard Paul's question.

"Or with a country cousin, didn't you tell me? I'm the country cousin!" she continued over her shoulder to Paul as their friend drew her toward a hansom to which he had signalled. The young man watched them get in; he returned, as he stood there, the friendly wave of the hand with which, ensconced in the vehicle beside her, St. George took leave of him. He even lingered to see the vehicle start away and lose itself in the confusion of Bond Street. He followed it with his eyes; it put to him embarrassing things. "She's not for *me*!" the great novelist had said emphatically at Summersoft; but his manner of conducting himself toward her appeared not quite in harmony with such a conviction. How could he have behaved differently if she *had* been for him? An indefinite envy rose in Paul Overt's heart as he took his way on foot alone; a feeling addressed alike, strangely enough, to each of the occupants of the hansom. How much he should like to rattle about London with such a girl! How much he should like to go and look at "types" with St. George!

The next Sunday at four o'clock he called in Manchester Square, where his secret wish was gratified by his finding Miss Fancourt alone. She was in a large bright friendly occupied room, which was painted red all over, draped with the quaint cheap florid stuffs that are represented as coming from southern and eastern countries, where they are fabled to serve as the counterpanes of the peasantry, and bedecked with pottery of vivid hues, ranged on casual shelves, and with many water-colour drawings from the hand (as the visitor learned) of the young lady herself, commemorating with a brave breadth the sunsets, the mountains, the temples and palaces of India. He sat an hour—more than an hour, two hours—and all the while no one came in. His hostess was so good as to remark, with her liberal humanity, that it was delightful they weren't interrupted: it was so rare in London, especially at that season, that people got a good talk. But luckily now, of a fine Sunday, half the world went out of town, and that made it better for those who didn't go, when these others were in sympathy. It was the defect of London—one or two or three, the very short list of those she recognised in the teeming world-city she adored—that there were too few good chances for talk: you never had time to carry anything far.

"Too many things, too many things!" Paul said, quoting St. George's exclamation of a few days before.

"Ah yes, for him there are too many—his life's too complicated."

"Have you seen it *near*? That's what I should like to do; it might explain some mysteries," her visitor went on. She asked him what mysteries he meant, and he said: "Oh peculiarities of his work, inequalities, superficialities. For one who looks at it from the artistic point of view it contains a bottomless ambiguity."

She became at this, on the spot, all intensity. "Ah do describe that more—it's so interesting. There are no such suggestive questions. I'm so fond of them. He thinks he's a failure—fancy!" she beautifully wailed.

"That depends on what his ideal may have been. With his gifts it ought to have been high. But till one knows what he really proposed to himself——! Do *you* know by chance?" the young man broke off.

"Oh he doesn't talk to me about himself. I can't make him. It's too provoking."

Paul was on the point of asking what, then, he did talk about, but discretion checked it and he said instead: "Do you think he's unhappy at home?"

She seemed to wonder. "At home?"

"I mean in his relations with his wife. He had a mystifying little way of alluding to her."

"Not to me," said Marian Fancourt with her clear eyes. "That wouldn't be right, would it?" she asked gravely.

"Not particularly; so I'm glad he doesn't mention her to you. To praise her might bore you, and he has no business to do anything else. Yet he knows you better than me."

"Ah but he respects *you* !" the girl cried as with envy.

Her visitor stared a moment, then broke into a laugh. "Doesn't he respect you?"

"Of course, but not in the same way. He respects what you've done —he told me so the other day."

Paul drank it in, but retained his faculties. "When you went to look at types?"

"Yes—we found so many: he has such an observation of them ! He talked a great deal about your book. He says it's really important."

"Important ! Ah the grand creature !"—and the author of the work in question groaned for joy.

"He was wonderfully amusing, he was inexpressibly droll, while we walked about. He sees everything; he has so many compassions and images, and they're always exactly right. *C'est d'un trouvé*, as they say !"

"Yes, with his gifts, such things as he ought to have done !" Paul sighed.

"And don't you think he *has* done them?"

Ah it was just the point. "A part of them, and of course even that part's immense. But he might have been one of the greatest. However, let us not make this an hour of qualifications. Even as they stand," our friend earnestly concluded, "his writings are a mine of gold."

To this proposition she ardently responded, and for half an hour the pair talked over the Master's principal productions. She knew them well—she knew them even better than her visitor, who was struck with her critical intelligence and with something large and bold in the movement in her mind. She said things that startled him and that evidently had come to her directly; they weren't picked-up phrases—she placed them too well. St. George had been right about her being first-rate, about her not being afraid to gush, not remembering that she must be proud. Suddenly something came back to her, and she said: "I recollect that he did speak of Mrs. St. George to me once. He said, apropos of something or other, that she didn't care for perfection."

"That's a great crime in an artist's wife," Paul returned.

"Yes, poor thing!" and the girl sighed with a suggestion of many reflexions, some of them mitigating. But she presently added: "Ah perfection, perfection—how one ought to go in for it! I wish I could."

"Every one can in his way," her companion opined.

"In *his* way, yes—but not in hers. Women are so hampered—so condemned! Yet it's a kind of dishonour if you don't, when you want to *do* something, isn't it?" Miss Fancourt pursued, dropping one train in her quickness to take up another, an accident that was common with her. So these two young persons sat discussing high themes in their eclectic drawing-room, in their London "season"—discussing, with extreme seriousness, the high theme of perfection. It must be said in extenuation of this eccentricity that they were interested in the business. Their tone had truth and their emotion beauty; they weren't posturing for each other or for someone else.

The subject was so wide that they found themselves reducing it; the perfection to which for the moment they agreed to confine their speculations was that of the valid, the exemplary work of art. Our young woman's imagination, it appeared, had wandered far in that direction, and her guest had the rare delight of feeling in their conversation a full interchange. This episode will have lived for years in his memory and even in his wonder; it had the quality that fortune distils in a single drop at a time—the quality that lubricates many ensuing frictions. He still, whenever he likes, has a vision of the room, the bright red sociable talkative room with the curtains that, by a stroke of successful audacity, had the note of vivid blue. He remembers where certain things stood, the particular book open on the table and the almost intense odour of the flowers placed, at the left, somewhere behind him. These facts were the fringe, as it were, of a fine special agitation which had its birth in those two hours and of which perhaps the main sign was in its leading him inwardly and repeatedly to breathe, "I had no idea there was any one like this—I had no idea there was any one like this!" Her freedom amazed him and charmed him—it seemed so to simplify the practical question. She was on the footing of an independent personage—a motherless girl who had passed out of her teens and had a position and responsibilities, who wasn't held down to the limitations of a little miss. She came and went with no dragged duenna, she received people alone, and, though she was totally without hardness, the question of protection or patronage had no relevancy in

52

regard to her. She gave such an impression of the clear and the noble combined with the easy and the natural that in spite of her eminent modern situation she suggested no sort of sisterhood with the "fast" girl. Modern she was indeed, and made Paul Overt, who loved old colour, the golden glaze of time, think with some alarm of the muddled palette of the future. He couldn't get used to her interest in the arts he cared for; it seemed too good to be real—it was so unlikely an adventure to tumble into such a well of sympathy. One might stray into the desert easily—that was on the cards and that was the law of life; but it was too rare an accident to stumble on a crystal well. Yet if her aspirations seemed at one moment too extravagant to be real they struck him at the next as too intelligent to be false. They were both high and lame, and, whims for whims, he preferred them to any he had met in a like relation. It was probable enough she would leave them behind—exchange them for politics or "smartness" or mere prolific maternity, as was the custom of scribbling daubing educated flattered girls in an age of luxury and a society of leisure. He noted that the water-colours on the walls of the room she sat in had mainly the quality of being naïves, and reflected that naïveté in art is like a zero in a number: its importance depends on the figure it is united with. Meanwhile, however, he had fallen in love with her. Before he went away, at any rate, he said to her: "I thought St. George was coming to see you to-day, but he doesn't turn up."

For a moment he supposed she was going to cry "*Comment donc?* Did you come here only to meet him?" But the next he became aware of how little such a speech would have fallen in with any note of flirtation he had as yet perceived in her. She only replied: "Ah yes, but I don't think he'll come. He recommended me not to expect him." Then she gaily but all gently added: "He said it wasn't fair to you. But I think I could manage two."

"So could I," Paul Overt returned, stretching the point a little to meet her. In reality his appreciation of the occasion was so completely an appreciation of the woman before him that another figure in the scene, even so esteemed a one as St. George, might for the hour have appealed to him vainly. He left the house wondering what the great man had meant by its not being fair to him; and, still more than that, whether he had actually stayed away from the force of that idea. As he took his course through the Sunday solitude of Manchester Square, swinging his stick and with a good deal of emotion fermenting in his soul, it appeared to him he was living in a world strangely magnanimous.

Miss Fancourt had told him it was possible she should be away, and that her father should be, on the following Sunday, but that she had the hope of a visit from him in the other event. She promised to let him know should their absence fail, and then he might act accordingly. After he had passed into one of the streets that open from the Square he stopped, without definite intentions, looking sceptically for a cab. In a moment he saw a hansom roll through the place from the other side and come a part of the way toward him. He was on the point of hailing the driver when he noticed a "fare" within; then he waited, seeing the man prepare to deposit his passenger by pulling up at one of the houses. The house was apparently the one he himself had just quitted ; at least he drew that inference as he recognised Henry St. George in the person who stepped out of the hansom. Paul turned off as quickly as if he had been caught in the act of spying. He gave up his cab—he preferred to walk; he would go nowhere else. He was glad St. George hadn't renounced his visit altogether—that would have been too absurd. Yes, the world was magnanimous, and even he himself felt so as, on looking at his watch, he noted but six o'clock, so that he could mentally congratulate his successor on having an hour still to sit in Miss Fancourt's drawing-room. He himself might use that hour for another visit, but by the time he reached the Marble Arch the idea of such a course had become incongruous to him. He passed beneath that architectural effort and walked into the Park till he had got upon the spreading grass. Here he continued to walk; he took his way across the elastic turf and came out by the Serpentine. He watched with a friendly eye the diversions of the London people, he bent a glance almost encouraging on the young ladies paddling their sweethearts about the lake and the guardsmen tickling tenderly with their bearskins the artificial flowers in the Sunday hats of their partners. He prolonged his meditative walk; he went into Kensington Gardens, he sat upon the penny chairs, he looked at the little sail-boats launched upon the round pond and was glad he had no engagement to dine. He repaired for this purpose, very late, to his club, where he found himself unable to order a repast and told the waiter to bring whatever there was. He didn't even observe what he was served with, and he spent the evening in the library of the establishment, pretending to read an article in an American magazine. He failed to discover what it was about; it appeared in a dim way to be about Marian Fancourt.

Quite later in the week she wrote to him that she was not to go into the country—it had only just been settled. Her father, she added, would never settle anything, but put it all on her. She felt her responsibility—she had to—and since she was forced this was the way she had decided. She mentioned no reasons, which gave our friend all the clearer field for bold conjecture about them. In Manchester Square on this second Sunday he esteemed his fortune less good, for she had three or four other visitors. But there were three or four compensations; perhaps the greatest of which was that, learning how her father had after all, at the last hour, gone out of town alone, the bold conjecture I just now spoke of found itself becoming a shade more bold. And then her presence was her presence, and the personal red room was there and was full of it, whatever phantoms passed and vanished, emitting incomprehensible sounds. Lastly, he had the resource of staying till every one had come and gone and of believing this grateful to her, though she gave no particular sign. When they were alone together she came to his point. "But St. George did come —last Sunday. I saw him as I looked back."

"Yes, but it was the last time."

"The last time?"

"He said he would never come again."

Paul Overt stared. "Does he mean he wishes to cease to see you?"

"I don't know what he means," the girl bravely smiled. "He won't at any rate see me here."

"And pray why not?"

"I haven't the least idea," said Marian Fancourt, whose visitor found her more perversely sublime than ever yet as she professed this clear helplessness.

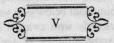

V

"OH I SAY, I want you to stop a little," Henry St. George said to him at eleven o'clock the night he dined with the head of the profession. The company—none of it indeed *of* the profession—had been numerous and was taking its leave; our young man, after bidding good night to his hostess, had put out his hand in farewell to the master of the house.

Besides drawing from the latter the protest I have cited this movement provoked a further priceless word about their chance now to have a talk, their going into his room, his having still everything to say. Paul Overt was all delight at this kindness; nevertheless he mentioned in weak jocose qualification the bare fact that he had promised to go to another place which was at a considerable distance.

"Well, then, you'll break your promise, that's all. You quite awful humbug!" St. George added in a tone that confirmed our young man's ease.

"Certainly I'll break it—but it was a real promise."

"Do you mean to Miss Fancourt? You're following her?" his friend asked.

He answered by a question. "Oh, is *she* going?"

"Base imposter!" his ironic host went on. "I've treated you handsomely on the article of that young lady: I won't make another concession. Wait three minutes—I'll be with you." He gave himself to his departing guests, accompanied the long-trained ladies to the door. It was a hot night, the windows were open, the sound of the quick carriages and of the linkmen's call came into the house. The affair had rather glittered; a sense of festal things was in the heavy air: not only the influence of that particular entertainment, but the suggestion of the wide hurry of pleasure which in London on summer nights fills so many of the happier quarters of the complicated town. Gradually Mrs. St. George's drawing-room emptied itself; Paul was left alone with his hostess, to whom he explained the motive of his waiting. "Ah yes, some intellectual, some *professional*, talk," she leered; "at this season doesn't one miss it? Poor dear Henry, I'm so glad!" The young man looked out of the window a moment, at the called hansoms that lurched up, at the smooth broughams that rolled away. When he turned round Mrs. St. George had disappeared; her husband's voice rose to him from below—he was laughing and talking, in the portico, with some lady who awaited her carriage. Paul had solitary possession, for some minutes, of the warm deserted rooms where the covered tinted lamplight was soft, the seats had been pushed about and the odour of flowers lingered. They were large, they were pretty, they contained objects of value; everything in the picture told of a "good house." At the end of five minutes a servant came in with a request from the Master that he would join him downstairs; upon which, descending, he followed his conductor through a long passage to an apartment thrown out, in the rear of the habitation, for the special requirements, as he guessed, of a busy man of letters.

St. George was in his shirt-sleeves in the middle of a large high room —a room without windows, but with a wide skylight at the top, that of a place of exhibition. It was furnished as a library, and the serried bookshelves rose to the ceiling, a surface of incomparable tone produced by dimly-gilt "backs" interrupted here and there by the suspension of old prints and drawings. At the end furthest from the door of admission was a tall desk, of great extent, at which the person using it could write only in the erect posture of a clerk in a counting-house; and stretched from the entrance to this structure was a wide plain band of crimson cloth, as straight as a garden-path and almost as long, where, in his mind's eye, Paul at once beheld the Master pace to and fro during vexed hours—hours, that is, of admirable composition. The servant gave him a coat, an old jacket with a hang of experience, from a cupboard in the wall, retiring afterwards with the garment he had taken off. Paul Overt welcomed the coat; it was a coat for talk, it promised confidences—having visibly received so many—and had tragic literary elbows. "Ah we're practical—we're practical!" St. George said as he saw his visitor look the place over. "Isn't it a good big cage for going round and round? My wife invented it and she locks me up here every morning."

Our young man breathed—by way of tribute—with a certain oppression. "You don't miss a window—a place to look out?"

"I did at first awfully; but her calculation was just. It saves time, it has saved me many months in these ten years. Here I stand, under the eye of day—in London of course, very often, it's rather a bleared old eye—walled in to my trade. I can't get away—so the room's a fine lesson in concentration. I've learnt the lesson, I think; look at that big bundle of proof and acknowledge it." He pointed to a fat roll of papers on one of the tables, which had not been undone.

"Are you bringing out another——?" Paul asked in a tone the fond deficiencies of which he didn't recognise till his companion burst out laughing, and indeed scarce even then.

"You humbug, you humbug!"—St. George appeared to enjoy caressing him, as it were, with that opprobrium. "Don't I know what you think of them?" he asked, standing there with his hands in his pockets and with a new kind of smile. It was as if he were going to let his young votary see him all now.

"Upon my word in that case you know more than I do!"

57

the latter ventured to respond, revealing a part of the torment of being able neither clearly to esteem nor distinctly to renounce him.

"My dear fellow," said the more and more interesting Master, "don't imagine I talk about my books specifically; they're not a decent subject—*il ne manquerait plus que ça!* I'm not so bad as you may apprehend. About myself, yes, a little, if you like; though it wasn't for that I brought you down here. I want to ask you something—very much indeed; I value this chance. Therefore sit down. We're practical, but there *is* a sofa, you see—for she does humour my poor bones so far. Like all really great administrators and disciplinarians she knows when wisely to relax." Paul sank into the corner of a deep leathern couch, but his friend remained standing and explanatory. "If you don't mind, in this room, this is my habit. From the door to the desk and from the desk to the door. That shakes up my imagination gently; and don't you see what a good thing it is that there's no window for her to fly out of? The eternal standing as I write (I stop at that bureau and put it down, when anything comes, and so we go on) was rather wearisome at first, but we adopted it with an eye to the long run: you're in better order—if your legs don't break down!—and you can keep it up for more years. Oh we're practical—we're practical!" St. George repeated, going to the table and taking up all mechanically the bundle of proofs. But, pulling off the wrapper, he had a change of attention that appealed afresh to our hero. He lost himself a moment, examining the sheets of his new book, while the younger man's eyes wandered over the room again.

"Lord, what good things I should do if I had such a charming place as this to do them in!" Paul reflected. The outer world, the world of accident and ugliness, was so successfully excluded, and within the rich protecting square, beneath the patronising sky, the dream-figures, the summoned company, could hold their particular revel. It was a fond prevision of Overt's rather than an observation on actual data, for which occasions had been too few, that the Master thus more closely viewed would have the quality, the charming gift, of flashing out, all surprisingly, in personal intercourse and at moments of suspended or perhaps even of diminished expectation. A happy relation with him would be a thing proceeding by jumps, not by traceable stages.

"Do you read them—really?" he asked, laying down the proofs on Paul's inquiring of him how soon the work would be published.

58

And when the young man answered, "Oh yes, always," he was moved to mirth again by something he caught in his manner of saying that. "You go to see your grandmother on her birthday—and very proper it is, especially as she won't last for ever. She has lost every faculty and every sense; she neither sees, nor hears, nor speaks; but all customary pieties and kindly habits are respectable. Only you're strong if you *do* read 'em ! *I* couldn't, my dear fellow. You *are* strong, I know; and that's just a part of what I wanted to say to you. You're very strong indeed. I've been going into your other things—they've interested me immensely. Some one ought to have told me about them before—some one I could believe. But whom can one believe ? You're wonderfully on the right road—it's awfully decent work. Now do you mean to keep it up ?—that's what I want to ask you."

"Do I mean to do others ?" Paul asked, looking up from his sofa at his erect inquisitor and feeling partly like a happy little boy when the schoolmaster is gay, and partly like some pilgrim of old who might have consulted a world-famous oracle. St. George's own performance had been infirm, but as an adviser he would be infallible.

"Others—others ? Ah the number won't matter; one other would do, if it were really a further step—a throb of the same effort. What I mean is have you it in your heart to go in for some sort of decent perfection ?"

"Ah decency, ah perfection—— !" the young man sincerely sighed. "I talked of them the other Sunday with Miss Fancourt."

It produced on the Master's part a laugh of odd acrimony. "Yes, they'll 'talk' of them as much as you like ! But they'll do little to help one to them. There's no obligation of course; only you strike me as capable," he went on. "You must have thought it all over. I can't believe you're without a plan. That's the sensation you give me, and it's so rare that it really stirs one up—it makes you remarkable. If you haven't a plan, if you *don't* mean to keep it up, surely you're within your rights; it's nobody's business, no one can force you, and not more than two or three people will notice you don't go straight. The others —*all* the rest, every blest soul in England, will think you do—will think you *are* keeping it up: upon my honour they will ! I shall be one of the two or three who know better. Now the question is whether you can do it for two or three. Is that the stuff you're made of ?"

It locked his guest a minute as in closed throbbing arms. "I could do it for one, if you were the one."

"Don't say that; I don't deserve it; it scorches me," he protested with eyes suddenly grave and glowing. "The 'one' is of course one's self, one's conscience, one's idea, the singleness of one's aim. I think of that pure spirit as a man thinks of a woman he has in some detested hour of his youth loved and forsaken. She haunts him with reproachful eyes, she lives for ever before him. As an artist, you know, I've married for money." Paul stared and even blushed a little, confounded by this avowal; whereupon his host, observing the expression of his face, dropped a quick laugh and pursued: "You don't follow my figure. I'm not speaking of my dear wife, who had a small fortune—which, however, was not my bribe. I fell in love with her, as many other people have done. I refer to the mercenary muse whom I led to the altar of literature. Don't, my boy, put your nose into *that* yoke. The awful jade will lead you a life!"

Our hero watched him, wondering and deeply touched. "Haven't you been happy?"

"Happy? It's a kind of hell."

"There are things I should like to ask you," Paul said after a pause.

"Ask me anything in all the world. I'd turn myself inside out to save you."

"To 'save' me?" he quavered.

"To make you stick to it—to make you see it through. As I said to you the other night at Summersoft, let my example be vivid to you."

"Why, your books are not so bad as that," said Paul, fairly laughing and feeling that if ever a fellow had breathed the air of art——!

"So bad as what?"

"Your talent's so great that it's in everything you do, in what's less good as well as in what's best. You've some forty volumes to show for it—forty volumes of wonderful life, of rare observation, of magnificent ability."

"I'm very clever, of course I know that"—but it was a thing, in fine, this author made nothing of. "Lord, what rot they'd all be if I hadn't been! I'm a successful charlatan," he went on—"I've been able to pass off my system. But do you know what it is? It's *carton-pierre*."

"*Carton-pierre?*" Paul was struck, and gaped.

"Lincrusta-Walton!"

"Ah don't say such things—you make me bleed!" the younger

man protested. "I see you in a beautiful fortunate home, living in comfort and honour."

"Do you call it honour?"—his host took him up with an intonation that often comes back to him. "That's what I want *you* to go in for. I mean the real thing. This is brummagem."

"Brummagem?" Paul ejaculated while his eyes wandered, by a movement natural at the moment, over the luxurious room.

"Ah they make it so well to-day—it's wonderfully deceptive!"

Our friend thrilled with the interest and perhaps even more with the pity of it. Yet he wasn't afraid to seem to patronise when he could still so far envy. "Is it deceptive that I find you living with every appearance of domestic felicity—blest with a devoted, accomplished wife, with children whose acquaintance I haven't yet had the pleasure of making, but who *must* be delightful young people, from what I know of their parents?"

St. George smiled as for the candour of his question. "It's all excellent, my dear fellow—heaven forbid I should deny it. I've made a great deal of money; my wife has known how to take care of it, to use it without wasting it, to put a good bit of it by, to make it fructify. I've got a loaf on the shelf; I've got everything in fact but the great thing."

"The great thing?" Paul kept echoing.

"The sense of having done the best—the sense which is the real life of the artist and the absence of which is his death, of having drawn from his intellectual instrument the finest music that nature had hidden in it, of having played it as it should be played. He either does that or he doesn't—and if he doesn't he isn't worth speaking of. Therefore, precisely, those who really know *don't* speak of him. He may still hear a great chatter, but what he hears most is the incorruptible silence of Fame. I've squared her, you may say, for my little hour—but what's my little hour? Don't imagine for a moment," the Master pursued, "that I'm such a cad as to have brought you down here to abuse or to complain of my wife to you. She's a woman of distinguished qualities, to whom my obligations are immense; so that, if you please, we'll say nothing about her. My boys—my children are all boys—are straight and strong, thank God, and have no poverty of growth about them, no penury of needs. I receive periodically the most satisfactory attestation from Harrow, from Oxford, from Sandhurst—oh we've done the best for them!—of their eminence as living thriving consuming organisms."

61

"It must be delightful to feel that the son of one's loins is at Sandhurst," Paul remarked enthusiastically.

"It is—it's charming. Oh I'm a patriot !"

The young man then could but have the greater tribute of questions to pay. "Then what did you mean—the other night at Summersoft— by saying that children are a curse ?"

"My dear youth, on what basis are we talking?" and St. George dropped upon the sofa at a short distance from him. Sitting a little sideways he leaned back against the opposite arm with his hands raised and interlocked behind his head. "On the supposition that a certain perfection's possible and even desirable—isn't it so ? Well, all I say is that one's children interfere with perfection. One's wife interferes. Marriage interferes."

"You think, then, the artist shouldn't marry ?"

"He does so at his peril—he does so at his cost."

"Not even when his wife's in sympathy with his work ?"

"She never is—she can't be ! Women haven't a conception of such things."

"Surely they on occasion work themselves," Paul objected.

"Yes, very badly indeed. Oh of course, often, they think they understand, they think they sympathise. Then it is they're most dangerous. Their idea is that you shall do a great lot and get a great lot of money. Their great nobleness and virtue, their exemplary conscientiousness as British females, is in keeping you up to that. My wife makes all my bargains with my publishers for me, and has done so for twenty years. She does it consummately well—that's why I'm really pretty well off. Aren't you the father of their innocent babes, and will you withhold from them their natural sustenance ? You asked me the other night if they're not an immense incentive. Of course they are—there's no doubt of that !"

Paul turned it over; it took, from eyes he had never felt open so wide, so much looking at. "For myself I've an idea I need incentives."

"Oh well, then, *n'en parlons plus* !" his companion handsomely smiled.

"*You* are an incentive, I maintain," the young man went on. "You don't affect me in the way you'd apparently like to. Your great success is what I see—the pomp of Ennismore Gardens !"

"Success ?"—St. George's eyes had a cold fine light. "Do you call it success to be spoken of as you'd speak of me if you were sitting here with another artist—a young man intelligent and sincere like yourself? Do you call it success to make you blush—as you *would* blush!—if some foreign critic (some fellow, of course I mean, who should know what he was talking about and should have shown you he did, as foreign critics like to show it) were to say to you: 'He's the one, in this country, whom they consider the most perfect, isn't he?' Is it success to be the occasion of a young Englishman's having to stammer as you would have to stammer at such a moment for old England? No, no; success is to have made people wriggle to another tune. Do try it!"

Paul continued all gravely to glow. "Try what?"

"Try to do some really good work."

"Oh I want to, heaven knows!"

"Well, you can't do it without sacrifices—don't believe that for a moment," the Master said. "I've made none. I've had everything. In other words, I've missed everything."

"You've had the full rich masculine human general life, with all the responsibilities and duties and burdens and sorrows and joys—all the domestic and social initiations and complications. They must be immensely suggestive, immensely amusing," Paul anxiously submitted.

"Amusing?"

"For a strong man—yes."

"They've given me subjects without number, if that's what you mean; but they've taken away at the same time the power to use them. I've touched a thousand things, but which one of them have I turned into gold? The artist has to do only with that—he knows nothing of any baser metal. I've led the life of the world, with my wife and my progeny; the clumsy conventional expensive materialised vulgarised brutalised life of London. We've got everything handsome, even a carriage—we're perfect Philistines and prosperous hospitable eminent people. But, my dear fellow, don't try to stultify yourself and pretend you don't know what we *haven't* got. It's bigger than all the rest. Between artists—come!" the Master wound up. "You know as well as you sit there that you'd put a pistol-ball into your brain if you had written my books!"

It struck his listener that the tremendous talk promised by him at Summersoft had indeed come off, and with a promptitude, a fulness, with which the latter's young imagination had scarcely reckoned. His impression fairly shook him and he throbbed with the excitement of such deep soundings and such strange confidences. He throbbed indeed with the conflict of his feelings—bewilderment and recognition and alarm, enjoyment and protest and assent, all commingled with tenderness (and a kind of shame in the participation) for the sores and bruises exhibited by so fine a creature, and with a sense of the tragic secret nursed under his trappings. The idea of *his*, Paul Overt's, becoming the occasion of such an act of humility made him flush and pant, at the same time that his consciousness was in certain directions too much alive not to swallow—and not intensely to taste—every offered spoonful of the revelation. It had been his odd fortune to blow upon the deep waters, to make them surge and break in waves of strange eloquence. But how couldn't he give out a passionate contradiction of his host's last extravagance, how couldn't he enumerate to him the parts of his work he loved, the splendid things he had found in it, beyond the compass of any other writer of the day ? St. George listened a while, courteously; then he said, laying his hand on his visitor's: "That's all very well; and if your idea's to do nothing better there's no reason you shouldn't have as many good things as I—as many human and material appendages, as many sons or daughters, a wife with as many gowns, a house with as many servants, a stable with as many horses, a heart with as many aches." The Master got up when he had spoken thus—he stood a moment—near the sofa, looking down on his agitated pupil. "Are you possessed of any property ?" it occurred to him to ask.

"None to speak of."

"Oh well then there's no reason why you shouldn't make a goodish income—if you set about it the right way. Study *me* for that—study me well. You may really have horses."

Paul sat there some minutes without speaking. He looked straight before him—he turned over many things. His friend had wandered away, taking up a parcel of letters from the table where the roll of proofs had lain. "What was the book Mrs. St. George made you burn—the one she didn't like ?" our young man brought out.

"The book she made me burn—how did you know that ?" The Master looked up from his letters quite without the facial convulsion the pupil had feared.

"I heard her speak of it at Summersoft."

"Ah yes—she's proud of it. I don't know—it was rather good."

"What was it about ?"

"Let me see." And he seemed to make an effort to remember.

"Oh yes—it was about myself." Paul gave an irrepressible groan for the disappearance of such a production, and the elder man went on: "Oh but *you* should write it—*you* should do me." And he pulled up —from the restless motion that had come upon him; his fine smile a generous glare. "There's a subject, my boy: no end of stuff in it!"

Again Paul was silent, but it was all tormenting. "Are there no women who really understand—who can take part in a sacrifice?"

"How can they take part? They themselves are the sacrifice. They're the idol and the altar and the flame."

"Isn't there even *one* who sees further?" Paul continued.

For a moment St. George made no answer; after which, having torn up his letters, he came back to the point all ironic. "Of course I know the one you mean. But not even Miss Fancourt."

"I thought you admired her so much."

"It's impossible to admire her more. Are you in love with her?" St. George asked.

"Yes," Paul Overt presently said.

"Well, then, give it up."

Paul stared. "Give up my 'love'?"

"Bless me, no. Your idea." And then as our hero but still gazed: "The one you talked with her about. The idea of a decent perfection."

"She'd help it—she'd help it!" the young man cried.

"For about a year—the first year, yes. After that she'd be as a millstone round its neck."

Paul frankly wondered. "Why, she has a passion for the real thing, for good work—for everything you and I care for most."

"'You and I' is charming, my dear fellow!" his friend laughed. "She has it indeed, but she'd have a still greater passion for her children —and very proper too. She'd insist on everything's being made comfortable, advantageous, propitious for them. That isn't the artist's business."

"The artist—the artist! Isn't he a man all the same?"

St. George had a grand grimace. "I mostly think not. You know as well as I what he has to do: the concentration, the finish, the independence he must strive for from the moment he begins to wish his work really decent. Ah my young friend, his relation to women, and especially to the one he's most intimately concerned with, is at the mercy of the damning fact that whereas he can in the nature of things have but one standard, they have about fifty. That's what makes them so superior,"

St. George amusingly added. "Fancy an artist with a change of standards as you'd have a change of shirts or of dinner-plates. To *do* it—to do it and make it divine—is the only thing he has to think about. 'Is it done or not?' is his only question. Not 'Is it done as well as a proper solicitude for my dear little family will allow?' He has nothing to do with the relative—he has only to do with the absolute; and a dear little family may represent a dozen relatives."

"Then you don't allow him the common passions and affections of men?" Paul asked.

"Hasn't he a passion, an affection, which includes all the rest? Besides, let him have all the passions he likes—if he only keeps his independence. He must be able to be poor."

Paul slowly got up. "Why, then, did you advise me to make up to her?"

St. George laid a hand on his shoulder. "Because she'd make a splendid wife! And I hadn't read you then."

The young man had a strained smile. "I wish you had left me alone!"

"I didn't know that that wasn't good enough for you," his host returned.

"What a false position, what a condemnation of the artist, that he's a mere disfranchised monk and can produce his effect only by giving up personal happiness. What an arraignment of art!" Paul went on with a trembling voice.

"Ah you don't imagine by chance that I'm defending art? 'Arraignment'—I should think so! Happy the societies in which it hasn't made its appearance, for from the moment it comes they have a consuming ache, they have an incurable corruption, in their breast. Most assuredly is the artist in a false position! But I thought we were taking him for granted. Pardon me," St. George continued: "''Ginistrella' made me!"

Paul stood looking at the floor—one o'clock struck, in the stillness, from a neighbouring church-tower. "Do you think she'd ever look at me?" he put to his friend at last.

"Miss Fancourt—as a suitor? Why shouldn't I think it? That's why I've tried to favour you—I've had a little chance or two of bettering your opportunity."

"Forgive my asking you, but do you mean by keeping away yourself?" Paul said with a blush.

"I'm an old idiot—my place isn't there," St. George stated gravely.

"I'm nothing yet, I've no fortune; and there must be so many others," his companion pursued.

The Master took this considerably in, but made little of it. "You're a gentleman and a man of genius. I think you might do something."

"But if I must give that up—the genius?"

"Lots of people, you know, think I've kept mine," St. George wonderfully grinned.

"You've a genius for mystification!" Paul declared, but grasping his hand gratefully in attenuation of this judgement.

"Poor dear boy, I do worry you! But try, try, all the same. I think your chances are good and you'll win a great prize."

Paul held fast the other's hand a minute; he looked into the strange deep face. "No, I *am* an artist—I can't help it!"

"Ah show it then!" St. George pleadingly broke out. "Let me see before I die the thing I most want, the thing I yearn for: a life in which the passion—ours—is really intense. If you càn be rare don't fail of it! Think what it is—how it counts—how it lives!"

They had moved to the door and he had closed both his hands over his companion's. Here they paused again and our hero breathed deep. "I want to live!"

"In what sense?"

"In the greatest."

"Well, then, stick to it—see it through."

"With your sympathy—your help?"

"Count on that—you'll be a great figure to me. Count on my highest appreciation, my devotion. You'll give me satisfaction—if that has any weight with you!" After which, as Paul appeared still to waver, his host added: "Do you remember what you said to me at Summersoft?"

"Something infatuated, no doubt!"

"'I'll do anything in the world you tell me.' You said that."

"And you hold me to it?"

"Ah what am I?" the Master expressively sighed.

"Lord, what things I shall have to do!" Paul almost moaned as he departed.

67

"IT GOES on too much abroad—hang abroad !" These or something like them had been the Master's remarkable words in relation to the action of "Ginistrella"; and yet, though they had made a sharp impression on the author of that work, like almost all spoken words from the same source, he a week after the conversation I have noted left England for a long absence and full of brave intentions. It is not a perversion of the truth to pronounce that encounter the direct cause of his departure. If the oral utterance of the eminent writer had the privilege of moving him deeply it was especially on his turning it over at leisure, hours and days later, that it appeared to yield him its full meaning and exhibit its extreme importance. He spent the summer in Switzerland and, having in September begun a new task, determined not to cross the Alps till he should have made a good start. To this end he returned to a quiet corner he knew well, on the edge of the Lake of Geneva and within sight of the towers of Chillon: a region and a view for which he had an affection that sprang from old associations and was capable of mysterious revivals and refreshments. Here he lingered late, till the snow was on the nearer hills, almost down to the limit to which he could climb when his stint, on the shortening afternoons, was performed. The autumn was fine, the lake was blue, and his book took form and direction. These felicities, for the time, embroidered his life, which he suffered to cover him with its mantle. At the end of six weeks he felt he had learnt St. George's lesson by heart, had tested and proved its doctrine. Nevertheless he did a very inconsistent thing: before crossing the Alps he wrote to Marian Fancourt. He was aware of the perversity of this act, and it was only as a luxury, an amusement, the reward of a strenuous autumn, that he justified it. She had asked of him no such favour when, shortly before he left London, three days after their dinner in Ennismore Gardens, he went to take leave of her. It was true she had had no ground—he hadn't named his intention of absence. He had kept his counsel for want of due assurance: it was that particular visit that was, the next thing, to settle the matter. He had paid the visit to see how much he really cared for her, and quick departure, without so much as an explicit farewell, was the sequel to this inquiry, the answer to which had created within him a deep yearning. When he wrote her from Clarens he noted that he owed her an explanation (more than three months after !) for not having told her what he was doing.

She replied now briefly but promptly, and gave him a striking piece of news: that of the death, a week before, of Mrs. St. George. This exemplary woman had succumbed, in the country, to a violent attack of inflammation of the lungs—he would remember that for a long time she had been delicate. Miss Fancourt added that she believed her husband was overwhelmed by the blow; he would miss her too terribly—she had been everything in life to him. Paul Overt, on this, immediately wrote to St. George. He would from the day of their parting have been glad to remain in communication with him, but had hitherto lacked the right excuse for troubling so busy a man. Their long nocturnal talk came back to him in every detail, but this was no bar to an expression of proper sympathy with the head of the profession, for hadn't that very talk made it clear that the late accomplished lady was the influence that ruled his life ? What catastrophe could be more cruel than the extinction of such an influence ? This was to be exactly the tone taken by St. George in answering his young friend upwards of a month later. He made no allusion of course to their important discussion. He spoke of his wife as frankly and generously as if he had quite forgotten that occasion, and the feeling of deep bereavement was visible in his words. "She took everything off my hands—off my mind. She carried on our life with the greatest art, the rarest devotion, and I was free, as few men can have been, to drive my pen, to shut myself up with my trade. This was a rare service—the highest she could have rendered me. Would I could have acknowledged it more fitly !"

A certain bewilderment, for our hero, disengaged itself from these remarks: they struck him as a contradiction, a retractation, strange on the part of a man who hadn't the excuse of witlessness. He had certainly not expected his correspondent to rejoice in the death of his wife, and it was perfectly in order that the rupture of a tie of more than twenty years should have left him sore. But if she had been so clear a blessing what in the name of consistency had the dear man meant by turning *him* upside down that night—by dosing him to that degree, at the most sensitive hour of his life, with the doctrine of renunciation ? If Mrs. St. George was an irreparable loss, then her husband's inspired advice had been a bad joke and renunciation was a mistake. Overt was on the point of rushing back to London to show that, for his part, he was perfectly willing to consider it so, and he went so far as to take his manuscript of the first chapters of his new book out of his table-drawer and insert it into a pocket of his portmanteau. This led to his catching a glimpse of certain pages he hadn't looked at for months, and that accident, in turn, to his being struck with the high promise they revealed—a rare result of such retrospections, which it was his habit to avoid as much as possible: they usually brought home to him that the glow of composition might be purely subjective and misleading emotion. On this occasion a certain belief in himself disengaged itself whimsically from the serried erasures of his first draft, making him think it best after all to pursue his present trial to the end. If he could write so well under the rigour of privation it might be a mistake to change the conditions before that spell had spent itself. He would go back to London of course, but he would go back only when he should have finished his book. This was the vow he privately made, restoring his manuscript to the table-drawer. It may be added that it took him a long time to finish his book, for the subject was as difficult as it was fine, and he was literally embarrassed by the fulness of his notes. Something within him warned him he must make it supremely good—otherwise he should lack, as regards his private behaviour, a handsome excuse. He had a horror of this deficiency and found himself as firm as need be on the question of the lamp and the file. He crossed the Alps at last and spent the winter, the spring, the ensuing summer, in Italy, where still, at the end of a twelvemonth, his task was unachieved. "Stick to it— see it through": this general injunction of St. George's was good also for the particular case. He applied it to the utmost, with the result that when in its slow order the summer had come round again he felt he had given all that was in him. This time he put his papers into his portmanteau, with the address of his publisher attached, and took his way northward.

He had been absent from London for two years; two years which, seeming to count as more, had made such a difference in his own life —through the production of a novel far stronger, he believed, than "Ginistrella"—that he turned out into Piccadilly, the morning after his arrival, with a vague expectation of changes, of finding great things had happened. But there were few transformations in Piccadilly— only three or four big red houses where there had been low black ones —and the brightness of the end of June peeped through the rusty railings of the Green Park and glittered in the varnish of the rolling carriages as he had seen it in other, more cursory Junes. It was a greeting he appreciated; it seemed friendly and pointed, added to the exhilaration of his finished book, of his having his own country and the huge oppressive amusing city that suggested everything, that contained everything, under his hand again. "Stay at home and do things here—do subjects we can measure," St. George had said; and now it struck him he should ask nothing better than to stay at home for ever. Late in the afternoon he took his way to Manchester Square, looking out for a number he hadn't forgotten. Miss Fancourt, however, was not at home, so that he turned rather dejectedly from the door. His movement brought him face to face with a gentleman just approaching it and recognised on another glance as Miss Fancourt's father. Paul saluted this personage, and the General returned the greeting with his customary good manner—a manner so good, however, that you could never tell whether it meant he placed you. The disappointed caller felt the impulse to address him; then, hesitating, became both aware of having no particular remark to make, and convinced that though the old soldier remembered him he remembered him wrong. He therefore went his way without computing the irresistible effect his own evident recognition would have on the General, who never neglected a chance to gossip. Our young man's face was expressive, and observation seldom let it pass. He hadn't taken ten steps before he heard himself called after with a friendly semi-articulate "Er—I beg your pardon !" He turned round and the General, smiling at him from the porch, said: "Won't you come in ? I won't leave you the advantage of me !" Paul declined to come in, and then felt regret, for Miss Fancourt, so late in the afternoon, might return at any moment. But her father gave him no second chance; he appeared mainly to wish not to have struck him as ungracious. A further look at the visitor had recalled something, enough at least to enable him to say: "You've come back, you've come back ?" Paul was on the point of replying that he had come back the night before, but he suppressed, the next instant, this strong light on the immediacy of his visit and, giving merely a general assent, alluded to the young lady he deplored not having found. He had come late in the hope she would be in. "I'll tell her—I'll tell her," said the old man; and then he added quickly, gallantly: "You'll be giving us something new ? It's a long time, isn't it ?" Now he remembered him right.

"Rather long. I'm very slow," Paul explained. "I met you at Summersoft a long time ago."

"Oh yes—with Henry St. George. I remember very well. Before

71

his poor wife——" General Fancourt paused a moment, smiling a little less. "I daresay you know."

"About Mrs. St. George's death? Certainly—I heard at the time."

"Oh no, I mean—I mean he's to be married."

"Ah I've not heard that!" But just as Paul was about to add "To whom?" the General crossed his intention.

"When did you come back? I know you've been away—by my daughter. She was very sorry. You ought to give her something new."

"I came back last night," said our young man, to whom something had occurred which made his speech for the moment a little thick.

"Ah most kind of you to come so soon. Couldn't you turn up at dinner?"

"At dinner?" Paul just mechanically repeated, not liking to ask whom St. George was going to marry, but thinking only of that.

"There are several people, I believe. Certainly St. George. Or afterwards if you like better. I believe my daughter expects——" He appeared to notice something in the visitor's raised face (on his steps he stood higher) which led him to interrupt himself, and the interruption gave him a momentary sense of awkwardness, from which he sought a quick issue. "Perhaps, then, you haven't heard she's to be married."

Paul gaped again. "To be married?"

"To Mr. St. George—it has just been settled. Odd marriage, isn't it?" Our listener uttered no opinion on this point: he only continued to stare. "But I daresay it will do—she's so awfully literary!" said the General.

Paul had turned very red. "Oh it's a surprise—very interesting, very charming! I'm afraid I can't dine—so many thanks!"

"Well, you must come to the wedding!" cried the General. "Oh I remember that day at Summersoft. He's a great man, you know."

"Charming—charming!" Paul stammered for retreat. He shook hands with the General and got off. His face was red and he had the sense of its growing more and more crimson. All the evening at home— he went straight to his rooms and remained there dinnerless—his cheek burned at intervals as if it had been smitten. He didn't understand what had happened to him, what trick had been played him, what treachery practised. "None, none," he said to himself. "I've nothing to do with it. I'm out of it—it's none of my business." But that bewildered murmur was followed again and again by the incongruous ejaculation: "Was it a plan—was it a plan?" Sometimes he cried to himself, breathless, "Have I been duped, sold, swindled?" If at all, he was an absurd an abject victim. It was as if he hadn't lost her till now. He had renounced her, yes; but that was another affair—that was a closed but not a locked door. Now he seemed to see the door quite slammed in his face. Did he expect her to wait—was she to give him his time like that: two years at a stretch? He didn't know what he had expected—he only knew what he hadn't. It wasn't this—it wasn't this. Mystification, bitterness and wrath rose and boiled in him when he thought of the deference, the devotion, the credulity with which he had listened to St. George. The evening wore on and the light was long; but even when it had darkened he remained without a lamp. He had flung himself on the sofa, where he lay through the hours with his eyes either closed or gazing at the gloom, in the attitude of a man teaching himself to bear something, to bear having been made a fool of. He had made it too easy—that idea passed over him like a hot wave. Suddenly, as he heard eleven o'clock strike, he jumped up, remembering what General Fancourt had said about his coming after dinner. He'd go—he'd see her at least; perhaps he should see what it meant. He felt as if some of the elements of a hard sum had been given him and the others were wanting: he couldn't do his sum till he had got all his figures.

He dressed and drove quickly, so that by half-past eleven he was at Manchester Square. There were a good many carriages at the door—a party was going on; a circumstance which at the last gave him a slight relief, for now he would rather see her in a crowd. People passed him on the staircase; they were going away, going "on" with the hunted herdlike movement of London society at night. But sundry groups remained in the drawing-room, and it was some minutes, as she didn't hear him announced, before he discovered and spoke to her. In this short interval he had seen St. George talking to a lady before the fireplace; but he at once looked away, feeling unready for an encounter, and therefore couldn't be sure the author of "Shadowmere" noticed him. At all events he didn't come over; though Miss Fancourt did as soon as she saw him—she almost rushed at him, smiling rustling radiant beautiful. He had forgotten what her head, what her face offered to the sight; she was in white, there were gold figures on her dress and her hair was a casque of gold. He saw in a single moment that she was happy, happy with an aggressive splendour. But she wouldn't speak to him of that, she would speak only of himself.

"I'm so delighted; my father told me. How kind of you to come!" She struck him as so fresh and brave, while his eyes moved over her, that he said to himself irresistibly: "Why to *him*, why not to youth, to strength, to ambition, to a future? Why, in her rich young force, to failure, to abdication, to superannuation?" In his thought at that sharp moment he blasphemed even against all that had been left of his faith in the peccable master. "I'm so sorry I missed you," she went on. "My father told me. How charming of you to have come so soon!"

"Does that surprise you?" Paul Overt asked.

"The first day? No, from you—nothing that's nice." She was interrupted by a lady who bade her good-night, and he seemed to read that it cost her nothing to speak to him in that tone; it was her old liberal lavish way, with a certain added amplitude that time had brought; and if this manner began to operate on the spot, at such a juncture in her history, perhaps in the other days too it had meant just as little or as much—a mere mechanical charity, with the difference now that she was satisfied, ready to give but in want of nothing. Oh she was satisfied—and why shouldn't she be? Why shouldn't she have been surprised at his coming the first day—for all the good she had ever got from him? As the lady continued to hold her attention Paul turned from her with a strange irritation in his complicated artistic soul and a sort of disinterested disappointment. She was so happy that it was almost stupid —a disproof of the extraordinary intelligence he had formerly found in her. Didn't she know how bad St. George could be, hadn't she recognised the awful thinness——? If she didn't she was nothing, and if she did why such an insolence of serenity? This question expired as our young man's eyes settled at last on the genius who had advised him in a great crisis. St. George was still before the chimney-piece, but now he was alone—fixed, waiting, as if he meant to stop after every one— and he met the clouded gaze of the young friend so troubled as to the degree of his right (the right his resentment would have enjoyed) to regard himself as a victim. Somehow the ravage of the question was checked by the Master's radiance. It was as fine in its way as Marian Fancourt's, it denoted the happy human being; but also it represented to Paul Overt that the author of "Shadowmere" had now definitely ceased to count—ceased to count as a writer. As he smiled a welcome across the place he was almost *banal*, was almost smug. Paul fancied that for a moment he hesitated to make a movement, as if, for all the world, he *had* his bad conscience; then they had already met in the middle of the room and had shaken hands—expressively, cordially on St. George's part. With which they had passed back together to where the elder man had been standing, while St. George said: "I hope

you're never going away again. I've been dining here; the General told
me." He was handsome, he was young, he looked as if he had still a
great fund of life. He bent the friendliest, most unconfessing eyes on
his disciple of a couple of years before; asked him about everything,
his health, his plans, his late occupations, the new book. "When will
it be out—soon, soon, I hope? Splendid, eh? That's right; you're a
comfort, you're a luxury! I've read you all over again these last six
months." Paul waited to see if he'd tell him what the General had told
him in the afternoon and what Miss Fancourt, verbally at least, of
course hadn't. But as it didn't come out he at last put the question,
"Is it true, the great news I hear—that you're to be married?"

"Ah you *have* heard it, then?"

"Didn't the General tell you?" Paul asked.

The Master's face was wonderful. "Tell me what?"

"That he mentioned it to me this afternoon?"

"My dear fellow, I don't remember. We've been in the midst of
people. I'm sorry, in the case, that I lose the pleasure, myself, of
announcing to you a fact that touches me so nearly. It *is* a fact, strange
as it may appear. It has only just become one. Isn't it ridiculous?"
St. George made this speech without confusion, but on the other hand,
so far as our friend could judge, without latent impudence. It struck
his interlocutor that, to talk so comfortably and coolly, he must simply
have forgotten what had passed between them. His next words, however, showed he hadn't, and they produced, as an appeal to Paul's
own memory, an effect which would have been ludicrous if it hadn't
been cruel. "Do you recall the talk we had at my house that night,
into which Miss Fancourt's name entered? I've often thought of it
since."

"Yes; no wonder you said what you did"—Paul was careful to
meet his eyes.

"In the light of the present occasion? Ah but there was no light then.
How could I have foreseen this hour?"

"Didn't you think it probable?"

"Upon my honour, no," said Henry St. George. "Certainly I owe
you that assurance. Think how my situation has changed."

"I see—I see," our young man murmured.

His companion went on as if, now that the subject had been broached,
he was, as a person of imagination and tact, quite ready to give every
satisfaction—being both by his genius and his method so able to enter
into everything another might feel. "But it's not only that; for honesty,

at my age, I never dreamed—a widower with big boys and with so little else ! It has turned out differently from anything one could have dreamed, and I'm fortunate beyond all measure. She has been so free, and yet she consents. Better than any one else perhaps—for I remember how you liked her before you went away, and how she liked you—you can intelligently congratulate me."

"She has been so free ! " Those words made a great impression on Paul Overt, and he almost writhed under that irony in them as to which it so little mattered whether it was designed or casual. Of course she had been free, and appreciably perhaps by his own act; for wasn't the Master's allusion to her having liked him a part of the irony too ? "I thought that by your theory you disapproved of a writer's marrying."

"Surely—surely. But you don't call me a writer ?"

"You ought to be ashamed," said Paul.

"Ashamed of marrying again ?"

"I won't say that—but ashamed of your reasons."

The elder man beautifully smiled. "You must let me judge of them, my good friend."

"Yes; why not ? For you judged wonderfully of mine."

The tone of these words appeared suddenly, for St. George, to suggest the unsuspected. He stated as if divining a bitterness. "Don't you think I've been straight ?"

"You might have told me at the time perhaps."

"My dear fellow, when I say I couldn't pierce futurity——!"

"I mean afterwards."

The Master wondered. "After my wife's death ?"

"When this idea came to you."

"Ah never, never ! I wanted to save you, rare and precious as you are."

Poor Overt looked hard at him. "Are you marrying Miss Fancourt to save me ?"

"Not absolutely, but it adds to the pleasure. I shall be the making of you," St. George smiled. "I was greatly struck, after our talk, with the brave devoted way you quitted the country, and still more perhaps with your force of character in remaining abroad. You're very strong —you're wonderfully strong."

Paul tried to sound his shining eyes; the strange thing was that he seemed sincere—not a mocking fiend. He turned away, and as he did so heard the Master say something about his giving them all the proof,

76

being the joy of his old age. He faced him again, taking another look. "Do you mean to say you've stopped writing?"

"My dear fellow, of course I have. It's too late. Didn't I tell you?"

"I can't believe it!"

"Of course you can't—with your own talent! No, no; for the rest of my life I shall only read *you*."

"Does she know that—Miss Fancourt?"

"She will—she will." Did he mean this, our young man wondered, as a covert intimation that the assistance he should derive from that young lady's fortune, moderate as it was, would make the difference of putting it in his power to cease to work ungratefully an exhausted vein? Somehow, standing there in the ripeness of his successful manhood, he didn't suggest that any of his veins were exhausted. "Don't you remember the moral I offered myself to you that night as pointing?" St. George continued. "Consider at any rate the warning I am at present."

This was too much—he *was* the mocking fiend. Paul turned from him with a mere nod for good-night and the sense in a sore heart that he might come back to him and his easy grace, his fine way of arranging things, some time in the far future, but couldn't fraternise with him now. It was necessary to his soreness to believe for the hour in the intensity of his grievance—all the more cruel for its not being a legal one. It was doubtless in the attitude of hugging this wrong that he descended the stairs without taking leave of Miss Fancourt, who hadn't been in view at the moment he quitted the room. He was glad to get out into the honest dusky unsophisticating night, to move fast, to take his way home on foot. He walked a long time, going astray, paying no attention. He was thinking of too many other things. His steps recovered their direction, however, and at the end of an hour he found himself before his door in the small inexpensive empty street. He lingered, questioning himself still before going in, with nothing around and above him but moonless blackness, a bad lamp or two and a few far-away dim stars. To these last faint features he raised his eyes; he had been saying to himself that he should have been "sold" indeed, diabolically sold, if now, on his new foundation, at the end of a year, St. George were to put forth something of his prime quality—something of the type of "Shadowmere" and finer than his finest. Greatly as he admired his talent Paul literally hoped such an incident wouldn't occur; it seemed to him just then that he shouldn't be able to bear it. His late adviser's words were still in his ears—"You're very strong, wonderfully strong." Was he really? Certainly he would have to be, and it might a little serve for revenge. *Is* he? the reader may ask in turn, if his interest has followed the perplexed young man so far. The best answer to that perhaps is that he's doing his best, but that it's too soon to say. When the new book came out in the autumn Mr. and Mrs. St. George found it really magnificent. The former still has published nothing, but Paul doesn't even yet feel safe. I may say for him, however, that if this event were to occur he would really be the very first to appreciate it: which is perhaps a proof that the Master was essentially right and that Nature had dedicated him to intellectual, not to personal passion.

THE DEATH OF THE LION

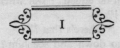

I

I HAD SIMPLY, I suppose, a change of heart, and it must have begun when I received my manuscript back from Mr. Pinhorn. Mr. Pinhorn was my "chief," as he was called in the office: he had accepted the high mission of bringing the paper up. This was a weekly periodical, which had been supposed to be almost past redemption when he took hold of it. It was Mr. Deedy who had let the thing down so dreadfully: he was never mentioned in the office now save in connection with that misdemeanour. Young as I was, I had been in a manner taken over from Mr. Deedy, who had been owner as well as editor; forming part of a promiscuous lot, mainly plant and office-furniture, which poor Mrs. Deedy, in her bereavement and depression, parted with at a rough valuation. I could account for my continuity but on the supposition that I had been cheap. I rather resented the practice of fathering all flatness on my late protector, who was in his unhonoured grave; but as I had my way to make I found matter enough for complacency in being on a "staff." At the same time I was aware of my exposure to suspicion as a product of the old lowering system. This made me feel I was doubly bound to have ideas, and had doubtless been at the bottom of my proposing to Mr. Pinhorn that I should lay my lean hands on Neil Paraday. I remember how he looked at me—quite, to begin with, as if he had never heard of this celebrity, who indeed at that moment was by no means in the centre of the heavens; and even when I had knowingly explained he expressed but little confidence in the demand for any such stuff. When I had reminded him that the great principle on which we were supposed to work was just to create the demand we required, he considered a moment and then returned: "I see—you want to write him up."

"Call it that if you like."

"And what's your inducement?"

"Bless my soul—my admiration!"

Mr. Pinhorn pursed up his mouth. "Is there much to be done with him?"

"Whatever there is we should have it all to ourselves, for he hasn't been touched."

This argument was effective and Mr. Pinhorn responded. "Very well, touch him." Then he added: "But where can you do it?"

"Under the fifth rib!"

Mr. Pinhorn stared. "Where's that?"

"You want me to go down and see him?" I asked when I had enjoyed his visible search for the obscure suburb I seemed to have named.

"I don't 'want' anything—the proposal's your own. But you must remember that that's the way we do things *now*," said Mr. Pinhorn with another dig at Mr. Deedy.

Unregenerate as I was, I could read the queer implications of this speech. The present owner's superior virtue as well as his deeper craft spoke in his reference to the late editor as one of that baser sort who deal in false representations. Mr. Deedy would as soon have sent me to call on Neil Paraday as he would have published a "holiday-number"; but such scruples presented themselves as mere ignoble thrift to his successor, whose own sincerity took the form of ringing door-bells and whose definition of genius was the art of finding people at home. It was as if Mr. Deedy had published reports without his young men's having, as Pinhorn would have said, really been there. I was unregenerate, as I have hinted, and couldn't be concerned to straighten out the journalistic morals of my chief, feeling them indeed to be an abyss over the edge of which it was better not to peer. Really to be there this time, moreover, was a vision that made the idea of writing something subtle about Neil Paraday only the more inspiring. I would be as considerate as even Mr. Deedy could have wished, and yet I should be as present as only Mr. Pinhorn could conceive. My allusion to the sequestered manner in which Mr. Paraday lived—it had formed part of my explanation, though I knew of it only by hearsay—was, I could divine, very much what had made Mr. Pinhorn nibble. It struck him as inconsistent with the success of his paper that any one should be so sequestered as that. And then wasn't an immediate exposure of everything just what the public wanted? Mr. Pinhorn effectually called me to order by reminding me of the promptness with which I had met Miss Braby at Liverpool on her return from her fiasco in the States. Hadn't we published, while its freshness and flavour were unimpaired, Miss Braby's own version of that great international episode? I felt somewhat uneasy at this lumping of the actress and the author, and I confess that after having enlisted Mr. Pinhorn's sympathies I procrastinated a little. I had succeeded better than I wished, and I had, as it happened, work nearer at hand. A few days later I called on Lord Crouchley and carried off in triumph the most unintelligible statement that had yet appeared of his lordship's reasons for his change of front. I thus set in motion in the daily papers columns of virtuous verbiage. The following week I ran down to Brighton for a chat, as Mr. Pinhorn called it, with Mrs. Bounder, who gave me, on the subject of her divorce, many curious particulars that had not been articulated in court. If ever an article flowed from the primal fount it was that article on Mrs. Bounder. By this time, however, I became aware that Neil Paraday's new book was on the point of appearing and that its approach had been the ground of my original appeal to Mr. Pinhorn, who was now annoyed with me for having lost so many days. He bundled me off—we would at least not lose another. I've always thought his sudden alertness a remarkable example of the journalistic instinct. Nothing had occurred, since I first spoke to him, to create a visible urgency, and no enlightenment could possibly have reached him. It was a pure case of professional *flair*—he had smelt the coming glory as an animal smells its distant prey.

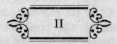

II

I MAY AS well say at once that this little record pretends in no degree to be a picture either of my introduction to Mr. Paraday or of certain proximate steps and stages. The scheme of my narrative allows no space for these things, and in any case a prohibitory sentiment would hang about my recollection of so rare an hour. These meagre notes are essentially private, so that if they see the light the insidious forces that, as my story itself shows, make at present for publicity will simply have overmastered my precautions. The curtain fell lately enough on the lamentable drama. My memory of the day I alighted at Mr. Paraday's door is a fresh memory of kindness, hospitality, compassion, and of the wonderful illuminating talk in which the welcome was conveyed. Some voice of the air had taught me the right moment, the moment of his life at which an act of unexpected young allegiance might most come home to him. He had recently recovered from a long grave illness. I had gone to the neighbouring inn for the night, but I spent the evening in his company, and he insisted the next day on my sleeping under his roof. I hadn't an indefinite leave: Mr. Pinhorn supposed us to put our victims through on the gallop. It was later, in the office, that the rude motions of the jig were set to music. I fortified myself, however, as my training had taught me to do, by the conviction that nothing could be more advantageous for my article than to be written in the very atmosphere. I said nothing to Mr. Paraday about it, but in the morning, after my removal from the inn, while he was occupied in his study, as he notified me he should need to be, I committed to paper the main heads of my impression. Then thinking to commend myself to Mr. Pinhorn by my celerity, I walked out and posted my little packet before luncheon. Once my paper was written I was free to stay on, and if it was calculated to divert attention from my levity in so doing I could reflect with satisfaction that I had never been so clever. I don't mean to deny of course that I was aware it was much too good for Mr. Pinhorn; but I was equally conscious that Mr. Pinhorn had the supreme shrewdness of recognising from time to time the cases in which an article was not too bad only because it was too good. There was nothing he loved so much as to print on the right occasion a thing he hated. I had begun my visit to the great man on a Monday, and on the Wednesday his book came out. A copy of it arrived by the first post, and he let me go out into the garden with it immediately after breakfast. I read it from beginning to end that day, and in the evening he asked me to remain with him the rest of the week and over the Sunday.

That night my manuscript came back from Mr. Pinhorn, accompanied with a letter the gist of which was the desire to know what I meant by trying to fob off on him such stuff. That was the meaning of the question, if not exactly its form, and it made my mistake immense to me. Such as this mistake was I could now only look it in the face and accept it. I knew where I had failed, but it was exactly where I couldn't have succeeded. I had been sent down to be personal and then in point of fact hadn't been personal at all: what I had despatched to London was just a little finicking feverish study of my author's talent. Anything less relevant to Mr. Pinhorn's purpose couldn't well be imagined, and he was visibly angry at my having (at his expense, with a second-class ticket) approached the subject of

THE DEATH OF THE LION

ur enterprise only to stand off so helplessly. For myself, I knew
ut too well what had happened, and how a miracle—as pretty as
ome old miracle of legend—had been wrought on the spot to save me.
here had been a big brush of wings, the flash of an opaline robe, and
hen, with a great cool stir of the air, the sense of an angel's having
wooped down and caught me to his bosom. He held me only till the
anger was over, and it all took place in a minute. With my manu-
cript back on my hands I understood the phenomenon better, and the
eflexions I made on it are what I meant, at the beginning of this
necdote, by my change of heart. Mr. Pinhorn's note was not only a
ebuke decidedly stern, but an invitation immediately to send him—it
as the case to say so—the genuine article, the revealing and rever-
erating sketch to the promise of which, and of which alone, I owed
y squandered privilege. A week or two later I recast my peccant
aper, and giving it a particular application to Mr. Paraday's new book,
btained for it the hospitality of another journal, where, I must admit,
Ir. Pinhorn was so far vindicated as that it attracted not the least
ttention.

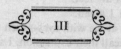

III

WAS FRANKLY, at the end of three days, a very prejudiced critic, so
at one morning when, in the garden, my great man had offered to
ead me something I quite held my breath as I listened. It was the
ritten scheme of another book—something put aside long ago, before
is illness, but that he had lately taken out again to reconsider. He
ad been turning it round when I came down on him, and it had grown
agnificently under this second hand. Loose liberal confident, it
ight have passed for a great gossiping eloquent letter—the overflow
to talk of an artist's amorous plan. The theme I thought singularly
ch, quite the strongest he had yet treated; and this familiar state-
ent of it, full too of fine maturities, was really, in summarised
lendour, a mine of gold, a precious independent work. I remember
ther profanely wondering whether the ultimate production could
ossibly keep at the pitch. His reading of the fond epistle, at any rate,
ade me feel as if I were, for the advantage of posterity, in close

correspondence with him—were the distinguished person to whom it ha
been affectionately addressed. It was a high distinction simply to b
told such things. The idea he now communicated had all the freshnes.
the flushed fairness, of the conception untouched and untried: it wa
Venus rising from the sea and before the airs had blown upon her.
had never been so throbbingly present at such an unveiling. But whe
he had tossed the last bright word after the others, as I had see
cashiers in banks, weighing mounds of coin, drop a final sovereig
into the tray, I knew a sudden prudent alarm.

"My dear master, how, after all, are you going to do it? It's infinitel
noble, but what time it will take, what patience and independenc
what assured, what perfect conditions! Oh for a lone isle in a tepi
sea!"

"Isn't this practically a lone isle, and aren't you, as an encirclin
medium, tepid enough?" he asked, alluding with a laugh to the wor
der of my young admiration and the narrow limits of his little pro
vincial home. "Time isn't what I've lacked hitherto: the question hasn
been to find it, but to use it. Of course my illness made, while it laste
a great hole —but I daresay there would have been a hole at any rat
The earth we tread has more pockets than a billiard-table. The grea
thing is now to keep on my feet."

"That's exactly what I mean."

Neil Paraday looked at me with eyes—such pleasant eyes as he ha
—in which, as I now recall their expression, I seem to have seen a di
imagination of his fate. He was fifty years old, and his illness ha
been cruel, his convalescence slow. "It isn't as if I weren't all right

"Oh if you weren't all right I wouldn't look at you!" I tenderly sai
We had both got up, quickened as by this clearer air, and he ha
lighted a cigarette. I had taken a fresh one, which with an intens
smile, by way of answer to my exclamation, he applied to the flame o
his match. "If I weren't better I shouldn't have thought of *that*!
He flourished his script in his hand.

"I don't want to be discouraging, but that's not true," I returne
"I'm sure that during the months you lay here in pain you had vis
tations sublime. You thought of a thousand things. You think of mo
and more all the while. That's what makes you, if you'll pardon m
familiarity, so respectable. At a time when so many people are spen
you come into your second wind. But, thank God, all the same, you'
better! Thank God too you're not, as you were telling me yesterda
'successful.' If *you* weren't a failure what would be the use of trying

That's my one reserve on the subject of your recovery—that it makes you 'score,' as the newspapers say. It looks well in the newspapers, and almost anything that does that's horrible. 'We are happy to announce that Mr. Paraday, the celebrated author, is again in the enjoyment of excellent health.' Somehow I shouldn't like to see it."

"You won't see it; I'm not in the least celebrated—my obscurity protects me. But couldn't you bear even to see I was dying or dead?" my host inquired.

"Dead—*passe encore*; there's nothing so safe. One never knows what living artist may do—one has mourned so many. However, one must make the worst of it. You must be as dead as you can."

"Don't I meet that condition in having just published a book?"

"Adequately, let us hope; for the book's verily a masterpiece."

At this moment the parlour-maid appeared in the door that opened from the garden: Paraday lived at no great cost, and the frisk of petticoats, with a timorous "Sherry, sir?" was about his modest mahogany. He allowed half his income to his wife, from whom he had succeeded in separating without redundancy of legend. I had a general faith in his having behaved well, and I had once, in London, taken Mrs. Paraday down to dinner. He now turned to speak to the maid, who offered him, on a tray, some card or note, while, agitated, excited, I wandered to the end of the precinct. The idea of his security became supremely clear to me, and I asked myself if I were the same young man who had come down a few days before to scatter him to the four winds. When I retraced my steps he had gone into the house, and the woman—the second London post had come in—had placed my letters and a newspaper on a bench. I sat down there to the letters, which were a brief business, and then, without heeding the address, took the paper from its envelope. It was the journal of highest renown, The Empire of that morning. It regularly came to Paraday, but I remembered that neither of us had yet looked at the copy already delivered. This one had a great mark on the "editorial" page, and, uncrumpling the wrapper, I saw it to be directed to my host and stamped with the name of his publishers. I instantly divined that The Empire had spoken of him, and I've not forgotten the odd little shock of the circumstance. It checked all eagerness and made me drop the paper a moment. As I sat there conscious of a palpitation I think I had a vision of what was to be. I had also a vision of the letter I would presently address to Mr. Pinhorn, breaking, as it were, with Mr. Pinhorn. Of course, however, the next minute the voice of The Empire was in my ears.

The article wasn't, I thanked heaven, a review; it was a "leader,"
the last of three, presenting Neil Paraday to the human race. His new
book, the fifth from his hand, had been but a day or two out, and *The
Empire*, already aware of it, fired, as if on the birth of a prince, a salute
of a whole column. The guns had been booming these three hours in
the house without our suspecting them. The big blundering newspaper
had discovered him, and now he was proclaimed and anointed and
crowned. His place was assigned him as publicly as if a fat usher with
a wand had pointed to the topmost chair; he was to pass up and still
up, higher and higher, between the watching faces and the envious
sounds—away up to the dais and the throne. The article was "epoch
making," a landmark in his life; he had taken rank at a bound, waked
up a national glory. A national glory was needed, and it was an immense convenience he was there. What all this meant rolled over me,
and I fear I grew a little faint—it meant so much more than I could say
"yea" to on the spot. In a flash, somehow, all was different; the
tremendous wave I speak of had swept something away. It had knocked
down, I suppose, my little customary altar, my twinkling tapers and my
flowers, and had reared itself into the likeness of a temple vast and
bare. When Neil Paraday should come out of the house he would come
out a contemporary. That was what had happened: the poor man was
to be squeezed into his horrible age. I felt as if he had been overtaken
on the crest of the hill and brought back to the city. A little more and
he would have dipped down the short cut to posterity and escaped.

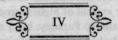

IV

WHEN HE came out it was exactly as if he had been in custody, for
beside him walked a stout man with a big black beard, who, saw
that he wore spectacles, might have been a policeman, and in
whom at a second glance I recognised the highest contemporary
enterprise.

"This is Mr. Morrow," said Paraday, looking, I thought, rather
white: "he wants to publish heaven knows what about me."

I winced as I remembered that this was exactly what I myself had wanted. "Already?" I cried, with a sort of sense that my friend had fled to me for protection.

Mr. Morrow glared, agreeably, through his glasses: they suggested the electric headlights of some monstrous modern ship, and I felt as if Paraday and I were tossing terrified under his bows. I saw his momentum was irresistible. "I was confident that I should be the first in the field. A great interest is naturally felt in Mr. Paraday's surroundings," he heavily observed.

"I hadn't the least idea of it," said Paraday, as if he had been told he had been snoring.

"I find he hasn't read the article in *The Empire*," Mr. Morrow remarked to me. "That's so very interesting—it's something to start with," he smiled. He had begun to pull off his gloves, which were violently new, and to look encouragingly round the little garden. As a "surrounding" I felt how I myself had already been taken in; I was a little fish in the stomach of a bigger one. "I represent," our visitor continued, "a syndicate of influential journals, no less than thirty-seven, whose public—whose publics, I may say—are in peculiar sympathy with Mr. Paraday's line of thought. They would greatly appreciate any expression of his views on the subject of the art he so nobly exemplifies. In addition to my connexion with the syndicate just mentioned I hold a particular commission from *The Tatler*, whose most prominent department, 'Smatter and Chatter'—I daresay you've often enjoyed it—attracts such attention. I was honoured only last week, as a representative of *The Tatler*, with the confidence of Guy Walsingham, the brilliant author of 'Obsessions.' She pronounced herself thoroughly pleased with my sketch of her method; she went so far as to say that I had made her genius more comprehensible even to herself."

Neil Paraday had dropped on the garden-bench and sat there at once detached and confounded; he looked hard at a bare spot in the lawn, as if with an anxiety that had suddenly made him grave. His movement had been interpreted by his visitor as an invitation to sink sympathetically into a wicker chair that stood hard by, and while Mr. Morrow so settled himself I felt he had taken official possession and that there was no undoing it. One had heard of unfortunate people's having "a man in the house," and this was just what *we* had. There was a silence of a moment, during which we seemed to acknowledge in the only way that was possible the presence of universal fate; the sunny stillness took no pity, and my thought, as I was sure Paraday's was doing, performed within the minute a great distant revolution. I saw just how emphatic I should make my rejoinder to Mr. Pinhorn, and that having come, like Mr. Morrow, to betray, I must remain as long as possible to save. Not because I had brought my mind back, but because our visitor's last words were in my ear, I presently inquired with gloomy irrelevance if Guy Walsingham were a woman.

"Oh yes, a mere pseudonym—rather pretty, isn't it?—and convenient, you know, for a lady who goes in for the larger latitude. '"Obsessions," by Miss So-and so,' would look a little odd, but men are more naturally indelicate. Have you peeped into 'Obsessions'?" Mr. Morrow continued sociably to our companion.

Paraday, still absent, remote, made no answer, as if he hadn't heard the question: a form of intercourse that appeared to suit the cheerful Mr. Morrow as well as any other. Imperturbably bland, he was a man of resources—he only needed to be on the spot. He had pocketed the whole poor place while Paraday and I were wool-gathering, and I could imagine that he had already got his "heads." His system, at any rate, was justified by the inevitability with which I replied, to save my friend the trouble: "Dear no—he hasn't read it. He doesn't read such things!" I unwarily added.

"Things that are *too* far over the fence, eh?" I was indeed a godsend to Mr. Morrow. It was the psychological moment; it determined the appearance of his note-book, which, however, he at first kept slightly behind him, even as the dentist approaching his victim keeps the horrible forceps. "Mr. Paraday holds with the good old proprieties —I see!" And thinking of the thirty-seven influential journals, I found myself, as I found poor Paraday, helplessly assisting at the promulgation of this ineptitude. "There's no point on which distinguished views are so acceptable as on this question—raised perhaps more strikingly than ever by Guy Walsingham—of the permissibility of the larger latitude. I've an appointment, precisely in connexion with it, next week, with Dora Forbes, author of 'The Other Way Round,' which everybody's talking about. Has Mr. Paraday glanced at 'The Other Way Round'?" Mr. Morrow now frankly appealed to me. I took on myself to repudiate the supposition, while our companion, still silent, got up nervously and walked away. His visitor paid no heed to his withdrawal, but opened out the note-book with a more fatherly pat. "Dora Forbes, I gather, takes the ground, the same as Guy Walsingham's, that the larger latitude has simply got to come. He holds that it has got to be squarely faced. Of course his sex makes him a less prejudiced witness. But an authoritative word from Mr. Paraday—from the point of view of *his* sex, you know—would go right round the globe. He takes the line that we *haven't* got to face it ?"

I was bewildered: it sounded somehow as if there were three sexes. My interlocutor's pencil was poised, my private responsibility great. I simply sat staring, none the less, and only found presence of mind to say: "Is this Miss Forbes a gentleman ?"

Mr. Morrow had a subtle smile. "It wouldn't be 'Miss'—there's a wife !"

"I mean is she a man ?"

"The wife ?"—Mr. Morrow was for a moment as confused as myself. But when I explained that I alluded to Dora Forbes in person he informed me, with visible amusement at my being so out of it, that this was the "pen-name" of an indubitable male—he had a big red moustache. "He goes in for the slight mystification because the ladies are such popular favourites. A great deal of interest is felt in his acting on that idea—which *is* clever, isn't it ?—and there's every prospect of its being widely imitated." Our host at this moment joined us again, and Mr. Morrow remarked invitingly that he should be happy to make a note of any observation the movement in question, the bid for success under a lady's name, might suggest to Mr. Paraday. But the poor man, without catching the allusion, excused himself, pleading that, though greatly honoured by his visitor's interest, he suddenly felt unwell and should have to take leave of him—have to go and lie down and keep quiet. His young friend might be trusted to answer for him, but he hoped Mr. Morrow didn't expect great things even of his young friend. His young friend, at this moment, looked at Neil Paraday with an anxious eye, greatly wondering if he were doomed to be ill again; but Paraday's own kind face met his question reassuringly, seemed to say in a glance intelligible enough: "Oh I'm not ill, but I'm scared; get him out of the house as quietly as possible." Getting newspaper-men out of the house was odd business for an emissary of Mr. Pinhorn, and I was so exhilarated by the idea of it that I called after him as he left us: "Read the article in *The Empire* and you'll soon be all right !"

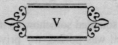

V

"DELICIOUS MY having come down to tell him of it !" Mr. Morrow ejaculated. "My cab was at the door twenty minutes after *The Empire* had been laid on my breakfast-table. Now what have you got for me ?" he continued, dropping again into his chair, from which, however, he the next moment eagerly rose. "I was shown into the drawing-room, but there must be more to see—his study, his literary sanctum, the little things he has about, or other domestic objects and features. He wouldn't be lying down on his study-table ? There's a great interest always felt in the scene of an author's labours. Sometimes we're favoured with very delightful peeps. Dora Forbes showed me all his table-drawers, and almost jammed my hand into one into which I made a dash ! I don't ask that of you, but if we could talk things over right there where he sits I feel as if I should get the keynote."

I had no wish whatever to be rude to Mr. Morrow, I was much too initiated not to tend to more diplomacy; but I had a quick inspiration, and I entertained an insurmountable, an almost superstitious objection to his crossing the threshold of my friend's little lonely shabby consecrated workshop. "No, no—we shan't get at his life that way," I said. "The way to get at his life is to—— But wait a moment !" I broke off and went quickly into the house, whence I in three minutes reappeared before Mr. Morrow with the two volumes of Paraday's new book. "His life's here," I went on, "and I'm so full of this admirable thing that I can't talk of anything else. The artist's life's his work, and this is the place to observe him. What he has to tell us he tells us with *this* perfection. My dear sir, the best interviewer's the best reader."

Mr. Morrow good-humouredly protested. "Do you mean to say that no other source of information should be open to us ?"

"None other till this particular one—by far the most copious—has been quite exhausted. Have you exhausted it, my dear sir ? Had you exhausted it when you came down here ? It seems to me in our time almost wholly neglected, and something should surely be done to restore its ruined credit. It's the course to which the artist himself at every step, and with such pathetic confidence, refers us. This last book of Mr. Paraday's is full of revelations."

"Revelations?" panted Mr. Morrow, whom I had forced again into his chair.

"The only kind that count. It tells you with a perfection that seems to me quite final all the author thinks, for instance, about the advent of the 'larger latitude.'"

"Where does it do that?" asked Mr. Morrow, who had picked up the second volume and was insincerely thumbing it.

"Everywhere—in the whole treatment of his case. Extract the opinion, disengage the answer—those are the real acts of homage."

Mr. Morrow, after a minute, tossed the book away. "Ah, but you mustn't take me for a reviewer."

"Heaven forbid I should take you for anything so dreadful! You came down to perform a little act of sympathy, and so, I may confide to you, did I. Let us perform our little act together. These pages overflow with the testimony we want: let us read them and taste them and interpret them. You'll of course have perceived for yourself that one scarcely does read Neil Paraday till one reads him aloud; he gives out to the ear an extraordinary full tone, and it's only when you expose it confidently to that test that you really get near his style. Take up your book again and let me listen, while you pay it out, to that wonderful fifteenth chapter. If you feel you can't do it justice, compose yourself to attention while I produce for you—I think I can!—this scarcely less admirable ninth."

Mr. Morrow gave me a straight look which was as hard as a blow between the eyes; he had turned rather red, and a question had formed itself in his mind which reached my sense as distinctly as if he had uttered it: "What sort of a damned fool are *you*?" Then he got up, gathering together his hat and gloves, buttoning his coat, projecting hungrily all over the place the big transparency of his mask. It seemed to flare over Fleet Street and somehow made the actual spot distressingly humble: there was so little for it to feed on unless he counted the blisters of our stucco or saw his way to do something with the roses. Even the poor roses were common kinds. Presently his eyes fell on the manuscript from which Paraday had been reading to me and which still lay on the bench. As my own followed them I saw it looked promising, looked pregnant, as if it gently throbbed with the life the reader had given it. Mr. Morrow indulged in a nod at it and a vague thrust of his umbrella. "What's that?"

"Oh it's a plan—a secret."

"A secret!" There was an instant's silence, and then Mr. Morrow made another movement. I may have been mistaken, but it affected me as the translated impulse of the desire to lay hands on the manuscript, and this led me to indulge in a quick anticipatory grab which may very well have seemed ungraceful, or even impertinent, and which at any rate left Mr. Paraday's two admirers very erect, glaring at each other while one of them held a bundle of papers well behind him. An instant later Mr. Morrow quitted me abruptly, as if he had really carried something off with him. To reassure myself, watching his broad back recede, I only grasped my manuscript the tighter. He went to the back door of the house, the one he had come out from, but on trying the handle he appeared to find it fastened. So he passed round into the front garden, and by listening intently enough I could presently hear the outer gate close behind him with a bang. I thought again of the thirty-seven influential journals and wondered what would be his revenge. I hasten to add that he was magnanimous: which was just the most dreadful thing he could have been. *The Tatler* published a charming chatty familiar account of Mr. Paraday's "Home-life," and on the wings of the thirty-seven influential journals it went, to use Mr. Morrow's own expression, right round the globe.

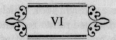

VI

A WEEK later, early in May, my glorified friend came up to town, where, it may be veraciously recorded, he was the king of the beasts of the year. No advancement was ever more rapid, no exaltation more complete, no bewilderment more teachable. His book sold but moderately, though the article in *The Empire* had done unwonted wonders for it; but he circulated in person to a measure that the libraries might well have envied. His formula had been found—he was a "revelation." His momentary terror had been real, just as mine had been—the overclouding of his passionate desire to be left to finish his work. He was far from unsociable, but he had the finest conception of being let alone that I've ever met. For the time, none the less, he took his profit where it seemed most to crowd on him, having in his pocket the portable sophistries about the nature of the artist's task. Observation too was a kind of work and experience a kind of success; London dinners were all material and London ladies were fruitful toil. "No one has the faintest conception of what I'm trying for," he said to me, "and not many have read three pages that I've written; but I must dine with them first—they'll find out why when they've time." It was rather rude justice perhaps; but the fatigue had the merit of being a new sort, while the phantasmagoric town was probably after all less of a battlefield than the haunted study. He once told me that he had had no personal life to speak of since his fortieth year, but had had more than was good for him before. London closed the parenthesis and exhibited him in relations; one of the most inevitable of these being that in which he found himself to Mrs. Weeks Wimbush, wife of the boundless brewer and proprietress of the universal menagerie. In this establishment, as everybody knows, on occasions when the crush is great, the animals rub shoulders freely with the spectators and the lions sit down for whole evenings with the lambs.

It had been ominously clear to me from the first that in Neil Paraday this lady, who, as all the world agreed, was tremendous fun, considered that she had secured a prime attraction, a creature of almost heraldic oddity. Nothing could exceed her enthusiasm over her capture, and nothing could exceed the confused apprehensions it excited in me. I had an instinctive fear of her which I tried without effect to conceal from her victim, but which I let her notice with perfect impunity. Paraday heeded it, but she never did, for her conscience was that of a romping child. She was a blind violent force to which I could attach no more idea of responsibility than to the creaking of a sign in the wind. It was difficult to say what she conduced to but circulation. She was constructed of steel and leather, and all I asked of her for our tractable friend was not to do him to death. He had consented for a time to be of india-rubber, but my thoughts were fixed on the day he should resume his shape or at least get back into his box. It was evidently all right, but I should be glad when it was well over. I had a special fear—the impression was ineffaceable of the hour when, after Mr. Morrow's departure, I found him on the sofa in his study. That pretext of indisposition had not in the least been meant as a snub to the envoy of *The Tatler*—he had gone to lie down in very truth. He had felt a pang of his old pain, the result of the agitation wrought in him by this forcing open of a new period. His old programme, his old ideal even had to be changed. Say what one would, success was a complication and recognition had to be reciprocal. The monastic life, the pious illumination of the missal in the convent-cell were things of the gathered past. It didn't engender despair, but at least it required adjustment. Before I left him on that occasion we had passed a bargain, my part of which was that I should make it my business to take care of him. Let whoever would represent the interest in his presence (I must have had a mystical prevision of Mrs. Weeks Wimbush) I should represent the interest in his work—or otherwise expressed in his absence. These two interests were in their essence opposed; and I doubt, as youth is fleeting, if I shall ever again know the intensity of joy with which I felt that in so good a cause I was willing to make myself odious.

One day in Sloane Street I found myself questioning Paraday's landlord, who had come to the door in answer to my knock. Two vehicles, a barouche and a smart hansom, were drawn up before the house.

"In the drawing-room, sir? Mrs. Weeks Wimbush."

"And in the dining-room?"

"A young lady, sir—waiting: I think a foreigner."

It was three o'clock, and on days when Paraday didn't lunch out he attached a value to these appropriated hours. On which days, however, didn't the dear man lunch out? Mrs. Wimbush, at such a crisis, would have rushed round immediately after her own repast. I went into the dining-room first, postponing the pleasure of seeing how, upstairs, the lady of the barouche would, on my arrival, point the moral of my sweet solicitude. No one took such an interest as herself in his doing only what was good for him, and she was always on the spot to see that he did it. She made appointments with him to discuss the best means of economising his time and protecting his privacy. She further made his health her special business, and had so much sympathy with my own zeal for it that she was the author of pleasing fictions on the subject of what my devotion had led me to give up. I gave up nothing (I don't count Mr. Pinhorn) because I had nothing, and all I had as yet achieved was to find myself also in the menagerie. I had dashed in to save my friend, but I had only got domesticated and wedged; so that I could do little more for him than exchange with him over people's heads looks of intense but futile intelligence.

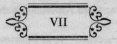

VII

THE YOUNG lady in the dining-room had a brave face, black hair, blue eyes, and in her lap a big volume. "I've come for his autograph," she said when I had explained to her that I was under bonds to see people for him when he was occupied. "I've been waiting half an hour, but I'm prepared to wait all day." I don't know whether it was this that told me she was American, for the propensity to wait all day is not in general characteristic of her race. I was enlightened probably not so much by the spirit of the utterance as by some quality of its sound. At any rate I saw she had an individual patience and a lovely frock, together with an expression that played among her pretty features like a breeze among flowers. Putting her book on the table she showed me a massive album, showily bound and full of autographs of price. The collection of faded notes, of still more faded "thoughts," of quotations, platitudes, signatures, represented a formidable purpose.

I could only disclose my dread of it. "Most people apply to Mr. Paraday by letter, you know."

"Yes, but he doesn't answer. I've written three times."

"Very true," I reflected; "the sort of letter you mean goes straight into the fire."

"How do you know the sort I mean?" My interlocutress had blushed and smiled, and in a moment she added: "I don't believe he gets many like them!"

"I'm sure they're beautiful, but he burns without reading." I didn't add that I had convinced him he ought to.

"Isn't he then in danger of burning things of importance?"

"He would perhaps be so if distinguished men hadn't an infallible nose for nonsense."

She looked at me a moment—her face was sweet and gay. "Do *you* burn without reading too?"—in answer to which I assured her that if she'd trust me with her repository I'd see that Mr. Paraday should write his name in it.

She considered a little. "That's very well, but it wouldn't make me see him."

"Do you want very much to see him?" It seemed ungracious to

95

catechise so charming a creature, but somehow I had never yet taken my duty to the great author so seriously.

"Enough to have come from America for the purpose."

I stared. "All alone?"

"I don't see that that's exactly your business, but if it will make me more seductive I'll confess that I'm quite by myself. I had to come alone or not come at all."

She was interesting; I could imagine she had lost parents, natural protectors—could conceive even she had inherited money. I was at a pass of my own fortunes when keeping hansoms at doors seemed to me pure swagger. As a trick of this bold and sensitive girl, however, it became romantic—a part of the general romance of her freedom, her errand, her innocence. The confidence of young Americans was notorious, and I speedily arrived at a conviction that no impulse could have been more generous than the impulse that had operated here. I foresaw at that moment that it would make her my peculiar charge, just as circumstances had made Neil Paraday. She would be another person to look after, so that one's honour would be concerned in guiding her straight. These things became clearer to me later on; at the instant I had scepticism enough to observe to her, as I turned the pages of her volume, that her net had all the same caught many a big fish. She appeared to have had fruitful access to the great ones of the earth; there were people, moreover, whose signatures she had presumably secured without a personal interview. She couldn't have worried George Washington and Friedrich Schiller and Hannah More. She met this argument, to my surprise, by throwing up the album without a pang. It wasn't even her own; she was responsible for none of its treasures. It belonged to a girl-friend in America, a young lady in a western city. This young lady had insisted on her bringing it, to pick up more autographs: she thought they might like to see, in Europe, in what company they would be. The "girl-friend," the western city, the immortal names, the curious errand, the idyllic faith, all made a story as strange to me, and as beguiling, as some tale in the *Arabian Nights*. Thus it was that my informant had encumbered herself with the ponderous tome; but she hastened to assure me that this was the first time she had brought it out. For her visit to Mr. Paraday it had simply been a pretext. She didn't really care a straw that he should write his name; what she did want was to look straight into his face.

I demurred a little. "And why do you require to do that?"

"Because I just love him!" Before I could recover from the agitating effect of this crystal ring my companion had continued: "Hasn't there ever been any face that *you've* wanted to look into?"

How could I tell her so soon how much I appreciated the opportunity of looking into hers? I could only assent in general to the proposition that there were certainly for every one such yearnings, and even such faces; and I felt the crisis demand all my lucidity, all my wisdom. "Oh yes, I'm a student of physiognomy. Do you mean," I pursued, "that you've a passion for Mr. Paraday's books?"

"They've been everything to me and a little more beside—I know them by heart. They've completely taken hold of me. There's no author about whom I'm in such a state as I'm in about Neil Paraday."

"Permit me to remark, then," I presently returned, "that you're one of the right sort."

"One of the enthusiasts? Of course I am!"

"Oh there are enthusiasts who are quite of the wrong. I mean you're one of those to whom an appeal can be made."

"An appeal?" Her face lighted as if with the chance of some great sacrifice.

If she was ready for one it was only waiting for her, and in a moment I mentioned it. "Give up this crude purpose of seeing him. Go away without it. That will be far better."

She looked mystified, then turned visibly pale. "Why, hasn't he any personal charm?" The girl was terrible and laughable in her bright directness.

"Ah, that dreadful word 'personal'!" I wailed; "we're dying of it, for you women bring it out with murderous effect. When you meet with a genius as fine as this idol of ours, let him off the dreary duty of being a personality as well. Know him only by what's best in him and spare him for the same sweet sake."

My young lady continued to look at me in confusion and mistrust, and the result of her reflexion on what I had just said was to make her suddenly break out: "Look here, sir—what's the matter with him?"

"The matter with him is that if he doesn't look out people will eat a great hole in his life."

She turned it over. "He hasn't any disfigurement?"

"Nothing to speak of!"

"Do you mean that social engagements interfere with his occupations?"

"That but feebly expresses it."

"So that he can't give himself up to his beautiful imagination?"

"He's beset, badgered, bothered—he's pulled to pieces on the pretext of being applauded. People expect him to give them his time, his golden time, who wouldn't themselves give five shillings for one of his books."

"Five? I'd give five thousand!"

"Give your sympathy—give your forbearance. Two-thirds of those who approach him only do it to advertise themselves."

"Why, it's too bad!" the girl exclaimed, with the face of an angel. "It's the first time I was ever called crude!" she laughed.

I followed up my advantage. "There's a lady with him now who's a terrible complication, and who yet hasn't read, I'm sure, ten pages he ever wrote."

My visitor's wide eyes grew tenderer. "Then how does she talk——?"

"Without ceasing. I only mention her as a single case. Do you want to know how to show a superlative consideration? Simply avoid him."

"Avoid him?" she despairingly breathed.

"Don't force him to have to take account of you; admire him in silence, cultivate him at a distance and secretly appropriate his message. Do you want to know," I continued, warming to my idea, "how to perform an act of homage really sublime?" Then as she hung on my words: "Succeed in never seeing him at all!"

"Never at all?"—she suppressed a shriek for it.

"The more you get into his writings the less you'll want to, and you'll be immensely sustained by the thought of the good you're doing him."

She looked at me without resentment or spite, and at the truth I had put before her with candour, credulity, pity. I was afterwards happy to remember that she must have gathered from my face the liveliness of my interest in herself. "I think I see what you mean."

"Oh I express it badly, but I should be delighted if you'd let me come to see you—to explain it better."

She made no response to this, and her thoughtful eyes fell on the big album, on which she presently laid her hands as if to take it away. "I did use to say out West that they might write a little less for autographs—to all the great poets, you know—and study the thoughts and style a little more."

"What do they care for the thoughts and style? They didn't even

98

understand you. I'm not sure," I added, "that I do myself, and I daresay that you by no means make me out."

She had got up to go, and though I wanted her to succeed in not seeing Neil Paraday I wanted her also, inconsequently, to remain in the house. I was at any rate far from desiring to hustle her off. As Mrs. Weeks Wimbush, upstairs, was still saving our friend in her own way, I asked my young lady to let me briefly relate, in illustration of my point, the little incident of my having gone down into the country for a profane purpose and been converted on the spot to holiness. Sinking again into her chair to listen she showed a deep interest in the anecdote. Then thinking it over gravely she returned with her odd intonation: "Yes, but you do see him!" I had to admit that this was the case; and I wasn't so prepared with an effective attenuation as I could have wished. She eased the situation off, however, by the charming quaintness with which she finally said: "Well, I wouldn't want him to be lonely!" This time she rose in earnest, but I persuaded her to let me keep the album to show Mr. Paraday. I assured her I'd bring it back to her myself. "Well, you'll find my address somewhere in it on a paper!" she sighed all resignedly at the door.

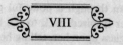

VIII

BLUSH to confess it, but I invited Mr. Paraday that very day to transcribe into the album one of his most characteristic passages. I told him how I had got rid of the strange girl who had brought it— her ominous name was Miss Hurter and she lived at an hotel; quite agreeing with him, moreover, as to the wisdom of getting rid with equal promptitude of the book itself. This was why I carried it to Albemarle Street no later than on the morrow. I failed to find her at home, but she wrote to me and I went again: she wanted so much to hear more about Neil Paraday. I returned repeatedly, I may briefly declare, to supply her with this information. She had been immensely taken, the more she thought of it, with that idea of mine about the act of homage: it had ended by filling her with a generous rapture. She positively desired to do something sublime for him, though indeed

I could see that, as this particular flight was difficult, she appreciated the fact that my visits kept her up. I had it on my conscience to keep her up; I neglected nothing that would contribute to it, and her conception of our cherished author's independence became at last as fine as his very own. "Read him, read him—*that* will be an education in decency," I constantly repeated; while, seeking him in his works even as God in nature, she represented herself as convinced that, according to my assurance, this was the system that had, as she expressed it, weaned her. We read him together when I could find time, and the generous creature's sacrifice was fed by our communion. There were twenty selfish women about whom I told her and who stirred her to a beautiful rage. Immediately after my first visit her sister, Mrs. Milsom, came over from Paris, and the two ladies began to present, as they called it, their letters. I thanked our stars that none had been presented to Mr. Paraday. They received invitations and dined out, and some of these occasions enabled Fanny Hurter to perform, for consistency's sake, touching feats of submission. Nothing indeed would now have induced her even to look at the object of her admiration. Once, hearing his name announced at a party, she instantly left the room by another door and then straightway quitted the house. At another time when I was at the opera with them—Mrs. Milsom had invited me to their box—I attempted to point Mr. Paraday out to her in the stalls. On this she asked her sister to change places with her and, while that lady devoured the great man through a powerful glass, presented, all the rest of the evening, her inspired back to the house. To torment her tenderly I pressed the glass upon her, telling her how wonderfully near it brought our friend's handsome head. By way of answer she simply looked at me in charged silence, letting me see that tears had gathered in her eyes. These tears, I may remark, produced an effect on me of which the end is not yet. There was a moment when I felt it my duty to mention them to Neil Paraday, but I was deterred by the reflexion that there were questions more relevant to his happiness.

These questions indeed, by the end of the season, were reduced to a single one—the question of reconstituting so far as might be possible the conditions under which he had produced his best work. Such conditions could never all come back, for there was a new one that took up too much place; but some perhaps were not beyond recall. I wanted above all things to see him sit down to the subject he had, on my making his acquaintance, read me that admirable sketch of. Something told me there was no security but in his doing so before the new factor, as we used to say at Mr. Pinhorn's, should render the problem incalculable. It only half-reassured me that the sketch itself was so copious and so eloquent that even at the worst there would be the making of a small but complete book, a tiny volume which, for the faithful, might well become an object of adoration. There would even not be wanting critics to declare, I foresaw, that the plan was a thing to be more thankful for than the structure to have been read on it. My impatience for the structure, none the less, grew and grew with the interruptions. He had on coming up to town begun to sit for his portrait to a young painter, Mr. Rumble, whose little game, as we also used to say at Mr. Pinhorn's, was to be the first to perch on the shoulders of renown. Mr. Rumble's studio was a circus in which the man of the hour, and still more the woman, leaped through the hoops of his showy frames almost as electrically as they burst into telegrams and "specials." He pranced into the exhibitions on their back; he was the reporter on canvas, the Vandyke up to date, and there was one roaring year in which Mrs. Bounder and Miss Braby, Guy Walsingham and Dora Forbes proclaimed in chorus from the same pictured walls that no one had yet got ahead of him.

Paraday had been promptly caught and saddled, accepting with characteristic good humour his confidential hint that to figure in his show was not so much a consequence as a cause of immortality. From Mrs. Wimbush to the last "representative" who called to ascertain his twelve favourite dishes, it was the same ingenuous assumption that he would rejoice in the repercussion. There were moments when I fancied I might have had more patience with them if they hadn't been so fatally benevolent. I hated at all events Mr. Rumble's picture, and had my bottled resentment ready when, later on, I found my distracted friend had been stuffed by Mrs. Wimbush into the mouth of another cannon. A young artist in whom she was intensely interested, and who had no connexion with Mr. Rumble, was to show how far *he* could make him go. Poor Paraday, in return, was naturally to write something somewhere about the young artist. She played her victims against each other with admirable ingenuity, and her establishment was a huge machine in which the tiniest and the biggest wheels went round to the same treadle. I had a scene with her in which I tried to express that the function of such a man was to exercise his genius— not to serve as a hoarding for pictorial posters. The people I was perhaps angriest with were the editors of magazines who had intro- duced what they called new features, so aware were they that the newest feature of all would be to make him grind their axes by contributing his views on vital topics and taking part in the periodical prattle about the future of fiction. I made sure that before I should have done with him there would scarcely be a current form of words left me to be sick of; but meanwhile I could make surer still of my animosity to bustling ladies for whom he drew the water that irrigated their social flower-beds.

I had a battle with Mrs. Wimbush over the artist she protected, and another over the question of a certain week, at the end of July, that Mr. Paraday appeared to have contracted to spend with her in the country. I protested against this visit; I intimated that he was too unwell for hospitality without a *nuance*, for caresses without imagination; I begged he might rather take the time in some restorative way. A sultry air of promises, of ponderous parties, hung over his August, and he would greatly profit by the interval of rest. He hadn't told me he was ill again—that he had had a warning; but I hadn't needed this, for I found his reticence his worst symptom. The only thing he said to me was that he believed a comfortable attack of something or other would set him up: it would put out of the question everything but the exemptions he prized. I'm afraid I shall have presented him as a martyr in a very small cause if I fail to explain that he surrendered himself much more liberally than I surrendered him. He filled his lungs, for the most part, with the comedy of his queer fate: the tragedy was in the spectacles through which I chose to look. He was conscious of inconvenience, and above all of a great renouncement; but how could he have heard a mere dirge in the bells of his accession? The sagacity and the jealousy were mine, and his the impressions and the harvest. Of course, as regards Mrs. Wimbush, I was worsted in my encounters, for wasn't the state of his health the very reason for his coming to her at Prestidge? Wasn't it precisely at Prestidge that he was to be coddled, and wasn't the dear Princess coming to help her to coddle him? The dear Princess, now on a visit to England, was of a famous foreign house, and, in her gilded cage, with her retinue of keepers and feeders, was the most expensive specimen in the good lady's collection. I don't think her august presence had had to do with Paraday's consenting to go, but it's not impossible he had operated as a bait to the illustrious stranger. The party had been made up for him, Mrs. Wimbush averred, and every one was counting on it, the dear Princess most of all. If he was well enough he was to read them something absolutely fresh, and it was on that particular prospect the Princess had set her heart. She was so fond of genius in *any* walk of life, and was so used to it and understood it so well: she was the greatest of Mr. Paraday's admirers, she devoured everything he wrote. And then he read like an angel. Mrs. Wimbush reminded me that he had again and again given her, Mrs. Wimbush, the privilege of listening to him.

I looked at her a moment. "What has he read to you?" I crudely inquired.

For a moment too she met my eyes, and for the fraction of a moment she hesitated and coloured. "Oh all sorts of things!"

I wondered if this were an imperfect recollection or only a perfect fib, and she quite understood my unuttered comment on her measure of such things. But if she could forget Neil Paraday's beauties she could of course forget my rudeness, and three days later she invited me, by telegraph, to join the party at Prestidge. This time she might indeed have had a story about what I had given up to be near the master. I addressed from that fine residence several communications to a young lady in London, a young lady whom, I confess, I quitted with reluctance and whom the reminder of what she herself could give up was required to make me quit at all. It adds to the gratitude I owe her on other grounds that she kindly allows me to transcribe from my letters a few of the passages in which that hateful sojourn is candidly commemorated.

IX

"I SUPPOSE I ought to enjoy the joke of what's going on here," I wrote, "but somehow it doesn't amuse me. Pessimism on the contrary possesses me and cynicism deeply engages. I positively feel my own flesh sore from the brass nails in Neil Paraday's social harness. The house is full of people who like him, as they mention, awfully, and with whom his talent for talking nonsense has prodigious success. I delight in his nonsense myself; why is it therefore that I grudge these happy folk their artless satisfaction? Mystery of the human heart—abyss of the critical spirit! Mrs. Wimbush thinks she can answer that question, and as my want of gaiety has at last worn out her patience she has given me a glimpse of her shrewd guess. I'm made restless by

the selfishness of the insincere friend—I want to monopolise Paraday
in order that he may push me on. To be intimate with him's a feather
in my cap ; it gives me an importance that I couldn't naturally
pretend to, and I seek to deprive him of social refreshment because
I fear that meeting more disinterested people may enlighten him as to
my real motive. All the disinterested people here are his particular
admirers and have been carefully selected as such. There's supposed
to be a copy of his last book in the house, and in the hall I come upon
ladies, in attitudes, bending gracefully over the first volume. I dis-
creetly avert my eyes, and when I next look round the precarious joy
has been superseded by the book of life. There's a sociable circle or a
confidential couple, and the relinquished volume lies open on its face
and as dropped under extreme coercion. Somebody else presently
finds it and transfers it, with its air of momentary desolation, to
another piece of furniture. Every one's asking every one about it all
day, and everyone's telling every one where they put it last. I'm sure it's
rather smudgy about the twentieth page. I've a strong impression too
that the second volume is lost—has been packed in the bag for some
departing guest; and yet everybody has the impression that somebody
else has read to the end. You see therefore that the beautiful book plays
a great part in our existence. Why should I take the occasion of such
distinguished honours to say that I begin to see deeper into Gustave
Flaubert's doleful refrain about the hatred of literature ? I refer you
again to the perverse constitution of man.   •

"The Princess is a massive lady with the organisation of an athlete
and the confusion of tongues of a *valet de place*. She contrives to commit herself extraordinarily little in a great many languages, and is
entertained and conversed with in detachments and relays, like an
institution which goes on from generation to generation or a big
building contracted for under a forfeit. She can't have a personal
taste any more than, when her husband succeeds, she can have a
personal crown, and her opinion on any matter is rusty and heavy and
plain—made, in the night of ages, to last and be transmitted. I feel as
if I ought to 'tip' some *custode* for my glimpse of it. She had been
told everything in the world and has never perceived anything, and the
echoes of her education respond awfully to the rash footfall—I mean
the casual remark—in the cold Valhalla of her memory. Mrs. Wimbush delights in her wit and says there's nothing so charming as to hear
Mr. Paraday draw it out. He's perpetually detailed for this job, and
he tells me it has a peculiarly exhausting effect. Every one's beginning

—at the end of two days—to sidle obsequiously away from her, and Mrs. Wimbush pushes him again into the breach. None of the uses I have yet seen him put to infuriate me quite so much. He looks very fagged and has at last confessed to me that his condition makes him uneasy—has even promised me he'll go straight home instead of returning to his final engagement in town. Last night I had some talk with him about going to-day, cutting his visit short; so sure am I that he'll be better as soon as he's shut up in his lighthouse. He told me that this is what he would like to do; reminding me, however, that the first lesson of his greatness has been precisely that he can't do what he likes. Mrs. Wimbush would never forgive him if he should leave her before the Princess has received the last hand. When I hint that a violent rupture with our hostess would be the best thing in the world for him he gives me to understand that if his reason assents to the proposition his courage hangs woefully back. He makes no secret of being mortally afraid of her, and when I ask what harm she can do him that she hasn't already done he simply repeats: 'I'm afraid, I'm afraid ! Don't inquire too closely,' he said last night; 'only believe that I feel a sort of terror. It's strange, when she's so kind ! At any rate, I'd as soon overturn that piece of priceless Sèvres as tell her I must go before my date.' It sounds dreadfully weak, but he has some reason, and he pays for his imagination, which puts him (I should hate it) in the place of others and makes him feel, even against himself, their feelings, their appetites, their motives. It's indeed inveterately against himself that he makes his imagination act. What a pity he has such a lot of it ! He's too beastly intelligent. Besides, the famous reading's still to come off, and it has been postponed a day to allow Guy Walsingham to arrive. It appears this eminent lady's staying at a house a few miles off, which means of course that Mrs. Wimbush has forcibly annexed her. She's to come over in a day or two—Mrs. Wimbush wants her to hear Mr. Paraday.

"To-day's wet and cold, and several of the company, at the invitation of the Duke, have driven over to luncheon at Bigwood. I saw poor Paraday wedge himself, by command, into the little supplementary seat of a brougham in which the Princess and our hostess were already ensconced. If the front glass isn't open on his dear old back perhaps he'll survive. Bigwood, I believe, is very grand and frigid, all marble and precedence, and I wish him well out of the adventure. I can't tell you how much more and more *your* attitude to him, in the midst of all this, shines out by contrast. I never willingly talk to these people about him, but see what a comfort I find it to scribble to you! I appreciate it—it keeps me warm; there are no fires in the house. Mrs. Wimbush goes by the calendar, the temperature goes by the weather, the weather goes by God knows what, and the Princess is easily heated. I've nothing but my acrimony to warm me, and have been out under an umbrella to restore my circulation. Coming in an hour ago I found Lady Augusta Minch rummaging about the hall. When I asked her what she was looking for she said she had mislaid something that Mr. Paraday had lent her. I ascertained in a moment that the article in question is a manuscript, and I've a foreboding that it's the noble morsel he read me six weeks go. When I expressed my surprise that he should have bandied about anything so precious (I happen to know it's his only copy—in the most beautiful hand in all the world) Lady Augusta confessed to me that she hadn't had it from himself, but from Mrs. Wimbush, who had wished to give her a glimpse of it as a salve for her not being able to stay and hear it read.

"'Is that the piece he's to read,' I asked, 'when Guy Walsingham arrives?'

"'It's not for Guy Walsingham they're waiting now, it's for Dora Forbes,' Lady Augusta said. 'She's coming, I believe, early to-morrow. Meanwhile Mrs. Wimbush has found out about *him*, and is actively wiring to him. She says he also must hear him.'

"'You bewilder me a little,' I replied; 'in the age we live in one gets lost among the genders and the pronouns. The clear thing is that Mrs. Wimbush doesn't guard such a treasure so jealously as she might.'

"'Poor dear, she has the Princess to guard! Mr. Paraday lent her the manuscript to look over.'

"'She spoke, you mean, as if it were the morning paper?'

"Lady Augusta stared—my irony was lost on her. 'She didn't have time, so she gave me a chance first; because unfortunately I go to-morrow to Bigwood.'

"'And your chance has only proved a chance to lose it?'

"'I haven't lost it. I remember now—it was very stupid of me to have forgotten. I told my maid to give it to Lord Dorimont—or at least to his man.'

"'And Lord Dorimont went away directly after luncheon.'

"'Of course he gave it back to my maid—or else his man did,' said Lady Augusta. 'I daresay it's all right.'

"The conscience of these people is like a summer sea. They haven't time to 'look over' a priceless composition; they've only time to kick

106

it about the house. I suggested that the 'man,' fired with a noble emulation, had perhaps kept the work for his own perusal; and her ladyship wanted to know whether, if the thing shouldn't reappear for the grand occasion appointed by our hostess, the author wouldn't have something else to read that would do just as well. Their questions are too delightful ! I declared to Lady Augusta briefly that nothing in the world can ever do so well as the thing that does best; and at this she looked a little disconcerted. But I added that if the manuscript had gone astray our little circle would have the less of an effort of attention to make. The piece in question was very long—it would keep them three hours.

"'Three hours ! Oh the Princess will get up ! ' said Lady Augusta.

"'I thought she was Mr. Paraday's greatest admirer.'

"'I daresay she is—she's so awfully clever. But what's the use of being a Princess——'

"'If you can't dissemble your love ?' I asked as Lady Augusta was vague. She said at any rate that she'd question her maid; and I'm hoping that when I go down to dinner I shall find the manuscript has been recovered.''

X

"It has *not* been recovered," I wrote early the next day, "and I'm moreover much troubled about our friend. He came back from Bigwood with a chill and, being allowed to have a fire in his room, lay down a while before dinner. I tried to send him to bed and indeed thought I had put him in the way of it; but after I had gone to dress Mrs. Wimbush came up to see him, with the inevitable result that when I returned I found him under arms and flushed and feverish, though decorated with the rare flower she had brought him for his button-hole. He came down to dinner, but Lady Augusta Minch was very shy of him. To-day he's in great pain, and the advent of *ces dames*—I mean of Guy Walsingham and Dora Forbes—doesn't at all console me. It does Mrs. Wimbush, however, for she has consented to his remaining in bed so that he may be all right to-morrow for the listening circle. Guy Walsingham's already on the scene, and the doctor for Paraday also arrived early. I haven't yet seen the author of 'Obsessions,' but of course I've had a moment by myself with the Doctor. I tried to get him to say that our invalid must go straight home—I mean to-morrow or next day; but he quite refuses to talk about the future. Absolute quiet and warmth and the regular administration of an important remedy are the points he mainly insists on. He returns this afternoon, and I'm to go back to see the patient at one o'clock, when he next takes his medicine. It consoles me a little that he certainly won't be able to read—an exertion he was already more than unfit for. Lady Augusta went off after breakfast, assuring me her first care would be to follow up the lost manuscript. I can see she thinks me a shocking busybody and doesn't understand my alarm, but she'll do what she can, for she's a good-natured woman. 'So are they all honourable men.' That was precisely what made her give the thing to Lord Dorimont and made Lord Dorimont bag it. What use *he* has for it God only knows. I've the worst forebodings, but somehow I'm strangely without passion—desperately calm. As I consider the unconscious, the well-meaning ravages of our appreciative circle, I bow my head in submission to some great natural, some universal accident; I'm rendered almost indifferent, in fact quite gay (ha-ha !) by the sense of immitigable fate. Lady Augusta promises me to trace the precious object and let me have it through the post by the time Paraday's well enough to play his part with it. The last evidence is that her maid did give it to his lordship's valet. One would suppose it some thrilling number of *The Family Budget*. Mrs. Wimbush, who's aware of the accident, is much less agitated by it than she would doubtless be were she not for the hour inevitably engrossed with Guy Walsingham."

Later in the day I informed my correspondent, for whom indeed I kept a loose diary of the situation, that I had made the acquaintance of this celebrity and that she was a pretty little girl who wore her hair in what used to be called a crop. She looked so juvenile and so innocent that if, as Mr. Morrow had announced, she was resigned to the larger latitude, her superiority to prejudice must have come to her early. I spent most of the day hovering about Neil Paraday's room, but it was communicated to me from below that Guy Walsingham, at Prestidge, was a success. Toward evening I became conscious somehow that her superiority was contagious, and by the time the company separated for the night I was sure the larger latitude had been generally accepted. I thought of Dora Forbes and felt that he had no time to lose. Before

dinner I received a telegram from Lady Augusta Minch. "Lord Dorimont thinks he must have left bundle in train—inquire." How could
I inquire—if I was to take the word as a command? I was too worried
and now too alarmed about Neil Paraday. The Doctor came back,
and it was an immense satisfaction to me to be sure he was wise and
interested. He was proud of being called to so distinguished a patient,
but he admitted to me that night that my friend was gravely ill. It was
really a relapse, a recrudescence of his old malady. There could be no
question of moving him: we must at any rate see first, on the spot,
what turn his condition would take. Meanwhile, on the morrow, he
was to have a nurse. On the morrow the dear man was easier, and
my spirits rose to such cheerfulness that I could almost laugh over
Lady Augusta's second telegram: "Lord Dorimont's servant been
to station—nothing found. Push inquiries." I did laugh, I'm sure, as
I remember this to be the mystic scroll I had scarcely allowed poor
Mr. Morrow to point his umbrella at. Fool that I had been; the
thirty-seven influential journals wouldn't have destroyed it, they'd only
have printed it. Of course I said nothing to Paraday.

When the nurse arrived she turned me out of the room, on which I
went downstairs. I should premise that at breakfast the news that
our brilliant friend was doing well excited universal complacency, and
the Princess graciously remarked that he was only to be commiserated
for missing the society of Miss Collop. Mrs. Wimbush, whose social
gift never shone brighter than in the dry decorum with which she
accepted this fizzle in her fireworks, mentioned to me that Guy Walsingham had made a very favourable impression on her Imperial
Highness. Indeed I think every one did so, and that, like the money-
market or the national honour, her Imperial Highness was constitution-
ally sensitive. There was a certain gladness, a perceptible bustle in the
air, however, which I thought slightly anomalous in a house where
a great author lay critically ill. "*Le roy est mort—vive le roy*": I was
reminded that another great author had already stepped into his shoes.
When I came down again after the nurse had taken possession I found
a strange gentleman hanging about the hall and pacing to and fro by
the closed door of the drawing-room. This personage was florid and
bald; he had a big red moustache and wore showy knickerbockers—
characteristics all that fitted to my conception of the identity of Dora
Forbes. In a moment I saw what had happened: the author of "The
Other Way Round" had just alighted at the portals of Prestidge, but
had suffered a scruple to restrain him from penetrating further. I

recognised his scruple when, pausing to listen at his gesture of caution, I heard a shrill voice lifted in a sort of rhythmic uncanny chant. The famous reading had begun, only it was the author of "Obsessions" who now furnished the sacrifice. The new visitor whispered to me that he judged something was going on he oughtn't to interrupt.

"Miss Collop arrived last night," I smiled, "and the Princess has a thirst for the *inédit*."

Dora Forbes raised his bushy brows. "Miss Collop?"

"Guy Walsingham, your distinguished *confrére*—or shall I say your formidable rival?"

"Oh!" growled Dora Forbes. Then he added: "Shall I spoil it if I go in?"

"I should think nothing could spoil it!" I ambiguously laughed.

Dora Forbes evidently felt the dilemma; he gave an irritated crook to his moustache. "*Shall* I go in?" he presently asked.

We looked at each other hard a moment; then I expressed something bitter that was in me, expressed it in an infernal "Do!" After this I got out into the air, but not so fast as not to hear, when the door of the drawing-room opened, the disconcerted drop of Miss Collop's public manner: she must have been in the midst of the larger latitude. Producing with extreme rapidity, Guy Walsingham has just published a work in which amiable people who are not initiated have been pained to see the genius of a sister-novelist held up to unmistakable ridicule; so fresh an exhibition does it seem to them of the dreadful way men have always treated women. Dora Forbes, it's true, at the present hour, is immensely pushed by Mrs. Wimbush and has sat for his portrait to the young artists she protects, sat for it not only in oils but in monumental alabaster.

What happened at Prestidge later in the day is of course contemporary history. If the interruption I had whimsically sanctioned was almost a scandal, what is to be said of that general scatter of the company which, under the Doctor's rule, began to take place in the evening? His rule was soothing to behold, small comfort as I was to have at the end. He decreed in the interest of his patient an absolutely soundless house and a consequent break-up of the party. Little country practitioner as he was, he literally packed off the Princess. She departed as promptly as if a revolution had broken out, and Guy Walsingham emigrated with her. I was kindly permitted to remain, and this was not denied even to Mrs. Wimbush. The privilege was withheld indeed from Dora Forbes; so Mrs. Wimbush kept her latest capture temporarily concealed. This was so little, however, her usual way of dealing with her eminent friends that a couple of days of it exhausted her patience and she went up to town with him in great publicity. The sudden turn for the worse her afflicted guest had, after a brief improvement, taken on the third night raised an obstacle to her seeing him before her retreat; a fortunate circumstance doubtless, for she was fundamentally disappointed in him. This was not the kind of performance for which she had invited him to Prestidge, let alone invited the Princess. I must add that none of the generous acts marking her patronage of intellectual and other merit have done so much for her reputation as her lending Neil Paraday the most beautiful of her numerous homes to die in. He took advantage to the utmost of the singular favour. Day by day I saw him sink, and I roamed alone about the empty terraces and gardens. His wife never came near him, but I scarcely noticed it: as I paced there with rage in my heart I was too full of another wrong. In the event of his death it would fall to me perhaps to bring out in some charming form, with notes, with the tenderest editorial care, that precious heritage of his written project. But where *was* that precious heritage, and were both the author and the book to have been snatched from us? Lady Augusta wrote me she had done all she could and that poor Lord Dorimont, who had really been worried to death, was extremely sorry. I couldn't have the matter out with Mrs. Wimbush, for I didn't want to be taunted by her with desiring to aggrandise myself by a public connexion with Mr. Paraday's sweepings. She had signified her willingness to meet the expense of all advertising, as indeed she was already ready to do. The last night of the horrible series, the night before he died, I put my ear closer to his pillow.

"That thing I read you that morning, you know."

"In your garden that dreadful day? Yes!"

"Won't it do as it is?"

"It would have been a glorious book."

"It *is* a glorious book," Neil Paraday murmured. "Print it as it stands—beautifully."

"Beautifully!" I passionately promised.

It may be imagined whether, now that he's gone, the promise seems to me less sacred. I'm convinced that if such pages had appeared in his lifetime the Abbey would hold him to-day. I've kept the advertising in my own hands, but the manuscript has not been recovered. It's impossible, and at any rate intolerable, to suppose it can have been wantonly destroyed. Perhaps some hazard of a blind hand, some brutal fatal ignorance has lighted kitchen-fires with it. Every stupid and hideous accident haunts my meditations. My undiscourageable search for the lost treasure would make a long chapter. Fortunately I've a devoted associate in the person of a young lady who has every day a fresh indignation and a fresh idea, and who maintains with intensity that the prize will still turn up. Sometimes I believe her, but I've quite ceased to believe myself. The only thing for us at all events is to go on seeking and hoping together, and we should be closely united by this firm tie even were we not at present by another.

THE NEXT TIME

MRS. HIGHMORE'S errand this morning was odd enough to deserve commemoration: she came to ask me to write a notice of her great forthcoming work. Her great works have come forth so frequently without my assistance that I was sufficiently entitled on this occasion to open my eyes; but what really made me stare was the ground on which her request reposed, and what prompts a note of the matter is the train of memory lighted by that explanation. Poor Ray Limbert, while we talked, seemed to sit there between us: she reminded me that my acquaintance with him had begun, eighteen years ago, with her having come in, precisely as she came to-day before luncheon, to bespeak my charity for him. If she didn't know then how little my charity was worth she's at least enlightened now, and this is just what makes the drollery of her visit. As I hold up the torch to the dusky years—by which I mean as I cipher up with a pen that stumbles and stops the figured column of my reminiscences—I see that Limbert's public hour, or at least my small apprehension of it, is rounded by those two occasions. It was *finis*, with a little moralising flourish, that Mrs. Highmore seemed to trace to-day at the bottom of the page. "One of the most voluminous writers of the time," she has often repeated this sign; but never, I daresay, in spite of her professional command of appropriate emotion, with an equal sense of that mystery and that sadness of things which to people of imagination generally hover over the close of human histories. This romance at any rate is bracketed by her early and her late appeal; and when its melancholy protrusions had caught the declining light again from my half-hour's talk with her I took a private vow to recover while that light still lingers something of the delicate flush, to pick out with a brief patience the perplexing lesson.

It was wonderful to see how for herself Mrs. Highmore had already done so: she wouldn't have hesitated to announce to me what was the matter with Ralph Limbert, or at all events to give me a glimpse of the high admonition she had read in his career. There could have been no better proof of the vividness of this parable, which we were really in our pleasant sympathy quite at one about, than that Mrs. Highmore of all hardened sinners, should have been converted. It wasn't indeed news to me: she impressed on me that for the last ten years she had wanted to do something artistic, something as to which she was prepared not to care a rap whether or no it should sell. She brought home to me further that it had been mainly seeing what her brother-in-law did and how he did it that had wedded her to this perversity. As *he* didn't sell, dear soul, and as several persons, of whom I was one, thought highly of that, the fancy had taken her—taken her even quite early in her prolific course—of reaching, if only once, the same heroic eminence. She yearned to be, like Limbert, but of course only once, an exquisite failure. There was something a failure was, a failure in the market, that a success somehow wasn't. A success was as prosaic as a good dinner: there was nothing more to be said about it than that you had had it. Who but vulgar people, in such a case, made gloating remarks about the courses? It was often by such vulgar people that a success was attested. It made, if you came to look at it, nothing but money; that is, it made so much that any other result showed small in comparison. A failure now could make—oh with the aid of immense talent of course, for there were failures and failures—such a reputation! She did me the honour—she had often done it—to intimate that what she meant by reputation was seeing *me* toss a flower. If it took a failure to catch a failure I was by my own admission well qualified to place the laurel. It was because she had made so much money and Mr. Highmore had taken such care of it that she could treat herself to an hour of pure glory. She perfectly remembered that as often as I had heard her heave that sigh I had been prompt with my declaration that a book sold might easily be as glorious as a book unsold. Of course she knew this, but she knew also that it was the age of trash triumphant and that she had never heard me speak of anything that had "done well" exactly as she had sometimes heard me speak of something that hadn't—with just two or three words of respect which, when I used them, seemed to convey more than they commonly stood for, seemed to hush the discussion up a little, as for the very beauty of the secret.

I may declare in regard to these allusions that, whatever I then thought of myself as a holder of the scales, I had never scrupled to laugh out at the humour of Mrs. Highmore's pursuit of quality at any price. It had never rescued her even for a day from the hard doom of popularity, and though I never gave her my word for it there was no reason at all why it should. The public *would* have her, as her husband used roguishly to remark; not indeed that, making her bargains, standing up to her publishers, and even in his higher flights to her reviewers, he ever had a glimpse of her attempted conspiracy against her genius, or rather, as I may say, against mine. It wasn't that when she tried to be what she called subtle (for wasn't Limbert subtle, and wasn't I?) her fond consumers, bless them, didn't suspect the trick nor show what they thought of it: they straightway rose on the contrary to the morsel she had hoped to hold too high, and, making but a big cheerful bite of it, wagged their great collective tail artlessly for more. It was not given to her not to please, not granted even to her best refinements to affright. I had always respected the mystery of those humiliations, but I was fully aware this morning that they were practically the reason why she had come to me. Therefore when she said with the flush of a bold joke in her kind coarse face, "What I feel is, you know, that *you* could settle me if you only would," I knew quite well what she meant. She meant that of old it had always appeared to be the fine blade (as some one had hyperbolically called it) of my particular opinion that snapped the silken thread by which Limbert's chance in the market was wont to hang. She meant that my favour was compromising, that my praise indeed was fatal. I had cultivated the queer habit of seeing nothing in certain celebrities, of seeing overmuch in an occasional nobody, and of judging from a point of view that, say what I would for it (and I had a monstrous deal to say), mostly remained perverse and obscure. Mine was in short the love that killed, for my subtlety, unlike Mrs. Highmore's, produced no tremor of the public tail. She hadn't forgotten how, toward the end, when his case was worst, Limbert would absolutely come to me with an odd shy pathos in his eyes and say: "My dear fellow, I think I've done it this time, if you'll only keep quiet." If my keeping quiet in those days was to help him to appear to have hit the usual taste, for the want of which he was starving, so now my breaking-out was to help Mrs. Highmore to appear to have hit the unusual.

The moral of all this was that I had frightened the public too much for our late friend, but that as she was not starving this was exactly what her grosser reputation required. And then, she good-naturedly and delicately intimated, there would always be, if further reasons were wanting, the price of my clever little article. I think she gave that hint with a flattering impression—spoiled child of the booksellers as she is—that the offered fee for my clever little articles is heavy. Whatever it is, at any rate, she had evidently reflected that poor Limbert's anxiety for his own profit used to involve my sacrificing mine. Any inconvenience that my obliging her might entail would not in fine be pecuniary. Her appeal, her motive, her fantastic thirst for quality and her ingenious theory of my influence struck me all as excellent comedy, and when I consented at hazard to oblige her she left me the sheets of her new novel. I could plead no inconvenience and have been looking them over; but I'm frankly appalled at what she expects of me. What's she thinking of, poor dear, and what has put it into her head that the muse of "quality" has ever sat with her for so much as three minutes? Why does she suppose that she has been "artistic"? She hasn't been anything whatever, I surmise, that she hasn't inveterately been. What does she imagine she has left out? What does she conceive she has put in? She has neither left out nor put in anything. I shall have to write her an embarrassed note. The book doesn't exist and there's nothing in life to say about it. How can there be anything but the same old faithful rush for it?

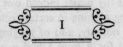

I

THIS RUSH had already begun when, early in the seventies, in the interest of her prospective brother-in-law, she approached me on the singular ground of the unencouraged sentiment I had entertained for her sister. Pretty pink Maud had cast me out, but I appear to have passed in the flurried little circle for a magnanimous youth. Pretty pink Maud, so lovely then, before her troubles, that dusky Jane was gratefully conscious of all she made up for, Maud Stannace, very literary too, very languishing and extremely bullied by her mother, had yielded, invidiously as it might have struck me, to Ray Limbert's suit, which Mrs. Stannace wasn't the woman to stomach. Mrs. Stannace was seldom the woman to do anything: she had been shocked at the way her children, with the grubby taint of their father's blood— he had published pale Remains or flat Conversations of *his* father— breathed the alien air of authorship. If not the daughter, nor even the niece, she was, if I'm not mistaken, the second cousin of a hundred earls and a great stickler for relationship, so that she had other views for her brilliant child, especially after her quiet one—such had been her original discreet forecast of the producer of eighty volumes— became the second wife of an ex-army-surgeon, already the father of 'our children. Mrs. Stannace had too manifestly dreamed it would be given to pretty pink Maud to detach some one of the noble hundred, who wouldn't be missed, from the cluster. It was because she cared only for cousins that I unlearnt the way to her house, which she had once reminded me was one of the few paths of gentility I could hope to tread. Ralph Limbert, who belonged to nobody and had done nothing—nothing even at Cambridge—had only the uncanny spell he had cast on her younger daughter to recommend him; but if her younger daughter had a spark of filial feeling she wouldn't commit the indecency of deserting for his sake a deeply dependent and intensely aggravated mother.

These things I learned from Jane Highmore, who, as if her books had been babies—they remained her only ones—had waited till after marriage to show what she could do, and now bade fair to surround her satisfied spouse (he took, for some mysterious reason, a part of the credit) with a little family, in sets of triplets, which properly handled would be the support of his declining years. The young couple, neither of whom had a penny, were now virtually engaged: the thing was subject to Ralph's putting his hand on some regular employment. People more enamoured couldn't be conceived, and Mrs. Highmore, honest woman, who had moreover a professional sense for a love-story, was eager to take them under her wing. What was wanted was a decent opening for Limbert, which it had occurred to her I might assist her to find, though indeed I had not yet found any such matter for myself. But it was well known that I was too particular, whereas poor Ralph, with the easy manners of genius, was ready to accept almost anything to which a salary, even a small one, was attached. If he could only for instance get a place on a newspaper the rest of his maintenance would come freely enough. It was true that his two novels, one of which she had brought to leave with me, had passed unperceived, and that to her, Mrs. Highmore personally, they didn't irresistibly appeal; but she could all the same assure me that I should have only to spend ten minutes with him—and our encounter must speedily take place—to receive an impression of latent power.

Our encounter took place soon after I had read the volumes Mrs. Highmore had left with me, in which I recognised an intention of a sort that I had then pretty well given up the hope of meeting. I daresay that without knowing it I had been looking out rather hungrily for an altar of sacrifice: however that may be, I submitted when I came across Ralph Limbert to one of the rarest emotions of my literary life, the sense of an activity in which I could critically rest. The rest was deep and salutary, and has not been disturbed to this hour. It has been a long large surrender, the luxury of dropped discriminations. He couldn't trouble me, whatever he did, for I practically enjoyed him as much when he was worse as when he was better. It was a case, I suppose, of natural prearrangement, in which, I hasten to add, I keep excellent company. We're a numerous band, partakers of the same repose, who sit together in the shade of the tree, by the plash of the fountain, with the glare of the desert round us and no great vice that I know of but the habit perhaps of estimating people a little too much by what they think of a certain style. If it had been laid upon these few pages, none the less, to be the history of an enthusiasm, I shouldn't have undertaken them: they're concerned with Ralph Limbert in relations to which I was a stranger or in which I participated but by sympathy. I used to talk about his work, but I seldom talk now: the brotherhood of the faith have become, like the Trappists, a silent order. If to the day of his death, after mortal disenchantments, the impression he first produced always evoked the word "ingenuous," those to whom his face was familiar can easily imagine what it must have been when it still had the light of youth. I had never seen a man of genius show so for passive, a man of experience so off his guard. At the time I made his acquaintance this freshness was all unbrushed. His foot had begun to stumble, but he was full of big intentions and of sweet Maud Stannace. Black-haired and pale, deceptively languid, he had the eyes of a clever child and the voice of a bronze bell. He saw more even than I had done in the girl he was engaged to; as time went on I became conscious that we had both, properly enough, seen rather more than there was. Our odd situation, that of the three of us, became perfectly possible from the moment I recognised how much more patience he had with her than I should have had. I was happy at not having to supply this quantity, and she, on her side, found pleasure in being able to be impertinent to me without incurring the reproach of the bad wife.

Limbert's novels appeared to have brought him no money: they had only brought him, so far as I could then make out, tributes that took up his time. These indeed brought him from several quarters some other things, and on my part at the end of three months *The Blackport Beacon*. I don't to-day remember how I obtained for him the London correspondence of the great northern organ, unless it was through somebody's having obtained it for myself. I seem to recall that I got rid of it in Limbert's interest, urging on the editor that he was much the better man. The better man was naturally the man who had pledged himself at the altar to provide for a charming woman. We were neither of us good, as the event proved, but he had the braver badness. *The Blackport Beacon* rejoiced in two London correspondents —one a supposed haunter of political circles, the other a votary of questions sketchily classified as literary. They were both expected to be lively, and what was held out to each was that it was honourably open to him to be livelier than the other. I recollect the political correspondent of that period and how the problem offered to Ray Limbert was to try to be livelier than Pat Moyle. He had not yet seemed to me so candid as when he undertook this exploit, which brought matters to a head with Mrs. Stannace, inasmuch as her opposition to the marriage now logically fell to the ground. It's all tears and laughter as I look back upon that admirable time, in which nothing was so romantic as our intense vision of the real. No fool's paradise ever rustled such a cradle-song. It was anything but Bohemia —it was the very temple of Mrs. Grundy. We knew we were too critical, and that made us sublimely indulgent; we believed we did our duty or wanted to, and that made us free to dream. But we dreamed over the multiplication-table; we were nothing if not practical. Oh the long smokes and sudden happy thoughts, the knowing hints and banished scruples! The great thing was for Limbert to bring out his next book, which was just what his delightful engagement with the *Beacon* would give him leisure and liberty to do. The kind of work, all human and elastic and suggestive, was capital experience: in picking up things for his bi-weekly letter he would pick up life as well, he would pick up literature. The new publications, the new pictures, the new people—there would be nothing too novel for us and nobody too sacred. We introduced everything and everybody into Mrs. Stannace's drawing-room, of which I again became a familiar.

Mrs. Stannace, it was true, thought herself in strange company; she didn't particularly mind the new books, though some of them seemed queer enough, but to the new people she had decided objections. It was notorious, however, that poor Lady Robeck secretly wrote for one of the papers, and the thing had certainly, in its glance at the doings of the great world, a side that might be made attractive. But we were going to make every side attractive and we had everything to say about the sort of thing a paper like the *Beacon* would want. To give it what it would want and to give it nothing else was not doubtless an inspiring but was a perfectly respectable task, especially for a man with an appealing bride and a contentious mother-in-law. I thought Limbert's first letters as charming as the type allowed, though I won't deny that in spite of my sense of the importance of concessions I was just a trifle disconcerted at the way he had caught the tone. The tone was of course to be caught, but need it have been caught so in the act? The creature was even cleverer, as Maud Stannace said, than she had ventured to hope. Verily it was a good thing to have a dose of the wisdom of the serpent. If it had to be journalism—well, it *was* journalism. If he had to be "chatty"—well, he *was* chatty. Now and then he made a hit that—it was stupid of me—brought the blood to my face. I hated him to be so personal; but still, if it would make his fortune——! It wouldn't of course directly, but the book would, practically and in the sense to which our pure ideas of fortune were confined; and these things were all for the book. The daily balm meanwhile was in what one knew of the book—there were exquisite things to know; in the quiet monthly cheques from Blackport and in the deeper rose of Maud's little preparations, which were as dainty, on their tiny scale, as if she had been a humming-bird building a nest. When at the end of three months her betrothed had fairly settled down to his correspondence—in which Mrs. Highmore was the only person, so far as we could discover, disappointed, even she moreover being in this particular tortuous and possibly jealous; when the situation had assumed such a comfortable shape it was quite time to prepare. I published at that moment my first volume, mere faded ink to-day, a little collection of literary impressions, odds and ends of criticism contributed to a journal less remunerative but also less chatty than the *Beacon*, small ironies and ecstasies, great phrases and mistakes; and the very week it came out poor Limbert devoted half of one of his letters to it, with the happy sense this time of gratifying both himself and me as well as the Blackport breakfast-tables. I remember his saying it wasn't literature, the stuff, superficial stuff, he had to write about me; but what did that matter if it came back, as we knew, to the making for literature in the roundabout way? I had sold the thing, I recall, for ten pounds, and with the money I bought in Vigo Street a quaint piece of old silver for Maud Stannace, which I carried her with my own hand as a wedding-gift. In her mother's small drawing-room, a faded bower of photography fenced in and bedimmed by folding screens out of which sallow persons of fashion with dashing signatures looked at you from re-touched eyes and little windows of plush, I was left to wait long enough to feel in the air of the house a hushed vibration of disaster. When our young lady came in she was very pale and *her* eyes too had been retouched.

"Something horrid has happened," I at once said; and having really all along but half-believed in her mother's meagre permission, I risked with an unguarded groan the introduction of Mrs. Stannace's name.

"Yes, she has made a dreadful scene; she insists on our putting it off again. We've very unhappy: poor Ray has been turned off." Her tears recommenced to flow.

I had such a good conscience that I stared. "Turned off what?"

"Why, his paper of course. The *Beacon* has given him what he calls the sack. They don't like his letters—they're not the style of thing they want."

My blankness could only deepen. "Then what style of thing, in God's name, *do* they want?"

"Something more chatty."

"More?" I cried, aghast.

"More gossipy, more personal. They want 'journalism.' They want tremendous trash."

"Why, that's just what his letters have *been*!" I broke out.

This was strong, and I caught myself up, but the girl offered me the pardon of a beautiful wan smile. "So Ray himself declares. He says he has stooped so low."

"Very well—he must stoop lower. He *must* keep the place."

"He can't!" poor Maud wailed. "He says he has tried all he knows, has been abject, has gone on all-fours, has crawled like a worm; and that if they don't like that——"

"He accepts his dismissal?" I interposed in dismay.

She gave a tragic shrug. "What other course is open to him? He wrote to them that such work as he has done is the very worst he can do for the money."

"Therefore," I pressed with a flash of hope, "they'll offer him more for worse?"

"No indeed," she answered, "they haven't even offered him to go on at a reduction. He isn't funny enough."

I reflected a moment. "But surely such a thing as his notice of my book—— !"

"It was your wretched book that was the last straw! He should have treated it superficially."

121

"Well, if he didn't——!" I began. Then I checked myself. "*Je vous porte malheur.*"

She didn't deny this; she only went on: "What on earth is he to do?"

"He's to do better than the monkeys! He's to write!"

"But what on earth are we to marry on?"

I considered once more. "You're to marry on 'The Major Key.'"

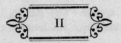

II

"THE MAJOR KEY" was the new novel, and the great thing accordingly was to finish it; a consummation for which three months of the *Beacon* had in some degree prepared the way. The action of that journal was indeed a shock, but I didn't know then the worst, didn't know that in addition to being a shock it was also a symptom. It was the first hint of the difficulty to which poor Limbert was eventually to succumb. His state was the happier, of a truth, for his not immediately seeing all it meant. Difficulty was the law of life, but one could thank heaven it was quite abnormally present in that awful connexion. There was the difficulty that inspired, the difficulty of "The Major Key" to wit, which it was after all base to sacrifice to the turning of somersaults for pennies. These convictions my friend beguiled his fresh wait by blandly entertaining: not indeed, I think, that the failure of his attempt to be chatty didn't leave him slightly humiliated. If it was bad enough to have grinned through a horse-collar it was very bad indeed to have grinned in vain. Well, he would try no more grinning or at least no more horse-collars. The only success worth one's powder was success in the line of one's idiosyncrasy. Consistency was in itself distinction, and what was talent but the art of being completely whatever it was that one happened to be? One's things were characteristic or they were nothing. I look back rather fondly on our having exchanged in those days these admirable remarks and many others; on our having been very happy too, in spite of postponements and obscurities, in spite also of such occasional hauntings as could spring from our lurid glimpse of the fact that even twaddle cunningly calculated was far above people's heads. It was easy to wave away spectres by the reflexion that all one had to do was not to write for people; it was certainly not for people that Limbert wrote while he hammered at "The Major Key." The taint of literature was fatal only in a certain kind of air, which was precisely the kind against which we had now closed our window. Mrs. Stannace rose from her crumpled cushions as soon as she had obtained an adjournment, and Maud looked pale and proud, quite victorious and superior, at her having obtained nothing more. Maud behaved well, I thought, to her mother, and well indeed, for a girl who had mainly been taught to be flowerlike, to every one. What she gave Ray Limbert for her fine abundant needs made him then and ever pay for; but the gift was liberal, almost wonderful—an assertion I make even while remembering to how many clever women, early and late, his work has been dear. It was not only that the woman he was to marry was in love with him, but that—this was the strangeness— she had really seen almost better than any one what he could do. The greatest strangeness was that she didn't want him to do something different. This boundless belief was indeed the main way of her devotion; and as an act of faith it naturally asked for miracles. She was a rare wife for a poet, if she was not perhaps the best to have been picked out for a poor man.

Well, we were to have the miracles of all events and we were in a perfect state of mind to receive them. There were more of us every day, and we thought highly even of our friend's odd jobs and pot-boilers. The *Beacon* had had no successor, but he found some quiet corners and stray chances. Perpetually poking the fire and looking out of the window, he was certainly not a monster of facility, but he was, thanks perhaps to a certain method in that madness, a monster of certainty. It wasn't every one, however, who knew him for this: many editors printed him but once. He was getting a small reputation as a man it was well to have the first time; he created obscure apprehensions as to what might happen the second. He was good for making an impression, but no one seemed exactly to know what the impression was good for when made. The reason was simply that they had not seen yet "The Major Key," that fiery-hearted rose as to which we watched in private the formation of petal after petal and flame after flame. Nothing mattered but this, for it had already elicited a splendid bid, much talked about in Mrs. Highmore's drawing-room, where at this point my reminiscences grow particularly thick. *Her* roses bloomed all the year and her sociability increased with her row of prizes. We had an idea that we "met every one" there—so we naturally thought when we met each other. Between our hostess and Ray Limbert flourished the happiest relation, the only cloud on which was that her husband eyed him rather askance. When he was called clever this personage wanted to know what he had to "show"; and it was certain that he showed nothing that could compare with Jane Highmore. Mr. Highmore took his stand on accomplished work and, turning up his coat-tails, warmed his rear with a good conscience at the neat book-case in which the generations of triplets were chronologically arranged. The harmony between his companions rested on the fact that, as I have already hinted, each would have liked so much to be the other. Limbert couldn't but have a feeling about a woman who in addition to being the best creature and her sister's backer would have made, could she have condescended, such a success with the *Beacon*. On the other hand Mrs. Highmore used freely to say: "Do you know, he'll do exactly the thing that *I* want to do? I shall never do it myself, but he'll do it instead. Yes, he'll do *my* thing, and I shall hate him for it—the wretch." Hating him was her pleasant humour, for the wretch was personally to her taste.

She prevailed on her own publisher to promise to take "The Major Key" and to engage to pay a considerable sum down, as the phrase is, on the presumption of its attracting attention. This was good news for the evening's end at Mrs. Highmore's when there were only four or five left and cigarettes ran low; but there was better to come, and I have never forgotten how, as it was I who had the good fortune to bring it, I kept it back on one of those occasions, for the sake of my effect, till only the right people remained. The right people were now more and more numerous, but this was a revelation addressed only to a choice residuum—a residuum including of course Limbert himself, with whom I haggled for another cigarette before I announced that as a consequence of an interview I had had with him that afternoon, and of a subtle argument I had brought to bear, Mrs. Highmore's pearl of publishers had agreed to put forth the new book as a serial. He was to "run" it in his magazine and he was to pay ever so much more for the privilege. I produced a fine gasp which presently found a more articulate relief, but poor Limbert's voice failed him once for all—he knew he was to walk away with me—and it was some one else who asked me what my subtle argument had been. I forget what florid description I then gave of it: to-day I've no reason not to confess that it had resided in the simple plea that the book was exquisite. I had said: "Come, my dear friend, be original; just risk it for that !" My dear friend seemed to rise to the chance, and I followed up my advantage, permitting him honestly no illusion as to the nature of the thing. He clutched interrogatively at two or three attenuations, but I dashed them aside, leaving him face to face with the formidable truth. It was just a pure gem: was he the man not to flinch ? His danger appeared to have acted on him as the anaconda acts on the rabbit; fascinated and paralysed, he had been engulfed in the long pink throat. When a week before, at my request, Limbert had left with me for a day the complete manuscript, beautifully copied out by Maud Stannace, I had flushed with indignation at its having to be said of the author of such pages that he hadn't the common means to marry. I had taken the field in a great glow to repair this scandal, and it was therefore quite directly my fault if three months later, when "The Major Key" began to run, Mrs. Stannace was driven to the wall. She had made a condition of a fixed income, and at last a fixed income was achieved.

She had to recognise it, and after much prostration among the photographs she recognised it to the extent of accepting some of the convenience of it in the form of a project for a common household, to the expenses of which each party should proportionately contribute. Jane Highmore made a great point of her not being left alone, but Mrs. Stannace herself determined the proportion, which on Limbert's side at least and in spite of many other fluctuations was never altered. His income had been "fixed" with a vengeance: having painfully stooped to the comprehension of it Mrs. Stannace rested on this effort to the end and asked no further question on the subject. "The Major Key" in other words ran ever so long, and before it was half out Limbert and Maud had been married and the common household set up. These first months were probably the happiest in the family annals, with wedding-bells and budding laurels, the quiet assured course of the book and the friendly familiar note, round the corner, of Mrs. Highmore's big guns. They gave Ralph time to block in another picture as well as to let me know after a while that he had the happy prospect of becoming a father. We had at times some dispute as to whether "The Major Key" was making an impression, but our difference could only be futile so long as we were not agreed as to what an impression consisted of. Several persons wrote to the author and several others asked to be introduced to him: wasn't that an impression ? One of the lively "weeklies," snapping at the deadly "monthlies," said the whole thing was "grossly inartistic"—wasn't *that*? It was somewhere else proclaimed "a wonderfully subtle character-study"—wasn't that too? The strongest effect doubtless was produced on the publisher when, in its lemon-coloured volumes, like a little dish of three custards, the book was at last served cold: he never got his money back and so far as I know has never got it back to this day. "The Major Key" was rather a great performance than a great success. It converted readers into friends and friends into lovers; it placed the author, as the phrase is—placed him all too definitely; but it shrank to obscurity in the account of sales eventually rendered. It was in short an exquisite thing, but it was scarcely a thing to have published and certainly not a thing to have married on. I heard all about the matter, for my intervention had much exposed me. Mrs. Highmore was emphatic as to the second volume's having given her ideas, and the ideas are probably to be found in some of her works, to the circulation of which they have even perhaps contributed. This was not absolutely yet the very thing she wanted to do—though on the way to it. So much, she informed me, she particularly perceived in the light of a critical study that I put forth in a little magazine; a thing the publisher in his advertisements quoted from profusely, and as to which there sprang up some absurd story that Limbert himself had written it. I remember that on my asking some one why such an idiotic thing had been said my interlocutor replied: "Oh because, you know, it's just the way he *would* have written!" My spirit sank a little perhaps as I reflected that with such analogies in our manner there might prove to be some in our fate.

It was during the next four or five years that our eyes were open to what, unless something could be done, that fate, at least on Limbert's part, might be. The thing to be done was of course to write the book, the book that would make the difference, really justify the burden he had accepted and consummately express his power. For the works that followed upon "The Major Key" he had inevitably to accept conditions the reverse of brilliant, at a time too when the strain upon his resources had begun to show sharpness. With three babies in due course, an ailing wife and a complication still greater than these, it became highly important that a man should do only his best. Whatever Limbert did was his best; so at least each time I thought and so I unfailingly said somewhere, though it was not my saying it, heaven knows, that made the desired difference. Every one else indeed said it, and there was among multiplied worries always the comfort that his position was quite assured. The two books that followed "The Major Key" did more than anything else to assure it, and Jane Highmore was always crying out: "You stand alone, dear Ray; you stand absolutely alone !" Dear Ray used to leave me in no doubt of how he felt the truth of this in feebly-attempted discussions with his bookseller. His sister-in-law gave him good advice into the bargain; she was a repository of knowing hints, of esoteric learning. These things were doubtless not the less valuable to him for bearing wholly on the question of how a reputation might be with a little gumption, as Mrs. Highmore said, "worked." Save when she occasionally bore testimony to her desire to do, as Limbert did, something some day for her own very self, I never heard her speak of the literary motive as if it were distinguishable from the pecuniary. She cocked up his hat, she pricked up his prudence for him, reminding him that as one seemed to take one's self so the silly world was ready to take one. It was a fatal mistake to be too candid even with those who were all right—not to look and to talk prosperous, not at least to pretend one had beautiful sales. To listen to her you would have thought the profession of letters a wonderful game of bluff. Wherever one's idea began it ended somehow in inspired paragraphs in the newspapers. "*I* pretend, I assure you, that you're going off like wildfire—I can at least do that for you !" she often declared, prevented as she was from doing much else by Mr. Highmore's insurmountable objection to *their* taking Mrs. Stannace.

I couldn't help regarding the presence of this latter lady in Limbert's life as the major complication: whatever he attempted it appeared given to him to achieve as best he could in the mere margin of the space in which she swung her petticoats. I may err in the belief that she practically lived on him, for though it was not in him to follow adequately Mrs. Highmore's counsel there were exasperated confessions he never made, scant domestic curtains he rattled on their rings. I may exaggerate in the retrospect his apparent anxieties, for these after all were the years when his talent was freshest and when as a writer he most laid down his line. It wasn't of Mrs. Stannace nor even as time went on of Mrs. Limbert that we mainly talked when I got at longer intervals a smokier hour in the little grey den from which we could step out, as we used to say, to the lawn. The lawn was the back-garden, and Limbert's study was behind the dining-room, with folding doors not impervious to the clatter of the children's tea. We sometimes took refuge from it in the depths—a bush and a half deep—of the shrubbery, where was a bench that gave us while we gossiped a view of Mrs. Stannace's tiara-like headdress nodding at an upper window. Within doors and without Limbert's life was overhung by an awful region that figured in his conversation, comprehensively and with unpremeditated art, as Upstairs. It was Upstairs that the thunder gathered, that Mrs. Stannace kept her accounts and her state, that Mrs. Limbert had her babies and her headaches, that the bells for ever jangled at the maids, that everything imperative in short took place—everything that he had somehow, pen in hand, to meet, to deal with and dispose of, in the little room on the garden-level. I don't think he liked to go Upstairs, but no special burst of confidence was needed to make me feel that a terrible deal of service went. It was the habit of the ladies of the Stannace family to be extremely waited on, and I've never been in a house where three maids and a nursery-governess gave such an impression of a retinue. "Oh they're so deucedly, so hereditarily fine !"—I remember how that dropped from him in some worried hour. Well, it was because Maud was so universally fine that we had both been in love with her. It was not an air, moreover, for the plaintive note : no private inconvenience could long outweigh for him the great happiness of these years—the happiness that sat with us when we talked and that made it always amusing to talk, the sense of his being on the heels of success, coming closer and closer, touching it at last, knowing that he should touch it again and hold it fast and hold it high. Of course when we said success we didn't mean exactly what Mrs. Highmore for instance meant. He used to quote at me as a definition something from a nameless page of my own, some stray dictum to the effect that the man of his craft had achieved it when of a beautiful subject his expression was complete. Well, wasn't Limbert's in all conscience complete ?

IT WAS bang upon this completeness all the same that the turn arrived, the turn I can't say of his fortune—for what was that ?—but of his confidence, of his spirits and, what was more to the point, of his system. The whole occasion on which the first symptom flared out is before me as I write. I had met them both at dinner: they were diners who had reached the penultimate stage—the stage which in theory is a rigid selection and in practice a wan submission. It was late in the season and stronger spirits than theirs were broken; the night was close and the air of the banquet such as to restrict conversation to the refusal of dishes and consumption to the sniffing of a flower. It struck me all the more that Mrs. Limbert was flying her flag. As vivid as a page of her husband's prose, she had one of those flickers of freshness that are the miracle of her sex and one of those expensive dresses that are the miracle of ours. She had also a neat brougham in which she had offered to rescue an old lady from the possibilities of a queer cab-horse; so that when she had rolled away with her charge I proposed a walk home with her husband, whom I had overtaken on the door-step. Before I had gone far with him he told me he had news for me—he had accepted, of all people and of all things, an "editorial position." It had come to pass that very day, from one hour to another, without time for appeals or ponderations: Mr. Bousefield, the proprietor of a "high-class monthly," making, as they said, a sudden change, had dropped on him heavily out of the blue. It was all right—there was a salary and an idea, and both of them, as such things went, rather high. We took our way slowly through the vacant streets, and in the explanations and revelations that as we lingered under lamp-posts I drew from him I found with an apprehension that I tried to gulp down a foretaste of the bitter end. He told me more than he had ever told me yet. He couldn't balance accounts—that was the trouble: his expenses were too rising a tide. It was imperative he should at last make money, and now he must work only for that. The need this last year had gathered the force of a crusher: it had rolled over him and laid him on his back. He had his scheme; this time he knew what he was about; on some good occasion, with leisure to talk it over, he would tell me the blest whole. His editorship would help him, and for the rest he must help himself. If he couldn't they would have to do something fundamental —change their life altogether, give up London, move into the country, take a house at thirty pounds a year, send their children to the Board-school. I saw he was excited, and he admitted he was: he had waked out of a trance. He had been on the wrong tack; he had piled mistake on mistake. It was the vision of his remedy that now excited him: ineffably, grotesquely simple, it had yet come to him only within a day or two. No, he wouldn't tell me what it was; he would give me the night to guess, and if I shouldn't guess it would be because I was as big an ass as himself. However, a lone man might be an ass: he had room in his life for his ears. Ray had a burden that demanded a back: the back must therefore now be properly instituted. As to the editor-ship, it was simply heaven-sent, being not at all another case of *The Blackport Beacon* but a case of the very opposite. The proprietor, the great Mr. Bousefield, had approached him precisely because his name, which was to be on the cover, *didn't* represent the chatty. The whole thing was to be—oh on fiddling little lines of course—a protest against the chatty. Bousefield wanted him to be himself; it was for himself Bousefield had picked him out. Wasn't it beautiful and brave of Bouse-field? He wanted literature, he saw the great reaction coming, the way the cat was going to jump. "Where will you get literature?" I woefully asked; to which he replied with a laugh that what he had to get was not literature but only what Bousefield would take for it.

In that single phrase I without more ado discovered his famous remedy. What was before him for the future was not to do his work but to do what somebody else would take for it. I had the question out with him on the next opportunity, and of all the lively discussions into which we had been destined to drift it lingers in my mind as the liveliest. This was not, I hasten to add, because I disputed his con-clusions: it was an effect of the very force with which, when I had fathomed his wretched premises, I took them to my soul. It was very well to talk with Jane Highmore about his standing alone: the eminent relief of this position had brought him to the verge of ruin. Several persons admired his books—nothing was less contestable; but they appeared to have a mortal objection to acquiring them by subscription or by purchase; they begged or borrowed or stole, they delegated one of the party perhaps to commit the volumes to memory and repeat them, like the bards of old, to listening multitudes. Some ingenious theory was required at any rate to account for the inexorable limits of his circulation. It wasn't a thing for five people to live on; therefore either the objects circulated must change their nature or the organisms to be nourished must. The former change was perhaps the easier to consider first. Limbert considered it with sovereign ingenuity from that time on, and the ingenuity, greater even than any I had yet had occasion to admire in him, made the whole next stage of his career rich in curiosity and suspense.

"I've been butting my skull against a wall," he had said in those hours of confidence; "and, to be as sublime a blockhead, if you'll allow me the word, you, my dear fellow, have kept sounding the charge. We've sat prating here of 'success,' heaven help us, like chanting monks in a cloister, hugging the sweet delusion that it lies somewhere in the work itself, in the expression, as you said, of one's subject or the intensification, as somebody else somewhere says, of one's note. One has been going on in short as if the only thing to do were to accept the law of one's talent, and thinking that if certain consequences didn't follow it was only because one wasn't logical enough. My disaster has served me right—I mean for using that ignoble word at all. It's a mere distributor's, a mere hawker's word. What *is* 'success' anyhow? When a book's right it's right—shame to it surely if it isn't. When it sells it sells—it brings money like potatoes or beer. If there's dishonour one way and inconvenience the other, it certainly is comfortable, but it as certainly isn't glorious, to have escaped them. People of delicacy don't brag either about their probity or about their luck. Success be hanged!—I want to sell. It's a question of life and death. I must study the way. I've studied too much the other way—I know the other way now, every inch of it. I must cultivate the market—it's a science like another. I must go in for an infernal cunning. It will be very amusing, I foresee that; I shall lead a dashing life and drive a roaring trade. I haven't been obvious—I must *be* obvious. I haven't been popular—I must *be* popular. It's another art—or perhaps it isn't an art at all. It's something else; one must find out *what* it is. Is it something awfully queer?—you blush!—something barely decent? All the greater incentive to curiosity! Curiosity's an immense motive, we shall have tremendous sport. 'They all do it'—doesn't somebody sing at a music hall?—it's only a question of how. Of course I've everything to unlearn; but what's life, as Jane Highmore says, but a lesson? I must get all I can, all she can give me, from Jane. She can't explain herself much; she's all intuition; her processes are obscure; it's the spirit that swoops down and catches her up. But I must study her reverently in her works. Yes, you've defied me before, but now my loins are girded: I declare I'll *read* one of them—I really will; I'll put it through if I perish!"

I won't pretend he made all these remarks at once; but there wasn't one that he didn't make at one time or another, for suggestion and occasion were plentiful enough, his life being now given up altogether to his new necessity. It wasn't a question of his having or not having, as they say, my intellectual sympathy: the brute force of the pressure left no room for judgement; it made all emotion a mere recourse to the spyglass. I watched him as I should have watched a long race or a long chase, irresistibly siding with him, yet much occupied with the calculation of odds. I confess indeed that my heart, for the endless stretch he covered so fast, was often in my throat. I saw him peg away over the sun-dappled plain, I saw him double and wind and gain and lose; and all the while I secretly entertained a conviction. I wanted him to feed his many mouths, but at the bottom of all things was my sense that if he should succeed in doing so in this particular way I should think less well of him. Now I had an absolute terror of that. Meanwhile so far as I could I backed him up, I helped him: all the more that I had warned him immensely at first, smiled with a compassion it was very good of him not to have found exasperating over the complacency of his assumption that a man could escape from himself. Ray Limbert at all events would certainly never escape; but one could make believe for him, make believe very hard—an undertaking in which at first Mr. Bousefield was visibly a blessing. Ralph was delightful on the business of this being at last my chance too—my chance, so miraculously vouchsafed, to appear with a certain luxuriance. He didn't care how often he printed me, for wasn't it exactly in my direction Mr. Bousefield held the cat was going to jump? This was the least he could do for me. I might write on anything I liked—on anything at least but Mr. Limbert's second manner. He didn't wish attention strikingly called to his second manner; it was to operate insidiously; people were to be left to believe they had discovered it long ago. "Ralph Limbert? Why, when did we ever live without him?"—that's what he wanted them to say. Besides, they hated manners—let sleeping dogs lie. His understanding with Mr. Bousefield—on which he had had not at all to insist; it was the excellent man who insisted—was that he should run one of his beautiful stories in the magazine. As to the beauty of his story, however, Limbert was going to be less admirably straight than as to the beauty of everything else. That was another

132

reason why I mustn't write about his new line: Mr. Bousefield was not to be too definitely warned that such a periodical was exposed to prostitution. By the time he should find it out for himself the public— *le gros public*—would have bitten, and then perhaps he would be conciliated and forgive. Everything else would be literary in short, and above all *I* would be; only Ralph Limbert wouldn't—he'd chuck up the whole thing sooner. He'd be vulgar, he'd be vile, he'd be abject: he'd be elaborately what he hadn't been before.

I duly noticed that he had more trouble in making "everything else" literary than he had at first allowed for; but this was largely counter-acted by the ease with which he was able to obtain that his mark shouldn't be overshot. He had taken well to heart the old lesson of the *Beacon*; he remembered that he was after all there to keep his contri-butors down much rather than to keep them up. I thought at times that he kept them down a trifle too far, but he assured me that I needn't be nervous: he had his limit—his limit was inexorable. He would reserve pure vulgarity for his serial, over which he was sweating blood and water; elsewhere it should be qualified by the prime qualifications, the mediocrity that attaches, that endears. Bousefield, he allowed, was proud, was difficult, nothing was really good enough for him but the middling good: he himself, however, was prepared for adverse com-ment, resolute for his noble course. Hadn't Limbert, moreover, in the event of a charge of laxity from headquarters the great strength of being able to point to my contributions ? Therefore I must let myself go, I must abound in my peculiar sense, I must be a resource in case of accidents. Limbert's vision of accidents hovered mainly over the sudden awakening of Mr. Bousefield to the stuff that in the department of fiction his editor was palming off. He would then have to confess in all humility that this was not what the old boy wanted, but I should be all the more there as a salutary specimen. I would cross the scent with something showily impossible, splendidly unpopular—I must be sure to have something on hand. I always had plenty on hand—poor Lim-bert needn't have worried: the magazine was forearmed each month by my care with a retort to any possible accusation of trifling with Mr. Bousefield's standard. He had admitted to Limbert, after much consideration indeed, that he was prepared to be perfectly human; but he had added that he was not prepared for an abuse of this ad-mission. The thing in the world I think I least felt myself was an abuse, even though—as I had never mentioned to my friendly editor—I too had my project for a bigger reverberation. I daresay I trusted mine more than I trusted Limbert's; at all events the golden mean in which, for the special case, he saw his salvation as an editor was something I should be most sure of were I to exhibit it myself. I exhibited it month after month in the form of a monstrous levity, only praying heaven that my editor might now not tell me, as he had so often told me, that my result was awfully good. I knew what that would signify—it would signify, sketchily speaking, disaster. What he did tell me heartily was that it was just what his game required; his new line had brought with it an earnest assumption—earnest save when we privately laughed about it—of the locutions proper to real bold enterprise. If I tried to keep him in the dark even as he kept Mr. Bousefield there was nothing to show that I wasn't tolerably successful: each case therefore presented a promising analogy for the other. He never noticed my descent, and it was accordingly possible Mr. Bousefield would never notice his. But would nobody notice it at all?—that was a question that added a prospective zest to one's possession of a critical sense. So much depended upon it that I was rather relieved than otherwise not to know the answer too soon. I waited in fact a year—the trial-year for which Limbert had cannily engaged with Mr. Bousefield; the year as to which, through the same sharpened shrewdness, it had been conveyed in the agreement between them that Mr. Bousefield wasn't to intermeddle. It had been Limbert's general prayer that we would during this period let him quite alone. His terror of my direct rays was a droll dreadful force that always operated: he explained it by the fact that I understood him too well, expressed too much of his intention, saved him too little from himself. The less he was saved the more he didn't sell: I positively interpreted, and that was simply fatal.

I held my breath accordingly; I did more—I closed my eyes, I guarded my treacherous ears. He induced several of us to do that—of such devotions we were capable—so that, not even glancing at the thing from month to month and having nothing but his shamed anxious silence to go by, I participated only vaguely in the little hum that surrounded his act of sacrifice. It was blown about the town that the public would be surprised; it was hinted, it was printed, that he was making a desperate bid. His new work was spoken of as "more calculated for general acceptance." These tidings produced in some quarters much reprobation, and nowhere more, I think, than on the part of certain persons who had never read a word of him, or assuredly had never spent a shilling on him, and who hung for hours over the other attractions of the newspaper that announced his abasement. So much asperity cheered me a little—seemed to signify that he might really be doing something. On the other hand, I had a distinct alarm; some one sent me for some alien reason an American journal—containing frankly more than that source of affliction—in which was quoted a passage from our friend's last instalment. The passage—I couldn't for my life help reading it—was simply superb. Ah he *would* have to move to the country if that was the worst he could do ! It gave me a pang to see how little after all he had improved since the days of his competition with Pat Moyle. There was nothing in the passage quoted in the American paper that Pat would for a moment have owned.

During the last weeks, as the opportunity of reading the complete thing drew near, one's suspense was barely endurable, and I shall never forget the July evening on which I put it to rout. Coming home to dinner I found the two volumes on my table, and I sat up with them half the night, dazed, bewildered, rubbing my eyes, wondering at the monstrous joke. *Was* it a monstrous joke, his second manner—was *this* the new line, the desperate bid, the scheme for more general acceptance and the remedy for material failure ? Had he made a fool of all his following, or had he most injuriously made a still bigger fool of himself ? Obvious ?—where the deuce was it obvious ? Popular ?— how on earth could it be popular ? The thing was charming with all his charm and powerful with all his power : it was an unscrupulous, an unsparing, a shameless merciless masterpiece. It was, no doubt, like the old letters to the *Beacon*, the worst he could do; but the perversity of the effort, even though heroic, had been frustrated by the purity of the gift. Under what illusion had he laboured, with what wavering treacherous compass had he steered ? His honour was inviolable, his measurements were all wrong. I was thrilled with the whole impression and with all that came crowding in its train. It was too grand a collapse —it was too hideous a triumph; I exulted almost with tears—I lamented with a strange delight. Indeed as the short night waned and, threshing about in my emotion, I fidgeted to my high-perched window for a glimpse of the summer dawn, I became at last aware that I was staring at it out of eyes that had compassionately and admiringly filled. The eastern sky, over the London house tops, had a wonderful tragic crimson. That was the colour of his magnificent mistake.

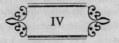

IV

IF SOMETHING less had depended on my impression I daresay I should have communicated it as soon as I had swallowed my breakfast; but the case was so embarrassing that I spent the first half of the day in reconsidering it, dipping into the book again, almost feverishly turning its leaves and trying to extract from them, for my friend's benefit, some symptom of reassurance, some ground for felicitation. This rash challenge had consequences merely dreadful; the wretched volumes, imperturbable and impeccable, with their shyer secrets and their second line of defence, were like a beautiful woman more denuded or a great symphony on a new hearing. There was something quite sinister in the way they stood up to me. I couldn't, however, be dumb —that was to give the wrong tinge to my disappointment; so that later in the afternoon, taking my courage in both hands, I approached with a vain tortuosity poor Limbert's door. A smart victoria waited before it, in which, from the bottom of the street, I saw that a lady who had apparently just issued from the house was settling herself. I recognised Jane Highmore and instantly paused till she should drive down to me. She soon met me halfway and directly she saw me stopped her carriage in agitation. This was a relief—it postponed a moment the sight of that pale fine face of our friend's fronting me for the right verdict. I gathered from the flushed eagerness with which Mrs. Highmore asked me if I had heard the news that a verdict of some sort had already been rendered.

"What news ?—about the book ? "

"About that horrid magazine. They're shockingly upset. He has lost his position—he has had a fearful flare-up with Mr. Bousefield."

I stood there blank, but not unaware in my blankness of how history repeats itself. There came to me across the years Maud's announcement of their ejection from the *Beacon*, and dimly, confusedly, the same explanation was in the air. This time, however, I had been on my guard; I had had my suspicion. "He has made it too flippant ?" I found breath after an instant to inquire.

Mrs. Highmore's vacuity exceeded my own. "Too 'flippant' ? He had made it too oracular; Mr. Bousefield says he has killed it." Then perceiving my stupefaction: "Don't you know what has happened?" she pursued; "isn't it because in his trouble, poor love, he has sent for you that you've come? You've heard nothing at all? Then you had better know before you see them. Get in here with me—I'll take you a turn and tell you." We were close to the Park, the Regent's, and when with extreme alacrity I had placed myself beside her and the carriage had begun to enter it she went on: "It was what I feared, you know. It reeked with culture. He keyed it up too high."

I felt myself sinking in the general collapse. "What are you talking about?"

"Why, about that beastly magazine. They're all on the streets. I shall have to take mamma."

I pulled myself together. "What on earth, then, did Bousefield want? He said he wanted intellectual power."

"Yes, but Ray overdid it."

"Why, Bousefield said it was a thing he *couldn't* overdo."

"Well, Ray managed: he took Mr. Bousefield too literally. It appears the thing has been doing dreadfully, but the proprietor couldn't say anything, because he had covenanted to leave the editor quite free. He describes himself as having stood there in a fever and seen his ship go down. A day or two ago the year was up, so he could at last break out. Maud says he did break out quite fearfully—he came to the house and let poor Ray have it. Ray gave it him back—he reminded him of his own idea of the way the cat was going to jump."

I gasped with dismay. "Has Bousefield abandoned that idea? *Isn't* the cat going to jump?"

Mrs. Highmore hesitated. "It appears she doesn't seem in a hurry. Ray at any rate has jumped too far ahead of her. He should have temporised a little, Mr. Bousefield says; but I'm beginning to think, you know," said my companion, "that Ray *can't* temporise." Fresh from my emotion of the previous twenty-four hours I was scarcely in a position to disagree with her. "He published too much pure thought."

"Pure thought?" I cried. "Why, it struck me so often—certainly in a due proportion of cases—as pure drivel!"

"Oh you're more keyed up than he! Mr. Bousefield says that of course he wanted things that were suggestive and clever, things that he could point to with pride. But he contends that Ray didn't allow for human weakness. He gave everything in too stiff doses."

Sensibly, I fear, to my neighbour, I winced at her words—I felt a prick that made me meditate. Then I said: "Is that, by chance, the way he gave *me*?" Mrs. Highmore remained silent so long that I had somehow the sense of a fresh pang; and after a minute, turning in my seat, I laid my hand on her arm, fixed my eyes on her face, and pursued pressingly: "Do you suppose it to be to my 'Occasional Remarks' that Mr. Bousefield refers?"

At last she met my look. "Can you bear to hear it?"

"I think I can bear anything now."

"Well then, it was really what I wanted to give you an inkling of. It's largely over you that they've quarrelled. Mr. Bousefield wants him to chuck you."

I grabbed her arm again. "And our friend *won't*?"

"He seems to cling to you. Mr. Bousefield says no magazine can afford you."

I gave a laugh that agitated the very coachman. "Why, my dear lady, has he any idea of my price?"

"It isn't your price—he says you're dear at any price: you do so much to sink the ship. Your 'Remarks' are called 'Occasional,' but nothing could be more deadly regular; you're there month after month and you're never anywhere else. And you supply no public want."

"I supply the most delicious irony."

"So Ray appears to have declared. Mr. Bousefield says that's not in the least a public want. No one can make out what you're talking about and no one would care if he could. I'm only quoting *him*, mind."

"Quote, quote—if Ray holds out. I think I must leave you now, please: I must rush back to express to him what I feel."

"I'll drive you to his door. That isn't all," said Mrs. Highmore. And on the way, when the carriage had turned, she communicated the rest. "Mr. Bousefield really arrived with an ultimatum: it had the form of something or other by Minnie Meadows."

"Minnie Meadows?" I was stupefied.

"The new lady-humourist every one seems talking about. It's the first of a series of screaming sketches for which poor Ray was to find a place."

"Is *that* Mr. Bousefield's idea of literature?"

"No, but he says it's the public's, and you've got to take *some* account of the public. *Aux grands maux les grands remèdes.* They had a tremendous lot of ground to make up, and no one would make it up like Minnie. She would be the best concession they could make to human weakness; she would strike at least this note of showing that it wasn't going to be quite all—well, all *you*. Now Ray draws the line at

Minnie; he won't stoop to Minnie; he declines to touch, to look at Minnie. When Mr. Bousefield—rather imperiously, I believe—made Minnie a *sine qua non* of his retention of his post he said something rather violent, told him to go to some unmentionable place and take Minnie with him. That of course put the fat on the fire. They had really a considerable scene."

"So had he with the *Beacon* man," I musingly replied. "Poor dear, he seems born for considerable scenes ! It's on Minnie, then, they've really split ?" Mrs. Highmore exhaled her despair in a sound which I took for an assent, and when we had rolled a little further I rather inconsequently and to her visible surprise broke out of my reverie. "It will never do in the world—he *must* stoop to Minnie !"

"It's too late—and what I've told you still isn't all. Mr. Bousefield raises another objection."

"What other, pray ?"

"Can't you guess ?"

I wondered. "No more of Ray's fiction ?"

"Not a line. That's something else no magazine can stand. Now that his novel has run its course Mr. Bousefield's distinctly disappointed."

I fairly bounded in my place. "Then it may do ?"

Mrs. Highmore looked bewildered. "Why so, if he finds it too dull ?"

"Dull ? Ralph Limbert ? He's as fine as the spray of a lawn-irrigator."

"It comes to the same thing, when your lawn's as coarse as a turnip field. Mr. Bousefield had counted on something that *would* do, something that would have a wider acceptance. Ray says he wants gutter-pipes and slop-buckets." I collapsed again; my flicker of elation dropped to a throb of quieter comfort; and after a moment's silence I asked my neighbour if she had herself read the work our friend had just put forth. "No," she returned, "I gave him my word at the beginning, on his urgent request, that I wouldn't."

"Not even as a book ?"

"He begged me never to look at it at all. He said he was trying a low experiment. Of course I knew what he meant and I entreated him to let me just for curiosity take a peep. But he was firm, he declared he couldn't bear the thought that a woman like me should see him in the depths."

"He's only, thank God, in the depths of distress," I answered. "His experiment's nothing worse than a failure."

"Then Bousefield *is* right—his circulation won't budge ?"

"It won't move one, as they say in Fleet Street. The book has extraordinary beauty."

"Poor duck—after trying so hard !" Jane Highmore sighed with real tenderness. "What *will*, then, become of them ?"

I was silent an instant. "You must take your mother."

She was silent too. "I must speak of it to Cecil !" she presently said. Cecil is Mr. Highmore, who then entertained, I knew, strong views on the inadjustability of circumstances in general to the idiosyncrasies of Mrs. Stannace. He held it supremely happy that in an important relation she should have met her match. Her match was Ray Limbert—not much of a writer but a practical man. "The dear things still think, you know," my companion continued, "that the book will be the beginning of their fortune. Their illusion, if you're right, will be rudely dispelled."

"That's what makes me dread to face them. I've just spent with his volumes an unforgettable night. His illusion has lasted because so many of us have been pledged till this moment to turn our faces the other way. We haven't known the truth and have therefore had nothing to say. Now that we do know it indeed we have practically quite as little. I hang back from the threshold. How can I follow up with a burst of enthusiasm such a catastrophe as Mr. Bousefield's visit ?"

As I turned uneasily about my neighbour more comfortably snuggled. "Well, I'm glad, then, I haven't read him and have nothing unpleasant to say !" We had come back to Limbert's door, and I made the coachman stop short of it. "But he'll try again, with that determination of his : he'll build his hopes on the next time."

"On what else has he built them from the very first ? It's never the present for him that bears the fruit; that's always postponed and for somebody else : there has always to be another try. I admit that his idea of a 'new line' has made him try harder than ever. It makes no difference," I brooded, still timorously lingering; "his achievement of his necessity, his hope of a market, will continue to attach itself to the future. But the next time will disappoint him as each last time has done —and then the next and the next and the next !"

I found myself seeing it all with a clearness almost inspired : it evidently cast a chill on Mrs. Highmore. "Then what on earth will become of him ?" she plaintively repeated.

"I don't think I particularly care what may become of *him*," I returned with a conscious reckless increase of my exaltation; "I feel it almost enough to be concerned with what may become of one's

140

enjoyment of him. I don't know in short what will become of his circulation; I'm only quite at my ease as to what will become of his work. It will simply keep all its quality. He'll try again for the common with what he'll believe to be a still more infernal cunning, and again the common will fatally elude him, for his infernal cunning will have been only his genius in an ineffectual disguise." We sat drawn up by the pavement, facing poor Limbert's future as I saw it. It relieved me in a manner to know the worst, and I prophesied with an assurance which as I look back upon it strikes me as rather remarkable. "*Que voulez-vous?*" I went on; "you can't make a sow's ear of a silk purse ! It's grievous indeed if you like—there are people who can't be vulgar for trying. *He* can't—it wouldn't come off, I promise you, even once. It takes more than trying—it comes by grace. It happens not to be given to Limbert to fall. He belongs to the heights—he breathes there, he lives there, and it's accordingly to the heights I must ascend," I said as I took leave of my conductress, "to carry him this wretched news from where *we* move !"

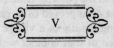

V

A few months were sufficient to show how right I had been about his circulation. It didn't move one, as I had said; it stopped short in the same place, fell off in a sheer descent, like some precipice gaped up at by tourists. The public, in other words, drew the line for him as sharply as he had drawn it for Minnie Meadows. Minnie has skipped with a flouncing caper over his line, however; whereas the mark traced by a lustier cudgel has been a barrier insurmountable to Limbert. Those next times I had spoken of to Jane Highmore, I see them simplified by retrocession. Again and again he made his desperate bid—again and again he tried to. His rupture with Mr. Bousefield caused him in professional circles, I fear, to be thought impracticable, and I'm perfectly aware, to speak candidly, that no sordid advantage ever accrued to him from such public patronage of my performances as he had occasionally been in a position to offer. I reflect for my comfort that any injury I may have done him by untimely application of a faculty of analysis which could point to no converts gained by honourable exercise was at least equalled by the injury he did himself. More than once, as I have hinted, I held my tongue at his request, but my frequent plea that such favours weren't politic never found him, when in other connexions there was an opportunity to give me a lift, anything but indifferent to the danger of the association. He let them have me, in a word, whenever he could; sometimes in periodicals in which he had credit, sometimes only at dinner. He talked about me when he couldn't get me in, but it was always part of the bargain that I shouldn't make him a topic. "How can I successfully serve you if you do?" he used to ask: he was more afraid than I thought he ought to have been of the charge of tit for tat. I didn't care, for I never could distinguish tat from tit; but, as I've intimated, I dropped into silence really more than anything else because there was a certain fascinated observation of his course which was quite testimony enough and to which in this huddled conclusion of it he practically reduced me.

I see it all foreshortened, his wonderful remainder—see it from the end backward, with the direction widening toward me as if on a level with the eye. The migration to the country promised him at first great things—smaller expenses, larger leisure, conditions eminently conducive on each occasion to the possible triumph of the next time. Mrs. Stannace, who altogether disapproved of it, gave as one of her reasons that her son-in-law, living mainly in a village on the edge of a goose-green, would be deprived of that contact with the great world which was indispensable to the painter of manners. She had the showiest arguments for keeping him in touch, as she called it, with good society; wishing to know with some force where, from the moment he ceased to represent it from observation, the novelist could be said to be. In London fortunately a clever man was just a clever man; there were charming houses in which a person of Ray's undoubted ability, even though without the knack of making the best use of it, could always be sure of a quiet corner for watching decorously the social kaleidoscope. But the kaleidoscope of the goose-green, what in the world was that, and what such delusive thrift as drives about the land (with a fearful account for flys from the inn) to leave cards on the country magnates? This solicitude for Limbert's subject-matter was the specious colour with which, deeply determined not to affront mere tolerance in a cottage, Mrs. Stannace overlaid her indisposition to place herself under the heel of Cecil Highmore. She knew that he ruled Upstairs as well as down, and she clung to the fable of the association of interests in the north of London. The Highmores had a better address, they lived now in Stanhope Gardens; but Cecil was fearfully artful—he wouldn't hear of an association of interests nor treat with his mother-in-law save as a visitor. She didn't like false positions; but on the other hand she didn't like the sacrifice of everything she was accustomed to. Her universe at all events was a universe of card-leavings and charming houses, and it was fortunate that she couldn't, Upstairs, catch the sound of the doom to which, in his little grey den, describing to me his diplomacy, Limbert consigned alike the country magnates and the opportunities of London. Despoiled of every guarantee she went to Stanhope Gardens like a mere maidservant, with restrictions on her very luggage, while during the year that followed this upheaval Limbert, strolling with me on the goose-green, to which I often ran down, played extravagantly over the theme that with what he was now going in for it was a positive comfort not to have the social kaleidoscope. With a cold-blooded trick in view, what had life or manners or the best society or flys from the inn to say to the question? It was as good a place as another to play his new game. He had found a quieter corner than any corner of the great world, and a damp old house at tenpence a year, which, beside leaving him all his margin to educate his children, would allow of the supreme luxury of his frankly presenting himself as a poor man. This was a convenience that *ces dames*, as he called them, had never yet fully permitted him.

It rankled in me at first to see his reward so meagre, his conquest so mean; but the simplification effected had a charm that I finally felt: it was a forcing-house for the three or four other fine miscarriages to which his scheme was evidently condemned. I limited him to three or four, having had my sharp impression, in spite of the perpetual broad joke of the thing, that a spring had really broken in him on the occasion of that deeply disconcerting sequel to the episode of his editorship. He never lost his sense of the grotesque want, in the difference made, of adequate relation to the effort that had been the intensest of his life. He had carried from that moment a charge of shot, and it slowly worked its way to a vital part. As he met his embarrassments each year with his punctual false remedy I wondered periodically where he found the energy to return to the attack. He did it every time with a rage more blanched, but it was clear to me that the tension must finally snap the cord. We got again and again the irrepressible work of art, but what did *he* get, poor man, who wanted something so different? There were likewise odder questions than this in the matter, phenomena more curious and mysteries more puzzling, which often for sympathy, if not for illumination, I intimately discussed with Mrs. Limbert. She had her burdens, dear lady: after the removal from London and a considerable interval she twice again became a mother. Mrs. Stannace too, in a more restricted sense, exhibited afresh, in relation to the home she had abandoned, the same exemplary character. In her poverty of guarantees at Stanhope Gardens there had been least of all, it appeared, a proviso that she shouldn't resentfully revert again from Goneril to Regan. She came down to the goose-green like Lear himself, with fewer knights, or at least baronets, and the joint household was at last patched up. It fell to pieces and was put together on various occasions before Ray Limbert died. He was ridden to the end by the superstition that he had broken up Mrs. Stannace's original home on pretences that had proved hollow, and that if he hadn't given Maud what she might have had he could at least give her back her mother. I was always sure that a sense of the compensations he owed was half the motive of the dogged pride with which he tried to wake up the libraries. I believed Mrs. Stannace still had money, though she pretended that, called upon at every turn to retrieve deficits, she had long since poured it into the general fund. This conviction haunted me; I suspected her of secret hoards, and I said to myself that she couldn't be so infamous as not some day on her deathbed to leave everything to her less opulent daughter. My compassion for the Limberts led me to hover perhaps indiscreetly round that closing scene, to dream of some happy time when such an accession of means would make up a little for their present penury.

This, however, was crude comfort, as in the first place I had nothing definite to go by and in the second I held it for more and more indicated that Ray wouldn't outlive her. I never ventured to sound him as to what in this particular he hoped or feared, for after the crisis marked by his leaving London I had new scruples about suffering him to be reminded of where he fell short. The poor man was in truth humiliated, and there were things as to which that kept us both silent. In proportion as he tried more fiercely for the market the old plaintive arithmetic, fertile in jokes, dropped from our conversation. We joked immensely still about the process, but our treatment of the results became sparing and superficial. He talked as much as ever, with monstrous arts and borrowed hints, of the traps he kept setting, but we all agreed to take merely for granted that the animal was caught. This propriety had really dawned upon me the day that, after Mr. Bousefield's visit, Mrs. Highmore put me down at his door. Mr. Bousefield at that juncture had been served up to me anew, but after we had disposed of him we came to the book, which I was obliged to confess I had already rushed through. It was from this moment—the moment at which my terrible impression of it had blinked out at his anxious query—that the image of his scared face was to abide with me. I couldn't attentuate then—the cat was out of the bag; but later, each of the next times, I did, I acknowledge, attentuate. We all did religiously, so far as was possible; we cast ingenious ambiguities over the strong places, the beauties that betrayed him most, and found ourselves in the queer position of admirers banded to mislead a confiding artist. If we stifled our cheers however, if we dissimulated our joy, our fond hypocrisy accomplished little, for Limbert's finger was on a pulse that told a plainer story. It was a satisfaction to have secured a greater freedom with his wife, who at last, much to her honour, entered into the conspiracy and whose sense of responsibility was flattered by the frequency of our united appeal to her for some answer to the marvellous riddle. We had all turned it over till we were tired of it, threshing out the question of why the note he strained every chord to pitch for common ears should invariably insist on addressing itself to the angels. Being, as it were, ourselves the angels, we had only a limited quarrel in each case with the event; but its inconsequent character, given the forces set in motion, was peculiarly baffling. It was like an interminable sum that wouldn't come straight; nobody had the time to handle so many figures. Limbert gathered, to make his pudding, dry bones and dead husks; how, then, was one to formulate the law that made the dish prove a feast? What was the cerebral treachery that defied his own vigilance? There was some obscure interference of taste, some obsession of the exquisite. All one could say was that genius was a fatal disturber or that the unhappy man had no effectual *flair*. When he went abroad to gather garlic he came home with heliotrope.

I hasten to add that if Mrs. Limbert was not directly illuminating she was yet rich in anecdote and example, having found a refuge from mystification exactly where the rest of us had found it, in a more devoted embrace and the sense of a finer glory. Her disappointments and eventually her privations had been many, her discipline severe; but she had ended by accepting the long grind of life and was now quite willing to take her turn at the mill. She was essentially one of us—she always understood. Touching and admirable at the last, when through the unmistakable change in Limbert's health her troubles were thickest, was the spectacle of the particular pride that she wouldn't have exchanged for prosperity. She had said to me once—only once, in a gloomy hour of London days when things were not going at all—that one really had to think him a very great man, since if one didn't one would be rather ashamed of him. She had distinctly felt it at first—and in a very tender place—that almost every one passed him on the road; but I believe that in these final years she would almost have been ashamed of him if he had suddenly gone into editions. It's certain indeed that her complacency was not subjected to that shock. She would have liked the money immensely, but she would have missed something she had taught herself to regard as rather rare. There's another remark I remember her making, a remark to the effect that of course if she could have chosen she would have liked him to be Shakespeare or Scott, but that failing this she was very glad he wasn't— well, she named the two gentlemen, but I won't. I daresay she sometimes laughed out to escape an alternative. She contributed passionately to the capture of the second manner, foraging for him further afield than he could conveniently go, gleaning in the barest stubble, picking up shreds to build the nest and in particular, in the study of the great secret of how, as we always said, they all did it, laying waste of the circulating libraries. If Limbert had a weakness he rather broke down in his reading. It was fortunately not till after the appearance of "The Hidden Heart" that he broke down in everything else. He had had rheumatic fever in the spring, when the book was but half-finished, and this ordeal had in addition to interrupting his work enfeebled his powers of resistance and greatly reduced his vitality. He recovered from the fever and was able to take up the book again, but the organ of life was pronounced ominously weak and it was enjoined upon him with some sharpness that he should lend himself to no worries. It might have struck me as on the cards that his worries would now be surmountable, for when he began to mend he expressed to me a conviction almost contagious that he had never yet made so adroit a bid as in the idea of "The Hidden Heart." It is grimly droll to reflect that this superb little composition, the shortest of his novels but perhaps the loveliest, was planned from the first as an "adventure-story" on approved lines. It was the way they all did the adventure-story that he had tried dauntlessly to emulate. I wonder how many readers ever divined to which of their book-shelves "The Hidden Heart" was so exclusively addressed. High medical advice early in the summer had been quite viciously clear as to the inconvenience that might ensue to him should he neglect to spend the winter in Egypt. He was not a man to neglect anything;

out Egypt seemed to us all then as unattainable as a second edition. He finished "The Hidden Heart" with the energy of apprehension and desire, for if the book should happen to do what "books of that class," as the publisher said, sometimes did, he might well have a fund to draw on. As soon as I read the fine deep thing I knew, as I had known in each case before, exactly how well it would do. Poor Limbert in this long business always figured to me an undiscourageable parent to whom only girls kept being born. A bouncing boy, a son and heir, was devoutly prayed for and almanacks and old wives consulted; but the spell was inveterate, incurable, and "The Hidden Heart" proved, so to speak, but another female child. When the winter arrived accordingly Egypt was out of the question. Jane Highmore, to my knowledge, wanted to lend him money, and there were even greater devotees who did their best to induce him to lean on them. There was so marked a "movement" among his friends that a very considerable sum would have been at his disposal; but his stiffness was invincible: it had its root, I think, in his sense, on his own side, of sacrifices already made. He had sacrificed honour and pride, and he had sacrificed them precisely to the question of money. He would evidently, should he be able to go on, have to continue to sacrifice them, but it must be all in the way to which he had now, as he considered, hardened himself. He had spent years in plotting for favour, and since on favour he must live it could only be as a bargain and a price.

He got through the early part of the season better than we feared, and I went down in great elation to spend Christmas on the goose-green. He told me late on Christmas Eve, after our simple domestic revels had sunk to rest and we sat together by the fire, how he had been visited the night before in wakeful hours by the finest fancy for a really good thing that he had ever felt descend in the darkness. "It's just the vision of a situation that contains, upon my honour, everything," he said, "and I wonder I've never thought of it before." He didn't describe it further, contrary to his common practice, and I only knew later, by Mrs. Limbert, that he had begun "Derogation" and was completely full of his subject. It was, however, a subject he wasn't to live to treat. The work went on for a couple of months in quiet mystery, without revelations even to his wife. He hadn't invited her to help him to get up his case—she hadn't taken the field with him as on his previous campaigns. We only knew he was at it again, but that less even than ever had been said about the impression to be made on the market. I saw him in February and thought him sufficiently at ease.

147

The great thing was that he was immensely interested and was pleased
with the omens. I got a strange stirring sense that he had not consulted
the usual ones and indeed that he had floated away into a grand indifference, into a reckless consciousness of art. The voice of the market
had suddenly grown faint and far: he had come back at the last, as
people so often do, to one of the moods, the sincerities of his prime.
Was he really, with a blurred sense of the urgent, doing something now
only for himself? We wondered and waited—we felt he was a little
confused. What had happened, I was afterwards satisfied, was that he
had quite forgotten whether he generally sold or not. He had merely
waked up one morning again in the country of the blue and had stayed
there with a good conscience and a great idea. He stayed till death
knocked at the gate, for the pen dropped from his hand only at the
moment when, from sudden failure of the heart, his eyes, as he sank
back in his chair, closed for ever. "Derogation" is a splendid fragment;
it evidently would have been one of his high successes. I am now
prepared to say it would have waked up the libraries.

THE FIGURE IN THE
CARPET

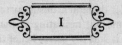

I

HAD done a few things and earned a few pence—I had perhaps even had time to begin to think I was finer than was perceived by the patronising; but when I take the little measure of my course (a fidgety habit, for it's none of the longest yet) I count my real start from the evening George Corvick, breathless and worried, came in to ask me a service. He had done more things than I, and earned more pence, though there were chances for cleverness I thought he sometimes missed. I could only, however, that evening declare to him that he never missed one for kindness. There was almost rapture in hearing it proposed to me to prepare for *The Middle*, the organ of our lucubrations, so called from the position in the week of its day of appearance, an article for which he had made himself responsible and of which, tied up with a stout string, he laid on my table the subject. I pounced upon my opportunity—that is on the first volume of it—and paid scant attention to my friend's explanation of his appeal. What explanation could be more to the point than my obvious fitness for the task? I had written on Hugh Vereker, but never a word in *The Middle*, where my dealings were mainly with the ladies and the minor poets. This was his new novel, an advance copy, and whatever much or little it should do for his reputation I was clear on the spot as to what it should do for mine. Moreover, if I always read him as soon as I could get hold of him I had a particular reason for wishing to read him now: I had accepted an invitation to Bridges for the following Sunday, and it had been mentioned in Lady Jane's note that Mr. Vereker was to be there. I was young enough for a flutter at meeting a man of his renown, and innocent enough to believe the occasion would demand the display of an acquaintance with his "last."

Corvick, who had promised a review of it, had not even had time to read it; he had gone to pieces in consequence of news requiring—as on precipitate reflexion he judged—that he should catch the night-mail to Paris. He had had a telegram from Gwendolen Erme in answer

to his letter offering to fly to her aid. I knew already about Gwendolen
Erme; I had never seen her, but I had my ideas, which were mainly to
the effect that Corvick would marry her if her mother would only die.
That lady seemed now in a fair way to oblige him; after some dreadful
mistake about a climate or a "cure" she had suddenly collapsed on the
return from abroad. Her daughter, unsupported and alarmed, desiring
to make a rush for home but hesitating at the risk, had accepted our
friend's assistance, and it was my secret belief that at sight of him Mrs.
Erme would pull round. His own belief was scarcely to be called
secret; it discernibly at any rate differed from mine. He had showed
me Gwendolen's photograph with the remark that she wasn't pretty
but was awfully interesting; she had published at the age of nineteen
a novel in three volumes, "Deep Down," about which, in *The Middle*,
he had been really splendid. He appreciated my present eagerness and
undertook that the periodical in question should do no less; then at
the last, with his hand on the door, he said to me: "Of course you'll
be all right, you know." Seeing I was a trifle vague he added: "I
mean you won't be silly."

"Silly—about Vereker! Why, what do I ever find him but awfully
clever?"

"Well, what's that but silly? What on earth does 'awfully clever'
mean? For God's sake try to get *at* him. Don't let him suffer by our
arrangement. Speak of him, you know, if you can, as *I* should have
spoken of him."

I wondered an instant. "You mean as far and away the biggest of
the lot—that sort of thing?"

Corvick almost groaned. "Oh you know, I don't put them back to
back that way; it's the infancy of art! But he gives me a pleasure so
rare; the sense of"—he mused a little—"something or other."

I wondered again. "The sense, pray, of what?"

"My dear man, that's just what I want *you* to say!"

Even before he had banged the door I had begun, book in hand, to
prepare myself to say it. I sat up with Vereker half the night; Corvick
couldn't have done more than that. He was awfully clever—I stuck
to that, but he wasn't a bit the biggest of the lot. I didn't allude to the
lot, however; I flattered myself that I emerged on this occasion from
the infancy of art. "It's all right," they declared vividly at the office;
and when the number appeared I felt there was a basis on which I
could meet the great man. It gave me confidence for a day or two—then
that confidence dropped. I had fancied him reading it with relish, but

if Corvick wasn't satisfied how could Vereker himself be? I reflected indeed that the heat of the admirer was sometimes grosser even than the appetite of the scribe. Corvick at all events wrote me from Paris a little ill-humouredly. Mrs. Erme was pulling round, and I hadn't at all said what Vereker gave him the sense of.

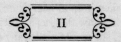

II

THE EFFECT of my visit to Bridges was to turn me out for more profundity. Hugh Vereker, as I saw him there, was of a contact so void of angles that I blushed for the poverty of imagination involved in my small precautions. If he was in spirits it wasn't because he had read my review; in fact on the Sunday morning I felt sure he hadn't read it, though *The Middle* had been out three days and bloomed. I assured myself, in the stiff garden of periodicals which gave one of the ormolu tables the air of a stand at a station. The impression he made on me personally was such that I wished him to read it, and I corrected to this end with a surreptitious hand what might be wanting in the careless conspicuity of the sheet. I'm afraid I even watched the result of my manœuvre, but up to luncheon I watched in vain.

When afterwards, in the course of our gregarious walk, I found myself for half an hour, not perhaps without another manœuvre, at the great man's side, the result of his affability was a still livelier desire that he shouldn't remain in ignorance of the peculiar justice I had done him. It wasn't that he seemed to thirst for justice; on the contrary I hadn't yet caught in his talk the faintest grunt of a grudge—a note for which my young experience had already given me an ear. Of late he had had more recognition, and it was pleasant, as we used to say in *The Middle*, to see how it drew him out. He wasn't of course popular, but I judged one of the sources of his good humour to be precisely that his success was independent of that. He had none the less become in a manner the fashion; the critics at least had put on a spurt and caught up with him. We had found out at last how clever he was, and he had had to make the best of the loss of his mystery. I was strongly tempted, as I walked beside him, to let him know how much of that unveiling was my act; and there was a moment when I probably should have done so had not one of the ladies of our party, snatching a place at his other elbow, just then appealed to him in a spirit comparatively selfish. It was very discouraging: I almost felt the liberty had been taken with myself.

I had had on my tongue's end, for my own part, a phrase or two about the right word at the right time; but later on I was glad not to have spoken, for when on our return we clustered at tea I perceived Lady Jane, who had not been out with us, brandishing *The Middle* with her longest arm. She had taken it up at her leisure; she was delighted with what she had found, and I saw that, as a mistake in a man may often be a felicity in a woman, she would practically do for me what I hadn't been able to do for myself. "Some sweet little truths that needed to be spoken," I heard her declare, thrusting the paper at rather a bewildered couple by the fireplace. She grabbed it away from them again on the reappearance of Hugh Vereker, who after our walk had been upstairs to change something. "I know you don't in general look at this kind of thing, but it's an occasion really for doing so. You *haven't* seen it? Then you must. The man has actually got *at* you, at what *I* always feel, you know." Lady Jane threw into her eyes a look evidently intended to give an idea of what she always felt; but she added that she couldn't have expressed it. The man in the paper expressed it in a striking manner. "Just see there, and there, where I've dashed it, how he brings it out." She had literally marked for him the brightest patches of my prose, and if I was a little amused Vereker himself may well have been. He showed how much he was when before us all Lady Jane wanted to read something aloud. I liked at any rate the way he defeated her purpose by jerking the paper affectionately out of her clutch. He'd take it upstairs with him and look at it on going to dress. He did this half an hour later—I saw it in his hand when he repaired to his room. That was the moment at which, thinking to give her pleasure, I mentioned to Lady Jane that I was the author of the review. I did give her pleasure, I judged, but perhaps not quite so much as I had expected. If the author was "only me" the thing didn't seem quite so remarkable. Hadn't I had the effect rather of diminishing the lustre of the article than of adding to my own? Her ladyship was subject to the most extraordinary drops. It didn't matter; the only effect I cared about was the one it would have on Vereker up there by his bedroom fire.

At dinner I watched for the signs of this impression, tried to fancy some happier light in his eyes; but to my disappointment Lady Jane gave me no chance to make sure. I had hoped she'd call triumphantly down the table, publicly demand if she hadn't been right. The party was large—there were people from outside as well, but I had never seen a table long enough to deprive Lady Jane of a triumph. I was just reflecting in truth that this interminable board would deprive *me* of one when the guest next me, dear woman—she was Miss Poyle, the vicar's sister, a robust unmodulated person—had the happy inspiration and the unusual courage to address herself across it to Vereker, who was opposite, but not directly, so that when he replied they were both leaning forward. She inquired, artless body, what he thought of Lady Jane's "panegyric," which she had read—not connecting it, however, with her right-hand neighbour; and while I strained my ear for his reply I heard him, to my stupefaction, call back gaily, his mouth full of bread: "Oh it's all right—the usual twaddle!"

I had caught Vereker's glance as he spoke, but Miss Poyle's surprise was a fortunate cover for my own. "You mean he doesn't do you justice?" said the excellent woman.

Vereker laughed out, and I was happy to be able to do the same. "It's a charming article," he tossed us.

Miss Poyle thrust her chin half across the cloth. "Oh you're so deep!" she drove home.

"As deep as the ocean! All I pretend is that the author doesn't see——" But a dish was at this point passed over his shoulder, and we had to wait while he helped himself.

"Doesn't see what?" my neighbour continued.

"Doesn't see anything."

"Dear me—how stupid!"

"Not a bit," Vereker laughed again. "Nobody does."

The lady on his further side appealed to him and Miss Poyle sank back to myself. "Nobody sees anything!" she cheerfully announced; to which I replied that I had often thought so too, but had somehow taken the thought for a proof on my own part of a tremendous eye. I didn't tell her the article was mine; and I observed that Lady Jane, occupied at the end of the table, had not caught Vereker's words.

I rather avoided him after dinner, for I confess he struck me as cruelly conceited, and the revelation was a pain. "The usual twaddle" —my acute little study! That one's admiration should have had a reserve or two could gall him to that point? I had thought him placid, and he was placid enough; such a surface was the hard polished glass that encased the bauble of his vanity. I was really ruffled, and the only comfort was that if nobody saw anything George Corvick was quite as much out of it as I. This comfort, however, was not sufficient, after the ladies had dispersed, to carry me in the proper manner—I mean in a spotted jacket and humming an air—into the smoking-room. I took my way in some dejection to bed; but in the passage I encountered Mr. Vereker, who had been up once more to change, coming out of his room. *He* was humming an air and had on a spotted jacket, and as soon as he saw me his gaiety gave a start.

"My dear young man," he exclaimed, "I'm so glad to lay hands on you! I'm afraid I most unwittingly wounded you by those words of mine at dinner to Miss Poyle. I learned but half an hour ago from Lady Jane that you're the author of the little notice in *The Middle*."

I protested that no bones were broken; but he moved with me to my own door, his hand on my shoulder, kindly feeling for a fracture; and on hearing that I had come up to bed he asked leave to cross my threshold and just tell me in three words what his qualification of my remarks had represented. It was plain he really feared I was hurt, and the sense of his solicitude suddenly made all the difference to me. My cheap review fluttered off into space, and the best things I had said in it became flat enough beside the brilliancy of his being there. I can see him there still, on my rug, in the firelight and his spotted jacket, his fine clear face all bright with the desire to be tender to my youth. I don't know what he had at first meant to say, but I think the sight of my relief touched him, excited him, brought up words to his lips from far within. It was so these words presently conveyed to me something that, as I afterwards knew, he had never uttered to any one. I've always done justice to the generous impulse that made him speak; it was simply compunction for a snub unconsciously administered to a man of letters in a position inferior to his own, a man of letters, moreover, in the very act of praising him. To make the thing right he talked to me exactly as an equal and on the ground of what we both loved best. The hour, the place, the unexpectedness deepened the impression: he couldn't have done anything more intensely effective.

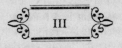

III

"I don't quite know how to explain it to you," he said, "but it was the very fact that your notice of my book had a spice of intelligence, it was just your exceptional sharpness, that produced the feeling—a very old story with me, I beg you to believe—under the momentary influence of which I used in speaking to that good lady the words you so naturally resent. I don't read the things in the newspapers unless they're thrust upon me as that one was—it's always one's best friend who does it ! But I used to read them sometimes—ten years ago. I daresay they were in general rather stupider then; at any rate it always struck me they missed my little point with a perfection exactly as admirable when they patted me on the back as when they kicked me in the shins. Whenever since I've happened to have a glimpse of them they were still blazing away—still missing it, I mean, deliciously. *You* miss it, my dear fellow, with inimitable assurance; the fact of your being awfully clever and your article's being awfully nice doesn't make a hair's breadth of difference. It's quite with you rising young men," Vereker laughed, "that I feel most what a failure I am !"

I listened with keen interest; it grew keener as he talked. "*You* a failure—heavens ! What then may your 'little point' happen to be ?"

"Have I got to *tell* you, after all these years and labours ?" There was something in the friendly reproach of this—jocosely exaggerated— that made me, as an ardent young seeker for truth, blush to the roots of my hair. I'm as much in the dark as ever, though I've grown used in a sense to my obtuseness; at that moment, however, Vereker's happy accent made me appear to myself, and probably to him, a rare dunce. I was on the point of exclaiming, "Ah, yes, don't tell me : for my honour for that of the craft, don't !" when he went on in a manner that showed he had read my thought and had his own idea of the probability of our some day redeeming ourselves. "By my little point I mean—what shall I call it ?—the particular thing I've written my books most *for*. Isn't there for every writer a particular thing of that sort, the thing that most makes him apply himself, the thing without the effort to achieve which he wouldn't write at all, the very passion of his passion, the part of the business in which, for him, the flame of art burns most intensely? Well, it's *that* !"

I considered a moment—that is, I followed at a respectful distance, rather gasping. I was fascinated—easily, you'll say; but I wasn't going after all to be put off my guard. "Your description's certainly beautiful, but it doesn't make what you describe very distinct."

"I promise you it would be distinct if it should dawn on you at all." I saw that the charm of our topic overflowed for my companion into an emotion as lively as my own. "At any rate," he went on, "I can speak for myself: there's an idea in my work without which I wouldn't have given a straw for the whole job. It's the finest fullest intention of the lot, and the application of it has been, I think, a triumph of patience, of ingenuity. I ought to leave that to somebody else to say; but that nobody does say it is precisely what we're talking about. It stretches, this little trick of mine, from book to book, and everything else, comparatively, plays over the surface of it. The order, the form, the texture of my books will perhaps some day constitute for the initiated a complete representation of it. So it's naturally the thing for the critic to look for. It strikes me," my visitor added, smiling, "even as the thing for the critic to find."

This seemed a responsibility indeed. "You call it a little trick?"

"That's only my little modesty. It's really an exquisite scheme."

"And you hold that you've carried the scheme out?"

"The way I've carried it out is the thing in life I think a bit well of myself for."

I had a pause. "Don't you think you ought—just a trifle—to assist the critic?"

"Assist him? What else have I done with every stroke of my pen? I've shouted my intention in his great blank face!" At this, laughing out again, Vereker laid his hand on my shoulder to show the allusion wasn't to my personal appearance.

"But you talk about the initiated. There must therefore, you see, *be* initiation."

"What else in heaven's name is criticism supposed to be?" I'm afraid I coloured at this too: but I took refuge in repeating that his account of his silver lining was poor in something or other that a plain man knows things by. "That's only because you've never had a glimpse of it," he returned. "If you had had one the element in question

156

would soon have become practically all you'd see. To me it's exactly as palpable as the marble of this chimney. Besides, the critic just *isn't* a plain man: if he were, pray, what would he be doing in his neighbours' garden? You're anything but a plain man yourself, and the very *raison d'être* of you all is that you're little demons of subtlety. If my great affair's a secret, that's only because it's a secret in spite of itself—the amazing event has made it one. I not only never took the smallest precaution to keep it so, but never dreamed of any such accident. If I had I shouldn't in advance have had the heart to go on. As it was, I only became aware little by little, and meanwhile I had done my work."

"And now you quite like it?" I risked.

"My work?"

"Your secret. It's the same thing."

"Your guessing that," Vereker replied, "is a proof that you're as clever as I say!" I was encouraged by this to remark that he would clearly be pained to part with it, and he confessed that it was indeed with him now the great amusement of life. "I live almost to see if it will ever be detected." He looked at me for a jesting challenge; something far within his eyes seemed to peep out. "But I needn't worry—it won't!"

"You fire me as I've never been fired," I declared; "you make me determined to do or die." Then I asked: "Is it a kind of esoteric message?"

His countenance fell at this—he put out his hand as if to bid me good-night. "Ah, my dear fellow, it can't be described in cheap journalese!"

I knew of course he'd be awfully fastidious, but our talk had made me feel how much his nerves were exposed. I was unsatisfied—I kept hold of his hand. "I won't make use of the expression, then," I said, "in the article in which I shall eventually announce my discovery, though I daresay I shall have hard work to do without it. But meanwhile, just to hasten that difficult birth, can't you give a fellow a clue?" I felt much more at my ease.

"My whole lucid effort gives him the clue—every page and line and letter. The thing's as concrete there as a bird in a cage, a bait on a hook, a piece of cheese in a mouse-trap. It's stuck into every volume as your foot is stuck into your shoe. It governs every line, it chooses every word, it dots every i, it places every comma."

157

I scratched my head. "Is it something in the style or something in the thought? An element of form or an element of feeling?"

He indulgently shook my hand again, and I felt my questions to be crude and my distinctions pitiful. "Good-night, my dear boy—don't bother about it. After all, you do like a fellow."

"And a little intelligence might spoil it?" I still detained him.

He hesitated. "Well, you've got a heart in your body. Is that an element of form or an element of feeling? What I contend that nobody has ever mentioned in my work is the organ of life."

"I see—it's some idea *about* life, some sort of philosophy. Unless it be," I added with the eagerness of a thought perhaps still happier, "some kind of game you're up to with your style, something you're after in the language. Perhaps it's a preference for the letter P!" I ventured profanely to break out. "Papa, potatoes, prunes—that sort of thing?" He was suitably indulgent: he only said I hadn't got the right letter. But his amusement was over; I could see he was bored. There was nevertheless something else I had absolutely to learn. "Should you be able, pen in hand, to state it clearly yourself—to name it, phrase it, formulate it?"

"Oh," he almost passionately sighed, "if I were only, pen in hand, one of *you* chaps!"

"That would be a great chance for you of course. But why should you despise us chaps for not doing what you can't do yourself?"

"Can't do?" He opened his eyes. "Haven't I done it in twenty volumes? I do it in my way," he continued. "Go *you* and do it in yours."

"Ours is so devilish difficult," I weakly observed.

"So's mine! We each choose our own. There's no compulsion. You won't come down and smoke?"

"No. I want to think this thing out."

"You'll tell me, then, in the morning that you've laid me bare?"

"I'll see what I can do; I'll sleep on it. But just one word more," I added. We had left the room—I walked again with him a few steps along the passage. "This extraordinary 'general intention,' as you call it—for that's the most vivid description I can induce you to make of it—is then, generally, a sort of buried treasure?"

His face lighted. "Yes, call it that, though it's perhaps not for me to do so."

"Nonsense!" I laughed. "You know you're hugely proud of it."

"Well, I didn't propose to tell you so; but it *is* the joy of my soul!"

"You mean it's a beauty so rare, so great?"

He waited a little again. "The loveliest thing in the world!" We had stopped, and on these words he left me; but at the end of the corridor, while I looked after him rather yearningly, he turned and caught sight of my puzzled face. It made him earnestly, indeed I thought quite anxiously, shake his head and wave his finger. "Give it up—give it up!"

This wasn't a challenge—it was fatherly advice. If I had had one of his books at hand I'd have repeated my recent act of faith—I'd have spent half the night with him. At three o'clock in the morning, not sleeping, remembering, moreover, how indispensable he was to Lady Jane, I stole down to the library with a candle. There wasn't, so far as I could discover, a line of his writing in the house.

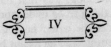

IV

RETURNING TO town I feverishly collected them all; I picked out each in its order and held it up to the light. This gave me a maddening month, in the course of which several things took place. One of these, the last, I may as well immediately mention, was that I acted on Vereker's advice: I renounced my ridiculous attempt. I could really make nothing of the business; it proved a dead loss. After all I had always, as he had himself noted, liked him; and what now occurred was simply that my new intelligence and vain preoccupation damaged my liking. I not only failed to run a general intention to earth, I found myself missing the subordinate intentions I had formerly enjoyed. His books didn't even remain the charming things they had been for me; the exasperation of my search put me out of conceit of them. Instead of being a pleasure the more they became a resource the less; for from the moment I was unable to follow up the author's hint I of course felt it a point of honour not to make use professionally of my knowledge of them. I *had* no knowledge—nobody had any. It was humiliating, but I could bear it—they only annoyed me now. At last they even bored me, and I accounted for my confusion—perversely, I allow—by the idea that Vereker had made a fool of me. The buried treasure was a bad joke, the general intention a monstrous *pose*.

The great point of it all is, however, that I told George Corvick what had befallen me and that my information had an immense effect on him. He had at last come back, but so, unfortunately, had Mrs. Erme, and there was as yet, I could see, no question of his nuptials. He was immensely stirred up by the anecdote I had brought from Bridges; it fell in so completely with the sense he had had from the first that there was more in Vereker than met the eye. When I remarked that the eye seemed what the printed page had been expressly invented to meet he immediately accused me of being spiteful because I had been foiled. Our commerce had always that pleasant latitude. The thing Vereker had mentioned to me was exactly the thing he, Corvick, had wanted me to speak of in my review. On my suggesting at last that with the assistance I had now given him he would doubtless be prepared to speak of it himself he admitted freely that before doing this there was more he must understand. What he would have said, had he reviewed the new book, was that there was evidently in the writer's inmost art something to *be* understood. I hadn't so much as hinted at that: no wonder the writer hadn't been flattered! I asked Corvick what he really considered he meant by his own supersubtlety, and, unmistakably kindled, he replied: "It isn't for the vulgar—it isn't for the vulgar!" He had hold of the tail of something: he would pull hard, pull it right out. He pumped me dry on Vereker's strange confidence and, pronouncing me the luckiest of mortals, mentioned half-a-dozen questions he wished to goodness I had had the gumption to put. Yet on the other hand he didn't want to be told too much—it would spoil the fun of seeing what would come. The failure of *my* fun was at the moment of our meeting not complete, but I saw it ahead, and Corvick saw that I saw it. I, on my side, saw likewise that one of the first things he would do would be to rush off with my story to Gwendolen.

On the very day after my talk with him I was surprised by the receipt of a note from Hugh Vereker, to whom our encounter at Bridges had been recalled, as he mentioned, by his falling, in a magazine, on some article to which my signature was attached. "I read it with great pleasure," he wrote, "and remembered under its influence our lively conversation by your bedroom fire. The consequence of this has been that I begin to measure the temerity of my having saddled you with a knowledge that you may find something of a burden. Now that the fit's over I can't imagine how I came to be moved so much beyond my wont. I had never before mentioned, no matter in what state of expansion, the fact of my little secret, and I shall never speak of that mystery again. I was accidentally so much more explicit with you than it had ever entered into my game to be, that I find this game— I mean the pleasure of playing it—suffers considerably. In short, if you can understand it, I've rather spoiled my sport. I really don't want to give anybody what I believe you clever young men call the tip. That's of course a selfish solicitude, and I name it to you for what it may be worth to you. If you're disposed to humour me don't repeat my revelation. Think me demented—it's your right; but don't tell anybody why."

The sequel to this communication was that as early on the morrow as I dared I drove straight to Mr. Vereker's door. He occupied in those years one of the honest old houses in Kensington Square. He received me immediately, and as soon as I came in I saw I hadn't lost my power to minister to his mirth. He laughed out at sight of my face, which doubtless expressed my perturbation. I had been indiscreet—my compunction was great. "I *have* told somebody," I panted, "and I'm sure that person will by this time have told somebody else! It's a woman, into the bargain."

"The person you've told ?"

"No, the other person. I'm quite sure he must have told her."

"For all the good it will do her—or do *me* ! A woman will never find out."

"No, but she'll talk all over the place: she'll do just what you don't want."

Vereker thought a moment, but wasn't so disconcerted as I had feared: he felt that if the harm was done it only served him right. "It doesn't matter—don't worry."

"I'll do my best, I promise you, that your talk with me shall go no further."

"Very good; do what you can."

"In the meantime," I pursued, "George Corvick's possession of the tip may, on his part, really lead to something."

"That will be a brave day."

I told him about Corvick's cleverness, his admiration, the intensity of his interest in my anecdote; and without making too much of the divergence of our respective estimates mentioned that my friend was already of opinion that he saw much further into a certain affair than most people. He was quite as fired as I had been at Bridges. He was, moreover, in love with the young lady: perhaps the two together would puzzle something out.

Vereker seemed struck with this. "Do you mean they're to be married?"

"I daresay that's what it will come to."

"That may help them," he conceded, "but we must give them time!"

I spoke of my own renewed assault and confessed my difficulties; whereupon he repeated his former advice: "Give it up, give it up!" He evidently didn't think me intellectually equipped for the adventure. I stayed half an hour, and he was most good-natured, but I couldn't help pronouncing him a man of unstable moods. He had been free with me in a mood, he had repented in a mood, and now in a mood he had turned indifferent. This general levity helped me to believe that, so far as the subject of the tip went, there wasn't much in it. I contrived, however, to make him answer a few more questions about it, though he did so with visible impatience. For himself, beyond doubt, the thing we were all so blank about was vividly there. It was something, I guessed, in the primal plan; something like a complex figure in a Persian carpet. He highly approved of this image when I used it, and he used another himself. "It's the very string," he said, "that my pearls are strung on!" The reason of his note to me had been that he really didn't want to give us a grain of succour—our density was a thing too perfect in its way to touch. He had formed the habit of depending on it, and if the spell was to break it must break by some force of its own. He comes back to me from that last occasion—for I was never to speak to him again—as a man with some safe preserve for sport. I wondered as I walked away where he had got *his* tip.

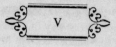

V

WHEN I spoke to George Corvick of the caution I had received he made me feel that any doubt of his delicacy would be almost an insult. He had instantly told Gwendolen, but Gwendolen's ardent response was in itself a pledge of discretion. The question would now absorb them and would offer them a pastime too precious to be shared with the crowd. They appeared to have caught instinctively at Vereker's high idea of enjoyment. Their intellectual pride, however, was not such as to make them indifferent to any further light I might throw on the affair they had in hand. They were indeed of the "artistic temperament," and I was freshly struck with my colleague's power to excite himself over a question of art. He'd call it letters, he'd call it life, but it was all one thing. In what he said I now seemed to understand that he spoke equally for Gwendolen, to whom, as soon as Mrs. Erme was sufficiently better to allow her a little leisure, he made a point of introducing me. I remember our going together one Sunday in August to a huddled house in Chelsea, and my renewed envy of Corvick's possession of a friend who had some light to mingle with his own. He could say things to her that I could never say to him. She had indeed no sense of humour and, with her pretty way of holding her head on one side, was one of those persons whom you want, as the phrase is, to shake, but who have learnt Hungarian by themselves. She conversed perhaps in Hungarian with Corvick; she had remarkably little English for his friend. Corvick afterwards told me that I had chilled her by my apparent indisposition to oblige them with the detail of what Vereker had said to me. I allowed that I felt I had given thought enough to that indication: hadn't I even made up my mind that it was vain and would lead nowhere? The importance they attached to it was irritating and quite envenomed my doubts.

That statement looks unamiable, and what probably happened was that I felt humiliated at seeing other persons deeply beguiled by an experiment that had brought me only chagrin. I was out in the cold while, by the evening fire, under the lamp, they followed the chase for which I myself had sounded the horn. They did as I had done, only more deliberately and sociably—they went over their author from the beginning. There was no hurry, Corvick said—the future was before them and the fascination could only grow; they would take him page by page, as they would take one of the classics, inhale him in slow draughts and let him sink all the way in. They would scarce have got so wound up, I think, if they hadn't been in love: poor Vereker's inner meaning gave them endless occasion to put and to keep their young heads together. None the less it represented the kind of problem for which Corvick had a special aptitude, drew out the particular pointed patience of which, had he lived, he would have given more striking and, it is to be hoped, more fruitful examples. He at least was, in Vereker's words, a little demon of subtlety. We had begun by disputing, but I soon saw that without my stirring a finger his infatuation would have its bad hours. He would bound off on false scents as I had done— he would clap his hands over new lights and see them blown out by the wind of the turned page. He was like nothing, I told him, but the maniacs who embrace some bedlamitical theory of the cryptic character of Shakespeare. To this he replied that if we had had Shakespeare's own word for his being cryptic he would at once have accepted it. The case there was altogether different—we had nothing but the word of Mr. Snooks. I returned that I was stupefied to see him attach such importance even to the word of Mr. Vereker. He wanted thereupon to know if I treated Mr. Vereker's word as a lie. I wasn't perhaps prepared, in my unhappy rebound, to go so far as that, but I insisted that till the contrary was proved I should view it as too fond an imagination. I didn't, I confess, say—I didn't at that time quite know—all I felt. Deep down, as Miss Erme would have said, I was uneasy, I was expectant. At the core of my disconcerted state—for my wonted curiosity lived in its ashes—was the sharpness of a sense that Corvick would at last probably come out somewhere. He made, in defence of his credulity, a great point of the fact that from of old, in his study of this genius, he had caught whiffs and hints of he didn't know what, faint wandering notes of a hidden music. That was just the rarity, that was the charm: it fitted so perfectly into what I reported.

If I returned on several occasions to the little house in Chelsea I daresay it was as much for news of Vereker as for news of Miss Erme's ailing parent. The hours spent there by Corvick were present to my fancy as those of a chessplayer bent with a silent scowl, all the lamplit winter, over his board and his moves. As my imagination filled it out the picture held me fast. On the other side of the table was a ghostlier form, the faint figure of an antagonist good-humouredly but a little wearily secure—an antagonist who leaned back in his chair with his hands in his pockets and a smile on his fine clear face. Close to Corvick, behind him, was a girl who had begun to strike me as pale and wasted and even, on more familiar view, as rather handsome, and who rested on his shoulder and hung on his moves. He would take up a chessman and hold it poised a while over one of the little squares, and then would put it back in its place with a long sigh of disappointment. The young lady, at this, would slightly but uneasily shift her position and look across, very hard, very long, very strangely, at their dim partici-pant. I had asked them at an early stage of the business if it mightn't contribute to their success to have some closer communication with him. The special circumstances would surely be held to have given me a right to introduce them. Corvick immediately replied that he had no wish to approach the altar before he had prepared the sacrifice. He quite agreed with our friend both as to the delight and as to the honour of the chase—he would bring down the animal with his own rifle. When I asked him if Miss Erme were as keen a shot he said after thinking: "No, I'm ashamed to say she wants to set a trap. She'd give anything to see him; she says she requires another tip. She's really quite morbid about it. But she must play fair—she *shan't* see him!" he emphatically added. I wondered if they hadn't even quarrel-led a little on the subject—a suspicion not corrected by the way he more than once exclaimed to me: "She's quite incredibly literary, you know—quite fantastically!" I remember his saying of her that she felt in italics and thought in capitals. "Oh when I've run him to earth," he also said, "then, you know, I shall knock at his door. Rather—I beg you to believe. I'll have it from his own lips: 'Right you are, my boy; you've done it this time!' He shall crown me victor —with the critical laurel."

Meanwhile he really avoided the chances London life might have given him of meeting the distinguished novelist; a danger, however, that disappeared with Vereker's leaving England for an indefinite absence, as the newspapers announced—going to the south for motives connected with the health of his wife, which had long kept her in retirement. A year—more than a year—had elapsed since the incident at Bridges, but I had had no further sight of him. I think I was at bottom rather ashamed—I hated to remind him that, though I had irremediably missed his point, a reputation for acuteness was rapidly overtaking me. This scruple led me a dance; kept me out of Lady Jane's house, made me even decline, when in spite of my bad manners she was a second time so good as to make me a sign, an invitation to her beautiful seat. I once became aware of her under Vereker's escort at a concert, and was sure I was seen by them, but I slipped out without being caught. I felt, as on that occasion I splashed along in the rain, that I couldn't have done anything else; and yet I remember saying to myself that it was hard, was even cruel. Not only had I lost the books, but I had lost the man himself: they and their author had been alike spoiled for me. I knew too which was the loss I most regretted. I had taken to the man still more than I had ever taken to the books.

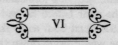

VI

SIX MONTHS after our friend had left England George Corvick, who made his living by his pen, contracted for a piece of work which imposed on him an absence for some length and a journey of some difficulty, and his undertaking of which was much of a surprise to me. His brother-in-law had become editor of a great provincial paper, and the great provincial paper, in a fine flight of fancy, had conceived the idea of sending a "special commissioner" to India. Special commissioners had begun, in the "metropolitan press," to be the fashion, and the journal in question must have felt it had passed too long for a mere country cousin. Corvick had no hand, I knew, for the big brush of the correspondent, but that was his brother-in-law's affair, and the fact that a particular task was not in his line was apt to be with himself exactly a reason for accepting it. He was prepared to out-Herod the metropolitan press; he took solemn precautions against priggishness, he exquisitely outraged taste. Nobody ever knew it—that offended principle was all his own. In addition to his expenses he was to be conveniently paid, and I found myself able to help him, for the usual fat book, to a plausible arrangement with the usual fat publisher. I naturally inferred that his obvious desire to make a little money was not unconnected with the prospect of a union with Gwendolen Erme. I was aware that her mother's opposition was largely addressed to his want of means and of lucrative abilities, but it so happened that, on my saying the last time I saw him something that bore on the question of his separation from our young lady, he brought out with an emphasis that startled me: "Ah, I'm not a bit engaged to her, you know!"

"Not overtly," I answered, "because her mother doesn't like you. But I've always taken for granted a private understanding."

"Well, there *was* one. But there isn't now." That was all he said save something about Mrs. Erme's having got on her feet again in the most extraordinary way—a remark pointing, as I supposed, the moral that private understandings were of little use when the doctor didn't share them. What I took the liberty of more closely inferring was that the girl might in some way have estranged him. Well, if he had taken the turn of jealousy, for instance, it could scarcely be jealousy of me. In that case—over and above the absurdity of it—he wouldn't have gone away just to leave us together. For some time before his going we had indulged in no allusion to the buried treasure, and from his silence, which my reserve simply emulated, I had drawn a sharp conclusion. His courage had dropped, his ardour had gone the way of mine—this appearance at least he left me to scan. More than that he couldn't do; he couldn't face the triumph with which I might have greeted an explicit admission. He needn't have been afraid, poor dear, for I had by this time lost all need to triumph. In fact I considered I showed magnanimity in not reproaching him with his collapse, for the sense of his having thrown up the game made me feel more than ever how much I at last depended on him. If Corvick had broken down I should never know; no one would be of any use if *he* wasn't. It wasn't a bit true I had ceased to care for knowledge; little by little my curiosity not only had begun to ache again, but had become the familiar torment of my days and my nights. There are doubtless people to whom torments of such an order appear hardly more natural than the contortions of disease; but I don't after all know why I should in this connexion so much as mention them. For the few persons, at any rate, abnormal or not, with whom my anecdote is concerned, literature was a game of skill, and skill meant courage, and courage meant honour, and honour meant passion, meant life. The stake on the table was of a special substance and our roulette the revolving mind, but we sat round the green board as intently as the grim gamblers at Monte Carlo. Gwendolen Erme, for that matter, with her white face and her fixed eyes, was of the very type of the lean ladies one had met in the temples of chance. I recognised in Corvick's absence that she made this analogy vivid. It was extravagant, I admit, the way she lived for the art of the pen. Her passion visibly preyed on her, and in her presence I felt almost tepid. I got hold of "Deep Down" again: it was a desert in which she had lost herself, but in which too she had dug a wonderful hole in the sand—a cavity out of which Corvick had still more remarkably pulled her.

Early in March I had a telegram from her, in consequence of which I repaired immediately to Chelsea, where the first thing she said to me was: "He has got it, he has got it !"

She was moved, as I could see, to such depths that she must mean the great thing. "Vereker's idea ?"

"His general intention. George has cabled from Bombay."

She had the missive open there; it was emphatic though concise. "Eureka. Immense." That was all—he had saved the cost of the signature. I shared her emotion, but I was disappointed. "He doesn't say what it is."

"How could he—in a telegram ? He'll write it."

"But how does he know ?"

"Know it's the real thing ? Oh I'm sure that when you see it you do know. *Vera incessu patuit dea !*"

"It's you, Miss Erme, who are a 'dear' for bringing me such news !" —I went all lengths in my high spirits. "But fancy finding our goddess in the temple of Vishnu ! How strange of George to have been able to go into the thing again in the midst of such different and such powerful solicitations !"

"He hasn't gone into it, I know; it's the thing itself, let severely alone for six months, that has simply sprung out at him like a tigress out of the jungle. He didn't take a book with him—on purpose; indeed he wouldn't have needed to—he knows every page, as I do, by heart. They all worked in him together, and some day somewhere, when he wasn't thinking, they fell, in all their superb intricacy, into the one right combination. The figure in the carpet came out. That's the way he knew it would come and the real reason—you didn't in the least understand, but I suppose I may tell you now—why he went and why I consented to his going. We knew the change would do it—that the difference of thought, of scene, would give the needed touch, the magic shake. We had perfectly, we had admirably calculated. The elements were all in his mind, and in the *secousse* of a new and intense experience they just struck light." She positively struck light herself—

she was literally, facially luminous. I stammered something about unconscious cerebration, and she continued: "He'll come right home —this will bring him."

"To see Vereker, you mean?"

"To see Vereker—and to see *me*. Think what he'll have to tell me!"

I hesitated. "About India?"

"About fiddlesticks! About Vereker—about the figure in the carpet."

"But, as you say, we shall surely have that in a letter."

She thought like one inspired, and I remembered how Corvick had told me long before that her face was interesting. "Perhaps it can't be got into a letter if it's 'immense.'"

"Perhaps not if it's immense bosh. If he has hold of something that can't be got into a letter he hasn't hold of *the* thing. Vereker's own statement to me was exactly that the 'figure' *would* fit into a letter."

"Well, I cabled to George an hour ago—two words," said Gwendolen.

"Is it indiscreet of me to ask what they were?"

She hung fire, but at last brought them out. "'Angel, write.'"

"Good!" I cried. "I'll make it sure—I'll send him the same."

VII

MY WORDS, however, were not absolutely the same—I put something instead of "angel"; and in the sequel my epithet seemed the more apt, for when eventually we heard from our traveller it was merely, it was thoroughly to be tantalised. He was magnificent in his triumph, he described his discovery as stupendous; but his ecstasy only obscured it—there were to be no particulars till he should have submitted his conception to the supreme authority. He had thrown up his commission, he had thrown up his book, he had thrown up everything but the instant need to hurry to Rapallo, on the Genoese shore, where Vereker was making a stay. I wrote him a letter which was to await him at Aden—I besought him to relieve my suspense. That he had found my letter was indicated by a telegram which, reaching me after weary days and in the absence of any answer to my laconic despatch to him at Bombay, was evidently intended as a reply to both communications. Those few words were in familiar French, the French of the day, which Corvick often made use of to show he wasn't a prig. It had for some persons the opposite effect, but his message may fairly be paraphrased. "Have patience; I want to see, as it breaks on you, the face you'll make !" "*Tellement envie de voir ta tête !*"—that was what I had to sit down with. I can certainly not be said to have sat down, for I seem to remember myself at this time as rattling constantly between the little house in Chelsea and my own. Our impatience, Gwendolen's and mine, was equal, but I kept hoping her light would be greater. We all spent during this episode, for people of our means, a great deal of money in telegrams and cabs, and I counted on the receipt of news from Rapallo immediately after the junction of the discoverer with the discovered. The interval seemed an age, but late one day I heard a hansom precipitated to my door with the crash engendered by a hint of liberality. I lived with my heart in my mouth and accordingly bounded to the window—a movement which gave me a view of a young lady erect on the footboard of the vehicle and eagerly looking up at my house. At sight of me she flourished a paper with a movement that brought me straight down, the movement with which, in melodramas, handkerchiefs and reprieves are flourished at the foot of the scaffold.

"Just seen Vereker—not a note wrong. Pressed me to bosom—keeps me a month." So much I read on her paper while the cabby dropped a grin from his perch. In my excitement I paid him profusely and in hers she suffered it; then as he drove away we started to walk about and talk. We had talked, heaven knows, enough before, but this was a wondrous lift. We pictured the whole scene at Rapallo, where he would have written, mentioning my name, for permission to call; that is, *I* pictured it, having more material than my companion, whom I felt hang on my lips as we stopped on purpose before shop-windows we didn't look into. About one thing we were clear: if he was staying on for fuller communication we should at least have a letter from him that would help us through the dregs of delay. We understood his staying on, and yet each of us saw, I think, that the other hated it. The letter we were clear about arrived; it was for Gwendolen, and I called on her in time to save her the trouble of bringing it to me. She didn't read it out, as was natural enough; but she repeated to me what it chiefly embodied. This consisted of the remarkable statement that he'd tell her after they were married exactly what she wanted to know.

"Only *then*, when I'm his wife—not before," she explained. "It's tantamount to saying—isn't it ?—that I must marry him straight off !" She smiled at me while I flushed with disappointment, a vision of fresh delay that made me at first unconscious of my surprise. It seemed more than a hint that on me as well he would impose some tiresome condition. Suddenly, while she reported several more things from his letter, I remembered what he had told me before going away. He had found Mr. Vereker deliriously interesting and his own possession of the secret a real intoxication. The buried treasure was all gold and gems. Now that it was there it seemed to grow and grow before him; it would have been, through all time and taking all tongues, one of the most wonderful flowers of literary art. Nothing, in especial, once you were face to face with it, could show for more consummately *done*. When once it came out it came out, was there with a splendour that made you ashamed; and there hadn't been, save in the bottomless vulgarity of the age, with every one tasteless and tainted, every sense stopped, the smallest reason why it should have been overlooked. It was great, yet so simple, was simple, yet so great, and the final knowledge of it was an experience quite apart. He intimated that the charm of such an experience, the desire to drain it, in its freshness, to the last drop, was what kept him there close to the source. Gwendolen, frankly radiant as she tossed me these fragments, showed the elation of a prospect more assured than my own. That brought me back to the question of her marriage, prompted me to ask if what she meant by what she had just surprised me with was that she was under an engagement.

"Of course I am !" she answered. "Didn't you know it ?" She seemed astonished, but I was still more so, for Corvick had told me the exact contrary. I didn't mention this, however; I only reminded her how little I had been on that score in her confidence, or even in Corvick's, and that moreover I wasn't in ignorance of her mother's interdict. At bottom I was troubled by the disparity of the two accounts; but after a little I felt Corvick's to be the one I least doubted. This simply reduced me to asking myself if the girl had on the spot improvised an engagement—vamped up an old one or dashed off a new—in order to arrive at the satisfaction she desired. She must have had resources of which I was destitute, but she made her case slightly more intelligible by returning presently: "What the state of things has been is that we felt of course bound to do nothing in mamma's lifetime."

"But now you think you'll just dispense with mamma's consent?"

"Ah it mayn't come to that!" I wondered what it might come to, and she went on: "Poor dear, she may swallow the dose. In fact, you know," she added with a laugh, "she really *must* !"—a proposition of which, on behalf of every one concerned, I fully acknowledged the force.

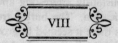

VIII

NOTHING MORE vexatious had ever happened to me than to become aware before Corvick's arrival in England that I shouldn't be there to put him through. I found myself abruptly called to Germany by the alarming illness of my younger brother, who, against my advice, had gone to Munich to study, at the feet indeed of a great master, the art of portraiture in oils. The near relative who made him an allowance had threatened to withdraw it if he should, under specious pretexts, turn for superior truth to Paris—Paris being somehow, for a Cheltenham aunt, the school of evil, the abyss. I deplored this prejudice at the time, and the deep injury of it was now visible—first in the fact that it hadn't saved the poor boy, who was clever frail and foolish, from congestion of the lungs, and second in the greater break with London to which the event condemned me. I'm afraid that what was uppermost in my mind during several anxious weeks was the sense that if we had only been in Paris I might have run over to see Corvick. This was actually out of the question from every point of view: my brother, whose recovery gave us both plenty to do, was ill for three months, during which I never left him and at the end of which we had to face the absolute prohibition of a return to England. The consideration of climate imposed itself, and he was in no state to meet it alone. I took him to Meran and there spent the summer with him, trying to show him by example how to get back to work and nursing a rage of another sort that I tried *not* to show him.

The whole business proved the first of a series of phenomena so strangely interlaced that, taken all together—which was how I had to take them—they form as good an illustration as I can recall of the manner in which, for the good of his soul doubtless, fate sometimes deals with a man's avidity. These incidents certainly had larger bearings than the comparatively meagre consequence we are here concerned with—though I feel that consequence also a thing to speak of with some respect. It's mainly in such a light, I confess, at any rate, that the ugly fruit of my exile is at this hour present to me. Even at first indeed the spirit in which my avidity, as I have called it, made me regard that term owed no element of ease to the fact that before coming back from Rapallo George Corvick addressed me in a way I objected to. His letter has none of the sedative action I must to-day profess myself sure he had wished to give it, and the march of occurrences was not so ordered as to make up for what it lacked. He had begun on the spot, for one of the quarterlies, a great last word on Vereker's writings, and this exhaustive study, the only one that would have counted, have existed, was to turn on the new light, to utter—oh so quietly !—the unimagined truth. It was, in other words, to trace the figure in the carpet through every convolution, to reproduce it in every tint. The result, according to my friend, would be the greatest literary portrait ever painted, and what he asked of me was just to be so good as not to trouble him with questions till he should hang up his masterpiece before me. He did me the honour to declare that, putting aside the great sitter himself, all aloft in his indifference, I was individually the connoisseur he was most working for. I was therefore to be a good boy and not try to peep under the curtain before the show was ready : I should enjoy it all the more if I sat very still.

I did my best to sit very still, but I couldn't help giving a jump on seeing in *The Times*, after I had been a week or two in Munich and before, as I knew, Corvick had reached London, the announcement of the sudden death of poor Mrs. Erme. I instantly, by letter, appealed to Gwendolen for particulars, and she wrote me that her mother had yielded to long-threatened failure of the heart. She didn't say, but I took the liberty of reading into her words, that from the point of view of her marriage and also of her eagerness, which was quite a match for mine, this was a solution more prompt than could have been expected and more radical than waiting for the old lady to swallow the dose. I candidly admit indeed that at the time—for I heard from her repeatedly—I read some singular things into Gwendolen's words and some still more extraordinary ones into her silences. Pen in hand, this way, I live the time over, and it brings back the oddest sense of my having been, both for months and in spite of myself, a kind of coerced spectator. All my life had taken refuge in my eyes, which the procession of events appeared to have committed itself to keep astare. There were days when I thought of writing to Hugh Vereker and simply throwing myself on his charity. But I felt more deeply that I hadn't fallen quite so low—besides which, quite properly, he would send me about my business. Mrs. Erme's death brought Corvick straight home, and within the month he was united "very quietly"—as quietly, I seemed to make out, as he meant in his article to bring out his *trouvaille* —to the young lady he had loved and quitted. I use this last term, I may parenthetically say, because I subsequently grew sure that at the time he went to India, at the time of his great news from Bombay, there had been no positive pledge between them whatever. There had been none at the moment she was affirming to me the very opposite. On the other hand, he had certainly become engaged the day he returned. The happy pair went down to Torquay for their honeymoon, and there, in a reckless hour, it occurred to poor Corvick to take his young bride a drive. He had no command of that business: this had been brought home to me of old in a little tour we had once made together in a dogcart. In a dogcart he perched his companion for a rattle over Devonshire hills, on one of the likeliest of which he brought his horse, who, it was true, had bolted, down with such violence that the occupants of the cart were hurled forward and that he fell horribly on his head. He was killed on the spot; Gwendolen escaped unhurt.

I pass rapidly over the question of this unmitigated tragedy, of what the loss of my best friend meant for me, and I complete my little history of my patience and my pain by the frank statement of my having, in a postscript to my very first letter to her after the receipt of the hideous news, asked Mrs. Corvick whether her husband mightn't at least have finished the great article on Vereker. Her answer was as prompt as my question: the article, which had been barely begun, was a mere heartbreaking scrap. She explained that our friend, abroad, had just settled down to it when interrupted by her mother's death, and that then, on his return, he had been kept from work by the engrossments into which that calamity was to plunge them. The opening pages were all that existed; they were striking, they were promising, but they didn't unveil the idol. That great intellectual feat was obviously to have formed his climax. She said nothing more, nothing to enlighten me as to the state of her own knowledge—the knowledge for the acquisition

174

of which I had fancied her prodigiously acting. This was above all what I wanted to know: had *she* seen the idol unveiled? Had there been a private ceremony for a palpitating audience of one? For what else but that ceremony had the nuptials taken place? I didn't like as yet to press her, though when I thought of what had passed between us on the subject in Corvick's absence her reticence surprised me. It was therefore not till much later, from Meran, that I risked another appeal, risked it in some trepidation, for she continued to tell me nothing. "Did you hear in those few days of your blighted bliss," I wrote, "what we desired so to hear?" I said "we" as a little hint; and she showed me she could take a little hint. "I heard everything," she replied, "and I mean to keep it to myself!"

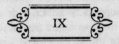

IX

It was impossible not to be moved with the strongest sympathy for her, and on my return to England I showed her every kindness in my power. Her mother's death had made her means sufficient, and she had gone to live in a more convenient quarter. But her loss had been great and her visitation cruel; it never would have occurred to me, moreover, to suppose she could come to feel the possession of a technical tip, of a piece of literary experience, a counterpoise to her grief. Strange to say, none the less, I couldn't help believing after I had seen her a few times that I caught a glimpse of some such oddity. I hasten to add that there had been other things I couldn't help believing, or at least imagining; and as I never felt I was really clear about these, so, as to the point I here touch on, I give her memory the benefit of the doubt. Stricken and solitary, highly accomplished and now, in her deep mourning, her maturer grace and her uncomplaining sorrow, incontestably handsome, she presented herself as leading a life of singular dignity and beauty. I had at first found a way to persuade myself that I should soon get the better of the reserve formulated, the week after the catastrophe, in her reply to an appeal as to which I was not unconscious that it might strike her as mistimed. Certainly that reserve was something of a shock to me—certainly it puzzled me the more I thought of it and even though I tried to explain it (with moments of success) by an imputation of exalted sentiments, of superstitious scruples, of a refinement of loyalty. Certainly it added at the same time hugely to the price of Vereker's secret, precious as this mystery already appeared. I may as well confess abjectly that Mrs. Corvick's unexpected attitude was the final tap on the nail that was to fix fast my luckless idea, convert it into the obsession of which I'm for ever conscious.

But this only helped me the more to be artful, to be adroit, to allow time to elapse before renewing my suit. There were plenty of speculations for the interval, and one of them was deeply absorbing. Corvick had kept his information from his young friend till after the removal of the last barrier to their intimacy—then only had he let the cat out of the bag. Was it Gwendolen's idea, taking a hint from him, to liberate this animal only on the basis of the renewal of such a relation? Was the figure in the carpet traceable or describable only for husbands and wives—for lovers supremely united? It came back to me in a mystifying manner that in Kensington Square, when I mentioned that Corvick would have told the girl he loved, some word had dropped from Vereker that gave colour to this possibility. There might be little in it, but there was enough to make me wonder if I should have to marry Mrs. Corvick to get what I wanted. Was I prepared to offer her this price for the blessing of her knowledge? Ah that way madness lay!—so I at least said to myself in bewildered hours. I could see meanwhile the torch she refused to pass on flame away in her chamber of memory—pour through her eyes a light that shone in her lonely house. At the end of six months I was fully sure of what this warm presence made up to her for. We had talked again and again of the man who had brought us together—of his talent, his character, his personal charm, his certain career, his dreadful doom, and even of his clear purpose in that great study which was to have been a supreme literary portrait, a kind of critical Vandyke or Velasquez. She had conveyed to me in abundance that she was tongue-tied by her perversity, by her piety, that she would never break the silence it had not been given to the "right person," as she said, to break. The hour, however, finally arrived. One evening when I had been sitting with her longer than usual I laid my hand firmly on her arm. "Now at last what *is* it?"

She had been expecting me and was ready. She gave a long slow soundless headshake, merciful only in being inarticulate. This mercy didn't prevent its hurling at me the largest finest coldest "Never!" I had yet, in the course of a life that had known denials, had to take full in the face. I took it and was aware that with the hard blow the tears had come into my eyes. So for a while we sat and looked at each other; after which I slowly rose. I was wondering if some day she would accept me; but this was not what I brought out. I said as I smoothed down my hat: "I know what to think then. It's nothing!"

A remote disdainful pity for me gathered in her dim smile; then she spoke in a voice that I hear at this hour. "It's my *life*!" As I stood at the door she added: "You've insulted him!"

"Do you mean Vereker?"

"I mean the Dead!"

I recognised when I reached the street the justice of her charge. Yes, it was her life—I recognised that too; but her life none the less made room with the lapse of time for another interest. A year and a half after Corvick's death she published in a single volume her second novel, "Overmastered," which I pounced on in the hope of finding in it some tell-tale echo or some peeping face. All I found was a much better book than her younger performance, showing I thought the better company she had kept. As a tissue tolerably intricate it was a carpet with a figure of its own; but the figure was not the figure I was looking for. On sending a review of it to *The Middle* I was surprised to learn from the office that a notice was already in type. When the paper came out I had no hesitation in attributing this article, which I thought rather vulgarly overdone, to Drayton Deane, who in the old days had been something of a friend of Corvick's, yet had only within a few weeks made the acquaintance of his widow. I had had an early copy of the book, but Deane had evidently had an earlier. He lacked all the same the light hand with which Corvick had gilded the gingerbread—he laid on the tinsel in splotches.

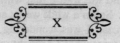

X

SIX MONTHS later appeared "The Right of Way," the last chance, though we didn't know it, that we were to have to redeem ourselves. Written wholly during Vereker's sojourn abroad, the book had been heralded, in a hundred paragraphs, by the usual ineptitudes. I carried it, as early a copy as any, I this time flattered myself, straightway to Mrs. Corvick. This was the only use I had for it; I left the inevitable tribute of *The Middle* to some more ingenious mind and some less irritated temper. "But I already have it," Gwendolen said. "Drayton Deane was so good as to bring it to me yesterday, and I've just finished it."

"Yesterday? How did he get it so soon?"

"He gets everything so soon! He's to review it in *The Middle*."

"He—Drayton Deane—review Vereker?" I couldn't believe my ears.

"Why not? One fine performance is as good as another."

I winced but I presently said: "You ought to review him yourself!"

"I don't 'review,'" she laughed. "I'm reviewed!"

Just then the door was thrown open. "Ah yes, here's your reviewer!" Drayton Deane was there with his long legs and his tall forehead: he had come to see what she thought of "The Right of Way," and to bring news that was singularly relevant. The evening papers were just out with a telegram on the author of that work, who, in Rome, had been ill for some days with an attack of malarial fever. It had at first not been thought grave, but had taken, in consequence of complications, a turn that might give rise to anxiety. Anxiety had indeed at the latest hour begun to be felt.

I was struck in the presence of these tidings with the fundamental detachment that Mrs. Corvick's overt concern quite failed to hide: it gave me the measure of her consummate independence. That independence rested on her knowledge, the knowledge which nothing now could destroy and which nothing could make different. The figure in the carpet might take on another twist or two, but the sentence had virtually been written. The writer might go down to his grave: she was the person in the world to whom—as if she had been his favoured heir—his continued existence was least of a need. This reminded me how I had observed at a particular moment—after Corvick's death— the drop of her desire to see him face to face. She had got what she wanted without that. I had been sure that if she hadn't got it she wouldn't have been restrained from the endeavour to sound him personally by those superior reflexions, more conceivable on a man's part than on a woman's, which in my case had served as a deterrent. It wasn't however, I hasten to add, that my case, in spite of this invidious comparison, wasn't ambiguous enough. At the thought that Vereker was perhaps at that moment dying there rolled over me a wave of anguish—a poignant sense of how inconsistently I still depended on him. A delicacy that it was my one compensation to suffer to rule me had left the Alps and the Apennines between us, but the sense of the waning occasion suggested that I might in my despair at last have gone to him. Of course I should really have done nothing of the sort. I remained five minutes, while my companions talked of the new book, and when Drayton Deane appealed to me for my opinion of it I made answer, getting up, that I detested Hugh Vereker and simply couldn't read him. I departed with the moral certainty that as the door closed behind me Deane would brand me for awfully superficial. His hostess wouldn't contradict *that* at least.

I continue to trace with a briefer touch our intensely odd successions. Three weeks after this came Vereker's death, and before the year was out the death of his wife. That poor lady I had never seen, but I had had a futile theory that, should she survive him long enough to be decorously accessible, I might approach her with the feeble flicker of my plea. Did she know and if she knew would she speak ? It was much to be presumed that for more reasons than one she would have nothing to say ; but when she passed out of all reach I felt renouncement indeed my appointed lot. I was shut up in my obsession for ever—my gaolers had gone off with the key. I find myself quite as vague as a captive in a dungeon about the time that further elapsed before Mrs. Corvick became the wife of Drayton Deane. I had foreseen, through my bars, this end of the business, though there was no indecent haste and our friendship had rather fallen off. They were both so "awfully in- tellectual" that it struck people as a suitable match, but I had measured better than any one of the wealth of understanding the bride would contribute to the union. Never, for a marriage in literary circles—so the newspapers described the alliance—had a lady been so bravely dowered. I began with due promptness to look for the fruit of the affair—that fruit, I mean, of which the premonitory symptoms would be peculiarly visible in the husband. Taking for granted the splendour of the other party's nuptial gift, I expected to see him make a show commensurate with his increase of means. I knew what his means had been—his article on "The Right of Way" had distinctly given one the figure. As he was now exactly in the position in which still more exactly I was not I watched from month to month, in the likely periodicals, for the heavy message poor Corvick had been unable to deliver and the responsibility of which would have fallen on his successor. The widow and wife would have broken by the rekindled hearth the silence that only a widow and wife might break, and Deane would be as aflame with the knowledge as Corvick in his own hour, as Gwendolen in hers, had been. Well, he was aflame doubtless, but the fire was apparently not to become a public blaze. I scanned the periodicals in vain: Drayton Deane filled them with exuberant pages, but he withheld the page I most feverishly sought. He wrote on a thousand subjects, but never on the subject of Vereker. His special line was to tell truths that other people either "funked," as he said, or overlooked, but he never told the only truth that seemed to me in these days to signify. I met the couple in those literary circles referred to in the papers: I have sufficiently intimated that it was only in such circles we were all constructed to revolve. Gwendolen was more than ever committed to them by the publication of her third novel, and I myself definitely classed by holding the opinion that this work was inferior to its immediate predecessor. Was it worse because she had been keeping worse company? If her secret was, as she has told me, her life—a fact discernible in her increasing bloom, an air of conscious privilege that, cleverly corrected by pretty charities, gave distinction to her appearance—it had yet not a direct influence on her work. That only made one—everything only made one—yearn the more for it; only rounded it off with a mystery finer and subtler.

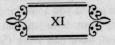
It was therefore from her husband I could never remove my eyes: I beset him in a manner that might have made him uneasy. I went even so far as to engage him in conversation. *Didn't* he know, hadn't he come into it as a matter of course ?—that question hummed in my brain. Of course he knew; otherwise he wouldn't return my stare so queerly. His wife had told him what I wanted and he was amiably amused at my impotence. He didn't laugh—he wasn't a laugher: his system was to present to my irritation, so that I should crudely expose myself, a conversational blank as vast as his big bare brow. It always happened that I turned away with a settled conviction from these unpeopled expanses, which seemed to complete each other geographically and to symbolise together Drayton Deane's want of voice, want of form. He simply hadn't the art to use what he knew; he literally was incompetent to take up the duty where Corvick had left it. I went still further—it was the only glimpse of happiness I had. I made up my mind that the duty didn't appeal to him. He wasn't interested, he didn't care. Yes, it quite comforted me to believe him too stupid to have joy of the thing I lacked. He was as stupid after as he had been before, and that deepened for me the golden glory in which the mystery was wrapped. I had of course none the less to recollect that his wife might have imposed her conditions and exactions. I had above all to remind myself that with Vereker's death the major incentive dropped. He was still there to be honoured by what might be done—he was no longer there to give it his sanction. Who alas but he had the authority ?

Two children were born to the pair, but the second cost the mother her life. After this stroke I seemed to see another ghost of a chance. I jumped at it in thought, but I waited a certain time for manners, and at last my opportunity arrived in a remunerative way. His wife had been dead a year when I met Drayton Deane in the smoking-room of a small club of which we both were members, but where for months— perhaps because I rarely entered it—I hadn't seen him. The room was empty and the occasion propitious. I deliberately offered him, to have done with the matter for ever, that advantage for which I felt he had long been looking.

"As an older acquaintance of your late wife's than even you were," I began, "you must let me say to you something I have on my mind. I shall be glad to make any terms with you that you see fit to name for the information she must have had from George Corvick—the information, you know, that had come to *him*, poor chap, in one of the happiest hours of his life, straight from Hugh Vereker."

He looked at me like a dim phrenological bust. "The information——?"

"Vereker's secret, my dear man—the general intention of his books: the string the pearls were strung on, the buried treasure, the figure in the carpet."

He began to flush—the numbers on his bumps to come out. "Vereker's books had a general intention?"

I stared in my turn. "You don't mean to say you don't know it?" I thought for a moment he was playing with me. "Mrs. Deane knew it; she had it, as I say, straight from Corvick, who had, after infinite search and to Vereker's own delight, found the very mouth of the cave. Where *is* the mouth? He told after their marriage—and told alone— the person who, when the circumstances were reproduced, must have told *you*. Have I been wrong in taking for granted that she admitted you, as one of the highest privileges of the relation in which you stood to her, to the knowledge of which she was after Corvick's death the sole depositary? All *I* know is that that knowledge is infinitely precious, and what I want you to understand is that if you'll in your turn admit me to it you'll do me a kindness for which I shall be lastingly grateful."

He had turned at last very red; I daresay he had begun by thinking I had lost my wits. Little by little he followed me; on my own side I stared with a livelier surprise. Then he spoke. "I don't know what you're talking about."

He wasn't acting—it was the absurd truth. "She *didn't* tell you——?"

"Nothing about Hugh Vereker."

I was stupefied; the room went round. It had been too good even for that! "Upon your honour?"

"Upon my honour. What the devil's the matter with you?" he growled.

"I'm astounded—I'm disappointed. I wanted to get it out of you."

"It isn't *in* me!" he awkwardly laughed. "And even if it were——"

"If it were you'd let me have it—oh yes, in common humanity. But I believe you. I see—I see!" I went on, conscious, with the full turn of the wheel, of my great delusion, my false view of the poor man's attitude. What I saw, though I couldn't say it, was that his wife hadn't thought him worth enlightening. This struck me as strange for a woman who had thought him worth marrying. At last I explained it by the reflexion that she couldn't possibly have married him for his understanding. She had married him for something else.

He was to some extent enlightened now, but he was even more astonished, more disconcerted: he took a moment to compare my story with his quickened memories. The result of his meditation was his presently saying with a good deal of rather feeble form: "This is the first I hear of what you allude to. I think you must be mistaken as to Mrs. Drayton Deane's having had any unmentioned, and still less any unmentionable, knowledge of Hugh Vereker. She'd certainly have wished it—should it have borne on his literary character—to be used."

"It *was* used. She used it herself. She told me with her own lips that she 'lived' on it."

I had no sooner spoken than I repented of my words; he grew so pale that I felt as if I had struck him. "Ah 'lived'——!" he murmured, turning short away from me.

My compunction was real; I laid my hand on his shoulder. "I beg you to forgive me—I've made a mistake. You *don't* know what I thought you knew. You could, if I had been right, have rendered me a service; and I had my reasons for assuming that you'd be in a position to meet me."

"Your reasons?" he echoed. "What were your reasons?"

I looked at him well; I hesitated; I considered. "Come and sit down with me here and I'll tell you." I drew him to a sofa, I lighted another cigar and, beginning with the anecdote of Vereker's one descent from the clouds, I recited to him the extraordinary chain of accidents that had, in spite of the original gleam, kept me till that hour in the dark. I told him in a word just what I've written out here. He listened with deepening attention, and I became aware, to my surprise, by his ejaculations, by his questions, that he would have been after all not unworthy to be trusted by his wife. So abrupt an experience of her want of trust had now a disturbing effect on him; but I saw the immediate shock throb away little by little and then gather again into waves of wonder and curiosity—waves that promised, I could perfectly judge, to break in the end with the fury of my own highest tides. I may say that to-day as victims of unappeased desire there isn't a pin to choose between us. The poor man's state is almost my consolation; there are really moments when I feel it to be quite my revenge.

THE COXON FUND

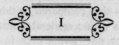

I

"THEY'VE got him for life!" I said to myself that evening on my way back to the station; but later on, alone in the compartment (from Wimbledon to Waterloo, before the glory of the District Railway) I amended this declaration in the light of the sense that my friends would probably after all not enjoy a monopoly of Mr. Saltram. I won't pretend to have taken his vast measure on that first occasion, but I think I had achieved a glimpse of what the privilege of his acquaintance might mean for many persons in the way of charges accepted. He had been a great experience, and it was this perhaps that had put me into the frame of foreseeing how we should all, sooner or later, have the honour of dealing with him as a whole. Whatever impression I then received of the amount of this total, I had a full enough vision of the patience of the Mulvilles. He was to stay all the winter: Adelaide dropped it in a tone that drew the sting from the inevitable emphasis. These excellent people might indeed have been content to give the circle of hospitality a diameter of six months; but if they didn't say he was to stay all summer as well it was only because this was more than they ventured to hope. I remember that at dinner that evening he wore slippers, new and predominantly purple, of some queer carpet-stuff; but the Mulvilles were still in the stage of supposing that he might be snatched from them by higher bidders. At a later time they grew, poor dears, to fear no snatching; but theirs was a fidelity which needed no help from competition to make them proud. Wonderful indeed as, when all was said, you inevitably pronounced Frank Saltram, it was not to be overlooked that the Kent Mulvilles were in their way still more extraordinary: as striking an instance as could easily be encountered of the familiar truth that remarkable men find remarkable conveniences.

They had sent for me from Wimbledon to come out and dine, and there had been an implication in Adelaide's note—judged by her notes alone she might have been thought silly—that it was a case in which something momentous was to be determined or done. I had never known them not be in a "state" about somebody, and I daresay I tried to be droll on this point in accepting their invitation. On finding myself in the presence of their latest discovery I had not at first felt irreverence droop—and, thank heaven, I have never been absolutely deprived of that alternative in Mr. Saltram's company. I saw, however —I hasten to declare it—that compared to this specimen their other phœnixes had been birds of inconsiderable feather, and I afterwards took credit to myself for not having even in primal bewilderments made a mistake about the essence of the man. He had an incomparable gift; I never was blind to it—it dazzles me still. It dazzles me perhaps even more in remembrance than in fact, for I'm not unaware that for so rare a subject the imagination goes to some expense, inserting a jewel here and there or giving a twist to a plume. How the art of portraiture would rejoice in this figure if the art of portraiture had only the canvas ! Nature, in truth, had largely rounded it, and if memory, hovering about it, sometimes holds her breath, this is because the voice that comes back was really golden.

Though the great man was an inmate and didn't dress, he kept dinner on this occasion waiting, and the first words he uttered on coming into the room were an elated announcement to Mulville that he had found out something. Not catching the allusion and gaping doubtless a little at his face, I privately asked Adelaide what he had found out. I shall never forget the look she gave me as she replied: "Everything !" She really believed it. At that moment, at any rate, he had found out that the mercy of the Mulvilles was infinite. He had previously of course discovered, as I had myself for that matter, that their dinners were *soignés*. Let me not indeed, in saying this, neglect to declare that I shall falsify my counterfeit if I seem to hint that there was in his nature any ounce of calculation. He took whatever came, but he never plotted for it, and no man who was so much of an absorbent can ever have been so little of a parasite. He had a system of the universe, but he had no system of sponging—that was quite hand-to-mouth. He had fine gross easy senses, but it was not his good-natured appetite that wrought confusion. If he had loved us for our dinners we could have paid with our dinners, and it would have been a great economy of finer matter. I make free in these connexions with the plural possessive because if I was never able to do what the Mulvilles did, and people with still bigger houses and simpler charities, I met, first and last, every demand of reflexion, of emotion—particularly perhaps those of gratitude and of resentment. No one, I think, paid the tribute of giving him up so often, and if it's rendering honour to borrow wisdom I've a right to talk of my sacrifices. He yielded lessons as the sea yields fish—I lived for a while on this diet. Sometimes it almost appeared to me that his massive monstrous failure—if failure after all it was—had been designed for my private recreation. He fairly pampered my curiosity; but the history of that experience would take me too far. This is not the large canvas I just now spoke of, and I wouldn't have approached him with my present hand had it been a question of all the features. Frank Saltram's features, for artistic purposes, are verily the anecdotes that are to be gathered. Their name is legion, and this is only one, of which the interest is that it concerns even more closely several other persons. Such episodes, as one looks back, are the little dramas that made up the innumerable facets of the big drama—which is yet to be reported.

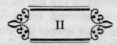

II

It is furthermore remarkable that though the two stories are distinct— my own, as it were, and this other—they equally began, in a manner, the first night of my acquaintance with Frank Saltram, the night I came back from Wimbledon so agitated with a new sense of life that, in London, for the very thrill of it, I could only walk home. Walking and swinging my stick, I overtook, at Buckingham Gate, George Gravener, and George Gravener's story may be said to have begun with my making him, as our paths lay together, come home with me for a talk. I duly remember, let me parenthesise, that it was still more that of another person, and also that several years were to elapse before it was to extend to a second chapter. I had much to say to him, none the less, about my visit to the Mulvilles, whom he more indifferently knew, and I was at any rate so amusing that for long afterwards he never encountered me without asking for news of the old man of the sea. I hadn't said Mr. Saltram was old, and it was to be seen that he was of an age to outweather George Gravener. I had at that time a lodging in Ebury Street, and Gravener was staying at his brother's empty house in Eaton Square. At Cambridge, five years before, even in our devastating set, his intellectual power had seemed to me almost awful.

Some one had once asked me privately, with blanched cheeks, what it was then that after all such a mind as that left standing. "It leaves itself!" I could recollect devoutly replying. I could smile at present for this remembrance, since before we got to Ebury Street I was struck with the fact that, save in the sense of being well set up on his legs, George Gravener had actually ceased to tower. The universe he laid low had somehow bloomed again—the usual eminences were visible. I wondered whether he had lost his humour, or only, dreadful thought, had never had any—not even when I had fancied him most Aristophanesque. What was the need of appealing to laughter, however, I could enviously inquire, where you might appeal so confidently to measurement? Mr. Saltram's queer figure, his thick nose and hanging lip, were fresh to me: in the light of my old friend's fine cold symmetry they presented mere success in amusing as the refuge of conscious ugliness. Already, at hungry twenty-six, Gravener looked as blank and parliamentary as if he were fifty and popular. In my scrap of a residence—he had a worldling's eye for its futile conveniences, but never a comrade's joke—I sounded Frank Saltram in his ears; a circumstance I mention in order to note that even then I was surprised at his impatience of my enlivenment. As he had never before heard of the personage it took indeed the form of impatience of the preposterous Mulvilles, his relation to whom, like mine, had had its origin in an early, a childish intimacy with the young Adelaide, the fruit of multiplied ties in the previous generation. When she married Kent Mulville, who was older than Gravener and I and much more amiable, I gained a friend, but Gravener practically lost one. We reacted in different ways from the form taken by what he called their deplorable social action—the form (the term was also his) of nasty second-rate gush. I may have held in my *for intérieur* that the good people at Wimbledon were beautiful fools, but when he sniffed at them I couldn't help taking the opposite line, for I already felt that even should we happen to agree it would always be for reasons that differed. It came home to me that he was admirably British as, without so much as a sociable sneer at my bookbinder, he turned away from the serried rows of my little French library.

"Of course I've never seen the fellow, but it's clear enough he's a humbug."

"Clear 'enough' is just what it isn't," I replied; "if it only were!" That ejaculation on my part must have been the beginning of what was to be later a long ache for final frivolous rest. Gravener was profound enough to remark after a moment that in the first place he couldn't be anything but a Dissenter, and when I answered that the very note of his fascination was his extraordinary speculative breadth my friend retorted that there was no cad like your cultivated cad, and that I might depend upon discovering—since I had had the levity not already to have inquired—that my shining light proceeded, a generation back, from a Methodist cheesemonger. I confess I was struck with his insistence, and I said, after reflexion: "It may be—I admit it may be; but why on earth are you so sure?"—asking the question mainly to lay him the trap of saying that it was because the poor man didn't dress for dinner. He took an instant to circumvent my trap and come blandly out the other side.

"Because the Kent Mulvilles have invented him. They've an infallible hand for frauds. All their geese are swans. They were born to be duped, they like it, they cry for it, they don't know anything from anything, and they disgust one—luckily perhaps!—with Christian charity." His vehemence was doubtless an accident, but it might have been a strange foreknowledge. I forget what protest I dropped; it was at any rate something that led him to go on after a moment: "I only ask one thing—it's perfectly simple. Is a man, in a given case, a real gentleman?"

"A real gentleman, my dear fellow—that's so soon said!"

"Not so soon when he isn't! If they've got hold of one this time he must be a great rascal!"

"I might feel injured," I answered, "if I didn't reflect that they don't rave about *me*."

"Don't be too sure! I'll grant that he's a gentleman," Gravener presently added, "if you'll admit that he's a scamp."

"I don't know which to admire most, your logic or your benevolence."

My companion coloured at this, but he didn't change the subject. "Where did they pick him up?"

"I think they were struck with something he had published."

"I can fancy the dreary thing!"

"I believe they found out he had all sorts of worries and difficulties."

"That of course wasn't to be endured, so they jumped at the privilege of paying his debts!" I professed that I knew nothing about his debts, and I reminded my visitor that though the dear Mulvilles were angels they were neither idiots nor millionaires. What they mainly aimed at was reuniting Mr. Saltram to his wife. "I was expecting to hear he has

189

basely abandoned her," Gravener went on, at this, "and I'm too glad you don't disappoint me."

I tried to recall exactly what Mrs. Mulville had told me. "He didn't leave her—no. It's she who has left him."

"Left him to *us*?" Gravener asked. "The monster—many thanks! I decline to take him."

"You'll hear more about him in spite of yourself. I can't, no, I really can't resist the impression that he's a big man." I was already mastering—to my shame perhaps be it said—just the tone my old friend least liked.

"It's doubtless only a trifle," he returned, "but you haven't happened to mention what his reputation's to rest on."

"Why, on what I began by boring you with—his extraordinary mind."

"As exhibited in his writings?"

"Possibly in his writing, but certainly in his talk, which is far and away the richest I ever listened to."

"And what's it all about?"

"My dear fellow, don't ask me! About everything! About everything!" I pursued, reminding myself of poor Adelaide. "About his ideas of things," I then more charitably added. "You must have heard him to know what I mean—it's unlike anything that ever *was* heard." I coloured, I admit, I overcharged a little, for such a picture was an anticipation of Saltram's later development and still more of my fuller acquaintance with him. However, I really expressed, a little lyrically perhaps, my actual imagination of him when I proceeded to declare that, in a cloud of tradition, legend, he might very well go down to posterity as the greatest of all great talkers. Before we parted George Gravener had wondered why such a row should be made about a chatterbox the more and why he should be pampered and pensioned. The greater the wind-bag the greater the calamity. Out of proportion to everything else on earth had come to be this wagging of the tongue. We were drenched with talk—our wretched age was dying of it. I differed from him here sincerely, only going so far as to concede, and gladly, that we were drenched with sound. It was not, however, the mere speakers who were killing us—it was the mere stammerers. Fine talk was as rare as it was refreshing—the gift of the gods themselves, the one starry spangle on the ragged cloak of humanity. How many men were there who rose to this privilege, of how many masters of conversation could he boast the acquaintance? Dying of talk?—why, we were dying of the lack of it ! Bad writing wasn't talk, as many people seemed to think, and even good wasn't always to be compared to it. From the best talk indeed the best writing had something to learn. I fancifully added that we too should peradventure be gilded by the legend, should be pointed at for having listened, for having actually heard. Gravener, who had glanced at his watch and discovered it was midnight, found to all this a retort beautifully characteristic of him.

"There's one little fact to be borne in mind in the presence equally of the best talk and of the worst." He looked, in saying this, as if he meant great things, and I was sure he could only mean once more that neither of them mattered if a man wasn't a real gentleman. Perhaps it was what he did mean; he deprived me, however, of the exultation of being right by putting the truth in a slightly different way. "The only thing that really counts for one's estimate of a person is his conduct." He had his watch still in his palm, and I reproached him with unfair play in having ascertained beforehand that it was now the hour at which I always gave in. My pleasantry so far failed to mollify him that he promptly added that to the rule he had just enunciated there was absolutely no exception.

"None whatever ?"

"None whatever."

"Trust me then to try to be good at any price !" I laughed as I went with him to the door. "I declare I will be, if I have to be horrible !"

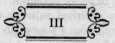

III

IF THAT first night was one of the liveliest, or at any rate was the freshest, of my exaltation, there was another, four years later, that was one of my great discomposures. Repetition, I well knew by this time, was the secret of Saltram's power to alienate, and of course one would never have seen him at his finest if one hadn't seen him in his remorses. They set in mainly at this season and were magnificent, elemental, orchestral. I was quite aware that one of these atmospheric disturbances was now due; but none the less, in our arduous attempt to set him on his feet as a lecturer, it was impossible not to feel that two failures were a large order, as we said, for a short course of five. This was the second time, and it was past nine o'clock; the audience, a muster unprecedented and really encouraging, had fortunately the attitude of blandness that might have been looked for in persons whom the promise of (if I'm not mistaken) An Analysis of Primary Ideas had drawn to the neighbourhood of Upper Baker Street. There was in those days in that region a petty lecture-hall to be secured on terms as moderate as the funds left at our disposal by the irrepressible question of the maintenance of five small Saltrams—I include the mother—and one large one. By the time the Saltrams, of different sizes, were all maintained we had pretty well poured out the oil that might have lubricated the machinery for enabling the most original of men to appear to maintain them.

It was I, the other time, who had been forced into the breach, standing up there for an odious lamplit moment to explain to half-a-dozen thin benches, where earnest brows were virtuously void of anything so cynical as a suspicion, that we couldn't so much as put a finger on Mr. Saltram. There was nothing to plead but that our scouts had been out from the early hours and that we were afraid that on one of his walks abroad—he took one, for meditation, whenever he was to address such a company—some accident had disabled or delayed him. The meditative walks were a fiction, for he never, that any one could discover, prepared anything but a magnificent prospectus; hence his circulars and programmes, of which I possess an almost complete collection, are the solemn ghosts of generations never born. I put the case, as it seemed to me, at the best; but I admit I had been angry, and Kent Mulville was shocked at my want of public optimism. This time therefore I left the excuses to his more practised patience, only relieving myself in response to a direct appeal from a young lady next whom, in the hall, I found myself sitting. My position was an accident, but if it had been calculated the reason would scarce have eluded an observer of the fact that no one else in the room had an approach to an appearance. Our philosopher's "tail" was deplorably limp. This visitor was the only person who looked at her ease, who had come a little in the spirit of adventure. She seemed to carry amusement in her handsome young head, and her presence spoke, a little mystifyingly, of a sudden extension of Saltram's sphere of influence. He was doing better than we hoped, and he had chosen such an occasion, of all occasions, to succumb to heaven knew which of his fond infirmities. The young lady produced an impression of auburn hair and black velvet, and had on her other hand a companion of obscurer type, presumably a waiting-maid. She herself might perhaps have been a foreign countess, and before she addressed me I had beguiled our sorry interval by finding in her a vague recall of the opening of some novel of Madame Sand. It didn't make her more fathomable to pass in a few minutes from this to the certitude that she was American; it simply engendered depressing reflexions as to the possible check to contributions from Boston. She asked me if, as a person apparently more initiated, I would recommend further waiting, and I answered that if she considered I was on my honour I would privately deprecate it. Perhaps she didn't; at any rate our talk took a turn that prolonged it till she became aware we were left almost alone. I presently ascertained she knew Mrs. Saltram, and this explained in a manner the miracle. The brotherhood of the friends of the husband was as nothing to the brotherhood, or perhaps I should say the sisterhood, of the friends of the wife. Like the Kent Mulvilles I belonged to both fraternities, and even better than they I think, I had sounded the abyss of Mrs. Saltram's wrongs. She bored me to extinction, and I knew but too well how she had bored her husband; but there were those who stood by her, the most efficient of whom were indeed the handful of poor Saltram's backers. They did her liberal justice, whereas her mere patrons and partisans had nothing but hatred for our philosopher. I'm bound to say it was we, however —we of both camps, as it were—who had always done most for her.

I thought my young lady looked rich—I scarcely knew why; and I hoped she had put her hand in her pocket. I soon made her out, however, not at all a fine fanatic—she was but a generous irresponsible inquirer. She had come to England to see her aunt, and it was at her aunt's she had met the dreary lady we had all so much on our mind. I saw she'd help to pass the time when she observed that it was a pity this lady wasn't intrinsically more interesting. That was refreshing, for it was an article of faith in Mrs. Saltram's circle—at least among those who scorned to know her horrid husband—that she was attractive on her merits. She was in truth a most ordinary person, as Saltram himself would have been if he hadn't been a prodigy. The question of vulgarity had no application to him, but it was a measure his wife kept challenging you to apply. I hasten to add that the consequences of your doing so were no sufficient reason for his having left her to starve. "He doesn't seem to have much force of character," said my young lady; at which I laughed out so loud that my departing friends looked

193

back at me over their shoulders as if I were making a joke of their dis-comfiture. My joke probably cost Saltram a subscription or two, but it helped me on with my interlocutress. "She says he drinks like a fish," she sociably continued, "and yet she allows that his mind's wonderfully clear." It was amusing to converse with a pretty girl who could talk of the clearness of Saltram's mind. I expected next to hear she had been assured he was awfully clever. I tried to tell her—I had it almost on my conscience—what was the proper way to regard him; an effort attended perhaps more than ever on this occasion with the usual effect of my feeling that I wasn't after all very sure of it. She had come tonight out of high curiosity—she had wanted to learn this proper way for herself. She had read some of his papers and hadn't understood them; but it was at home, at her aunt's, that her curiosity had been kindled—kindled mainly by his wife's remarkable stories of his want of virtue. "I suppose they ought to have kept me away," my companion dropped, and "I suppose they'd have done so if I hadn't somehow got an idea that he's fascinating. In fact Mrs. Saltram herself says he is."

"So you came to see where the fascination resides? Well, you've seen!"

My young lady raised fine eyebrows. "Do you mean in his bad faith?"

"In the extraordinary effects of it; his possession that is, of some quality or other that condemns us in advance to forgive him the humiliation, as I may call it, to which he has subjected us."

"The humiliation?"

"Why, mine, for instance, as one of his guarantors, before you as the purchaser of a ticket."

She let her charming gay eyes rest on me. "You don't look humili-ated a bit, and if you did I should let you off, disappointed as I am; for the mysterious quality you speak of is just the quality I came to see."

"Oh you can't 'see' it!" I cried.

"How then do you get at it?"

"You don't! You mustn't suppose he's good-looking," I added.

"Why, his wife says he's lovely!"

My hilarity may have struck her as excessive, but I confess it broke out afresh. Had she acted only in obedience to this singular plea, so characteristic, on Mrs. Saltram's part, of what was irritating in the narrowness of that lady's point of view? "Mrs. Saltram," I explained, "undervalues him where he's strongest, so that, to make up for it perhaps, she overpraises him where he's weak. He's not, assuredly, superficially attractive: he's middle-aged, fat, featureless save for his great eyes."

"Yes, his great eyes," said my young lady attentively. She had evidently heard all about his great eyes—the *beaux yeux* for which alone we had really done it all.

"They're tragic and splendid—lights on a dangerous coast. But he moves badly and dresses worse, and altogether he's anything but smart."

My companion, who appeared to reflect on this, after a moment appealed. "Do you call him a real gentleman?"

I started slightly at the question, for I had a sense of recognising it: George Gravener, years before, that first flushed night, had put me face to face with it. It had embarrassed me then, but it didn't embarrass me now, for I had lived with it and overcome it and disposed of it. "A real gentleman? Emphatically not!"

My promptitude surprised her a little, but I quickly felt how little it was to Gravener I was now talking. "Do you say that because he's—what do you call it in England?—of humble extraction?"

"Not a bit. His father was a country schoolmaster and his mother the widow of a sexton, but that has nothing to do with it. I say it simply because I know him well."

"But isn't it an awful drawback?"

"Awful—quite awful."

"I mean isn't it positively fatal?"

"Fatal to what? Not to his magnificent vitality."

Again she had a meditative moment. "And is his magnificent vitality the cause of his vices?"

"Your questions are formidable, but I'm glad you put them. I was thinking of his noble intellect. His vices, as you say, have been much exaggerated: they consist mainly after all in one comprehensive defect."

"A want of will?"

"A want of dignity."

"He doesn't recognise his obligations?"

"On the contrary, he recognises them with effusion, especially in public: he smiles and bows and beckons across the street to them. But when they pass over he turns away, and he speedily loses them in the crowd. The recognition's purely spiritual—it isn't in the least social. So he leaves all his belongings to other people to take care of. He accepts favours, loans, sacrifices—all with nothing more deterrent than an agony of shame. Fortunately we're a little faithful band and we do what we can." I held my tongue about the natural children engendered, to the number of three, in the wantonness of his youth. I only remarked that he did make efforts—often tremendous ones. "But the efforts," I said, "never come to much: the only things that come to much are the abandonments, the surrenders."

"And how much do they come to?"

"You're right to put it as if we had a big bill to pay, but, as I've told you before, your questions are rather terrible. They come, these mere exercises of genius, to a great sum total of poetry, of philosophy, a mighty mass of speculation, notation, quotation. The genius is there, you see, to meet the surrender; but there's no genius to support the defence."

"But what is there, after all, at his age, to show?"

"In the way of achievement recognised and reputation established?" I asked. "To 'show' if you will, there isn't much, since his writing, mostly, isn't as fine, isn't certainly as showy, as his talk. Moreover, two-thirds of his work are merely colossal projects and announcements. 'Showing' Frank Saltram is often a poor business," I went on; "we endeavoured, you'll have observed, to show him to-night! However, if he *had* lectured he'd have lectured divinely. It would just have been his talk."

"And what would his talk just have been?"

I was conscious of some ineffectiveness, as well perhaps as of a little impatience, as I replied: "The exhibition of a splendid intellect." My young lady looked not quite satisfied at this, but as I wasn't prepared for another question I hastily pursued: "The sight of a great suspended swinging crystal—huge lucid lustrous, a block of light—flashing back every impression of life and every possibility of thought!"

This gave her something to turn over till we had passed out to the dusky porch of the hall, in front of which the lamps of a quiet brougham were almost the only thing Saltram's treachery hadn't extinguished. I went with her to the door of her carriage, out of which she leaned a moment after she had thanked me and taken her seat. Her smile even in the darkness was pretty. "I do want to see that crystal!"

"You've only to come to the next lecture."

"I go abroad in a day or two with my aunt."

"Wait over till next week," I suggested. "It's quite worth it."

She became grave. "Not unless he really comes!" At which the brougham started off, carrying her away too fast, fortunately for my manners, to allow me to exclaim "Ingratitude!"

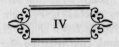

IV

MRS. SALTRAM made a great affair of her right to be informed where her husband had been the second evening he failed to meet his audience. She came to me to ascertain, but I couldn't satisfy her, for in spite of my ingenuity I remained in ignorance. It wasn't till much later that I found this had not been the case with Kent Mulville, whose hope for the best never twirled the thumbs of him more placidly than when he happened to know the worst. He had known it on the occasion I speak of—that is immediately after. He was impenetrable then, but ultimately confessed. What he confessed was more than I shall now venture to make public. It was of course familiar to me that Saltram was incapable of keeping the engagements which, after their separation, he had entered into with regard to his wife, a deeply wronged, justly resentful, quite irreproachable and insufferable person. She often appeared at my chambers to talk over his lapses; for if, as she declared, she had washed her hands of him, she had carefully preserved the water of this ablution, which she handed about for analysis. She had arts of her own of exciting one's impatience, the most infallible of which was perhaps her assumption that we were kind to her because we liked her. In reality her personal fall had been a sort of social rise—since I had seen the moment when, in our little conscientious circle, her desolation almost made her the fashion. Her voice was grating and her children ugly; moreover she hated the good Mulvilles, whom I more and more loved. They were the people who by doing most for her husband had in the long run done most for herself; and the warm confidence with which he had laid his length upon them was a pressure gentle compared with her stiffer persuadability. I'm bound to say he didn't criticise his benefactors, though practically he got tired of them; she, however, had the highest standards about eleemosynary forms. She offered the odd spectacle of a spirit puffed up by dependence, and indeed it had introduced her to some excellent society. She pitied me for not knowing certain people who aided her and whom she doubtless patronised in turn for their luck in not knowing me. I daresay I should have got on with her better if she had had a ray of imagination—if it had occasionally seemed to occur to her to view Saltram's expressions of his nature in any other manner than as separate subjects of woe. They were all flowers of his character, pearls strung on an endless thread; but she had a stubborn little way of challenging them one after the other, as if she never suspected that he *had* a character, such as it was, or that deficiencies might be organic; the irritating effect of a mind incapable of a generalisation. One might doubtless have overdone the idea that there was a general licence for such a man; but if this had happened it would have been through one's feeling that there could be none for such a woman.

I recognised her superiority when I asked her about the aunt of the disappointed young lady: it sounded like a sentence from an English-French or other phrase-book. She triumphed in what she told me and she may have triumphed still more in what she withheld. My friend of the other evening, Miss Anvoy, had but lately come to England; Lady Coxon, the aunt, had been established here for years in consequence of her marriage with the late Sir Gregory of that name. She had a house in the Regent's Park, a Bath-chair and a fernery; and above all she had sympathy. Mrs. Saltram had made her acquaintance through mutual friends. This vagueness caused me to feel how much I was out of it and how large an independent circle Mrs. Saltram had at her command. I should have been glad to know more about the disappointed young lady, but I felt I should know most by not depriving her of her advantage, as she might have mysterious means of depriving me of my knowledge. For the present, moreover, this experience was stayed, Lady Coxon having in fact gone abroad accompanied by her niece. The niece, beside being immensely clever, was an heiress, Mrs. Saltram said; the only daughter and the light of the eyes of some great American merchant, a man, over there, of endless indulgences and dollars. She had pretty clothes and pretty manners, and she had, what was prettier still, the great thing of all. The great thing of all for Mrs. Saltram was always sympathy, and she spoke as if during the absence of these ladies she mightn't know where to turn for it. A few months later indeed, when they had come back, her tone perceptibly changed: she alluded to them, on my leading her up to it, rather as to persons in her debt for favours received. What had happened I didn't know, but

I saw it would take only a little more or a little less to make her speak of them as thankless subjects of social countenance—people for whom she had vainly tried to do something. I confess I saw how it wouldn't be in a mere week or two that I should rid myself of the image of Ruth Anvoy, in whose very name, when I learnt it, I found something secretly to like. I should probably neither see her nor hear of her again: the knight's widow (he had been Mayor of Clockborough) would pass away and the heiress would return to her inheritance. I gathered with surprise that she had not communicated to his wife the story of her attempt to hear Mr. Saltram, and I founded this reticence on the easy supposition that Mrs. Saltram had fatigued by overpressure the spring of the sympathy of which she boasted. The girl at any rate would forget the small adventure, be distracted, take a husband; besides which she would lack occasion to repeat her experiment.

We clung to the idea of the brilliant course, delivered without an accident, that, as a lecturer, would still make the paying public aware of our great man; but the fact remained that in the case of an inspitraion so unequal there was treachery, there was fallacy at least, in the very conception of a series. In our scrutiny of ways and means we were inevitably subject to the old convention of the synopsis, the syllabus, partly of course not to lose the advantage of his grand free hand in drawing up such things; but for myself I laughed at our playbills even while I stickled for them. It was indeed amusing work to be scrupulous for Frank Saltram, who also at moments laughed about it, so far as the comfort of a sigh so unstudied as to be cheerful might pass for such a sound. He admitted with a candour all his own that he was in truth only to be depended on in the Mulvilles' drawing-room. "Yes," he suggestively allowed, "it's there, I think, that I'm at my best; quite late, when it gets toward eleven—and if I've not been too much worried." We all knew what too much worry meant; it meant too enslaved for the hour to the superstition of sobriety. On the Saturdays I used to bring my portmanteau, so as not to have to think of eleven o'clock trains. I had a bold theory that as regards this temple of talk and its altars of cushioned chintz, its pictures and its flowers, its large fireside and clear lamplight, we might really arrive at something if the Mulvilles would but charge for admission. Here it was, however, that they shamelessly broke down; as there's a flaw in every perfection this was the inexpugnable refuge of their egotism. They declined to make their saloon a market, so that Saltram's golden words continued the sole coin that rang there. It can have happened to no man, however, to be paid a greater price than such an enchanted hush as surrounded him on his greatest nights. The most profane, on these occasions, felt a presence; all minor eloquence grew dumb. Adelaide Mulville, for the pride of her hospitality, anxiously watched the door or stealthily poked the fire. I used to call it the music-room, for we had anticipated Bayreuth. The very gates of the kingdom of light seemed to open and the horizon of thought to flash with the beauty of a sunrise at sea.

In the consideration of ways and means, the sittings of our little board, we were always conscious of the creak of Mrs. Saltram's shoes. She hovered, she interrupted, she almost presided, the state of affairs being mostly such as to supply her with every incentive for inquiring what was to be done next. It was the pressing pursuit of this knowledge that, in concatenations of omnibuses and usually in very wet weather, led her so often to my door. She thought us spiritless creatures with editors and publishers, but she carried matters to no great effect when she personally pushed into back-shops. She wanted all moneys to be paid to herself: they were otherwise liable to such strange adventures. They trickled away into the desert—they were mainly at best, alas, a slender stream. The editors and the publishers were the last people to take this remarkable thinker at the valuation that has now pretty well come to be established. The former were half-distraught between the desire to "cut" him and the difficulty of finding a crevice for their shears; and when a volume on this or that portentous subject was proposed to the latter they suggested alternative titles which, as reported to our friend, brought into his face the noble blank melancholy that sometimes made it handsome. The title of an unwritten book didn't after all much matter, but some masterpiece of Saltram's may have died in his bosom of the shudder with which it was then convulsed. The ideal solution, failing the fee at Kent Mulville's door, would have been some system of subscription to projected treatises with their non-appearance provided for—provided for, I mean, by the indulgence of subscribers. The author's real misfortune was that subscribers were so wretchedly literal. When they tastelessly inquired why publication hadn't ensued I was tempted to ask who in the world had ever been so published. Nature herself had brought him out in voluminous form, and the money was simply a deposit on borrowing the work.

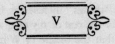

V

I WAS doubtless often a nuisance to my friends in those years; but there were sacrifices I declined to make, and I never passed the hat to George Gravener. I never forgot our little discussion in Ebury Street, and I think it stuck in my throat to have to treat him to the avowal I had found so easy to Miss Anvoy. It had cost me nothing to confide to this charming girl, but it would have cost me much to confide to the friend of my youth, that the character of the "real gentleman" wasn't an attribute of the man I took such pains for. Was this because I had already generalised to the point of perceiving that women are really the unfastidious sex? I knew at any rate that Gravener, already quite in view but still hungry and frugal, had naturally enough more ambition than charity. He had sharp aims for stray sovereigns, being in view most from the tall steeple of Clockborough. His immediate ambition was to occupy *à lui seul* the field of vision of that smokily-seeing city, and all his movements and postures were calculated for the favouring angle. The movement of the hand to the pocket had thus to alternate gracefully with the posture of the hand on the heart. He talked to Clockborough in short only less beguilingly than Frank Saltram talked to *his* electors; with the difference to our credit, however, that we had already voted and that our candidate had no antagonist but himself. He had more than once been at Wimbledon—it was Mrs. Mulville's work, not mine—and by the time the claret was served had seen the god descend. He took more pains to swing his censer than I had expected, but on our way back to town he forestalled any little triumph I might have been so artless as to express by the observation that such a man was—a hundred times!—a man to use and never a man to be used by. I remember that this neat remark humiliated me almost as much as if virtually, in the fever of broken slumbers, I hadn't often made it myself. The difference was that on Gravener's part a force attached to it that could never attach to it on mine. He was *able* to use people—he had the machinery; and the irony of Saltram's being made showy at Clockborough came out to me when he said, as if he had no memory of our original talk and the idea were quite fresh to him:

"I hate his type, you know, but I'll be hanged if I don't put some of those things in. I can find a place for them: we might even find a place for the fellow himself." I myself should have had some fear—not, I need scarcely say, for the "things" themselves, but for some other things very near them; in fine for the rest of my eloquence.

Later on I could see that the oracle of Wimbledon was not in this case so appropriate as he would have been had the politics of the gods only coincided more exactly with those of the party. There was a distinct moment when, without saying anything more distinct to me, Gravener entertained the idea of annexing Mr. Saltram. Such a project was delusive, for the discovery of analogies between his body of doctrine and that pressed from headquarters upon Clockborough— the bottling, in a word, of the air of those lungs for convenient public uncorking in corn-exchanges—was an experiment for which no one had the leisure. The only thing would have been to carry him massively about, paid, caged, clipped; to turn him on for a particular occasion in a particular channel. Frank Saltram's channel, however, was essentially not calculable, and there was no knowing what disastrous floods might have ensued. For what there would have been to do *The Empire*, the great newspaper, was there to look to; but it was no new misfortune that there were delicate situations in which *The Empire* broke down. In fine there was an instinctive apprehension that a clever young journalist commissioned to report on Mr. Saltram might never come back from the errand. No one knew better than George Gravener that that was a time when prompt returns counted double. If he therefore found our friend an exasperating waste of orthodoxy it was because of his being, as he said, poor Gravener, up in the clouds, not because he was down in the dust. The man would have been, just as he was, a real enough gentleman if he could have helped to put in a real gentleman. Gravener's great objection to the actual member was that he was not one.

Lady Coxon had a fine old house, a house with "grounds," at Clockborough, which she had let; but after she returned from abroad I learned from Mrs. Saltram that the lease had fallen in and that she had gone down to resume possession. I could see the faded red livery, the big square shoulders, the high-walled garden of this decent abode. As the rumble of dissolution grew louder the suitor would have pressed his suit, and I found myself hoping the politics of the late Mayor's widow wouldn't be such as to admonish her to ask him to dinner; perhaps indeed, I went so far as to pray, they would naturally form a bar to any contact. I tried to focus the many-buttoned page, in the daily airing, as he perhaps even pushed the Bath-chair over somebody's toes. I was destined to hear, none the less, through Mrs. Saltram—who, I afterwards learned, was in correspondence with Lady Coxon's house-keeper—that Gravener was known to have spoken of the habitation I had in my eye as the pleasantest thing at Clockborough. On his part, I was sure, this was the voice not of envy but of experience. The vivid scene was now peopled, and I could see him in the old-time garden with Miss Anvoy, who would be certain, and very justly, to think him good-looking. It would be too much to describe myself as troubled by this play of surmise; but I seem to remember the relief, singular enough, of feeling it suddenly brushed away by an annoyance really much greater; an annoyance the result of its happening to come over me about that time with a rush that I was simply ashamed of Frank Saltram. There were limits after all, and my mark at last had been reached.

I had had my disgusts, if I may allow myself to-day such an expression; but this was a supreme revolt. Certain things cleared up in my mind, certain values stood out. It was all very well to have an unfortunate temperament; there was nothing so unfortunate as to have, for practical purposes, nothing else. I avoided George Gravener at this moment and reflected that at such a time I should do so most effectually by leaving England. I wanted to forget Frank Saltram—that was all. I didn't want to do anything in the world to him but that. Indignation had withered on the stalk, and I felt that one could pity him as much as one ought only by never thinking of him again. It wasn't for anything he had done to me; it was for what he had done to the Mulvilles. Adelaide cried about it for a week, and her husband, profiting by the example so signally given him of the fatal effect of a want of character, left the letter, the drop too much, unanswered. The letter, an incredible one, addressed by Saltram to Wimbledon during a stay with the Pudneys at Ramsgate, was the central feature of the incident, which, however, had many features, each more painful than whichever other we com-pared it with. The Pudneys had behaved shockingly, but that was no excuse. Base ingratitude, gross indecency—one had one's choice only of such formulas as that the more they fitted the less they gave one rest. These are dead aches now, and I am under no obligation, thank heaven, to be definite about the business. There are things which if I had had to tell them—well, would have stopped me off here altogether.

I went abroad for the general election, and if I don't know how much, on the Continent, I forgot, I at least know how much I missed, him. At a distance, in a foreign land, ignoring, abjuring, unlearning him, I discovered what he had done for me. I owed him, oh unmistakably, certain noble conceptions ; I had lighted my little taper at his smoky lamp, and lo it continued to twinkle. But the light it gave me just showed me how much more I wanted. I was pursued of course by letters from Mrs. Saltram which I didn't scruple not to read, though quite aware her embarrassments couldn't but be now of the gravest. I sacrificed to propriety by simply putting them away, and this is how, one day as my absence drew to an end, my eye, while I rummaged in my desk for another paper, was caught by a name on a leaf that had detached itself from the packet. The allusion was to Miss Anvoy, who, it appeared, was engaged to be married to Mr. George Gravener ; and the news was two months old. A direct question of Mrs. Saltram's had thus remained unanswered—she had inquired of me in a post-script what sort of man this aspirant to such a hand might be. The great other fact about him just then was that he had been triumphantly returned for Clockborough in the interest of the party that had swept the country—so that I might easily have referred Mrs. Saltram to the journals of the day. Yet when I at last wrote her that I was coming home and would discharge my accumulated burden by seeing her, I but remarked in regard to her question that she must really put it to Miss Anvoy.

VI

I HAD ALMOST avoided the general election, but some of its consequences, on my return, had smartly to be faced. The season, in London, began to breathe again and to flap its folded wings. Confidence, under the new Ministry, was understood to be reviving, and one of the symptoms, in a social body, was a recovery of appetite. People once more fed together, and it happened that, one Sunday night, at somebody's house, I fed with George Gravener. When the ladies left the room I moved up to where he sat and begged to congratulate him. "On my election?" he asked after a moment; so that I could feign, jocosely, not to have heard of that triumph and to be alluding to the rumour of a victory still more personal. I daresay I coloured, however, for his political success had momentarily passed out of my mind. What was present to it was that he was to marry that beautiful girl; and yet his question made me conscious of some discomposure. I hadn't intended to put this before everything. He himself indeed ought gracefully to have done so, and I remember thinking the whole man was in this assumption that in expressing my sense of what he had won I had fixed my thoughts on his "seat." We straightened the matter out, and he was so much lighter in hand than I had lately seen him that his spirits might well have been fed from a twofold source. He was so good as to say that he hoped I should soon make the acquaintance of Miss Anvoy, who, with her aunt, was presently coming up to town. Lady Coxon, in the country, had been seriously unwell, and this had delayed their arrival. I told him I had heard the marriage would be a splendid one; on which, brightened and humanised by his luck, he laughed and said "Do you mean for *her*?" When I had again explained what I meant he went on: "Oh she's an American, but you'd scarcely know it; unless perhaps," he added, "by her being used to more money than most girls in England, even the daughters of rich men. That wouldn't in the least do for a fellow like me, you know, if it wasn't for the great liberality of her father. He really has been most kind, and everything's quite satisfactory." He added that his eldest brother had taken a tremendous fancy to her and that during a recent visit at Coldfield she had nearly won over Lady Maddock. I gathered from something he dropped later on that the free-handed gentleman beyond the seas had not made a settlement, but had given a handsome present and was apparently to be looked to, across the water, for other favours. People are simplified alike by great contentments and great yearnings, and, whether or no it was Gravener's directness that begot my own, I seem to recall that in some turn taken by our talk he almost imposed it on me as an act of decorum to ask if Miss Anvoy had also by chance expectations from her aunt. My question drew out that Lady Coxon, who was the oddest of women, would have in any contingency to act under her late husband's will, which was odder still, saddling her with a mass of queer obligations complicated with queer loopholes. There were several dreary people, Coxon cousins, old maids to whom she would have more or less to minister. Gravener laughed, without saying no, when I suggested that the young lady might come in through a loophole; then suddenly, as if he suspected my turning a lantern on him, he declared quite dryly: "That's all rot—one's moved by other springs!"

A fortnight later, at Lady Coxon's own house, I understood well enough the springs one was moved by. Gravener had spoken of me there as an old friend, and I received a gracious invitation to dine. The Knight's widow was again indisposed—she had succumbed at the eleventh hour; so that I found Miss Anvoy bravely playing hostess without even Gravener's help, since, to make matters worse, he had just sent up word that the House, the insatiable House, with which he supposed he had contracted for easier terms, positively declined to release him. I was struck with the courage, the grace and gaiety of the young lady left thus to handle the fauna and flora of the Regent's Park. I did what I could to help her to classify them, after I had recovered from the confusion of seeing her slightly disconcerted at perceiving in the guest introduced by her intended the gentleman with whom she had had that talk about Frank Saltram. I had at this moment my first glimpse of the fact that she was a person who could carry a responsibility; but I leave the reader to judge of my sense of the aggravation, for either of us, of such a burden, when I heard the servant announce Mrs. Saltram. From what immediately passed between the two ladies I gathered that the latter had been sent for post-haste to fill the gap created by the absence of the mistress of the house. "Good!" I remember crying, "she'll be put by *me*"; and my apprehension was promptly justified. Mrs. Saltram taken in to dinner, and taken in as a consequence of an appeal to her amiability, was Mrs. Saltram with a vengeance. I asked myself what Miss Anvoy meant by doing such things, but the only answer I arrived at was that Gravener was verily fortunate. She hadn't happened to tell him of her visit to Upper Baker Street, but she'd certainly tell him to-morrow; not indeed that this would make him like any better her having had the innocence to invite such a person as Mrs. Saltram on such an occasion. It could only strike me that I had never seen a young woman put such ignorance into her cleverness, such freedom into her modesty; this, I think, was when, after dinner, she said to me frankly, with almost jubilant mirth: "Oh you don't admire Mrs. Saltram?" Why should I? This was truly a young person without guile. I had briefly to consider before I could reply that my objection to the lady named was the objection often uttered about people met at the social board—I knew all her stories. Then as Miss Anvoy remained momentarily vague I added: "Those about her husband."

"Oh yes, but there are some new ones."

"None for me. Ah, novelty would be pleasant!"

"Doesn't it appear that of late he has been particularly horrid?"

"His fluctuations don't matter," I returned, "for at night all cats are grey. You saw the shade of this one the night we waited for him together. What will you have? He has no dignity."

Miss Anvoy, who had been introducing with her American distinctness, looked encouragingly round at some of the combinations she had risked. "It's too bad I can't see him."

"You mean Gravener won't let you?"

"I haven't asked him. He lets me do everything."

"But you know he knows him and wonders what some of us see in him."

"We haven't happened to talk of him," the girl said.

"Get him to take you some day out to see the Mulvilles."

"I thought Mr. Saltram had thrown the Mulvilles over."

"Utterly. But that won't prevent his being planted there again, to bloom like a rose, within a month or two."

Miss Anvoy thought a moment. Then, "I should like to see them," she said, with her fostering smile.

"They're tremendously worth it. You mustn't miss them."

"I'll make George take me," she went on as Mrs. Saltram came up to interrupt us. She smiled at this unfortunate as kindly as she had smiled at me and, addressing the question to her, continued: "But the chance of a lecture—one of the wonderful lectures? Isn't there another course announced?"

"Another? There are about thirty!" I exclaimed, turning away and feeling Mrs. Saltram's little eyes in my back. A few days after this I heard that Gravener's marriage was near at hand—was settled for Whitsuntide; but as no invitation had reached me I had my doubts, and there presently came to me in fact the report of a postponement. Something was the matter; what was the matter was supposed to be that Lady Coxon was now critically ill. I had called on her after my dinner in the Regent's Park, but I had neither seen her nor seen Miss Anvoy. I forget to-day the exact order in which, at this period, sundry incidents occurred and the particular stage at which it suddenly struck me, making me catch my breath a little, that the progression, the acceleration, was for all the world that of fine drama. This was probably rather late in the day, and the exact order doesn't signify. What had already occurred was some accident determining a more patient wait. George Gravener, whom I met again, in fact told me as much, but without signs of perturbation. Lady Coxon had to be constantly attended to, and there were other good reasons as well. Lady Coxon had to be so constantly attended to that on the occasion of a second attempt in the Regent's Park I equally failed to obtain a sight of her niece. I judged it discreet in all the conditions not to make a third; but this didn't matter, for it was through Adelaide Mulville that the side-wind of the comedy, though I was at first unwitting, began to reach me. I went to Wimbledon at times because Saltram was there, and I went at others because he wasn't. The Pudneys, who had taken him to Birmingham, had already got rid of him, and we had a horrible consciousness of his wandering roofless, in dishonour, about the smoky Midlands, almost as the injured Lear wandered on the storm-lashed heath. His room, upstairs, had been lately done up (I could hear the crackle of the new chintz) and the difference only made his smirches and bruises, his splendid tainted genius, the more tragic. If he wasn't barefoot in the mire he was sure to be unconventionally shod. These were the things Adelaide and I, who were old enough friends to stare at each other in silence, talked about when we didn't speak. When we spoke it was only about the brilliant girl George Gravener was to marry and whom he had brought out the other Sunday. I could see that this presentation had been happy, for Mrs. Mulville commemorated it after her sole fashion of showing confidence in a new relation. "She likes me—she likes me": her native humility exulted in that measure of success. We all knew for ourselves how she liked those who liked her, and as regards Ruth Anvoy she was more easily won over than Lady Maddock.

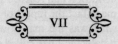

VII

ONE OF the consequences, for the Mulvilles, of the sacrifices they made for Frank Saltram was that they had to give up their carriage. Adelaide drove gently into London in a one-horse greenish thing, an early Victorian landau, hired, near at hand, imaginatively, from a broken-down jobmaster whose wife was in consumption—a vehicle that made people turn round all the more when her pensioner sat beside her in a soft white hat and a shawl, one of the dear woman's own. This was his position and I daresay his costume when on an afternoon in July she went to return Miss Anvoy's visit. The wheel of fate had now revolved, and amid silences deep and exhaustive, compunctions and condonations alike unutterable, Saltram was reinstated. Was it in pride or in penance that Mrs. Mulville had begun immediately to drive him about ? If he was ashamed of his ingratitude she might have been ashamed of her forgiveness; but she was incorrigibly capable of liking him to be conspicuous in the landau while she was in shops or with her acquaintance. However, if he was in the pillory for twenty minutes in the Regent's Park—I mean at Lady Coxon's door while his companion paid her call—it wasn't to the further humiliation of any one concerned that she presently came out for him in person, nor even to show either of them what a fool she was that she drew him in to be introduced to the bright young American. Her account of the introduction I had in its order, but before that, very late in the season, under Gravener's auspices, I met Miss Anvoy at tea at the House of Commons. The member for Clockborough had gathered a group of pretty ladies, and the Mulvilles were not of the party. On the great terrace, as I strolled off with her a little, the guest of honour immediately exclaimed to me : "I've seen him, you know—I've seen him !" She told me about Saltram's call.

"And how did you find him ?"

"Oh so strange !"

"You didn't like him ?"

"I can't tell till I see him again."

"You want to do that ?"

She had a pause. "Immensely."

We went no further; I fancied she had become aware Gravener was looking at us. She turned back toward the knot of the others, and I said : "Dislike him as much as you will—I see you're bitten."

"Bitten ?" I thought she coloured a little.

"Oh, it doesn't matter !" I laughed; "one doesn't die of it."

"I hope I shan't die of anything before I've seen more of Mrs. Mulville." I rejoiced with her over plain Adelaide, whom she pronounced the loveliest woman she had met in England; but before we separated I remarked to her that it was an act of mere humanity to warn her that if she should see more of Frank Saltram—which would be likely to follow on any increase of acquaintance with Mrs. Mulville —she might find herself flattening her nose against the clear hard pane of an eternal question—that of the relative, that of the opposed, importances of virtue and brains. She replied that this was surely a subject on which one took everything for granted; whereupon I admitted that I had perhaps expressed myself ill. What I referred to was that I had referred to the night we met in Upper Baker Street—the relative importance (relative to virtue) of other gifts. She asked me if I called virtue a gift—a thing handed to us in a parcel on our first birthday; and I declared that this very inquiry proved to me the problem had already caught her by the skirt. She would have help however, the same help I myself had once had, in resisting its tendency to make one cross.

"What help do you mean?"

"That of the member for Clockborough."

She stared, smiled, then returned: "Why my idea has been to help *him* !"

She *had* helped him—I had his own word for it that at Clockborough her bedevilment of the voters had really put him in. She would do so doubtless again and again, though I heard the very next month that this fine faculty had undergone a temporary eclipse. News of the catastrophe first came to me from Mrs. Saltram, and it was afterwards confirmed at Wimbledon: poor Miss Anvoy was in trouble—great disasters in America had suddenly summoned her home. Her father, in New York, had suffered reverses, lost so much money that it was really vexatious as showing how much he had had. It was Adelaide who told me she had gone off alone at less than a week's notice.

"Alone? Gravener has permitted that?"

"What will you have? The House of Commons !"

I'm afraid I cursed the House of Commons: I was so much interested. Of course he'd follow her as soon as he was free to make her his wife; only she mightn't now be able to bring him anything like the marriage-portion of which he had begun by having the virtual promise. Mrs. Mulville let me know what was already said: she was charming, this American girl, but really those American fathers—— ! What was a man to do? Mr. Saltram, according to Mrs. Mulville, was of opinion that a man was never to suffer his relation to money to become a spiritual relation—he was to keep it exclusively material. "*Moi pas comprendre !*" I commented on this; in rejoinder to which Adelaide, with her beautiful sympathy, explained that she supposed he simply meant that the thing was to use it, don't you know? but not to think too much about it. "To take it, but not to thank you for it ?" I still more profanely inquired. For a quarter of an hour afterwards she wouldn't look at me, but this didn't prevent my asking her what had been the result, that afternoon in the Regent's Park, of her taking our friend to see Miss Anvoy.

"Oh so charming!" she answered, brightening. "He said he recognised in her a nature he could absolutely trust."

"Yes, but I'm speaking of the effect on herself."

Mrs. Mulville had to remount the stream. "It was everything one could wish."

Something in her tone made me laugh. "Do you mean she gave him—a dole?"

"Well, since you ask me!"

"Right there on the spot?"

Again poor Adelaide faltered. "It was to me of course she gave it."

I stared; somehow I couldn't see the scene. "Do you mean a sum of money?"

"It was very handsome." Now at last she met my eyes, though I could see it was with an effort. "Thirty pounds."

"Straight out of her pocket?"

"Out of the drawer of a table at which she had been writing. She just slipped the folded notes into my hand. He wasn't looking; it was while he was going back to the carriage. Oh," said Adelaide reassuringly, "I take care of it for him!" The dear practical soul thought my agitation, for I confess I was agitated, referred to the employment of the money. Her disclosure made me for a moment muse violently, and I daresay that during that moment I wondered if anything else in the world makes people so gross as unselfishness. I uttered, I suppose, some vague, synthetic cry, for she went on as if she had had a glimpse of my inward amaze at such passages. "I assure you, my dear friend, he was in one of his happy hours."

But I wasn't thinking of that. "Truly indeed these Americans!" I said. "With her father in the very act, as it were, of swindling her betrothed!"

Mrs. Mulville stared. "Oh I suppose Mr. Anvoy has scarcely gone bankrupt—or whatever he has done—on purpose. Very likely they won't be able to keep it up, but there it was, and it was a very beautiful impulse."

"You say Saltram was very fine?"

"Beyond everything. He surprised even me."

"And I know what *you've* enjoyed." After a moment I added: "Had he peradventure caught a glimpse of the money in the table-drawer?"

At this my companion honestly flushed. "How can you be so cruel when you know how little he calculates?"

"Forgive me, I do know it. But you tell me things that act on my nerves. I'm sure he hadn't caught a glimpse of anything but some splendid idea."

Mrs. Mulville brightly concurred. "And perhaps even of her beautiful listening face."

"Perhaps even! And what was it all about?"

"His talk? It was apropos of her engagement, which I had told him about: the idea of marriage, the philosophy, the poetry, the sublimity of it." It was impossible wholly to restrain one's mirth at this, and some rude ripple that I emitted again caused my companion to admonish me. "It sounds a little stale, but you know his freshness."

"Of illustration? Indeed I do!"

"And how he has always been right on that great question."

"On what great question, dear lady, hasn't he been right?"

"Of what other great men can you equally say it?—and that he has never, but *never*, had a deflexion?" Mrs. Mulville exultantly demanded.

I tried to think of some other great man, but I had to give it up. "Didn't Miss Anvoy express her satisfaction in any less diffident way than by her charming present?" I was reduced to asking instead.

"Oh yes, she overflowed to me on the steps while he was getting into the carriage." These words somehow brushed up a picture of Saltram's big shawled back as he hoisted himself into the green landau. "She said she wasn't disappointed," Adelaide pursued.

I turned it over. "Did he wear his shawl?"

"His shawl?" She hadn't even noticed.

"I mean yours."

"He looked very nice, and you know he's really clean. Miss Anvoy used such a remarkable expression—she said his mind's like a crystal!"

I pricked up my ears. "A crystal?"

"Suspended in the moral world—swinging and shining and flashing there. She's monstrously clever, you know."

I thought again. "Monstrously!"

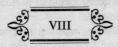

VIII

GEORGE GRAVENER didn't follow her, for late in September, after the House had risen, I met him in a railway-carriage. He was coming up from Scotland and I had just quitted some relations who lived near Durham. The current of travel back to London wasn't yet strong; at any rate on entering the compartment I found he had had it for some time to himself. We fared in company, and though he had a blue-book in his lap and the open jaws of his bag threatened me with the white teeth of confused papers, we inevitably, we even at last sociably conversed. I saw things weren't well with him, but I asked no question till something dropped by himself made, as it had made on another occasion, an absence of curiosity invidious. He mentioned that he was worried about his good old friend Lady Coxon, who, with her niece likely to be detained some time in America, lay seriously ill at Clockborough, much on his mind and on his hands.

"Ah, Miss Anvoy's in America?"

"Her father has got into horrid straits—has lost no end of money."

I waited, after expressing due concern, but I eventually said: "I hope that raises no objection to your marriage."

"None whatever; moreover it's my trade to meet objections. But it may create tiresome delays, of which there have been too many, from various causes, already. Lady Coxon got very bad, then she got much better. Then Mr. Anvoy suddenly began to totter, and now he seems quite on his back. I'm afraid he's really in for some big reverse. Lady Coxon's worse again, awfully upset by the news from America, and she sends me word that she *must* have Ruth. How can I supply her with Ruth? I haven't got Ruth myself!"

"Surely you haven't lost her?" I returned.

"She's everything to her wretched father. She writes me every post —telling me to smooth her aunt's pillow. I've other things to smooth; but the old lady, save for her servants, is really alone. She won't receive her Coxon relations—she's angry at so much of her money going to them. Besides, she's hopelessly mad," said Gravener very frankly.

I don't remember whether it was this, or what it was, that made me ask if she hadn't such an appreciation of Mrs. Saltram as might render that active person of some use.

He gave me a cold glance, wanting to know what had put Mrs. Saltram into my head, and I replied that she was unfortunately never out of it. I happened to remember the wonderful accounts she had given me of the kindness Lady Coxon had shown her. Gravener declared this to be false; Lady Coxon, who didn't care for her, hadn't seen her three times. The only foundation for it was that Miss Anvoy, who used, poor girl, to chuck money about in a manner she must now regret, had for an hour seen in the miserable woman—you could never know what she'd see in people—an interesting pretext for the liberality with which her nature overflowed. But even Miss Anvoy was now quite tired of her. Gravener told me more about the crash in New York and the annoyance it had been to him, and we also glanced here and there in other directions; but by the time we got to Doncaster the principal thing he had let me see was that he was keeping something back. We stopped at that station, and, at the carriage-door, some one made a movement to get in. Gravener uttered a sound of impatience, and I felt sure that but for this I should have had the secret. Then the intruder, for some reason, spared us his company; we started afresh, and my hope of a disclosure returned. My companion held his tongue, however, and I pretended to go to sleep; in fact I really dozed for discouragement. When I reopened my eyes he was looking at me with an injured air. He tossed away with some vivacity the remnant of a cigarette and then said: "If you're not too sleepy I want to put you a case." I answered that I'd make every effort to attend, and welcomed the note of interest when he went on: "As I told you a while ago, Lady Coxon, poor dear, is demented." His tone had much behind it —was full of promise. I asked if her ladyship's misfortune were a trait of her malady or only of her character, and he pronounced it a product of both. The case he wanted to put to me was a matter on which it concerned him to have the impression—the judgement, he might also say—of another person. "I mean of the average intelligent man, but you see I take what I can get." There would be the technical, the strictly legal view; then there would be the way the question would strike a man of the world. He had lighted another cigarette while he talked, and I saw he was glad to have it to handle when he brought out at last, with a laugh slightly artificial: "In fact it's a subject on which Miss Anvoy and I are pulling different ways."

"And you want me to decide between you? I decide in advance for Miss Anvoy."

"In advance—that's quite right. That's how I decided when I proposed to her. But my story will interest you only so far as your mind isn't made up." Gravener puffed his cigarette a minute and then continued: "Are you familiar with the idea of the Endowment of Research?"

"Of Research?" I was at sea a moment.

"I give you Lady Coxon's phrase. She has it on the brain."

"She wishes to endow——?"

"Some earnest and 'loyal' seeker," Gravener said. "It was a sketchy design of her late husband's, and he handed it on to her; setting apart in his will a sum of money of which she was to enjoy the interest for life, but of which, should she eventually see her opportunity—the matter was left largely to her discretion—she would best honour his memory by determining the exemplary public use. This sum of money, no less than thirteen thousand pounds, was to be called the Coxon Fund; and poor Sir Gregory evidently proposed to himself that the Coxon Fund should cover his name with glory—be universally desired and admired. He left his wife a full declaration of his views, so far at least as that term may be applied to views vitiated by a vagueness really infantine. A little learning's a dangerous thing, and a good citizen who happens to have been an ass is worse for a community than bad sewerage. He's worst of all when he's dead, because then he can't be stopped. However, such as they were, the poor man's aspirations are now in his wife's bosom, or fermenting rather in her foolish brain: it lies with her to carry them out. But of course she must first catch her hare."

"Her earnest loyal seeker?"

"The flower that blushes unseen for want of such a pecuniary independence as may aid the light that's in it to shine upon the human race. The individual, in a word, who, having the rest of the machinery, the spiritual, the intellectual, is most hampered in his search."

"His search for what?"

"For Moral Truth. That's what Sir Gregory calls it."

I burst out laughing. "Delightful munificent Sir Gregory! It's a charming idea."

"So Miss Anvoy thinks."

"Has she a candidate for the Fund?"

215

"Not that I know of—and she's perfectly reasonable about it. But Lady Coxon has put the matter before her, and we've naturally had a lot of talk."

"Talk that, as you've so interestingly intimated, has landed you in a disagreement."

"She considers there's something in it," Gravener said.

"And you consider there's nothing?"

"It seems to me a piece of solemn twaddle—which can't fail to be attended with consequences certainly grotesque and possibly immoral. To begin with, fancy constituting an endowment without establishing a tribunal—a bench of competent people, of judges."

"The sole tribunal is Lady Coxon?"

"And any one she chooses to invite."

"But she has invited you," I noted.

"I'm not competent—I hate the thing. Besides, she hasn't," my friend went on. "The real history of the matter, I take it, is that the inspiration was originally Lady Coxon's own, that she infected him with it, and that the flattering option left her is simply his tribute to her beautiful, her aboriginal enthusiasm. She came to England forty years ago, a thin transcendental Bostonian, and even her odd happy frumpy Clockborough marriage never really materialised her. She feels indeed that she has become very British—as if that, as a process, as a *Werden*, as anything but an original sign of grace, were conceivable; but it's precisely what makes her cling to the notion of the 'Fund'—cling to it as to a link with the ideal."

"How can she cling if she's dying?"

"Do you mean how can she act in the matter?" Gravener asked. "That's precisely the question. She can't ! As she has never yet caught her hare, never spied out her lucky impostor—how should she, with the life she has led ?—her husband's intention has come very near lapsing. His idea, to do him justice, was that it *should* lapse if exactly the right person, the perfect mixture of genius and chill penury, should fail to turn up. Ah the poor dear woman's very particular—she says there must be no mistake."

I found all this quite thrilling—I took it in with avidity. "And if she dies without doing anything, what becomes of the money?" I demanded.

"It goes back to his family, if she hasn't made some other disposition of it."

"She may do that then—she may divert it ?"

"Her hands are not tied. She has a grand discretion. The proof is that three months ago she offered to make the proceeds over to her niece."

"For Miss Anvoy's own use?"

"For Miss Anvoy's own use—on the occasion of her prospective marriage. She was discouraged—the earnest seeker required so earnest a search. She was afraid of making a mistake; every one she could think of seemed either not earnest enough or not poor enough. On the receipt of the first bad news about Mr. Anvoy's affairs she proposed to Ruth to make the sacrifice for her. As the situation in New York got worse she repeated her proposal."

"Which Miss Anvoy declined?"

"Except as a formal trust."

"You mean except as committing herself legally to place the money?"

"On the head of the deserving object, the great man frustrated," Gravener said. "She only consents to act in the spirit of Sir Gregory's scheme."

"And you blame her for that?" I asked with some intensity.

My tone couldn't have been harsh, but he coloured a little and there was a queer light in his eye. "My dear fellow, if I 'blamed' the young lady I'm engaged to I shouldn't immediately say it even to so old a friend as you." I saw that some deep discomfort, some restless desire to be sided with, reassuringly, approvingly mirrored, had been at the bottom of his drifting so far, and I was genuinely touched by his confidence. It was inconsistent with his habits; but being troubled about a woman was not, for him, a habit: that itself was an inconsistency. George Gravener could stand straight enough before any other combination of forces. It amused me to think that the combination he had succumbed to had an American accent, a transcendental aunt and an insolvent father; but all my old loyalty to him mustered to meet this unexpected hint that I could help him. I saw that I could from the insincere tone in which he pursued: "I've criticised her of course, I've contended with her, and it has been great fun." Yet it clearly couldn't have been such great fun as to make it improper for me presently to ask if Miss Anvoy had nothing at all settled on herself. To this he replied that she had only a trifle from her mother—a mere four hundred a year, which was exactly why it would be convenient to him that she shouldn't decline, in the face of this total change in her prospects, an accession of income which would distinctly help them to marry. When I inquired if there were no other

way in which so rich and so affectionate an aunt could cause the
weight of her benevolence to be felt, he answered that Lady Coxon
was affectionate indeed, but was scarcely to be called rich. She could
let her project of the Fund lapse for her niece's benefit, but she couldn't
do anything else. She had been accustomed to regard her as tremendously provided for, and she was up to her eyes in promises to anxious
Coxons. She was a woman of an inordinate conscience, and her
conscience was now a distress to her, hovering round her bed in irre-
concilable forms of resentful husbands, portionless nieces and undiscoverable philosophers.

We were by this time getting into the whirr of fleeting platforms, the
multiplication of lights. "I think you'll find," I said with a laugh,
"that your predicament will disappear in the very fact that the philosopher *is* undiscoverable."

He began to gather up his papers. "Who can set a limit to the
ingenuity of an extravagant woman?"

"Yes, after all, who indeed?" I echoed as I recalled the extravagance
commemorated in Adelaide's anecdote of Miss Anvoy and the thirty
pounds.

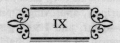

IX

THE THING I had been most sensible of in that talk with George Gravener was the way Saltram's name kept out of it. It seemed to me at
the time that we were quite pointedly silent about him; but afterwards
it appeared more probable there had been on my companion's part
no conscious avoidance. Later on I was sure of this, and for the best
of reasons—the simple reason of my perceiving more completely that,
for evil as well as for good, he said nothing to Gravener's imagination.
That honest man didn't fear him—he was too much disgusted with him.
No more did I, doubtless, and for very much the same reason. I treated
my friend's story as an absolute confidence; but when before Christmas,
by Mrs. Saltram, I was informed of Lady Coxon's death without
having had news of Miss Anvoy's return, I found myself taking for
granted we should hear no more of these nuptials, in which, as obscurely
unnatural, I now saw I had never *too* disconcertedly believed. I began

to ask myself how people who suited each other so little could please each other so much. The charm was some material charm, some affinity, exquisite doubtless, yet superficial; some surrender to youth and beauty and passion, to force and grace and fortune, happy accidents and easy contacts. They might dote on each other's persons, but how could they know each other's souls? How could they have the same prejudices, how could they have the same horizon? Such questions, I confess, seemed quenched but not answered when, one day in February, going out to Wimbledon, I found our young lady in the house. A passion that had brought her back across the wintry ocean was as much of a passion as was needed. No impulse equally strong indeed had drawn George Gravener to America; a circumstance on which, however, I reflected only long enough to remind myself that it was none of my business. Ruth Anvoy was distinctly different, and I felt that the difference was not simply that of her marks of mourning. Mrs. Mulville told me soon enough what it was: it was the difference between a handsome girl with large expectations and a handsome girl with only four hundred a year. This explanation indeed didn't wholly content me, not even when I learned that her mourning had a double cause— learned that poor Mr. Anvoy, giving way altogether, buried under the ruins of his fortune and leaving next to nothing, had died a few weeks before.

"So she has come out to marry George Gravener?" I commented. "Wouldn't it have been prettier of him to have saved her the trouble?"

"Hasn't the House just met?" Adelaide replied. "And for Mr. Gravener the House——!" Then she added: "I gather that her having come is exactly a sign that the marriage is a little shaky. If it were quite all right a self-respecting girl like Ruth would have waited for him over there."

I noted that they were already Ruth and Adelaide, but what I said was: "Do you mean she'll have had to return to *make* it so?"

"No, I mean that she must have come out for some reason independent of it." Adelaide could only surmise, however, as yet, and there was more, as we found, to be revealed. Mrs. Mulville, on hearing of her arrival, had brought the young lady out in the green landau for the Sunday. The Coxons were in possession of the house in Regent's Park and Miss Anvoy was in dreary lodgings. George Gravener had been with her when Adelaide called, but had assented graciously enough to the little visit at Wimbledon. The carriage, with Mr. Saltram in it but not mentioned, had been sent off on some errand from which it was to return and pick the ladies up. Gravener had left them together, and at the end of an hour, on the Saturday afternoon, the party of three had driven out to Wimbledon. This was the girl's second glimpse of our great man, and I was interested in asking Mrs. Mulville if the impression made by the first appeared to have been confirmed. On her replying, after consideration, that of course with time and opportunity it couldn't fail to be, but that she was disappointed, I was sufficiently struck with her use of this last word to question her further.

"Do you mean you're disappointed because you judge Miss Anvoy to be?"

"Yes; I hoped for a greater effect last evening. We had two or three people, but he scarcely opened his mouth."

"He'll be all the better to-night," I opined after a moment. Then I pursued: "What particular importance do you attach to the idea of her being impressed?"

Adelaide turned her mild pale eyes on me as for rebuke of my levity. "Why the importance of her being as happy as *we* are!"

I'm afraid that at this my levity grew. "Oh that's a happiness almost too great to wish a person!" I saw she hadn't yet in her mind what I had in mine, and at any rate the visitor's actual bliss was limited to a walk in the garden with Kent Mulville. Later in the afternoon I also took one, and I saw nothing of Miss Anvoy till dinner, at which we failed of the company of Saltram, who had caused it to be reported that he was indisposed and lying down. This made us, most of us— for there were other friends present—convey to each other in silence some of the unutterable things that in those years our eyes had inevitably acquired the art of expressing. If a fine little American inquirer hadn't been there we would have expressed them otherwise, and Adelaide would have pretended not to hear. I had seen her, before the very fact, abstract herself nobly; and I knew that more than once, to keep it from the servants, managing, dissimulating cleverly, she had helped her husband to carry him bodily to his room. Just recently he had been so wise and so deep and so high that I had begun to get nervous—to wonder if by chance there were something behind it, if he were kept straight for instance by the knowledge that the hated Pudneys would have more to tell us if they chose. He was lying low, but unfortunately it was common wisdom with us in this connexion that the biggest splashes took place in the quietest pools. We should have had a merry life indeed if all the splashes had sprinkled us as refreshingly as the waters we were even then to feel about our ears. Kent Mulville had been up to his room, but had come back with a face that told as few tales as I had seen it succeed in telling on the evening I waited in the lecture-room with Miss Anvoy. I said to myself that our friend had gone out, but it was a comfort that the presence of a comparative stranger deprived us of the dreary duty of suggesting to each other, in respect of his errand, edifying possibilities in which we didn't ourselves believe. At ten o'clock he came into the drawing-room with his waistcoat much awry but his eyes sending out great signals. It was precisely with his entrance that I ceased to be vividly conscious of him. I saw that the crystal, as I had called it, had begun to swing, and I had need of my immediate attention for Miss Anvoy.

Even when I was told afterwards that he had, as we might have said to-day, broken the record, the manner in which that attention had been rewarded relieved me of a sense of loss. I had of course a perfect general consciousness that something great was going on: it was a little like having been etherised to hear Herr Joachim play. The old music was in the air; I felt the strong pulse of thought, the sink and swell, the flight, the poise, the plunge; but I knew something about one of the listeners that nobody else knew, and Saltram's monologue could reach me only through that medium. To this hour I'm of no use when, as a witness, I'm appealed to—for they still absurdly contend about it—as to whether or no on that historic night he was drunk; and my position is slightly ridiculous, for I've never cared to tell them what it really was I was taken up with. What I got out of it is the only morsel of the total experience that is quite my own. The others were shared, but this is incommunicable. I feel that now, I'm bound to say, even in thus roughly evoking the occasion, and it takes something from my pride of clearness. However, I shall perhaps be as clear as is absolutely needful if I remark that our young lady was too much given up to her own intensity of observation to be sensible of mine. It was plainly *not* the question of her marriage that had brought her back. I greatly enjoyed this discovery and was sure that had that question alone been involved she would have stirred no step. In this case doubtless Gravener would, in spite of the House of Commons, have found means to rejoin her. It afterwards made me uncomfortable for her that, alone in the lodging Mrs. Mulville had put before me as dreary, she should have in any degree the air of waiting for her fate; so that I was presently relieved at hearing of her having gone to stay at Coldfield. If she was in England at all while the engagement stood the only proper place for her was under Lady Maddock's wing. Now that she was unfortunate and relatively poor, perhaps her prospective sister-in-law would be wholly won over.

There would be much to say, if I had space, about the way her behaviour, as I caught gleams of it, ministered to the image that had taken birth in my mind, to my private amusement, while that other night I listened to George Gravener in the railway-carriage. I watched her in the light of this queer possibility—a formidable thing certainly to meet—and I was aware that it coloured, extravagantly perhaps, my interpretation of her very looks and tones. At Wimbledon for instance it had appeared to me she was literally afraid of Saltram, in dread of a coercion that she had begun already to feel. I had come up to town with her the next day and had been convinced that, though deeply interested, she was immensely on her guard. She would show as little as possible before she should be ready to show everything. What this final exhibition might be on the part of a girl perceptibly so able to think things out I found it great sport to forecast. It would have been exciting to be approached by her, appealed to by her for advice; but I prayed to heaven I mightn't find myself in such a predicament. If there was really a present rigour in the situation of which Gravener had sketched for me the elements, she would have to get out of her difficulty by herself. It wasn't I who had launched her and it wasn't I who could help her. I didn't fail to ask myself why, since I couldn't help her, I should think so much about her. It was in part my suspense that was responsible for this; I waited impatiently to see whether she wouldn't have told Mrs. Mulville a portion at least of what I had learned from Gravener. But I saw Mrs. Mulville was still reduced to wonder what she had come out again for if she hadn't come as a conciliatory bride. That she had come in some other character was the only thing that fitted all the appearances. Having for family reasons to spend some time that spring in the west of England, I was in a manner out of earshot of the great oceanic rumble—I mean of the continuous hum of Saltram's thought—and my uneasiness tended to keep me quiet. There was something I wanted so little to have to say that my prudence surmounted my curiosity. I only wondered if Ruth Anvoy talked over the idea of the Coxon Fund with Lady Maddock, and also somewhat why I didn't hear from Wimbledon. I had a reproachful note about something or other from Mrs. Saltram, but it contained no mention of Lady Coxon's niece, on whom her eyes had been much less fixed since the recent untoward events.

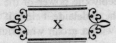

X

Poor Adelaide's silence was fully explained later—practically explained when in June, returning to London, I was honoured by this admirable woman with an early visit. As soon as she arrived I guessed everything, and as soon as she told me that darling Ruth had been in her house nearly a month I had my question ready. "What in the name of maidenly modesty is she staying in England for?"

"Because she loves me so!" cried Adelaide gaily. But she hadn't come to see me only to tell me Miss Anvoy loved her: that was quite sufficiently established, and what was much more to the point was that Mr. Gravener had now raised an objection to it. He had protested at least against her being at Wimbledon, where in the innocence of his heart he had originally brought her himself: he called on her to put an end to their engagement in the only proper, the only happy manner.

"And why in the world doesn't she do so?" I asked.

Adelaide had a pause. "She says you know." Then on my also hesitating she added: "A condition he makes."

"The Coxon Fund?" I panted.

"He has mentioned to her his having told you about it."

"Ah, but so little! Do you mean she has accepted the trust?"

"In the most splendid spirit—as a duty about which there can be no two opinions." To which my friend added: "Of course she's thinking of Mr. Saltram."

I gave a quick cry at this, which, in its violence, made my visitor turn pale. "How very awful!"

"Awful?"

"Why, to have anything to do with such an idea one's self."

"I'm sure *you* needn't!" And Mrs. Mulville tossed her head.

"He isn't good enough!" I went on; to which she opposed a sound almost as contentious as my own had been. This made me, with genuine immediate horror, exclaim: "You haven't influenced her, I hope!" and my emphasis brought back the blood with a rush to poor Adelaide's face. She declared while she blushed—for I had frightened her again—that she had never influenced anybody and that the girl had only seen and heard and judged for herself. *He* had influenced her, if I would, as he did every one who had a soul: that word, as we knew, even expressed feebly the power of the things he said to haunt the mind. How could she, Adelaide, help it if Miss Anvoy's mind was haunted? I demanded with a groan what right a pretty girl engaged to a rising M.P. had to *have* a mind; but the only explanation my bewildered friend could give me was that she was so clever. She regarded Mr. Saltram naturally as a tremendous force for good. She was intelligent enough to understand him and generous enough to admire.

"She's many things enough, but is she, among them, rich enough?" I demanded. "Rich enough, I mean, to sacrifice such a lot of good money?"

"That's for herself to judge. Besides, it's not her own money; she doesn't in the least consider it so."

"And Gravener does, if not *his* own? and that's the whole difficulty?"

"The difficulty that brought her back, yes: she had absolutely to see her poor aunt's solicitor. It's clear that by Lady Coxon's will she may have the money, but it's still clearer to her conscience that the original condition, definite, intensely implied on her uncle's part, is attached to the use of it. She can only take one view of it. It's for the Endowment or it's for nothing."

"The Endowment," I permitted myself to observe, "is a conception superficially sublime, but fundamentally ridiculous."

"Are you repeating Mr. Gravener's words?" Adelaide asked.

"Possibly, though I've not seen him for months. It's simply the way it strikes me too. It's an old wife's tale. Gravener made some reference to the legal aspect, but such an absurdly loose arrangement has *no* legal aspect."

"Ruth doesn't insist on that," said Mrs. Mulville; "and it's, for her, exactly this technical weakness that constitutes the force of the moral obligation."

"Are you repeating *her* words?" I inquired. I forget what else Adelaide said, but she said she was magnificent. I thought of George Gravener confronted with such magnificence as that, and I asked what could have made two such persons ever suppose they understood each other. Mrs. Mulville assured me the girl loved him as such a woman could love and that she suffered as such a woman could suffer. Nevertheless she wanted to see *me*. At this I sprang up with a groan. "Oh I'm so sorry!—when?" Small though her sense of humour, I think

Adelaide laughed at my sequence. We discussed the day, the nearest it would be convenient I should come out; but before she went I asked my visitor how long she had been acquainted with these prodigies.

"For several weeks, but I was pledged to secrecy."

"And that's why you didn't write?"

"I couldn't very well tell you she was with me without telling you that no time had even yet been fixed for her marriage. And I couldn't very well tell you as much as that without telling you what I knew of the reason of it. It was not till a day or two ago," Mrs. Mulville went on, "that she asked me to ask you if you wouldn't come and see her. Then at last she spoke of your knowing about the idea of the Endowment."

I turned this over. "Why on earth does she want to see me?"

"To talk with you, naturally, about Mr. Saltram."

"As a subject for the prize?" This was hugely obvious, and I presently returned: "I think I'll sail to-morrow for Australia."

"Well then—sail!" said Mrs. Mulville, getting up.

But I frivolously continued. "On Thursday at five, we said?" The appointment was made definite and I inquired how, all this time, the unconscious candidate had carried himself.

"In perfection, really, by the happiest of chances: he has positively been a dear. And then, as to what we revere him for, in the most wonderful form. His very highest—pure celestial light. You *won't* do him an ill turn?" Adelaide pleaded at the door.

"What danger can equal for him the danger to which he's exposed from himself?" I asked. "Look out sharp, if he has lately been too prim. He'll presently take a day off, treat us to some exhibition that will make an Endowment a scandal."

"A scandal?" Mrs. Mulville dolorously echoed.

"Is Miss Anvoy prepared for that?"

My visitor, for a moment, screwed her parasol into my carpet. "He grows bigger every day."

"So do you!" I laughed as she went off.

That girl at Wimbledon, on the Thursday afternoon, more than justified my apprehensions. I recognised fully now the cause of the agitation she had produced in me from the first—the faint foreknowledge that there was something very stiff I should have to do for her. I felt more than ever committed to my fate as, standing before her in the big drawing-room where they had tactfully left us to ourselves, I tried with a smile to string together the pearls of lucidity which, from her chair, she successively tossed me. Pale and bright, in her monotonous mourning, she was an image of intelligent purpose, of the passion of duty; but I asked myself whether any girl had ever had so charming an instinct as that which permitted her to laugh out, as for the joy of her difficulty, into the priggish old room. This remarkable young woman could be earnest without being solemn, and at moments when I ought doubtless to have cursed her obstinacy I found myself watching the unstudied play of her eyebrows or the recurrence of a singularly intense whiteness produced by the parting of her lips. These aberrations, I hasten to add, didn't prevent my learning soon enough why she had wished to see me. Her reason for this was as distinct as her beauty: it was to make me explain what I had meant, on the occasion of our first meeting, by Mr. Saltram's want of dignity. It wasn't that she couldn't imagine, but she desired it there from my lips. What she really desired of course was to know whether there was worse about him than what she had found out for herself. She hadn't been a month so much in the house with him without discovering that he wasn't a man of monumental bronze. He was like a jelly *minus* its mould, he had to be embanked; and that was precisely the source of her interest in him and the ground of her project. She put her project boldly before one: there it stood in its preposterous beauty. She was as willing to take the humorous view of it as I could be: the only difference was that for her the humorous view of a thing wasn't necessarily prohibitive, wasn't paralysing.

Moreover she professed that she couldn't discuss with me the primary question—the moral obligation: that was in her own breast. There were things she couldn't go into—injunctions, impressions she had received. They were a part of the closest intimacy of her intercourse with her aunt, they were absolutely clear to her; and on questions of delicacy, the interpretation of a fidelity, of a promise, one had always in the last resort to make up one's mind for one's self. It was the idea of the application to the particular case, such a splendid one at last, that troubled her, and she admitted that it stirred very deep things. She didn't pretend that such a responsibility was a simple matter; if it *had* been she wouldn't have attempted to saddle me with any portion of it. The Mulvilles were sympathy itself, but were they absolutely candid? Could they indeed be, in their position—would it even have been to be desired? Yet, she had sent for me to ask no less than that of me—whether there was anything dreadful kept back. She made no allusion whatever to George Gravener—I thought her silence the only good taste and her gaiety perhaps a part of the very anxiety of that discretion, the effect of a determination that people shouldn't know from herself that her relations with the man she was to marry were strained. All the weight, however, that she left me to throw was a sufficient implication of the weight *he* had thrown in vain. Oh she knew the question of character was immense, and that one couldn't entertain any plan for making merit comfortable without running the gauntlet of that terrible procession of interrogation-points which, like a young ladies' school out for a walk, hooked their uniform noses at the tail of governess Conduct. But were we absolutely to hold that there was never, never, never an exception, never, never, never an occasion for liberal acceptance, for clever charity, for suspended pedantry—for letting one side, in short, outbalance another? When Miss Anvoy threw off this appeal I could have embraced her for so delightfully emphasising her unlikeness to Mrs. Saltram. "Why not have the courage of one's forgiveness," she asked, "as well as the enthusiasm of one's adhesion?"

"Seeing how wonderfully you've threshed the whole thing out," I evasively replied, "gives me an extraordinary notion of the point your enthusiasm has reached."

She considered this remark an instant with her eyes on mine, and I divined that it struck her I might possibly intend it as a reference to some personal subjection to our fat philosopher, to some aberration of sensibility, some perversion of taste. At least I couldn't interpret otherwise the sudden flush that came into her face. Such a manifestation, as the result of any word of mine, embarrassed me; but while I was thinking how to reassure her the flush passed away in a smile of exquisite good nature. "Oh you see one forgets so wonderfully how one dislikes him!" she said; and if her tone simply extinguished his strange figure with the brush of its compassion, it also rings in my ear to-day as the purest of all our praises. But with what quick response of fine pity such a relegation of the man himself made me privately sigh "Ah poor Saltram!" She instantly, with this, took the measure of all I didn't believe, and it enabled her to go on. "What can one do when a person has given such a lift to one's interest in life?"

"Yes, what can one do?" If I struck her as a little vague it was because I was thinking of another person. I indulged in another inarticulate murmur—"Poor George Gravener!" What had become of the lift *he* had given that interest? Later on I made up my mind that she was sore and stricken at the apperance he presented of wanting the miserable money. This was the hidden reason of her alienation. The probable sincerity, in spite of the illiberality, of his scruples about the particular use of it under discussion didn't efface the ugliness of his demand that they should buy a good house with it. Then, as for *his* alienation, he didn't, pardonably enough, grasp the lift Frank Saltram had given her interest in life. If a mere spectator could ask that last question, with what rage in his heart the man himself might ! He wasn't, like her, I was to see, too proud to show me why he was disappointed.

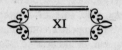

XI

I WAS unable this time to stay to dinner: such at any rate was the plea on which I took leave. I desired in truth to get away from my young lady, for that obviously helped me not to pretend to satisfy her. How *could* I satisfy her ? I asked myself—how could I tell her how much had been kept back ? I didn't even know and I certainly didn't desire to know. My own policy had ever been to learn the least about poor Saltram's weaknesses—not to learn the most. A great deal that I had in fact learned had been forced upon me by his wife. There was something even irritating in Miss Anvoy's crude conscientiousness, and I wondered why, after all, she couldn't have let him alone and been content to entrust George Gravener with the purchase of the good house. I was sure he would have driven a bargain, got something excellent and cheap. I laughed louder even than she, I temporised, I failed her; I told her I must think over her case. I professed a horror of responsibilities and twitted her with her own extravagant passion for them. It wasn't really that I was afraid of the scandal, the moral discredit for the Fund; what troubled me most was a feeling of a different order. Of course, as the beneficiary of the Fund was to enjoy a simple life-interest, as it was hoped that new beneficiaries would arise and come up to new standards, it wouldn't be a trifle that the first of these worthies shouldn't have been a striking example of the domestic virtues. The Fund would start badly, as it were, and the laurel would, in some respects at least, scarcely be greener from the brows of the original wearer. That idea, however, was at that hour, as I have hinted, not the source of solicitude it ought perhaps to have been, for I felt less the irregularity of Saltram's getting the money than that of this exalted young woman's giving it up. I wanted her to have it for herself, and I told her so before I went away. She looked graver at this than she had looked at all, saying she hoped such a preference wouldn't make me dishonest.

It made me, to begin with, very restless—made me, instead of going straight to the station, fidget a little about that many-coloured Common which gives Wimbledon horizons. There was a worry for me to work off, or rather keep at a distance, for I declined even to admit to myself that I had, in Miss Anvoy's phrase, been saddled with it. What could have been clearer indeed than the attitude of recognising perfectly what a world of trouble the Coxon Fund would in future save us, and of yet liking better to face a continuance of that trouble than see, and in fact contribute to, a deviation from attainable bliss in the life of two other persons in whom I was deeply interested? Suddenly, at the end of twenty minutes, there was projected across this clearness the image of a massive middle-aged man seated on a bench under a tree, with sad far-wandering eyes and plump white hands folded on the head of a stick—a stick I recognised, a stout gold-headed staff that I had given him in devoted days. I stopped short as he turned his face to me, and it happened that for some reason or other I took in as I had perhaps never done before the beauty of his rich blank gaze. It was charged with experience as the sky is charged with light, and I felt on the instant as if we had been overspanned and conjoined by the great arch of a bridge or the great dome of a temple. Doubtless I was rendered peculiarly sensitive to it by something in the way I had been giving him up and sinking him. While I met it I stood there smitten, and I felt myself responding to it with a sort of guilty grimace. This brought back his attention in a smile which expressed for me a cheerful weary patience, a bruised noble gentleness. I had told Miss Anvoy that he had no dignity, but what did he seem to me, all unbuttoned and fatigued as he waited for me to come up, if he didn't seem unconcerned with small things, didn't seem in short majestic? There was majesty in his mere unconsciousness of our little conferences and puzzlements over his maintenance and his reward.

After I had sat by him a few minutes I passed my arm over his big soft shoulder—wherever you touched him you found equally little firmness—and said in a tone of which the suppliance fell oddly on my own ear: "Come back to town with me, old friend—come back and spend the evening." I wanted to hold him, I wanted to keep him, and at Waterloo, an hour later, I telegraphed possessively to the Mulvilles. When he objected, as regards staying all night, that he had no things, I asked him if he hadn't everything of mine. I had abstained from ordering dinner, and it was too late for preliminaries at a club; so we were reduced to tea and fried fish at my rooms—reduced also to the transcendent. Something had come up which made me want him to feel at peace with me—and which, precisely, was all the dear man himself wanted on any occasion. I had too often had to press upon him considerations irrelevant, but it gives me pleasure now to think that of that particular evening I didn't even mention Mrs. Saltram and the children. Late into the night we smoked and talked; old shames and old rigours fell away from us; I only let him see that I was conscious of what I owed him. He was as mild as contrition and as copious as faith; he was never so fine as on a shy return, and even better at forgiving than at being forgiven. I daresay it was a smaller matter than that famous night at Wimbledon, the night of the problematical sobriety and of Miss Anvoy's initiation; but I was as much in it on this occasion as I had been out of it then. At about 1.30 he was sublime.

He never, in whatever situation, rose till all other risings were over, and his breakfasts, at Wimbledon, had always been the principal reason mentioned by departing cooks. The coast was therefore clear for me to receive her when, early the next morning, to my surprise, it was announced to me his wife had called. I hesitated, after she had come up, about telling her Saltram was in the house, but she herself settled the question, kept me reticent by drawing forth a sealed letter which, looking at me very hard in the eyes, she placed, with a pregnant absence of comment, in my hand. For a single moment there glimmered before me the fond hope that Mrs. Saltram had tendered me, as it were, her resignation and desired to embody the act in an unsparing form. To bring this about I would have feigned any humiliation; but after my eyes had caught the superscription I heard myself say with a flatness that betrayed a sense of something very different from relief: "Oh the Pudneys!" I knew their envelopes though they didn't know mine. They always used the kind sold at post-offices with the stamp affixed, and as this letter hadn't been posted they had wasted a penny on me. I had seen their horrid missives to the Mulvilles, but hadn't been in direct correspondence with them.

"They enclosed it to me, to be delivered. They doubtless explain to you that they hadn't your address."

I turned the thing over without opening it. "Why in the world should they write to me?"

"Because they've something to tell you. The worst," Mrs. Saltram dryly added.

It was another chapter, I felt, of the history of their lamentable quarrel with her husband, the episode in which, vindictively, disingenuously as they themselves had behaved, one had to admit that he had put himself more grossly in the wrong than at any moment of his life. He had begun by insulting the matchless Mulvilles for these more specious protectors, and then, according to his wont at the end of a few months, had dug a still deeper ditch for his aberration than the chasm left yawning behind. The chasm at Wimbledon was now blessedly closed; but the Pudneys, across their persistent gulf, kept up the nastiest fire. I never doubted they had a strong case, and I had been from the first for not defending him—reasoning that if they weren't contradicted they'd perhaps subside. This was above all what I wanted, and I so far prevailed that I did arrest the correspondence in time to save our little circle an infliction heavier than it perhaps would have borne. I knew, that is I divined, that their allegations had gone as yet only as far as their courage, conscious as they were in their own virtue of an exposed place in which Saltram could have planted a blow. It was a question with them whether a man who had himself so much to cover up would dare his blow; so that these vessels of rancour were in a manner afraid of each other. I judged that on the day the Pudneys should cease for some reason or other to be afraid they would treat us to some revelation more disconcerting than any of its predecessors. As I held Mrs. Saltram's letter in my hand it was distinctly communicated to me that the day had come—they had ceased to be afraid.

"I don't want to know the worst," I presently declared.

"You'll have to open the letter. It also contains an enclosure."

I felt it—it was fat and uncanny. "Wheels within wheels!" I exclaimed. "There's something for me too to deliver."

"So they tell me—to Miss Anvoy."

I stared; I felt a certain thrill. "Why don't they send it to her directly?"

Mrs. Saltram hung fire. "Because she's staying with Mr. and Mrs. Mulville."

"And why should that prevent?"

Again my visitor faltered, and I began to reflect on the grotesque, the unconscious perversity of her action. It was the only person save George

231

Gravener and the Mulvilles who was aware of Sir Gregory Coxon's and of Miss Anvoy's strange bounty. Where could there have been a more signal illustration of the clumsiness of human affairs than her having complacently selected this moment to fly in the face of it? "There's the chance of their seeing her letters. They know Mr. Pudney's hand."

Still I didn't understand; then it flashed upon me. "You mean they might intercept it? How can you imply anything so base?" I indignantly demanded.

"It's not I—it's Mr. Pudney!" cried Mrs. Saltram with a flush. "It's his own idea."

"Then why couldn't he send the letter to *you* to be delivered?"

Mrs. Saltram's embarrassment increased; she gave me another hard look. "You must make that out for yourself."

I made it out quickly enough. "It's a denunciation?"

"A real lady doesn't betray her husband!" this virtuous woman exclaimed.

I burst out laughing, and I fear my laugh may have had an effect of impertinence. "Especially to Miss Anvoy, who's so easily shocked? Why do such things concern *her*?" I asked, much at a loss.

"Because she's there, exposed to all his craft. Mr. and Mrs. Pudney have been watching this: they feel she may be taken in."

"Thank you for all the rest of us! What difference can it make when she has lost her power to contribute?"

Again Mrs. Saltram considered; then very nobly: "There are other things in the world than money." This hadn't occurred to her so long as the young lady had any; but she now added, with a glance at my letter, that Mr. and Mrs. Pudney doubtless explained their motives. "It's all in kindness," she continued as she got up.

"Kindness to Miss Anvoy? You took, on the whole, another view of kindness before her reverses."

My companion smiled with some acidity. "Perhaps you're no safer than the Mulvilles!"

I didn't want her to think that, nor that she should report to the Pudneys that they had not been happy in their agent; and I well remember that this was the moment at which I began, with considerable emotion, to promise myself to enjoin upon Miss Anvoy never to open any letter that should come to her in one of those penny envelopes. My emotion, and I fear I must add my confusion, quickly deepened; I presently should have been as glad to frighten Mrs. Saltram as to think I might by some diplomacy restore the Pudneys to a quieter vigilance.

"It's best you should take *my* view of my safety," I at any rate soon responded. When I saw she didn't know what I meant by this I added: "You may turn out to have done, in bringing me this letter, a thing you'll profoundly regret." My tone had a significance which, I could see, did make her uneasy, and there was a moment, after I had made two or three more remarks of studiously bewildering effect, at which her eyes followed so hungrily the little flourish of the letter with which I emphasised them that I instinctively slipped Mr. Pudney's communication into my pocket. She looked, in her embarrassed annoyance, capable of grabbing it to send it back to him. I felt, after she had gone, as if I had almost given her my word I wouldn't deliver the enclosure. The passionate movement, at any rate, with which, in solitude, I transferred the whole thing, unopened, from my pocket to a drawer which I double-locked would have amounted, for an initiated observer, to some such pledge.

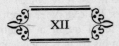

XII

MRS. SALTRAM left me drawing my breath more quickly and indeed almost in pain—as if I had just perilously grazed the loss of something precious. I didn't quite know what it was—it had a shocking resemblance to my honour. The emotion was the livelier surely in that my pulses even yet vibrated to the pleasure with which, the night before, I had rallied to the rare analyst, the great intellectual adventurer and pathfinder. What had dropped from me like a cumbersome garment as Saltram appeared before me in the afternoon on the heath was the disposition to haggle over his value. Hang it, one had to choose, one had to put that value somewhere; so I would put it really high and have done with it. Mrs. Mulville drove in for him at a discreet hour—the earliest she could suppose him to have got up; and I learned that Miss Anvoy would also have come had she not been expecting a visit from Mr. Gravener. I was perfectly mindful that I was under bonds to see this young lady, and also that I had a letter to hand to her; but I took my time, I waited from day to day. I left Mrs. Saltram to deal as her apprehensions should prompt with the Pudneys. I knew at last what I meant—I had ceased to wince at my responsibility. I gave this supreme impression of Saltram time to fade if it would; but it didn't fade, and, individually, it hasn't faded even now. During the month that I thus invited myself to stiffen again, Adelaide Mulville, perplexed by my absence, wrote to me to ask why I *was* so stiff. At that season of the year I was usually oftener "with" them. She also wrote that she feared a real estrangement had set in between Mr. Gravener and her sweet young friend—a state of things but half satisfactory to her so long as the advantage resulting to Mr. Saltram failed to disengage itself from the merely nebulous state. She intimated that her sweet young friend was, if anything, a trifle too reserved; she also intimated that there might now be an opening for another clever young man. There never was the slightest opening, I may here parenthesise, and of course the question can't come up to-day. These are old frustrations now. Ruth Anvoy hasn't married, I hear, and neither have I. During the month, towards the end, I wrote to George Gravener to ask if, on a special errand, I might come to see him, and his answer was to knock the very next day at my door. I saw he had immediately connected my inquiry with the talk we had had in the railway carriage, and his promptitude showed that the ashes of his eagerness weren't yet cold. I told him there was something I felt I ought in candour to let him know—I recognised the obligation his friendly confidence had laid on me.

"You mean Miss Anvoy has talked to you? She has told me so herself," he said.

"It wasn't to tell you so that I wanted to see you," I replied; "for it seemed to me that such a communication would rest wholly with herself. If, however, she did speak to you of our conversation she probably told you I was discouraging."

"Discouraging?"

"On the subject of a present application of the Coxon Fund."

"To the case of Mr. Saltram? My dear fellow, I don't know what you call discouraging," Gravener cried.

"Well, I thought I was, and I thought she thought I was."

"I believe she did, but such a thing's measured by the effect. She's not 'discouraged,'" he said.

"That's her own affair. The reason I asked you to see me was that it appeared to me I ought to tell you frankly that—decidedly !—I can't undertake to produce that effect. In fact I don't want to !"

"It's very good of you, damn you!" my visitor laughed, red and really grave. Then he said: "You'd like to see that scoundrel publicly glorified—perched on the pedestal of a great complimentary pension?"

I braced myself. "Taking one form of public recognition with another it seems to me on the whole I should be able to bear it. When I see the compliments that *are* paid right and left I ask myself why this one shouldn't take its course. This therefore is what you're entitled to have looked to me to mention to you. I've some evidence that perhaps would be really dissuasive, but I propose to invite Miss Anvoy to remain in ignorance of it."

"And to invite me to do the same?"

"Oh you don't require it—you've evidence enough. I speak of a sealed letter that I've been requested to deliver to her."

"And you don't mean to?"

"There's only one consideration that would make me," I said.

Gravener's clear handsome eyes plunged into mine a minute, but evidently without fishing up a clue to this motive—a failure by which I was almost wounded. "What does the letter contain?"

"It's sealed, as I tell you, and I don't know what it contains."

"Why is it sent through you?"

"Rather than you?" I wondered how to put the thing. "The only explanation I can think of is that the person sending it may have imagined your relations with Miss Anvoy to be at an end—may have been told this is the case by Mrs. Saltram."

"My relations with Miss Anvoy are not at an end," poor Gravener stammered.

Again for an instant I thought. "The offer I propose to make you gives me the right to address you a question remarkably direct. Are you still engaged to Miss Anvoy?"

"No, I'm not," he slowly brought out. "But we're perfectly good friends."

"Such good friends that you'll again become prospective husband and wife if the obstacle in your path be removed?"

"Removed?" he anxiously repeated.

"If I send Miss Anvoy the letter I speak of she may give up her idea."

"Then for God's sake send it!"

"I'll do so if you're ready to assure me that her sacrifice would now presumably bring about your marriage."

235

"I'd marry her the next day !" my visitor cried.

"Yes, but would she marry *you*? What I ask of you of course is nothing less than your word of honour as to your conviction of this. If you give it me," I said, "I'll engage to hand her the letter before night."

Gravener took up his hat; turning it mechanically round he stood looking a moment hard at its unruffled perfection. Then very angrily, honestly and gallantly, "Hand it to the devil !" he broke out; with which he clapped the hat on his head and left me.

"Will you read it or not ? " I said to Ruth Anvoy, at Wimbledon, when I had told her the story of Mrs. Saltram's visit.

She debated for a time probably of the briefest, but long enough to make me nervous. "Have you brought it with you ?"

"No indeed. It's at home, locked up."

There was another great silence, and then she said, "Go back and destroy it."

I went back, but I didn't destroy it till after Saltram's death, when I burnt it unread. The Pudneys approached her again pressingly, but, prompt as they were, the Coxon Fund had already become an operative benefit and a general amaze : Mr. Saltram, while we gathered about, as it were, to watch the manna descend, had begun to draw the magnificent income. He drew it as he had always drawn everything, with a grand abstracted gesture. Its magnificence, alas, as all the world now knows, quite quenched him; it was the beginning of his decline. It was also naturally a new grievance for his wife, who began to believe in him as soon as he was blighted, and who at this hour accuses us of having bribed him, on the whim of a meddlesome American, to renounce his glorious office, to become, as she says, like everybody else. The very day he found himself able to publish he wholly ceased to produce. This deprived us, as may easily be imagined, of much of our occupation, and especially deprived the Mulvilles, whose want of self-support I never measured till they lost their great inmate. They've no one to live on now. Adelaide's most frequent reference to their destitution is embodied in the remark that dear faraway Ruth's intentions were doubtless good. She and Kent are even yet looking for another prop, but no one presents a true sphere of usefulness. They complain that people are self-sufficing. With Saltram the fine type of the child of adoption was scattered, the grander, the elder style. They've got their carriage back, but what's an empty carriage ? In short I think we were all happier as well as poorer before; even including George Gravener, who by the deaths of his brother and his nephew has lately become Lord Maddock. His wife, whose fortune clears the property, is criminally dull; he hates being in the upper House and hasn't yet had high office. But what are these accidents, which I should perhaps apologise for mentioning, in the light of the great eventual boon promised the patient by the rate at which the Coxon Fund must be rolling up?